Dark Light Anthology

Edited by S.J. Davis

READ ORDER

459	59	7	257
213	119	31	303
219	291	91	365
131	405	139	
225	197	175	
451	71	233	
355		333	
395		429	
419			

Dark Light

Cover Art by Para Graphic Designs

Dark Light
By Alexia Purdy

A twisted path in disarray
A siege inside my head.
As darkness grips at my eyes
I feel the mortal dread

As wired barbs and thorns embed
The world's a different place
I shudder and remember when
The light shone on my face

The dusk relents to the night
My light that shuns and takes
Embraces me with its breath
Releasing what it makes

The path eludes as I go
An infinity of dead
Dark light immolates
Down pours on my head

Dawn expands its grip anew
As wild and cursed things
Retreat back into night
Light's sanctuary brings

Dark Light

Dark Light

CONTENTS

Dark Light

Headless Homecoming

by
Andrew Katz

Creepy. That was the only word one could use to describe the "trophy" I was looking at. The head of the infamous Headless Horseman, resting on the pike it had been shoved on by former North American King, Gavin Patronar. Looking at the grotesquely preserved head, I couldn't help but think back to some of my history lessons from when I was younger. My teacher, Old McGee (he had received that name by simply outliving whatever it had once been) had mostly liked to use the Horseman as a boogieman of sorts, but I had still managed to learn the story. Before we get into that though, some quick background is in order.

During King Arthur's rule he had succeeded in expanding Camelot to quite literally encompass the entire world. After the Great War between Mordred's and Arthur's armies ended with the deaths of their respective leaders, the people that the Knights of both sides were sworn to protect were left to fend for themselves. Now, this may not have been that much of a problem had it not been for the emergence of all the supernatural evils that Arthur and his legions of Knights had kept at bay. Most of the men and women being preyed on by the monsters that stalk the night were simple farmers and traders that felt nothing if not betrayed by the men that were meant to defend them… as opposed to slaughtering one another. Yet these Knights were men of honor and would protect those who could not protect themselves, even if they didn't want them to. So the warriors fought in the shadows, slowly but surely throwing the evils that threatened their world back down. Eventually memories of monsters, demons, and dark predators faded as the Knights crushed them, and soon knowledge of the Knights did as well. However, there were those that kept faith in their protectors and supported them, and in time the hidden Kingdoms actually began to flourish. Even though the majority of man doesn't know they exist, they have managed to turn into serious powers today through modern means. Don't get it twisted though, the Knights still don their armor and swords and destroy the supernatural threats of the world... whether people know it or not.

But I digress - back to the Headless Horseman. In the earliest days of the North American Kingdom there was a Knight, far more talented and stronger than the rest. He lived in the days when much of the unrest from the Great War was still astir and the newer Kingdoms had just been formed. It was noted that he was – displeased – by the appointment of the new King, Godfrey Patronar, so naturally he attempted a mutiny. However, there were no men that would join with him so soon after the tragedy of Camelot's downfall. This being the case, the Horseman was to be brought about on treason charges to surely be executed by his peers. But when the Knights came to bring the King's justice, instead of facing his punishment; the Horseman fought. As I said, he was an unbelievable warrior and slew fifteen Anointed Knights in his escape. After which he pretty much just fell off the face of the Earth.

It was assumed that the Horseman was dead, and inevitably he was forgotten along with his original name. Unfortunately, in a terrible turn of events, the Horseman had not in fact died. It seems that since he had gone to ground with no army to command, he had begun building one. There had always been whispers about the Horseman's extra-curricular activities away from his Knighthood, but no one ever truly found out what they were - until he emerged from the depths of his hideout. The specifics are still a mystery, but when he arose the Horseman did so with an army of walking dead. It turns out the Horseman had been a fairly talented practitioner of necromancy, a strictly forbidden art since even before Arthur came to power. His emergence came in a wave of sickening corruption and death that swept over the entire realm until he finally reached the King's castle with the intent to overthrow him.

Thousands of men and women had been slaughtered by the Horseman and his undead and it looked like he might actually overtake the Kingdom. That is until the King at the time, Gavin Patronar (Godfrey's great-great-great-grandson), took the field of battle to oppose the evildoer. Stories say that the King and a select few warriors drove all the way through the heart of the undead army and came upon the Horseman, reviling in all of his vile power. As his men fought off the surrounding horde, Gavin engaged the Necromancer directly. They say that their battle lasted for several hours, culminating with the King separating the Horseman's head from his shoulders. Yet somehow (it was eventually chalked up to the practice of necromancy), decapitation did not end the Horseman's life although his body fell. His power was released and his walking army fell. King Gavin took the severed head, grotesquely still breathing, and slammed it onto a pike as a message.

It's said that the damn head didn't stop screaming for revenge for over twelve hours before the King ordered it gagged. Finally, years later, the eyes rolled back into the severed head and the tedious cycle of chewing through gags and screaming abruptly ended. The head had, for some reason I still didn't understand, been passed down through the generations. Normally I avoided it, but I was bored today and had come to check out some of the cooler artifacts that King's of the past had claimed. For some reason I had been drawn over to this gross, creepy, decapitated head. My examination of the thing was coming to a close, when suddenly, something unexpected happened. The Horseman's head opened its eyes and grinned at me with a mouth full of decaying teeth.

I jumped back startled and looked at the thing, wide-eyed. "Well, that can't be good."

The Horseman's severed head licked its flaking lips and spoke with a voice that had clearly not been used in centuries. "I don't like your face. When I regain my powers I will make sure to kill you." It rasped.

There was nothing wrong with my face. I mean sure I was a little scruffy from a lack of shaving, and my hair was getting on the long side, but overall I think I'm a good-looking guy. I have a square jaw, rigid nose, and bright burgundy eyes (they're the same color as my hair). I stand five feet nine inches tall, and am layered in hard slabs of muscle. I'm not bad to look at. Sure I'm no model, but heading down this road could lead to some self-esteem problems later in life, so I'm going to let it go.

Pursing my lips and looking hard into its eyes, I said, "Yeah, I don't like your face either." And I didn't, so I punched it in said face.

The head squealed in surprise, and I made a show of skipping off as I went to get the King's Right Hand. Peter is a leonine man of below average height with ice blue eyes that burn with intelligence and exude authority. I found him sitting comfortably in his quarters, reading. Upon my approach he peered over his reading glasses at me and sighed. "What is it?"

I scratched my head nervously, "You might want to see this for yourself."

We heard it long before Peter saw the head. As soon as the screaming reached his ears he took off sprinting down the castle halls to the trophy room with me on his heels the whole way. We arrived to the head shouting out obscenities and Peter swearing under his breath. The older man turned to me with fury in his eyes.

"What happened here? Did you do this?"

I put my hands in the air like I was being arrested. "Whoa there big fella, the thing just woke up. I didn't do anything."

"This whelp punched me." The head snarled.

"Tattle tale." I muttered.

"It woke up... because you punched it?" Peter asked quietly, trying to contain his anger.

"Hang on just one second there." I said.

"It woke up and told me it didn't like my face. Then I punched it."

The head said a few words that would make a sailor blush, and addressed Peter. "I have awoken to regain my power. My body grows restless and will soon come to claim me and restore our full glory. Then I shall slaughter you foolish usurpers and take what is rightfully mine."

The King's Hand stared hard into the head's eyes and turned to me. "I can see why you punched it. Go get the King, I'll gag the head and then we'll figure out what to do"

Snapping off a mock salute, I started through the castle to the throne room. I found the King sitting his throne, staring off into space. He was a stocky, broad, and muscle-laden man of average height. His eyes were also burgundy and his close cut hair matched them (except where it was peppered with grey). The attire he chose wasn't exactly regal since he was currently wearing a maroon long-sleeve T-shirt and brown corduroy pants. Then of course there was the brilliant granite crown studded with emeralds that he wore to signify his office.

I strolled up and waved my hand in front of his face to get his attention. He snapped back into the real world and placed an annoyed look on me. "Yes?"

"The Horseman's head just woke up; figured you should know."

The King rolled his shoulders and stood. "I knew today wasn't going to be a fun one." He grunted. "Come along, we'll go talk to it."

"Yeah… beat you to that one; the head doesn't really like me."

He snorted. "Why shouldn't I be surprised?"

***

The King, Peter and I sat in the strategy room discussing what should be done.

"Do we have any possible way of locating the body?" I asked.

Peter let a heavy breath out through his nose. "I don't think we have to at all. Clearly the head isn't going anywhere, and it said that the body was going to come and reclaim it. I say we just wait for it to show up and kill it."

"How do we do that?" The King asked reluctantly. "The Headless Horseman was supposed to have been dead for many, many years. How do you suppose we actually put him down?"

"We gather the Knights of the continent and we hack off the rest of the limbs." Peter suggested.

"I'm OK with that plan." I chimed in.

The King shrugged. "Works for me too."

So we gathered the eight other active Knights of North America and filled them in on what was happening. There was Rudolph Richards, Marcus the Gruesome, Juan Corrales, Jacques Ribery, Trevor Wingback, Kellen Factarum, my best friend Devin Eversor, and the most terrifying of them all; Ashley Reyes. The King, Peter and I were all Anointed Warriors as well and now the majority of the most dangerous people on the continent were in the same room.

As Knight-Commander of the Realm, Peter gave them each their duties and told them to be ready to arrive at the castle to kill the Horseman. They nodded their understanding, exchanged a few pleasantries, and parted ways to resume their current activities. Only Devin stayed; mostly because he lived in the castle, but also because he had just returned from thwarting a nest of vampires outside of Houston responsible for ten recent homicides. Once the others had departed Dev came over and greeted me.

My best friend is a giant. Not literally of course, an actual giant wouldn't fit in the castle, but as humans go he's freaking huge. He goes about seven-two, two-sixty-five of pure rock hard muscle. He has dark blue eyes, a neat cut black goatee, and was wearing a dark brown leather jacket, white T-shirt, dark jeans, and his brutal steel headed mace. He may just as well swing a telephone pole with a fire hydrant attached to the end since they were probably about the same size.

"How were the vamps?" I asked.

"Nothing too tough." He replied nonchalantly. "It might have been a little easier if you had gotten off your lazy ass and helped though."

"You know I couldn't, plus it's not like there would have been space for me with you there, Tubbo."

"I'm not fat." He said sullenly (he was right of course, but I like to poke fun at him all the same).

"Sensitive." I accused.

"Whatever. Let's get some food... don't you dare say a word."

I laughed, clapped him on the back and set off.

***

Two weeks had passed without incident, and Peter had called Devin and me into the strategy room with an assignment.

"I need you two to go out to Denver. There have been reported decapitations there, and from what our people inside have told us it doesn't look like human work."

"What about the Horseman?" I asked bluntly.

Peter made a non-committal sound. "There's been no sign of him so we'll just put it on the backburner and continue to wait. It's not like there's much else we can do without more information, and the world isn't stopping awaiting his arrival. For all we know it could be years before he reveals himself to us. So get to Denver and look into what's going on, OK?"

Devin and I nodded and left the room to gather our gear. I didn't like to go out into the real world wearing my armor; not because I really care about all the stares and blatant judgment from people that see me, but because there's no need to draw unnecessary attention to yourself when you have as many enemies as I do. Stepping into my poster plastered bedroom, I put on my chainmail shirt, Kevlar vest, long-sleeve black T-shirt, and grey overcoat. I buckled on my sword; *Laniatus* (AKA my pride and joy), that I had forged myself. The blade was a wicked longsword made from my own special ice-blue alloy and a hand carved dragonbone hilt and pommel. My overcoat came just far enough down to properly conceal the blade when I walked, and no one would see it unless I need use it (which generally meant they wouldn't get to talk about it anyway).

As soon as I set foot out of my room Devin appeared in the hallway wearing his massive hunter green cloak over his usual attire. The cloak was a family heirloom from Devin's deceased father and had some serious magical protections on it. I have honestly come to believe that it would take a WMD to do damage to Dev while wearing that thing. We strolled along down the hallway towards the castle portal. The way this works is certain VIPs are awarded transport runes, certain Words take you to certain places, but you have to know the Word. Luckily I know most of the key locations for North America, and boy did it make traveling easy.

The two of us went up to the ever-stoic men that guarded the portal, and as always I flashed them an obnoxiously cheery grin and waved jovially. None of them batted an eyelash as we sauntered on by. I produced my rune; a small, circular stone tablet with a single very complex marking on it. I murmured a soft Word into it and suddenly the world blurred, tilted, spun, and Devin and I were standing in the Denver International Airport. Airports are always good to appear in, people are focused on getting to and from where they're going, and the terminals are so crowded no one ever really notices two new faces. One semi-aggravating transaction later with a fake ID (I'm not technically old enough to rent a car); Devin and I were cruising towards the Denver PD in a purple Chevy Impala.

"You are the worst person on the face of the planet." Devin complained.

"I honestly don't see what the big deal is."

"Peter let you have the King's own credit card, and you rent a purple Impala? You have the royal credit card, and you rent a *purple Impala.* We couldn't have gotten a Corvette? A Jaguar? I mean honestly. You're a disgrace."

I flicked my big friend in the forehead. "The idea is not to draw attention to ourselves you humungous moron. Plus this way you can rack the seat all the way back and I don't have to hear you bitch about legroom."

He rubbed at the spot on his head and puffed air through his nose. "Whatever." And he closed his eyes to sleep in the car as he always did.

***

We arrived at the station and stepped out of the Impala into the fresh cold air. Devin cracked every joint in his body and began moving towards the doors, until I stopped him.

"Forgetting something dum-dum?"

"What?" He asked me agitated. Dev was always cranky after his nap.

I patted my leg where his giant mace was bulging under his cloak. "You're not going through any metal detectors wearing that."

"You still have *Laniatus*." He said pointedly.

"Which you know full well won't set them off." Not to brag, but my sword was pretty special.

"Well what about your chainmail?"

"Same alloy, not a problem. But lucky for you I brought you a present." He tilted his head at me inquisitively and I tossed him the two large knuckledusters I had made for him.

He gave them an appreciative once over and tried them on. "Daddy likey."

"Yeah, I figured you would. Lose the cloak too, you'll kill our credibility."

He grunted acquiescence and dropped the cloak on the passenger seat. He put on his aviator sunglasses and fastened his badge to his belt. Devin and I had procured authentic FBI badges to help when we had to do investigations involving natural humans. I adjusted *Laniatus* to fit straight down my leg, put my badge in my inner lapel pocket, and we walked through the double doors into the station.

Anyone can tell you how important confidence is when pretending to be someone you're not, so Devin and I stalked into the station like we owned the place. A beat cop in full uniform scrambled up to us to say something, but then Devin removed his sunglasses and looked hard into his eyes. The cop literally stopped dead in his tracks.

Dev tapped the badge on his belt and asked with pure authority, "Who's in charge here?"

A bull of a man about six inches shorter than Devin, dressed in a clean navy blue suit stormed over to us. "Who the hell are you two?" He demanded.

Dev was about to get into one of his usual alpha male pissing contests when I placed my hand on his shoulder. "I'm Special Agent Korver," I said producing my badge, "and this is my partner Agent Mason. We're here regarding the decapitation cases." Using false identities is fun.

The man in the suit scratched at his nose and let out a deep sigh of relief. "Thank God. We've got absolutely nothing on these. Lieutenant Betts" He said sticking out his hand. I traded grips with him, and he led us down a cold hallway to the morgue.

"This is our forensic coroner, Dr. Stanley Trumont." Betts said. "Stan these gentlemen are Special Agents Korver and Mason. They're here about the decapitations; you're to offer them your full cooperation."

"Pleasure to meet you," said the coroner in a voice about two octaves too deep for his slight body.

"You as well, Doctor. What can you tell us about the heads being cut off?" I asked politely.

Trumont gave his Lieutenant a look, Betts nodded, said, "I'll leave you to it." And left.

The skinny doctor scratched at his neck nervously and spoke in his oddly deep voice. "Um, the head's weren't exactly cut off." Devin cocked one bushy eyebrow at the coroner. "They were – well – they were pulled off."

"Pulled off?" I asked with genuine surprise.

"Yes. All of the evidence says that this was done by a person. The funny thing is we now have three victims, no prints, and it seems that each time the culprit was of a different height."

"So you're saying that there are multiple murderers running around ripping people's heads off?" Devin asked.

"With their bare hands." Trumont added.

That made it more likely than not that our killer was decidedly not human. It was obvious that Devin had picked up on the very same thought, and he gave me a pretty

17

displeased look. We each shook the doctor's hand and briskly began our departure from the office. However, before we could take our leave we were cut off by the uniformed cop from before.

"Come with me." He said quietly. "Please."

"What is this about?" Devin asked in the same tone he had used earlier.

The poor guy looked like he might wet himself, but managed to choke out a few more words. "I need to show you something, it'll only take a moment."

I placed a reassuring hand on the guy's arm. "Lead on, Officer."

We followed him out of the building and around to the back of the building. "There is something very important you need to know about the recent murders that have taken place."

"And what might that be?" I asked.

"I'm coming for my head." Whispered the cop, and he sprung into action.

Devin and I should have both been dead. We were up against a warrior and necromancer that had defied death for centuries, and were caught completely off guard. But we're Anointed Warriors and are somewhat tougher than your average customer. When a person is raised into the ranks of Knighthood they are anointed in ancient oils that award that person certain – abilities. In the material world those abilities pretty much boil down to heightened senses and reflexes, but they are seriously heightened senses and reflexes. The cop came at us hard and fast, but I had sensed something was off with him since the second we laid eyes on him and had tensed for action upon leaving the building. He lunged for Devin first; they always think the larger opponent is more dangerous, unfortunately for him, our enemy may have been right. Even though our attacker was moving at supernatural speeds, Dev still managed to get hold of his wrists before the "cop" could rip his head off.

Of course as soon as the officer moved I had whipped *Laniatus* from its sheath, and had just used it to remove both of the pseudo cop's arms at the elbows. To my dismay, it didn't really help our cause.

There was no blood, no cry of pain, just a cracking noise and a sprouting of two new limbs.

"Wish I had my mace." Devin muttered and slammed the cop in the face with one of the knuckledusters I'd given him.

Whatever he was staggered and I always say if you're going to be bear be a grizzly, so I lopped off his head. There was a high frequency hissing and suddenly the body… changed. The "cop" grew to about nine feet tall, professional body-builder wide, turned completely jet black, and stood there headless.

"I think we found the body" I said stupidly.

As Devin and I stood dumbfounded, the body stooped down, snatched up its former head, and dropped it back onto its shoulders. The stump of neck attached to the head writhed and began reattaching itself to the body, and just like that the cop was standing in front of us again, grinning sadistically.

"Neat trick, huh?" He said slyly. "Your move."

Dev and I exchanged a quick glance and moved to enclose the Horseman, but he just laughed. "Tell your false King I am coming for my head – and his." With that he took off running. Faster than any car I'd ever seen, he just bolted around the building and was gone.

"If he can run like that why the hell do they call him the Headless *Horseman*?" I wondered aloud.

"Not the time, Jackass." Devin said. "We need to go warn the castle right now."

***

We arrived back through the portal and stormed past the guards there without acknowledgement. Devin went to find Peter, and I went straight to the King's private quarters to interrupt his reading.

He set his book down and looked at me with severe agitation. "This better be good."

I rolled my eyes at him. "Devin and I found the body; gather the Knights so we can explain please." With that I turned on my heel and stalked through the halls to the strategy room to await the arrival of the others. They returned through the portal one by one and joined us to confer. First came Marcus, then Rudolph, Ashley, Jacques, Kellen, Juan, and finally Trevor.

We met around what I always thought was a huge clichéd round table so that Devin and I could alert the others to what we'd encountered.

"The Horseman has found a way to become a Pugot." Juan Corrales said casually after hearing the events. He was a Latin man of just average height and build with a long braided black ponytail. He was in camouflage fatigues and combat boots with a Desert Eagle on one hip and a large Bowie knife on the other.

"A what?" Devin and I said unanimously.

"A Pugot, you dolts." Sneered Kellen Factarum; he and I don't usually see eye to eye. "There are only a few documented in history, and it is my understanding that they cannot be killed. They are headless shape shifters that can become any given person by wearing their head. Upon acquiring a new head the former one is absorbed and the Pugot grows more powerful."

Kellen's a lean six-footer, with sandy blonde hair, and like me he holds a preference for a traditional longsword. Mine's better (at least I'm not petty though).

"And the Pugot may retain any form of their previous victims upon absorbing the head." Juan added.

"So say the body has been killing one or two people a year, for centuries, it would have to be immensely powerful." Said Peter.

"And could be any number of people." Ash chimed in.

Ashley Reyes was by far the scariest of the Knights in the room. She stood five-foot-nine, one hundred twenty pounds soaking wet, with long brown hair and big bright brown eyes. Oh, and did I mention she was a freaking knockout? Ash put most Victoria Secret models to shame and swung a two handed warhammer with enough force to squash a rock golem's skull.

"Then how are we supposed to kill it?" Grunted Marcus the Gruesome.

The name said it all about Marcus. He was big. Only a few inches shorter than Devin and just as wide, he had earned the surname Gruesome from his horribly disfigured face. The ancient dragon Yragux had seared half of it off battling Marcus. He had killed Yragux with his battleaxe, but it was destroyed in the battle, so he ripped one of the dead dragon's canines out of its skull and fastened it to some of the dragon's scales that he later wove together. It left him with a twenty-three inch knife that he paired with a pretty nasty pump-action shotgun.

Peter furrowed his brow at the question. "We hack it to pieces. That's been the plan, and I say we stick to it."

"One problem with that." Devin interjected. "We chopped off its arms and they sort of... grew back."

"Fire?" Rudolph Richards asked.

Rudy's a black man about the same height as I am with a Mohawk hairdo that I admired more that you could believe. He was muscled and scarred everywhere; wearing an open combat vest and armed with just about every weapon imaginable. Grenades, knives, firearms, a spiked flail, dual katanas crossed on his back, and his coup de grace; gauntlets that I had rigged up with spring loaded claws like Wolverine from X-Men.

"We'll keep it in mind." Said Peter. "Anyone have anything else, or have we really boiled it down to decapitation and fire?"

"We could go for the heart." Suggested Jacques.

Ribery is a French-Canadian, and like Ash he could easily double as a model. He has wavy black hair, deep green eyes, and is built like Michelangelo's David. I would hate him if he weren't such a nice guy, but I don't think he's said a harsh word in his life. Don't be fooled though, he was hell on wheels in battle. He favored a broad sword and shield and wielded them like the Knights of old.

"The Horseman has survived all these years without a head; I'm not sure taking the heart would do much either." The King had finally broken from his trance. "Kellen, you said there's no documented way to kill one of these?" Factarum nodded his approval. "Then when it gets here, we get creative."

"Creative how?" I asked.

The King let out a deep breath. "I wish I had an answer to that. If the Horseman's in Denver then he's close and we need to think quickly. Trevor, you've been uncharacteristically quiet, any ideas?"

Trevor Wingback was known for mouthing off just as much as I was, and as such we got along famously. He has red hair, pale skin, freckles, and doesn't look very threatening at all – it's what makes him so dangerous. He is called Wingback because when he was a baby he was found abandoned at the castle with giant wing shaped birthmarks on his back. Trevor had only ever used one weapon; a blade forged in the very fires of Hell called the Harbinger. No one knew where he'd gotten it, and he had never been at liberty to share. It was rare for him to go a meeting without speaking, and he didn't disappoint. Trevor stood and stretched his back, his red plate armor shining beautifully.

"I only have one thing to say." Trevor yawned. "I want – my head." Then the slight man flipped over the round table and sprinted off towards the trophy room.

Even with his supernatural speed the Horseman didn't get far. Marcus had avoided the table completely and turned his shotgun on "Trevor" to blow away both his legs. Regenerative limbs or not, they still vanished for a second and with nothing to catch its weight, the torso crashed to the floor. Marcus kept the pressure on and soon we had the Horseman surrounded ten to one. He drew the Harbinger and slowly circled looking for his first attack.

"Juan, he doesn't deserve to hold that blade." I growled.

"I couldn't agree more." My fellow Knight replied, he then blew the hand holding the Harbinger off with his Desert Eagle.

The blade rang against the floor and the Horseman howled his rage. He charged Rudolph, but feigned left to strike out at Jacques, who promptly chopped his arm off at the shoulder.

"I don't think the limb thing is working here, Pete." Said the King.

"Fire it is!" Exclaimed Rudy producing a handheld flamethrower from inside his vest.

"Where in the blazes did you get that?" Ashley asked incredulously.

"A lady doesn't ask, and a gentleman doesn't tell." He replied coolly and opened up on the horseman with his toy.

About fifteen seconds later Rudolph took his finger from the trigger. When the smoke cleared the Horseman was standing in our circle examining his fingernails in a particularly bored fashion.

"Tell you what." The monster said. "Try for my heart so that you can discover I no longer even have one, realize that you'll eventually tire where as I won't, bring me my head, and maybe I'll let some of you live."

The rest of the Knights and I let out a group snort and the King twirled his three-headed flail through the air. "You should leave now. Go hide in whatever hole you've been in for all this time and never come out."

"Very well." Replied the Horseman. "You're lives are forfeit."

Suddenly Trevor's head began receding into his neck and vanished entirely. Then, standing where Trevor had been was the monster Devin and I had seen before. Huge, headless, and entirely black, the Headless Horseman was definitely something to be reckoned with. What made him even scarier was the next trick he pulled out. Ten different heads sprouted from the top of the Pugot's body along with just as many sets of limbs.

"This just got interesting." I muttered and braced myself.

The Horseman went to work attacking everywhere at once to the dismay of our elite group. First Jacques was batted into a far wall, Juan followed while reloading his pistol with one hand. Next went Rudy as he lunged at the body with his claws, shortly after Kellen had his ankle hooked and was thrown across the room next to Jacques. I chanced a look around at my fallen companions. They were all still breathing, but if our remaining force didn't do something soon none of us would be. Marcus tried another shotgun blast to the heads and an absolutely mind-numbingly stupid plan hit me.

"Heads and legs on my cue!" I shouted. The Horseman turned his full attention on me as I spoke. "Now would be nice guys!"

Marcus and Peter went to work on the legs feigning and altering attacks to distract, while the King, Devin, and Ash used any opening to smash a spare skull. I took the luxury of awaiting the opportunity to enact what was arguably the dumbest idea I've ever had (and that is truly saying something).

Finally, my opening appeared. Marcus caught half the Horseman's legs in a shotgun blast, toppling it just as Ashley and Devin struck a full six heads from the monster's shoulders. Now or never, I darted in under flailing arms and caught the remaining four with a broad sweep of *Laniatus*. In their stead was a gaping hole of darkness, and the missing legs put the Horseman at a height for me to dive into the gap. Unfortunately, that's exactly what I did.

***

I landed in a black abyss, realizing that I had probably just thrown away my life. There was nothing. Nothing to see, nothing to feel, nothing to kill.

"Jonah, meet the whale." I uttered to myself.

Turning three hundred and sixty degrees, I searched for something – anything – to harm the Horseman, but it seemed like a losing cause. But, I always try to be proactive, so instead of standing around with my thumb up my ass, I started walking. Which begs the question, why was there so much room in here? I guess that was really a moot point at the moment, but I needed to find a way out of here or it was safe to assume I'd just wind up feeding the Horseman's power.

I had been walking for what seemed like miles when I heard it. At first I wasn't even sure I had, but then there was another faint echo of what sounded like a man in agony. I waited in utter silence trying to pinpoint the direction of the sound.

"Gotcha." I said to no one, and sprinted off after the moaning.

It was appalling. I arrived to find a very ethereal looking Trevor Wingback sitting next to his own moaning head. The view was almost enough to make me sick. My friend, dead, inside of a monster, head severed and sitting pitifully in the darkness. The worst of it was the contrast to what Trevor had once been. Always radiant and jovial, quick with a joke, quicker to draw his blade. Wingback hadn't just been my friend, he had been my sworn brother-in-arms, and had saved my life on at least two different occasions. Seeing him this way made an anger I had rarely felt boil inside me, which I failed to contain.

"Trevor, get off of the floor." My fallen compadre's head looked at me with despair in its eyes. "I said get the fuck up from the floor, Trevor."

Trev was still in his gleaming red plate, although it was as opaque as my friend now was. His decapitated body gathered up his severed head and held it under its arm.

"What?" His ghost asked pitifully.

"What the hell do you think you're doing?" I asked him icily.

"I think I'm being dead, imprisoned inside of an ancient villain that killed me by taking me completely unaware. I was a Knight and I never even saw it coming. I clearly didn't deserve to live anyway."

If I thought I could make physical contact with the ghost, I would have made what the Horseman did look like a favor. "How did he get you? Tell me exactly."

"I was in the Caribbean, relaxing on the beach of a very tropical island, when I heard a woman call out for help. She appeared to be drowning, and you know how I react to damsels in distress, so I dove in after her. Dragged her out, gave her CPR, made sure she was OK, turned to leave, and 'pop' went my head. My body is probably floating off in the sea somewhere."

"How long ago?"

His headless body shrugged. "Time's pretty irrelevant when you're dead. It happened in September."

"You've been dead for three months?" I asked, flabbergasted.

"If September was three months ago."

"That means that the Horseman was already in the castle earlier today. He tricked us all."

"Yeah, I don't think it was quite as bad for you though." Said Trevor. "At least your ghost still has the head attached."

"I'm not dead, Trev. I hopped in here looking for a way to kill the Horseman."

His head sighed from under his arm. "Well, you'll be dead soon enough, just like me."

I tried to punch his body in the chest, but my hand phased through it. "That's enough god damn it! The Trevor I know would be pissed right now. He would want to get back at the piece of trash that killed him... that's trying to kill his friends. Instead of fighting back, you're sitting here, literally holding your head in your hands, letting your murderer feed on your soul."

A flash of anger passed through his eyes. "Do you think I didn't try? I searched high and low for anyway out of here. There is none. So now I get to spend eternity trapped in here feeding the Horseman's power."

"Why?" I asked.

"What do you mean *why?* What option do I have?"

"You can fight." I said through my clenched jaw.

"HOW?" His severed head screamed at me.

I took a deep breath to try and maintain my composure. "The Horseman feeds on the souls of the heads he consumes, correct?" Trevor performed what I think was supposed to be a nod so I continued. "If you're floating around here, I'm assuming there are more, where are they?"

Trevor's head lifted an eyebrow. "They're around here somewhere, no one really talks much. What do you have in mind?"

"Just bring me to the rest of the victims." I said with a vicious grin. "I've got a plan."

***

There weren't hundreds of victims – there were
thousands. Maybe even tens of thousands. Each and every
one of them was holding their own severed head, which
looked downright depressed. It was disgusting… none of
them had any fight left in them. There were ghosts here that
clearly dated back all the way to the days of Camelot, but
even the newer victims just looked totally resigned. I even
saw the cop that the Horseman had attacked us as in
Denver. He couldn't have been dead for more than a few
days, and he already had the look of someone who had
given up.

I couldn't stand it. "What is wrong with all of you?"
I shouted at them as their dead eyes all gaped at me. "You
were all killed by the same… thing, and none of you will
stand up and try to get even?"

"Who are you?" asked a young woman's head from
where her body was holding it. This spurned a cacophony
of other questions and I didn't see any way to get them to
shut up. Luckily for me, Trevor did.

He jammed two fingers in his detached head's
mouth and let out a brain-piercing whistle. The other ghosts
simultaneously shut their mouths and stared at the deceased
Knight intently.

He took a step in front of me and spoke like the man
I had known in life. "Friends, I feel that I can call you
friends because we all share something very intimate. Our
murderer. I'm sure by now you all know who he is, the
Headless Horseman. Now, based on your current
appearances, I believe it's safe to assume that you had your
heads ripped off by the same assailant; although I'm sure
he rarely looked the same while doing it. I can't speak for
any of you, but I for one am pissed off and would like to
cause him some pain."

He was interrupted by a little girl with her head under one arm and a teddy bear under the other. "Mister, what can we do?" she asked in a saddening, innocent voice.

The anger in Trevor visibly grew, and he seemed to turn a little bit more solid. "We kill him." He replied evenly.

Shouts of "how" rose from the crowd and Trevor furrowed his brow. This is where I come in.

"It's simple people." I shouted over the din of their combined voices." "Hey, listen up!" I shouted to no avail.

I turned to Trevor and tilted my head towards the ghosts. One more unbelievably shrill whistle later there was quiet, and it was my turn to speak again. "People, the Horseman needs *you* to power him. Don't you get it? Band together, cut off his power supply, and poof; no more Horseman."

"But how do we do that?" Yelled out the head of a man in a Spanish Conquistador's clothing.

Of course this led to another bout of "Who's the Loudest" from the ghosts, but no whistle was necessary this time. Trevor simply began to hover off the ground, and raised the hand not holding onto his head for silence. He seemed to grow more substantial with each passing moment, and his voice sounded off like a carrion call to the masses of ghosts before him.

"Join me friends. Together we can end this poor, captive existence, and with it our joint tormentor."

It was amazing. As his voice echoed all around, more and more ghosts began to float into the air around Trevor; leaving me standing alone while they hovered above. The name Wingback never seemed more appropriate as he floated gloriously, his red plate armor shining like an artificial sun.

He looked down on me. "Thank you, Godric, for everything." He said smiling.

"A little cheesy for my tastes there, Buddy, but you're welcome." I called up to him.

"Yeah, it felt a little too soft." He winked, flipped me off, and turned his attention back to the horde of ghosts before him.

Grinning broadly, he nodded and the rest of the ghosts began to glow and solidify. Soon I couldn't keep my eyes open against the glare, and was forced to screw them shut. There was shaking beneath my feet, and the lights went back to normal. When I opened my eyes I was staring at the ceiling of the castle strategy room with Devin, the King, and everyone else kneeling around me.

Upon noticing my consciousness, Devin dropped to the seat of his pants, let out a deep breath, and said just two words. "Thank God."

The King also breathed heavily, and then smiled fondly at me. "Nice work, Son. You had us pretty worried there for a second."

Oh, did I forget to mention that the King is my father? My bad, please allow me to introduce myself. My name is Sir Godric Patronar, Knight of the Realm, Anointed Warrior, Master Blacksmith, General Smartass, and Heir Apparent to the Kingship of North America.

First Boy
by
Dennis Sharpe

"Matthew, you know I love you, but…" Her voice hung there, digitally dangling in his cell phone. He could picture her in his head, mouth open, unable to continue, as he fought the heavy winter winds to keep his cruiser on the road.

"Why do we have to have this conversation at least once a year? C'mon, Holly. You knew what I did for a living when you married me." He was trying to use his at home voice with her. She hated talking to him while he was at work and using what she called his "cop voice". He was frustrated, but he loved her so he had to keep his tone as warm as he could.

"That doesn't make it any easier to deal with. I just can't keep letting you go to work not knowing if I'll see you again. I can't do it! Not anymore, I just can't! I won't! I'll be at my parent's house when you get home. Please, just let it be over. Let me go."

Five years of safe evening returns had done nothing to assuage her fears. She heard all the stories of close calls and violent encounters from the other wives of Forrest County deputies. It was like each story was a pebble in her shoe and now she was walking on gravel piles – painfully, and uncomfortably, every day.

"Honey, it was a car wreck, that's all. I was the first on scene, not actually in the wreck! I'm fine." His tone was steady, but only because he was keeping it that way with every ounce of self-control he had.

"Diane said you almost fell off the bridge. Matt, I'm not ready to be a widow. I just couldn't handle it." There was a torrent of tears in her voice, quivering on the other end of the line.

"I'm fine. I'll be fine. I have one more stop to make, and then I have paperwork. I'll be home for dinner. We can talk it over then. Two days off in a row starts tonight. Cut me some slack and let's just talk when I get home." He paused, wondering if she was even listening, before punctuating his words with "I love you."

The phone was silent for long enough that he had to look at it to see if she'd hung up.

"I'll be here. I won't promise I'll stay, but we'll talk. I love you, too." She ended the call before he could add anything.

He told himself it was better that way, as he shifted his focus back on the rain-slicked pavement in front of him. With their conversation on hold, there was no chance he'd upset her more before he'd be there to hold her and make everything all-better. Holding her close always did a world to make her forget how bad things had been and he intended to do a lot of that tonight.

He passed the road he was supposed to turn down, twice, mistaking it for a driveway. The rain was picking up and with the cloud cover, four in the afternoon could have almost been midnight. He finally made the turn and looked for the address on his paperwork, cursing the cold wet weather under his breath.

Dark Light

Forrest County had more middle of nowhere than anywhere he could remember having been in all of his thirty-two years. If not for the radio and computer in his cruiser, he'd still be getting lost, even after eleven years on the job.

The house, if you could even call it a house, was not as difficult to find as the road it sat on had been. It had clearly once been white, though that was likely more than half a century ago if the peeling paint was to serve as a sign. The rotting three-story mammoth loomed above the road, looking more than foreboding in the gray haze of the afternoon. Even at a quarter of a mile away, the place gave him a chill the weather couldn't compete with.

He shrugged it off and continued up the winding tree-lined drive. This was a routine check, likely nothing. He'd be on his way in no time, and then a pot of coffee and some paperwork were all that stood between him and Holly's arms.

The crunch of the caramel rock driveway sounded like static on a radio, he thought, as he pulled slowly to a stop in front of the wide, decaying porch. He flipped the papers up on his clipboard to look. Someone had called this morning to report a child, possibly two, living abandoned and uncared for in this old heap. He should have been here hours ago, but he'd practically stumbled into that accident, and it had cost him hours.

Holding his cell phone in front of him, he considered fighting his poncho to get it back in his pants pocket. It didn't seem worth the effort, but he wasn't about to replace another Smartphone. As he stepped out in the deluge he decided to simply toss it up onto the dash.

He slowly examined the outside of the house and its immediate surroundings as he stepped to the far side of the porch. There were no signs that anyone had been here in his lifetime. Even the driveway was growing green in large patches. This was a ridiculous waste of time.

As he made his way slowly around the cracks and holes in the porch, his weight on the ancient boards caused a series of unsettling creaks and moans that filled his mind with images of falling through into God only knows what down below. He took another moment's glance around as the hair on the back of his neck began to stand up, and then knocked firmly on the door. To his amazement, it didn't just fall in.

Even more astounding to him were the sounds that followed. He could swear he heard voices and footsteps inside. Then there was the loud clicking sound of a deadbolt sliding back. There was someone here. Instinctively, Matthew took a half step back and rested his weight on his left foot as his right hand unsnapped his holster. His eyes narrowed as the door creaked back into the dark, trying to identify any threat before it could react to him. Then his mouth fell open in shock.

Standing there in the open doorway was a clean, if not well dressed, little girl. She couldn't be more than six years old. She looked up at him with a profound sadness in her eyes, as if she were mourning the loss of a pet.

"You shouldn't be here." She said very softly as she stepped back away from the door.

Shaking his head slightly, as though it would help dislodge his shock, Matthew stepped forward as he bent down toward her. "What's your name, sweetie? Where are your parents?"

The smell of mildew and rot was almost overpowering, slapping him in the face as he dared to enter. It felt like a warning, but he was trained to ignore danger when it meant helping others.

A male voice from deeper in the darkness answered for her, "She's not supposed to talk to you. You really should go."

Matthew glanced around quickly, trying to locate the source of the voice. All he succeeded in doing, though, was losing sight of the little girl. He crept further into the house trying to let his eyes adjust to the near pitch black of the room.

As he began to make out a staircase opposite where he had entered, the door slamming shut behind him startled him again. He spun around on his heels, hand on his pistol, only to vaguely make out the girl's small shape standing in front of the door. He couldn't be sure, but he thought she was looking at the floor.

"Your name plate says 'Burroughs,' so should I call you 'Deputy Burroughs,' 'Officer,' 'Sir,' or would you prefer to have me call you by your first name in an attempt to endear me to you?" The male voice was also a young one, but old enough for the chiding tone to be annoying.

"Where are you?" Matthew asked, realizing he was quickly losing control of the situation. He needed to calm down. He was the authority here, not these children. He needed to take charge. "I'm not playing games with you. Step out where I can see you. Now!"

"Why, Deputy… you sound cross." He was sure this boy, somewhere in the dark, was mocking him.

"I said now!" He said firmly again, stepping back toward the door and putting his hand on the girl's shoulder. The clicks of light switches being flipped echoed in the room for a moment before the room was lit by the dim glow of a single, low-watt bulb in a lamp near the base of the stairs. In the amber light, he could now make out the boy. He sat on one of the lower steps, his left arm stretched up onto a panel of switches on the wall. He didn't look to be more than twelve. He also looked very clean, but shabby, with a wiry frame below his close-cropped dark hair.

"Do you feel safer now? More in control? Aren't they supposed to teach deputies not to be afraid of the dark?" The boy asked it with a face completely devoid of emotion.

"Where are your parents, son?" Matthew asked as he stepped toward the boy, leading the girl by the shoulder next to him.

"My parents? They're dead. Her parents are dead. What does that have to do with anything?" The boys looked up the stairs, and then back at Matthew. "Are you here to save us?"

"Save you? Are you living here alone? Are there any adults in the house?" The thought that there might be a violent, possibly armed adult in the house dawned on Matthew. He stopped near the center of the room and looked up the staircase behind the boy.

"Father is the only adult who comes here. But he's not actually our parent…just our caretaker. He doesn't

approve of visitors either. Not even if they have badges."
He nodded slightly at the wall off to Matthew's right.

In the faint yellow light, Matthew could make out a large, wet looking stain on the wall. As he stepped toward it, the dark red and black smears looked thick and putrid. "Is that…" Disbelief softened his words, but the boy heard him and interrupted.

"Blood? Yes. It was Boy. Father did it. He had to, otherwise we wouldn't learn."

Turning his eyes back to the boy on the stairs, Matthew noticed what he thought was a faint smile on his face. This kid was screwing with him, trying to freak him out – and it had almost worked. Almost.

"Look, kid, are you here alone or not? I need to talk to an adult, or you're both going to have to come with me." Matthew looked down at the girl next to him for a reaction, but got none.

"Father wouldn't like that at all. He'd have to punish us. You really should just leave. You don't know…" this time it was Matthew's turn to interrupt.

"Stop playing games! I don't have time for it. Where are your parents, or whoever is looking after you? This 'Father,' or whoever?" He was pulling the girl with him and quickly closing the distance to the base of the stairs.

"You don't understand. Father isn't anything you're prepared for. He's ancient, and powerful." He could see that the boy's face was awash in terror. The acting was almost impressive.

"Where is he?"

"He'll be here soon, and you don't want to be here when he gets here."

***

"He was born in Nuremberg in 1632." The boy stopped putting clothes in his bag and looked at Matthew. "Can you even imagine what that must have been like, Deputy? Like a fairytale land. Like something out of a Terry Brooks story."

"Keep packing. That was the deal," Matthew said, pointing back at the large plastic bag. The boy sighed and turned, but kept his eyes on Matthew for a moment longer.

"His parents weren't royal, but they weren't poor either," the boy continued, ignoring Matthew's persistence. "They were educated for their time, with enough money to travel. You know, just to travel. But on a trip, when he was twelve, his parents got themselves caught up in the English Civil War."

The boy was picking up each article of threadbare clothing from piles in the corner, to hold them out in front of him, and then gently refold them before placing them in the bag just so. He was stalling, and Matthew knew it. He was probably just biding his time, waiting for just the right moment to make a run for it. Matthew wasn't going to let that happen. Not on his watch, not in this weather, and most certainly not with Holly waiting on him.

"They were killed -- his parents I mean. They were killed, right before his thirteenth birthday, and he was ferried off to what he was told would be the 'safety of London' in 1645. He was put in an orphan's home, but an ambitious woman sold him to a blacksmith for the price of a pair of boots. He was the blacksmith's slave for almost a year before he escaped, only to be gathered up as a 'ne'er-do-well,' and shipped to the colonies to be a bound servant."

"I'm going to check on...her. Is she your sister?"

"Yes, she is. But not in a way you'd understand."

Matthew did his best to look sympathetic. This kid still saw children and adults as being in an 'us versus them' situation. "Hey, I was a kid once, too. I know you don't think grown-ups understand you, and what you're going through. I'm not your enemy though. I'm here to help."

Shaking his head slowly, he replied, "You really don't get it, Deputy."

***

Matthew looked into the cluttered bedroom where he'd left the little girl to pack up a bag of her things. He found her exactly where he'd left her, standing next to the bed in her long, dingy white t-shirt, staring at her feet. She glanced up at him only briefly as he walked over to her and opened the empty black garbage bag that had been crumpled on the filthy mattress.

He'd gotten the bags out of his cruiser, one for each of the children when he'd gone out to call in. The bags were enormous and durable, intended for yard waste. They were lucky he still had some in his trunk from cleaning out his garage. Because of the worsening weather, the social workers had asked the dispatcher to have him bring the children to them at the hospital on his way back into town.

Bringing them back with him didn't seem so bad an idea, but he'd been told to have them pack up personal items and clothes if they had any. That proved more difficult than anticipated. The only way he could get that boy to agree to anything was if he agreed to listen to the boy's tall tales, 'for his own good,' as a warning of the boogeyman that was going to get them if he didn't just leave the kids here and go.

"Why aren't you packing?" He asked her, glancing around the room for what she might want to take with her. "Are your clothes in these boxes here?"

She looked at him like it physically hurt her not to speak, and yet she stayed silent.

Matthew knelt down next to the two cardboard boxes on the floor next to the mattress. He opened each one and found nothing but paper – sheet after sheet of lined paper colored on in black and brown crayon. He thought those were probably the only two colors she had. He began to scan the room again for anything else that might contain clothing. It really was quite a mess.

"Where are your clothes, sweetie?" He asked, looking back at her. She just stood there staring at him, her eyes barely holding back the tears.

"If I leave you here, and go back and check on...him, will you promise me you'll put your clothes in this bag?"

She continued to stare at him catatonically, for several moments before finally nodding her agreement.

"Okay then. I'll go, but when I come back, I really want to see that bag have clothes in it. Please." He waited for her to nod again, and then stood. "Alright."

***

"He worked as a laborer, as in 'doing the hard work,' by hand, in Virginia for a while. This wasn't even the United States back then, did you know that?" The boy asked the question with a genuine sense of reverence, and wonder.

"What year was it?" Matthew asked the boy absently.

"1646. He was fourteen. He was bought by man and kept as slave, not as bound servant."

This kid had to have studied this in school recently, or seen it on TV. Matthew felt like kicking himself for not retaining more of the history he'd studied in school. He really wanted facts to shoot holes in the story he was being told. If he could break the story, maybe he could get the boy to tell him what he was really doing here, and where his parents were. Even just his name would be nice.

"So he was a slave again? Or did the little boy just feel like a slave?" Matthew asked, fishing for more personal information.

"Yes. Again." He stopped folding a pair of underwear and looked at Matthew as though he thought the deputy was feeble-minded. "The man bought him. That made him a slave. The man would only call him 'boy,' and beat him horribly all the time."

"Boy, huh? Is that why you won't tell me your name? Are you really the 'boy' in this story?"

He rolled his eyes at Matthew in disdain. "My name is gone. So is hers. They aren't coming back. Ever. That's just how it is."

"If you were abused, we can help you. There's never an excuse to beat kids. Never." Matthew rested his hand on the boy's shoulder and squeezed it gently.

The boy looked up at Matthew, smirking slightly with a glint in his eye. "Spare the rod, and spoil the child, Deputy."

The look in his eyes gave Matthew a chill, making him step back from the boy.

"Anyway, the man's wife was the only thing that made that time bearable. She educated him for a while, gave him books to read, and helped him get more of the German accent out of his voice. She gave him hope – for a while anyway. All good things must end though. Right, Deputy? She and the man took a trip to Europe, and when they returned she was not well. They called it the White Plague.

"You mean the Black Plague?" Matthew thought he had finally found the mistake that would let him break the kid's story.

"No. I mean the White Plague. Google it if you have to, Deputy." He was so cocky and sure. Matthew made a mental note to look up 'White Plague' on his phone when he got back in the cruiser.

"When she died, he killed the man. Beat him to death with a curtain rod while he slept. He just grabbed what money the man had on him and he took off."

"Did he take his sister with him?"

The boy stopped sharply and looked at Matthew. It was the first time in his life that Matthew really understood the old saying, 'If looks could kill.' The awkward pause

stretched on for several long moments before the boy
turned and continued talking and packing.

Matthew could tell he was having an effect on this
kid. He wasn't sure if the boy was getting tired of all the
lies and stories, and might be getting ready to tell the truth,
or if he was just tired of being interrupted.

***

The girl was still in the room where he'd left her,
but she wasn't packing like the boy was. He could see the
bag sitting open on the floor next to the mattress. It had a
few pairs of underwear in it, and she sat next to it with her
face in her hands.

"I thought we had a deal. If I left you alone, you'd
pack."

She didn't even look up at him. She just took the
bag in one hand and scooted over, tears pouring silently
down her face, and began to take socks from under the
mattress and put them into the bag. Whatever issues that
boy might have, were nothing compared to the mess that
was this little girl.

Someone had done something awful to this child.
He wasn't entirely sure that the boy hadn't also done things
to her. She was in a sorry state, and all he wanted to do was
scoop her up and hold her. He wanted to tell her everything
would be all right, but that wouldn't help her right now,
and he knew it. She just had to finish packing so he could
get her out of this place, and to someone who really could
help her.

He watched her for a few moments as she moved at
a snail's pace. She was doing what he asked of her – she

was simply doing it as slow as humanly possible. She had clearly been through a lot, so Matthew decided he'd let her move at her own pace. After all, she was at least moving. Matthew turned and walked down the dimly lit hallway to the stairs. Looking down across the front room where he'd come in, he thought it seemed even darker now than before. He kept seeing things move in the darkness. There were likely all shapes and sizes of rodent and vermin all around him. He couldn't wait to be out of this place.

He eased himself slowly down the stairs and made his way through the voluminous black of the empty room toward the door. He didn't like leaving the boy alone any longer than he had to. He was sure that kid was just sitting up there in that room, not packing, and devising some kind of escape plan.

As he opened the door, Matthew was shocked at how much the temperature had dropped outside. The cold hit him in the face like he'd walked into a freezer. It wasn't just the cold that made Matthew shudder, the rain had gotten worse, and ice had started to coat everything.

He left the door standing open so there was less likelihood that the kids would lock him out as he walked to his cruiser. The sounds of the porch and even the gravel had changed now, with a coating of ice. Driving back into town was going to be awful, and there would be more wrecks like the one this morning.

They would ask him to stay on and keep working into the next shift, but he couldn't. Not tonight. He had to get back to Holly, and sort things out. He'd already lost enough time dealing with how slowly these children moved.

He had to hit the door to his cruiser a few times to break it loose of the ice before he could get it to open. Everything was icing over too fast. This weather was going to be awful. As he settled down in the seat and started the car, he decided he'd leave the engine running with the heat on when he went back inside. Maybe then, he hoped, the windows and doors wouldn't freeze up, and he'd actually be able to get the kids into town a little easier when the time came.

Matthew glanced briefly back at the dark, imposing house. The building itself made him uneasy, as if every window was another set of eyes peering out at him, examining him. This place, he thought, could do with a good bulldozing, and soon.

He was about to head back inside when he noticed his phone still lying on the dash. He thought about it for a second before he retrieved it, second-guessing himself. He unlocked it, opened a web browser window, and began to type. His mouth opened slightly as he looked at the search results in front of him, but the only words that escaped his lips were "White Plague... tuberculosis."

***

"New York City is where I left off. That's where the monster found him." The boy immediately picked the story back up when Matthew appeared in the doorway. "He had made it to New York City from Virginia, and New York has always been full of monsters, whether people can see them or not."

"Monsters aren't real, son. The only real monsters are people who hurt other people, or hurt children,"

Matthew said, sure that if he kept it up, he'd eventually get through to this kid.

"It was a monster, Deputy. A real one. It ate people. It caught him, and kept him for four years. Enjoying his fear. Enjoying what his blood tasted like. Finally, it decided that it liked him, so it drained him, trained him, and made him into a proper and civilized monster as well."

"A civilized monster?" Matthew asked.

"How else can they blend in and hide around people? They can't just run around the streets looking like monsters. They'd be killed." The boy said it like it was common sense, and he couldn't believe that Matthew hadn't just known it.

"The monster was a man then?"

"It looked like a man. It had been a man once. It wasn't a man anymore."

"Oh, I see what you mean." Matthew said, believing this would finally be the key. This story was cracking. The monsters really were men, and now he'd find out more about who had abused this boy.

"After he became a monster too, he was taught to stalk people. Not stalking like there are laws against, but stalking like a hunter cat – one of the big ones –would do. He learned how to shut off his emotions, how not to care. He didn't care about much anyway, but this was the last step in making him completely into a monster, in his own right."

"So, this monster made him a monster?"

"Yeah…and he'd never have to be afraid of anything again." There was almost a dreamy reverence in the boy's voice when he said it.

Matthew took note of the slight shift in the boy's tone. This kid was still afraid and didn't want to be anymore. Matthew was growing more and more determined – he had to help him.

"And what did he do now that he was a monster?"

"The only thing he could do." The boy said matter-of-factly. "He killed the monster that made him a monster." The boy placed the last article of clothing in the bag, and then dragged the bag over to an old broken chest lying on its side. He forced it open, causing further splintering of the already cracked wood, and began to remove his few personal items. A series of trinkets that looked like little more than worthless junk passed through the boy's hands as Matthew watched. All the while, the boy was still telling his story, obviously taking his time in filling the bag. "He had now become the monster. Now, he had power, and he had no fear. He felt nothing, but he had everything. The world opened up to him. His sociopathic nature took over – stalking and killing."

"Sociopathic?" Matthew asked, puzzled to hear the word.

"I'm sorry, Deputy. Should I use smaller words, so you can understand me?"

They both stared at each other for a moment, neither one flinching, before the boy looked back at what he was doing and continued to speak.

"He made dark alleys and abandoned buildings his homes, and preyed upon anyone foolish enough to go alone in the dark places. He followed the sad and worthless to their homes and ended them. You could almost say he was doing the world a favor."

"How are killing people doing the world a favor?" Matthew asked in stunned disbelief.

"He was getting rid of the people who didn't deserve to live. The awful people, the kind of people that hurt others, and end up filling up the jails and graveyards anyway."

The boy dragged the bag behind him to the other side of the mattress, and Matthew stepped far enough over to see what he was now loading into it. There were stacks and stacks of paperback novels, all in varied conditions. Some were tattered, worn and missing their covers, while others looked pristine and well cared for. Matthew thought he finally understood where the boy's story was really coming from, as he read the author's names: Anne Rice, Neil Gaiman, Stephen King, and Thomas Amo. This kid was just blending together all sorts of scary fiction to hide himself behind.

"He kept everything fluid, changing his M.O. as he moved all over the country. It was how he never got caught. He collected funds and new identities as he went. He made himself impossible to track – new towns, new faces, new victims." The boy sounded more reverent than afraid describing this.

"This guy sounds like all the bad guys from the last ten years of murder movies all rolled into one. Like he might be the worst of those books you have there. If he was real, and really like that, then I should arrest him, right?" Matthew asked, hoping he could show the boy that he would protect him, and he could tell him the truth now.

"No, Deputy. Because he is real, and he is really like that, and you should run."

***

As he walked down the hall toward the girl's room, he could swear he heard whispering voices somewhere off in a distance corner of the house. He knew it was only the wind, but he stopped to listen anyway. He felt like there were eyes on him. This place was really giving him the creeps.

He walked into the room where the girl sat, looking at her half-filled bag. She seemed so distant, like she'd gotten lost in what she was doing as she sat, her face still wet with tears.

"C'mon, sweetie. You're almost finished. Let's keep packing, okay? We need to get going before the storm gets any worse out there." Matthew nudged her slightly and she went back to putting things in the big black bag.
This little girl was the reason Matthew had become a cop. She was a victim who needed to be helped – to be saved. He only wished he could offer her more comfort, and somehow make all her pain go away. He knew she would be better in time, but her silent tears broke his heart.

He stepped back out into the hall and could swear he saw something move in the shadows near the top of the stairs. As he started walking that way, he told himself that it had only been a rat or a raccoon, no real threat, but his hand still found its way to his sidearm.

He heard something moving downstairs. This was getting to be too much. He took out his flashlight and wandered down into the dark. The long, black flashlight's batteries were almost dead and he knew it, but having it in his hand made things seem more sane. He was hearing things off in the dark and seeing movement where he knew there shouldn't be any.

"This place is getting to me," he said aloud as he turned and started back up the stairs.

He thought that maybe it had been the boy's plan all along to shake him up, to rattle him enough that he'd make a mistake, and let them get away. Matthew was resolved. He wasn't going to let that happen. He owed it to both of these kids to get them out of this mess, this nightmare, and give them a chance at a normal life.

Matthew stood at the top of the stairs looking toward the front door. His eyes darted from corner to corner of the scarcely lit room that spread out below him. He was convinced that there was something moving in the shadows down there, he just couldn't ever get a look at what it was. Finally, unable to take any more of it, he turned away and headed back down the hallway. It was completely black outside now, and the lights inside all seemed dimmer. He had to get them all out of this place before he lost his mind.

The little girl was standing by the door when he got to her room. She had the bag closed up beside her. His gaze met hers and in answer she looked down at her feet again. He could tell that she was resigned to leaving, but she was still shaking. He didn't know if it was due to the cold or her fear. He guessed it was a little of both.

***

Matthew opened the door and was completely unsurprised to find the boy sitting instead of packing. He brought the girl into the room with him this time, her packed bag slung over his shoulder. He looked into the boy's bag and took it in the same hand as the girl's, and slung them both onto his back. He motioned for the boy to stand and join him in the hall.

"For the last time, Deputy, please…just go. Leave us alone. Forget you ever saw us." The boy sounded sad, almost broken now.

"I can't just leave you here alone. This is about what's best for you, not what you think you want," Matthew said, exasperation ringing clearly in his words.

"But what about what's best for you?" The kid seemed at his wit's end with Matthew. "Just leave. Just go," he pleaded.

Matthew stood up straighter and puffed out his chest as he shifted his voice back to the one Holly hated. He was no long speaking to the boy, as much as he was commanding him. "That's enough, kid. You're going with me. You can walk out of here on your own, or I can cuff and carry you. Your call."

The boy didn't back down. He simply stood in place staring at Matthew, daring him to do something. As he stepped into the room and took him by the arm, the boy piped up to continue his story. "One night in St. Charles, Missouri, Father…he came across a child being abused…"

"Aren't we done with all that now?" Matthew asked, as he tugged him out into the hall.

"I haven't told you everything! I'm not done! Deputy, you said you'd hear me out if I packed my things. I did what you asked, let me finish." He almost yelled.

There was almost a sense of panic in his voice, and it showed in his eyes. Matthew decided to let him keep talking, but he wasn't going to stop to listen anymore. "Fine. But walk while you talk." He said to the boy, as he pushed him toward the stairs at the end of the hall.

"Okay!" He said as he began to walk slowly down the hallway. "Father accidently came across a child being abused by his parents. He wasn't sure he was going to do anything, but he watched them. He watched and he waited, and once they were asleep that night, he decided to act. He broke into their house. He woke the sleeping boy up, and carried him into his parents' room. He took knives and…and he…he killed them. He killed the parents and he made him…the boy…he made the boy help."

As they reached the end of the hallway and turned down onto the stairs, the girl began crying aloud. Matthew put his hand on her shoulder to comfort her, but she wouldn't look up from her feet. Thankfully, she was still walking dutifully with them.

"He chops up the parents' bodies and makes a big mess." The boy tried to stop to emphasize the point, but Matthew continued to gently push him forward. "Then he lights the house on fire, and stands outside in the backyard, ya know, just watching it burn. When he left, he took the boy with him. He didn't really force him to go, but where else was the boy going to go, really? He called him 'boy,' like he was called 'boy' by the man in Virginia."

The boy looked up, to verify that he was still being listened to as they continued down the stairs. He searched Matthew's face for a response, but didn't find one.

"Again, kinda like you. Just called 'boy,' huh?" Matthew said, almost flippantly.

"This time, Deputy, yes. Exactly like me."

At the base of the stairs, the boy turned to face Matthew. He kept moving, walking backward as he continued to talk. Matthew thought that this would be the point where the boy got desperate. Now he had to know he wasn't going to get his opening to run, and he would likely try anything he could come up with to get away.

"He starts an orphanage with that boy, then he goes around and collects 'his children.' He's collected over thirty children now. Each of us is 'boy' or 'girl.' But I'm the first. I'm the first boy. Do you understand yet, Deputy?"

The boy stopped in the middle of the room and stared wild-eyed at Matthew.

"You're finally admitting that some of the story is about you?" He asked the boy with some concern, as he tried to keep him moving.

"This is the part of the story where Father comes close to getting found out by a stupid, backwoods, hick deputy! A deputy that tries to take a couple of his kids! But his children would never let that happen, Deputy. Do you understand? They'd never let that happen!" The boy screamed at Matthew as he jerked the girl away from him.

Lightning ripped across the sky outside and for a moment the room was lit in an electric blue glow. Matthew could've sworn that he saw children everywhere – lots of them, surrounding the three of them. Then all went dark again, but now there was a depth to the blackness, and it was crawling with movement. Matthew thought the boy's story was really getting to him, and he tried to simply shake it off again, but then he began to actually see the children inching forward into the yellow light of that single bulb. They moved inhumanly fast, and were on him in a flash – a flurry of fists and feet and teeth. Then there was only pain and noise, and finally, darkness.

***

Matthew's head throbbed and the vision in his right eye was blurry when he opened it. Everything in the room seemed to spin. He was bloody, naked, and handcuffed on a dirt floor. This was a living, waking nightmare. Who would have ever have expected, or believed this could happen. This must be the basement, he told himself.

There was only one light here - a giant floodlight, which was right over his head. The basement looked to be about the same size as the whole first floor, with no walls. It was huge, wet, and disgusting, and he was laying down in it naked and covered in blood. He could only hope the blood was his own, and not the children's. Holly could never find out about this.

He could see something moving near the edge of the light beyond his right foot. It lingered there in the dark for a moment before moving forward. The boy finally came into the light and walked over to check on Matthew's wounds.

"What's going on here? Where are my clothes?" Matthew demanded. The boy continued to look him over, saying nothing. "You lied to me. What's your name? Who are all those kids?"

"No! I warned you. I mocked you… I was rude to you… But I never lied to you." The boy said it smugly, but Matthew thought he could see a hint of sadness in his eyes.

"You said that you weren't the person in the story. You said that monster was 'Father,' or whatever. You lied."

"No, Deputy Burroughs, he didn't," a man's voice said. Matthew strained to look in the direction he thought the voice had come from and was instantly on fire with the pain of his broken limbs. A man's form seemed to appear from the shadows, waving a finger in a disapproving gesture at Matthew. "My boys and girls don't lie. I make it a point to punish dishonesty swiftly and with a kind of finality I doubt you'd be comfortable with."

The man was huge. He wasn't fat, or even well muscled. While he was extremely thin, he was easily over seven feet tall. His skin was pale almost to the point of being translucent, and his short, dark hair sat perfectly atop his head, not a single strand out of place. He wore a black, finely tailored suit that he began to slowly remove as he approached Matthew.

"I must make preparations to relocate again. The children knew they'd be packing as soon as they saw you, so you really haven't upset things too badly. People will come looking for you in time. A new location, a new orphanage with the children. Life will go on…for us." The man finished his statement as he folded his coat and pants, placing them on a wooden table just outside of the light's comfortable reach.

"Who are you?"

"The children call me 'Father.'"

"But who are you really? What's your name? We both know the story the boy told about you being born in Germany in the 1600s is crap."

"Do we?" The man looked down at Matthew with a blank face as he removed his shirt and placed it with his vest on the table. "How little you really know, Deputy."

"It's not possible. You're just a monster who kidnaps and frightens children. You don't scare me!" He lied, more for his own benefit than the man standing in front of him.

"I realize you were just doing your job, Matthew. I don't hold that against you. If it's of any consolation, you won't have to fight with Holly anymore." The man said all this in the same unflinching monotone.

Matthew's eyes grew wide. Panic ripped through him. It almost seemed like the man enjoyed that fear, as he now stood completely naked next to the table.

"How dare you! How do you know? Who are you?!" Matthew demanded as his mind swam with all sorts of fearful images.

"You are Matthew Curtis Burroughs, your birthday is July nineteenth, your parents both died in a car wreck when you were twenty-one. Your wife, Holly Marie, is the most important and valuable thing in your little world. You've heard my whole life's story, but I've seen yours." He examined Matthew's reaction closely as he tapped his temple. "I've watched your life play out in its entirety, as though I had lived it personally. I took all your memories – copied them, I should say – out of your mind. I took everything, in fact. I had no choice in doing so, however, if that helps. The die was cast, and my part decided for me, as yours was when you were told to come to this house."

"What…what are you going to do?" Matthew just couldn't take it all in, no matter how hard he tried. He struggled again to get to his feet and was painfully reminded that too many of his bones were broken to allow him to stand. He yelped, wincing in agony, as he looked back up at 'Father.' "Who are you? I mean, who are you, really?"

The man held up Matthew's uniform hooked on a single extended finger as his body shifted and contorted, reforming itself to change size and coloration. Matthew watched the man's face reorder itself until the face looking down at him was his own.

"Why, Deputy Burroughs. I'm you, of course," the man said as he put on Matthew's uniform pants. "I have to be you, otherwise people might find it odd that I'm driving your car, and in your house. Like your wife, perhaps?"

"You leave Holly alone! Do you hear me, you sicko? Don't you lay a hand on my wife!"

The man put the final pieces of the uniform in place and turned again to look down at Matthew. Looking up into his own eyes, Matthew was nearly hysterical, shaking with rage, and barely able to contain his suffering.

"I give you my word, Matthew. She will come to no harm by my hand. My word, Matthew, is solid. Take comfort in that. No harm…by my hand."

The man turned and started to walk away. It startled Matthew to hear him speak with Matthew's own voice as he said, "Children, you know the Deputy can't live, and he can't be found. Please eat him and powder his bones."

The children, more than thirty of them, all came forward out of the shadows where they had been lurking and began to encircle Matthew. As an afterthought, the man called back to them, "Bring me those handcuffs when you're finished."

***

The knocking on door was a small but persistent sound, the kind one might imagine an indolent, heavyset woodpecker would make.

The raven-haired woman slid the deadbolt over, and opened the door enough to peer out into the ominous black of the night. The rain had slowed to a drizzle, forming angelic coronas around the young boy and girl, dressed in ratty white t-shirts, who stood outside the door in the warm, bright glow of the porch light.

"Can… can I help you?" She asked, puzzled, as she looked around in vain for the adults these children were missing.

As the girl looked down at her feet, the boy stepped forward. pulling the woman's attention back to him. "I'm really, really sorry to bother you ma'am, but are you Mrs. Matthew Burroughs?"

A Scarlet Night
by
Megan J. Parker

Awakening

Serena opened the door and stepped out of her cabin, sensing a wave of energy. She stood, trying through the blackness beyond the trees in an effort to locate the source. A snapping branch sounded to the left and she turned her head towards it right before a flash of light to the right snapped her attention back.

She sneered, "SHIT!"

She shifted on her heels, bracing herself as the bright-red blast shot at her and lifted her hands. Though the approaching wave was fast, she had more than enough time to complete the fluid cycle with her hands. As the motions came together, her own purple energy began to grow in her palms and she pushed out with it, a wisp of violet smoke swirling in the night air as the two energies collided and violently neutralized one-another.

"Stop right there!" A loud, male voice called out past the lingering glow.

"Oh? And why would I do that?" Serena asked snidely. As the sound of heavy boots on the forest floor advanced, her lip curled at the familiar energy. "Leave now, vampire!"

The intruder growled at her hostility, "No! You're coming with me!" Then, as an afterthought: "Serena."

"You sound pretty confident there!" she mocked, smiling and licking her parched lips. "Tell me, vampire. . . have you fed from a human? Or do you settle for that *disgusting* potion?"

"Enough stalling!" A roar bellowed from his chest, "I don't answer YOUR questions!"

He took one final step towards her and she fought her instinctive blush. He was so beautiful. His pale skin was lit under the glow of the moon and his inky mane spilled onto his shoulders; like her own mass of silver hair, a sharply-contrasting streak--like a sliver of moonlight in an otherwise dark sky--hung over his forehead and between his piercing gaze. Each of his eyes was unique; a nearly metallic right and a blue left that shimmered as though electrified. She smirked as his aura, an excited match to the wave of red energy she'd just dispelled, spiked impatiently as she continued to take all of him in.

"Had your fill yet?" He frowned at his own words.

"Not yet." She chuckled, slowly glancing over his form one last time, "But you *do* seem to be in something of a hurry. Maybe later I'll let you tie me to the train tracks, eh Snidely?"

She thought she saw him blush but passed it off as a glow from his aura and smiled as he stepped toward her, growling.

"Now give up. I don't want to hit you!" He glared.

Her smile widened and she licked a fang, continuing to undress him with her purple eyes, "Oh you *are* kinky! I only hope you hit better than you throw! Seriously! If you're here to take me you're going to have to do better than an amateur blast. Now, if you'll excuse me"-- she smirked and turned her back to him--"you're interrupting my dinner."

She felt his icy gaze narrow and chill her back and his heavy boots followed, daring her to continue. She rolled her eyes and turned back, lunging at him.

"Enough of this!"

"Wai-"

His speech and his advance ceased as he was taken off guard and she took the opportunity to jump up and shoved both of her high-heeled boots into his chest, rocketing him off the balcony and sending him crashing into a nearby willow tree.

She landed with cat-like grace on her feet and began a cocky swagger towards and then past him. His mismatched and bewildered eyes followed her, taking in her teasing wink as she disappeared.

"Dinner time!" she purred.

***

The city was still several miles south of the cottage she was staying at--or, rather, *had* been staying at. Now that the vampires knew of that location, she'd have to find a new home.

She sighed, "On the road again. . ." she shook her head as the vampire's shocked face bobbed into her mind. "That bastard!"

"You hurt him pretty bad, you know." Devon chided her.

"So you finally decided to come out, huh?" She smiled, not bothering to glance over at her ghostly companion.

The warmth--an ever-constant reminder of his presence--wrapped around her. She exhaled, enjoying the otherworldly embrace for only a moment before looking over at him. Even as a ghost, he retained his beautiful looks: an eternal mirror of how he was--thankfully--before the accident. He smiled warmly at her. Despite everything she'd done to him, he was still so kind to her.

And that hurt more than he knew.

"I'll find a body for you, Devon. I promise." She said, biting her lip.

"That's not what I said." His voice hardened.

She nodded, "I know what you said. Doesn't change the fact that I'm going to find you a body."

She had been looking--always had been--but, when she drank from every human she thought would fit his soul, Devon would always stop their approaching death and save them at the last minute.

"Serena, you know how I feel about that." Devon said.

She ignored his words. Nothing he'd said or ever could say would sway her. She wanted to feel him again; be able to enjoy his physical embrace and not just some warm air. He was, and always would be, the only one for her. Hell, she'd give up drinking blood and start gagging down that synthetic crap if he asked her to. He was the only one to see her as her true self because she refused to show it to any other.

"Devon, I want to be with you again." She finally said, stifling her approaching tears before they could spill down her cheeks. She wouldn't let him see her cry. She knew how much that hurt him.

"What's the matter?" he asked softly as his warmth engulfed her. "I can see that you're upset."

She paused beside a sapling and enjoyed a cool summer night's breeze as it wrapped around her, teasing her senses as it mingled with Devon's warmth.

Devon's unwavering warmth. . .

No matter what, she knew that he would always be there for her. Not even the fire could stop him from finding his way back to her three years earlier. She looked down and shook her head.

She wanted to fix it. . .

She wanted to stop it!

Waves of intense heat pushed her back; pushed her away from him. Still down on one knee, Devon was unable to move fast enough to save them both. The hollow, echoing

*taunt of his offered ring hitting the floor chilled her heart
as he stood and planted himself protectively in front of her.*

They'd found her.

Those flames had been meant for her.

But that didn't stop them from taking him instead.

"Serena, I love you, always."

*His last words, spoken moments before the fire had
started, were already growing cold with grief as he'd used
the last of his strength to push her into the tugging hold of
the fleeing crowd. There was no pulling free from the
combined force of the group as they unknowingly dragged
her out of the ballroom, crying and screaming as the roof
collapsed behind her and taking her happiness with it.*

She blinked, still feeling the phantom flames burn
through the fabric of time, and wiped away the tears. She
couldn't stop them that time around. Not that she wouldn't
have tried, but it was useless. When the memory surfaced,
her awareness sank. Devon's aura, knowing and
sympathetic, was already wrapped tightly around her. And
though it was comforting, it wasn't enough for her.

Approaching footsteps sounded from the clearing
and instinctively brought out the fighter in her, the trails of
tears drying up on cue.

There, standing and watching her with those
wonderfully mismatched eyes, was her attacker.

Though his face didn't show it, his slouched body,
weighed down with agony, was in so much pain that it hurt
her to see him. Frowning, she looked away, realizing then
just how much damage she'd inflicted.

"What do you want?" she made no move to fight,
having no strength or desire to do so.

He stayed quiet for a moment and the breeze from
earlier came back, colder than before. She frowned at the
sudden chill; Devon and his warmth had disappeared,
leaving her alone with the vampire.

"I w-was watching" he said, partially choking on the pain as he did. Something about it made him seem honest now his voice was softer.

She looked up, daring to meet his gaze. His face was still filled with the same confusion she'd left him with and his aura sagged around him, mirroring his beaten form.

She had thought he had been there to arrest her, but she could see now that that wasn't the case.

"You need to come with me." He said, "You'll be safe."

Despite the confusion she felt from his words--and from the voice that carried them--she was surprised to find that she believed him.

Against every instinct she'd ever learned, she stepped towards him, still staring into his eyes.

More than anything else she needed Devon. But, feeling a whole new type of warmth emanating from those eyes, she realized that she needed something else. Something more than just warmth.

"Serena." the vampire called to her, his voice no longer his own. She took another step, driven by that voice and the promises behind it, something in that voice made her want it all the more. "Serena!" he called again, the tone and pitch cutting through the haze of arousal and startling her with the now-obvious truth. . .

She faltered, nearly collapsing, and stared with wide eyes at the suddenly rigid vampire; his once mismatched eyes now shone with the bright green of her former lover.

"Devon?"

The vampire's face twisted for a moment, experimenting with its own expressions before settling with a wide smile and nodding.

"But. . . how?" she stammered, still staring.

"His guard was down." he explained, "The gate was open so I. . . I just took it. I don't know how long I'll be able to hold it, but for now. . ." he bit his lip and blushed; his flood of emotions assaulting his stolen body's cheeks. Stolen or not, she rushed to him, wrapping her arms tightly around the broad back of the stranger that now housed her lover. Despite everything, with her eyes clenched and buried in the body's chest, she could feel him there. Her Devon!

Even in a different body, it still felt right. Large hands met her face and lifted her chin, a flood of his classic warmth and that of the new body's natural heat seeped into her as he brushed her cheeks and she closed her eyes to savor the feeling. Devon lifted her face further towards him and pressed his new lips to hers. Ignoring the subtle differences, she wrapped her arms tightly around his neck, turning the kiss from an exploration to a fierce, passion-filled attack.

She'd been so damn starved for it that the first taste had awakened a hunger she'd long since forgotten. She forgot how to breath then, but soon found it as he trailed kisses down her chin and a desperate gasp ripped from her burning lungs. Lips still wet with their combined moisture brushed down her neck. Another, weaker gasp seeped out, reaching a peak as a breathy whimper as his tongue ran across her collarbone.

Her senses grew more receptive to everything as their auras collided and mingled, creating a bright and pulsating wave of multicolored light that expanded and contracted rhythmically around them. Devon eased her to the forest floor, the gentle-yet-firm hold the same as she'd remembered it. He pulled away then, beginning to peel the shirt from his borrowed torso, and she reached out to trail her fingertips across the strong, tattoo-covered chest as it emerged. She wanted to reach past the flesh and into Devon, feel everything with him. Even after all those celibate years their passion proved strong, and she was willing to look past the flesh to once again experience who they had been when they had become one.

He began to explore her body all over again, clearly reminding himself of the dips and curves he had not traveled in so long, and she gasped and arched against the static shocks that lit up her nerve endings with each inch he took. Pressing his every essence into her, they once again became one.

Serena explored the new body, rubbing her hands across his entire being as he continued the dance above. The bliss was too much for her and soon her climax reached. As the sounds of her cries filled she felt his body release as well, together finally.

As their bodies entangled on the forest floor, their cries sounded together as they climbed their way to pure ecstasy.

***

"What the hell?"

Serena blinked at the outburst, shaking the sleep from her system as she sat up in a daze. For a moment she was reminded of the previous night as the body heat from her partner's naked body seeped into her own. Then, as her eyes finally met his mismatched own, she was thrown off of him and onto the dew-coated grass. She cried out as the chilled moisture assaulted her bare skin.

"Ow! You asshole!" She glared, trying to ignore the burning of her cheeks as she realized her situation.

"What did you drug me with?" He rose to his feet and began snatching up the clothes that lay scattered all over the clearing and throwing what didn't belong to him in her direction. "God dammit!" he snarled, yanking his pants up, "Where the hell is my belt?"

"Probably in the tree where you threw it last night, you dick!" Serena lifted her clothes and began to slip into them, keeping her eyes on his chest and the large tribal designs and fresh scratches littered about thereon. Only when his glare returned with laser-focus on her did she avert her gaze, "And for the record, I did NOT drug you!"

The vampire glanced skyward, his shoulders sagging as he spotted the length of leather dangling from a branch. Trying to remain intimidating, he hid his growing sense of defeat, failing to control his aura's all-too-clear reaction. "Then why, pray-tell, am I waking up NAKED with you? Why can't I remember anything from last night?" Serena clucked her tongue, unsure of how to explain the situation without sounding like part of a strange, ghostly date-raping.

"Look, call me 'old fashioned', but I make it an effort to *remember* how I come to be naked with somebody!" He gave up on retrieving his belt and ducked into his shirt, a growl emerging from his throat.

"Oh? I'm so goddamn sorry to have interfered with your obviously detailed and intimate list of skanks and whores!" She countered, "I'm sure it's very confusing to wake up in this sort of a situation and not have to PAY your partner!"

"You bitch!" he bared his fangs, "I am only that way with women I respect and care about! Neither which include you or undignified wretches *like* you!"

Serena's breath caught in her throat at that and she bit her lip, looking down.

He paused, his enraged features softening as he took in her reaction. After a silent moment, he cleared his throat and calmed his tone, "So, did we. . .?"

"We. . ." Serena blushed and dared a glance at him, seeing his confusion and understanding his apprehension. She nodded once, "Yes. We did."

"Dammit!" He rubbed the back of his neck and turned away from her, "this was not supposed to happen!"

"I. . . I'm sorry." The sincerity felt strange to Serena. "If it makes you feel any better, it wasn't exactly planned."

A morning breeze began to pick up and the vampire looked over to meet her apologetic gaze; a gaze she had a hard time maintaining. She had no right to blame him for her not reaction. There she stood, still *smelling* like him and not even *knowing* his name!

"Zane." He said with a sigh.

Her eyes shifted back towards him, "Wh-what?"

"My name. It's Zane. It's only right that you know that much." He frowned at her confusion, "You *were* wondering-"

"How could you know that?" she blushed, feeling strangely violated.

Zane frowned and glanced towards the shadowed depths of the forest, frowning.

"We're not alone."

Serena turned in that direction and squinted against the rising sun. "I can't see-"

At that moment, four unnaturally large, glowing-red wolves leapt into the clearing and raced out towards them.

"Shit! They've been possessed! Keep your guard up!" Zane warned, his familiar energy flaring up in defense.

"Right!" Serena nodded, mimicking the action with her purple energy and taking a fighting stance.

The nearest wolf chose a target and pounced, targeting Zane and coming down in a vicious arc with its unnaturally large fangs parted and hungry. Serena gaped as Zane calmly pulled back his hand--his fingers locked and elongated like a blade's tip--and drove it into wolf's throat. As the beast's momentum forced it downward, Zane's hand sank deeper into its core and Serena watched in horrified awe as it collapsed to the ground with her ally's arm buried inside it to his elbow. Slowly, Zane withdrew his hand, now clutching the fallen demon's black and still-beating heart. Appalled by the image, the vampire threw his prize to the ground and brought his boot down on it with a crushing force. The wolf, still writhing in pain, collapsed at that moment--finally dead--and the two watched as a shrieking demonic aura tore free from the corpse and began to drift away.

"Not that easy!" Zane growled as he lifted his hand in its direction and wrapped his own aura around the fleeing demon. In the grip of Zane's power, the evil aura dissolved and then, with ease, he threw his opposite hand out in the direction of the other wolf-demons and dissolving them all at once.

Serena stared a moment longer as Zane drew in his energy and let out a breath.

"How did you do that?"

"Because," he looked over, his mismatched eyes shimmering brighter than ever before, "I'm not what you think I am."

To be continued...Look for Megan J. Parker's full-length novel "A Scarlet Night" in Winter 2012

Dark Light

Empty The Bones For You
by
Char Hardin

Twilight closed her curtains as the last of the sun's rays faded away. I found myself all alone, now that my family's last car had gone. While Death misted her recently departed perfume throughout The Pearly Gates Cemetery, the gravedigger's task was handed over to the funeral home attendees. Gently they lowered me down into the Earth's dark, damp, bug-infested womb. Clumps of dirt filtered through the flowers blanketing my casket, in haste to chase after me. The pelting against my coffin finally ended with a loud thud. The dust clouds settled and I was laid to rest.

Hours passed slowly as the full moon rose into the sky. I imagined, the Man in the Moon wept at my passing. It was tears from another being, which was more distraught at my passing that I heard. Her tears fell from the heavens, great big dollops of silvery tears dripped-dropped, dripped-dropped, and dripped-dropped down through the freshly turned dirt, to land a-top my casket. The angel's anguish turned to anger that roared like thunder and caused those silvery tears to fall harder and slashed the ground with her pain. I heard her and yet, no one heard me.

I lay in my casket and remembered early this morning, during my wake, I had screamed! Terrified and alone, I yelled for help and no one came to my rescue, so I just screamed and screamed, "I AM HERE, HEAR ME! HELP ME!" I begged until, I was hoarse and my throat hurt. Something I found to be a bit ironic, that I could talk and feel pain, when everyone else, saw me as DEAD.

Lovely flowers graced my wake and followed me to the cemetery. I couldn't make them hear me. I felt my mother press her warm lips to my cool ones. I felt her tears fall on my skin only to scald me with their finality. I heard my father cry. It broke my heart, to know, that he was in pain.

"Oh, Daddy, I beseeched, "This wasn't supposed to happen to us…to me!"

I had heard my Aunt Ida as she talked to my cousin Ella-Claire. "I think Miss Celia did a wonderful job with your cousin's hair. I know Elaina would have been pleased with the care given by Miss Celia." Aunt Ida gushed on-and-on about how natural, my hair and make-up looked.

"I agree Aunt Ida. It's…just so spooky how life-like Elaina looks, as if she were only sleeping," whispered Ella-Claire.

"That child looked like at any moment, she would rise up and get out of that coffin." Aunt Ida replied with a shudder.

"Oh Aunt Ida, IF Elaina had sat up, I would have fainted dead away!" Ella-Claire responded in horror.

I heard the whole conversation; while I willed, with my whole heart, for my eyes to open so that they could see, I was not dead, asleep or anything but ALIVE as they were before me!

Family from all over the globe came to bid their farewells. Something I found ludicrous, that the only time our family came together was either for a marriage, a funeral or of course the reading of a will! I knew my twin sister mirrored my angst at the family's hypocrisy. She knew that I would have hated an open casket. She knew I would find it hypocritical that "NOW" people wanted to see me. Why not while I was breathing?

Hours passed slowly, until just before they closed my casket, an odd scent reached out and tickled my nose. Citrus topped with notes of sandalwood. It could be only one person … Zane. He came!

I would be rescued, Zane wouldn't let them close me up forever, I knew he would come and deliver me from the endless line of family torturers.

"My beloved Zane…Zane, I am here, help me," I cried out, "See me, release me, Zane!" I pleaded.

He passed through the line. I heard him. "I'm so sorry Barbara," Zane leaned over and embraced my mother. Then he stood up and shook hands with my father, "Jack, I'm so sorry for your loss."

Something was wrong with Zane. His *tone* sounded forced. His *tone* sounded HOLLOW? Where was his PASSION? Who was this indifferent person? Where was my loving Zane?

"NO! He can't believe I'm dead … I AM NOT DEAD! Zane, HEAR ME!" I commanded his attention and yet he ignored my begging.

His scent grew stronger; he stood over me. With delicate tenderness, I felt him reach down and brushed his fingers against my cheek. Cool to touch, I know, but there

73

was a fire beneath, if he would have just trusted his heart, and reached for MY light. My torch burned so bright.

"Zane, please," I begged "Help get me out of this hell!" A lone tear slipped down and landed on my cheek. I wracked my mind for a way, to reach him; to let him know 'I am still here,' but he pulled back suddenly and a stab of dread washed over my stilled heart.

My sister, Eileen had come to stand next to Zane. She put her arms around him and told him those soppy things people say when someone dies. Anger surged through my useless veins and threatened to erupt. Emotions roared with turmoil and yet, to their human eyes, I was as still then, as I when they first arrived.

My sister's whispered words of comfort, felt like daggers of betrayal aimed straight at my heart. There was alien warmth in her voice, one I had not detected before. She cared for him, but not as a future sister-in-law should. Damn it! Why didn't I see this before! She had been at me constantly over the last few months.

"Zane has been unfaithful," Eileen had told me on more than one occasion "and that Zane is a…well there just isn't a kinder way to say it, Elaina. Zane is a WOMANIZER! Honey, you really should really re-think your engagement."

"Oh Eileen, that is not true! And you know it. Where is all this coming from? I thought you liked Zane?" I questioned her.

"It is true. I only want what is best for you. I love you sis." she sulked.

"Eileen, Zane is my soul mate. He is my perfect match. Don't worry, you'll see." I replied with a hug.

It was as if Eileen thought...no... feared that after Zane and I married, we would move away and not remain close to each other.

I was so naïve. Eileen didn't care for me being with Zane, no, she wanted him for herself. And most likely had been the one Zane had been unfaithful with and not some other woman. I had put her fretfulness behind me and had gone forward with our engagement party plans. I figured she was going through a twins' separation phase.
Then the incidents had begun happening. Lipstick on Zane's collar in shades not like mine, hang-ups in the middle of the day and ghost pages on his beeper that were unanswered, missed appointments, longer hours at the office and other little things. I had become suspicious, and even approached Zane with my concerns.

"Darling, I am working longer hours so I will be caught up, when we go on our honeymoon." He soothed me and quickly I shelved my fears.

He had an answer for all the mishaps. When he could fit me into his busy schedule, he would spend the time making love and showering me with presents to take my mind off my suspicions. And it had worked. I knew Zane couldn't be untrue and that he loved me beyond a shadow of a doubt.

The afternoon of my accident, I had talked to Zane's secretary about a surprise dinner at Topela, our favorite Cajun cuisine restaurant. She cleared his late afternoon appointments and made the reservation. I had run a few errands, and it was later that day that I met my sister coming out of Carter's Pharmacy. She looked irritated and I could tell she had been crying. I tried to get her to talk to me but she just brushed past me and ran for her car. The weatherman had predicted cats and dogs to hit by four o'clock. At precisely four thirty the bottom fell out of the sky. I barely made it back to my car before the downpour caught me. Roads that moments before were safe, had become doused and slippery.

I focused all my attention on the road. I had felt the car swish a few times on small curves, but it was when I approached the bend, where so many car accidents occurred, I slowed the car and moved with trepidation and care around what the media had dubbed "Bloody 98, Dead Man's Curve". I had almost come out of the turn, when something red ran out in front of me. I panicked, slammed on the brakes, and spun out of control. The car went over the old wooden barricade and sent me splintering down the embankment. My sight was blurred and sound roared in my ears. My car landed at the bottom of the wooded ravine with a jarring crash.

I knew my bones were broken, I felt the pain as it ricocheted through my body. Blood splattered the interior of my car and dripped into my open eyes. My lungs had been punctured, my throat filled with blood. I just slipped away while my body drowned from extensive internal injuries.

Moments…mere…seconds before impact, a bright light had flared and filled the confines of the car. My last thoughts were of my fiancée as my soul entered the light. Angels embraced me and flew to Heaven's Door. Tears flooded my eyes and when the door opened. I shrugged myself free from the angelic arms and stood before the door to eternity. Expecting Jesus to be standing there, or some old man, I prepared to ram my fist down the throat of whoever appeared. The unexpected form who greeted me was a CHILD!

The child looked to be about ten years in age. He was of slight build with sandy blonde hair and crystal blue eyes swimming with unshed tears. His eyes betrayed more depth than eyes of a mere boy, but more like the souls of thousands. His eyes were ancient. He reached for my hand; I pushed his hand away. His reaction was instant and caused me to cringe. Tears leaked from those unfathomable eyes and a slight frown hid I his boyish lips. He stepped back.

A voice like none other I have ever heard roared from the mouth of this child. The thunderous pounding of the oceans' surf rushing ashore couldn't begin to describe the vibrations of his voice. As he spoke the angels bowed down and their wings touched the smoky white floor.

"Elaina, you are saddened, that I have brought you here. I am sorry for your pain. I tried to intervene sooner, but my Angel was blocked from your sight by a red-haired demon and cast aside. I had hoped to take you before impact, so that you would not break in body and spirit." I shook my head, this could not be real. Was this someone's sick idea of a joke perhaps? Could it be a nightmare? Just the same, I shuffled my feet and turned to pull the wizard's curtain aside and see who was behind the nightmare. I was stunned to find no curtain, nor any wizened old man pulling levers or pushing buttons. Only the child and three Angels I arrived with were present.

"HERE? Where is here and how do I get back to Zane?" I whimpered.

The child stepped closer and reached out for my hand. "Elaina, I know you are bewildered and I wanted, truly, I did want to shield you from this pain," he started, "but there is something you should know. It was not your time, but your Guardian Angel, who came to have council with me in your behalf…"

I interrupted, "I don't believe in Guardian Angels and I certainly didn't ask, it to intervene on my "behalf". Who are you? Why am I here? What kind of monster kills an innocent woman?

The child reached down deep in his pocket and produced a white worn handkerchief. He handed it to me and continued, "Crying, even disbelief is expected here, as it is on Earth. Only those who believe, ever truly make it to MY door. I know that as a child you believed. You knew your Guardian Angel. Elaina, you have called upon your Guardian Angel during many ills in your life. You know her as Aria." He finished with a smile.

"A-a-r-i-a … I thought … she was just an imaginary friend from childhood. I n-e-v-e-r t-h-o-ugh-t…" I stammered.

"Aria is real! She has always been there when you called her. She was the first being to see you enter this world and she was the last to carry you out. Turn and behold your Guardian Angel, Aria. She has cared for you, all through your earthly life and before, when your soul had yet been sent forth into your mother's womb."

I turned and gasped. Kneeling behind me, there was the most beautiful Angel. Her robe was iridescent with shimmery pinks and purple hues. Her long hair was the color of finely spun silk with golden flecks that sparkled and her eyes the most brilliant purple. She smiled. Aria rose from the floor and stood with open arms. A cry escaped my throat, "Aria! Aria you are real!" I ran to her like a child to a loved one.

The ethereal being who embraced me with first her love and then her arms smelled of sunshine and roses. A memory slowly took form of me: a moment as a child, who had fallen from her crib. I was the babe who cried for her mamma and reached up in the darkness for help, only the hands that lifted me up were not my mother's. They belonged to a beautiful young woman. The woman whispered her name as "Aria" to my infant ears. Aria had pressed me close to her bosom and rocked me back to sleep, singing an ancient lullaby. Other memories flooded my mind's eye, other moments in time spent with Aria. She was as real to me as any member of my family.

Greedily I hugged Aria to me. Aria's love seeped inside me and helped to lessen my pain. With her eyes she implored me to listen to the child. I turned around, never leaving the comfort of her arms, and gave the child my full attention.

The child went on to weave a tale so farfetched and wretched, I couldn't believe his words. I had only to turn and look up at the sympathetic face of Aria, to know he spoke the truth. I felt the angel shiver with horror as the tale continued. Time passed and yet it didn't. I listened for hours only to learn seconds had passed. Time at the door was not measured in seconds or minutes, it just was. The child told of deception and lust. His tale told of my murder. My automobile had been tampered with, the food that awaited my arrival at the restaurant poisoned; in case

the brakes hadn't failed. My biggest threat of all was not a
stranger.

"It is saddens and sickens me, that you sister took it
upon herself to play God with your emotions and your life,
so that she could replace you with herself and be free to
love Zane for her own. She conspired with Zane as he had
the choice of free will; he is not blameless in this murder,
he helped." He lamented.

The child went on to tell me why Eileen did it and
why Zane went along with her evil plan. "Elaina, Eileen
had discovered a clause in your grandmother's will that
caused distress not only to her emotions, but the way of
living she had grown accustomed to, on the verge of being
a wealthy woman."

"My sister conspired with my fiancée to kill me
over a clause in my grandmother's will?" The words left
me in a burst.

"Yes, I am afraid so. The will stated in the event of
your untimely death, that your sister, Eileen would inherit
your share of your grandmother's estate and money she left
to you both." He responded.

I let what he said sink in a bit before I began my
explanation, "My father's mother had long since favored
my sister and me over the rest of the family. If asked,
grandmother would have told you I was the favored one. I
was the one who had freely given my time spent with her,
all through her sickness. I was the one who sat up countless
nights when she couldn't catch her breath as the cancer
ravaged her. I devoted my time to her comfort in her final
days, not for riches beyond my wildest dreams, but because
I loved her. She was my *Granny Mag* and I *loved* her. She

was more like a second mother. I did what I could for HER, not for any riches! I did it out of love." Anger punctuated my every word. How could Eileen be so brutally selfish? The child walked nearer and put his hands on my shoulders while I cried and sagged against Aria.

"I had heard your grandmother and father argue just before her death. She wanted to leave her estate and money to you, Elaina," explained the child. "Your father said that would cause a rift in the family. He advised his mother to divide it up, as she had initially planned before she got so sick. It's not that your father was choosing your sister over you; he was trying to prevent future hurt and chaos for the family. I think she admired his compassion more than she gave him credit for, and in the end, she left the will divided. The clause over either of you prematurely dying being added is something only she knew to do." He continued. It broke my heart all over again to hear this child accuse my loved ones of conspiracy. Even more horrific, that they would attempt to kill me.

"I am her twin. Eileen and I were bonded since birth. We shared everything. The only thing or person I didn't share with her was Zane. I had thought in time, she would find someone to love. I never dreamed it would be over my dead body." I pulled away from Aria and walked around the child shaking my head. I tried to make myself understand the ramifications of what Eileen had done…No, what Eileen *and* Zane had done to me.

I braced myself and turned around and tried to explain to these beings that Zane would never do this to me…to us! I had to make them understand.

81

"Zane and I were high school sweethearts. We had
felt destined to be married and have children. Dear, sweet
Zane, who oozed southern charm and promised a happy
future, filled with a house full of children and security, I
loved Zane! I was prepared to give him my body and soul
for an eternity, however I was not prepared to lose him and
my life, and to lose him to my sister! I just can't wrap my
mind around that. Are you sure they did this to me?" I
questioned them and all that I knew to be true was suddenly
clear. They did conspire and they did kill me. Something
about that just pissed me off. A fire in my belly erupted and
I could feel the birth of vengeance flare up within me.
All of the incidents Eileen had told me replayed over in my
mind. Zane had had an answer for every little thing. He
smoothed over my ruffled feathers and allayed my fears
with soft kisses. FOOL! Fool that I was I had fallen in
perfect alignment with his and Eileen's devious plans. The
big pay off would surely ensure his future in politics. I had
turned a blind eye to the two people I trusted the most and
lost them both plus my life.

Aria bristled with anger at the hurt Eileen and Zane
had bestowed upon her charge. It was she that had asked
for council with the child. She didn't want to see me die at
their hands. She knew that my premature death was not in
God's design or what my grandmother had secretly wished.
The child stepped back toward the door and turned the
knob.

"No! I don't want to go through that door. Please,
don't make me! I am not ready! Please, don't let them get
away with murder. Please!" I begged the boy.

Aria spoke, but when she did, it was not in any kind of language I had ever heard. But the child heard and from his posture he understood her plea.

The child turned back to face us. There was a wicked glint in his ancient stare, a clearly defined look of something not known to me. Aria walked over to me and stepped between the boy and *her* charge, Elaina. She spoke again in the rapid bird squawk language. The child broke out into a mischievous grin. Something was about to happen, to change all things changed.

"Elaina, you have been misplaced. You are not ready to go through the door. I think I WILL send you back and right the wrong thrust upon you. I request only a few promises which you must keep."

"Yes, yes, I promise. I promise anything you want, if you just send me back." New hope flared inside my breast. A chance to reclaim my life, there wasn't anything I wouldn't promise to get there!

"You must promise to seek council and overcome your issues with God..."

I shook my head up and down and exclaimed, "Oh, I will, thank you—"

"Do not interrupt me! Listen to me." he said firmly. "You must promise to not seek revenge on your sister or Zane."

I bristled with that condition, because I had lots of ideas for revenge and being told to ignore vengeance was a tough promise. But to have another chance at life, "Yes I promise no revenge!"

The child smiled as he continued, "You must promise to return to school and fulfill your dreams with the

gift your grandmother left you. And most importantly, you
MUST not write a book about your near death experience
with God. If you agree to these things, then you may return
to reclaim your life."

A resounding "YES I PROMISE!" That earned me
a big smile from the child.

"As I was saying, I will return you to the time of
MY choosing. Vengeance is mine and mine alone!" He
said.

I was a little awed up until he said the "Vengeance
is mine" part; I couldn't let that slide, "You, a mere child,
expect much of me. I have promised to do as you ask. And
I am thankful for your help, but don't you think, you will
pay a hefty price for imitating God at Heaven's Door?"
The child tipped back his head and laughter erupted. "Silly
girl, I am not imitating Myself, I am myself, and I am
GOD!"

Confusion clearly written all over my face drained
away as I responded, "How dare you assume you are GOD!
If I were you, I wouldn't play GOD in front of his Angels!"
The angels turned aside and giggled. I turned around and
saw the looks of mirth on their angelic faces. Holy crap!
My assumption proved false, the child was no ordinary
child, but GOD indeed!

"Elaina, you bring light where ever you go and
laughter to an old man. If I had appeared to you in any
other form, I feared that you would attack with all that
anger at me that you have trapped within you. So, I chose
the most innocent form, which would beseech you to not
harm me ... a child."

Before I could marvel that God had a sense of humor, Aria had kissed my cheek and sent me funneling back down to reclaim my life. Moments passed and I stopped whirling at light speed and landed with a jarring thud.

I opened my eyes and couldn't believe where I had landed. I stood outside the very funeral home, where I recently had been viewed. There was an odd charge in the air. Hmm, this must be more of that Heavenly Humor.

"Hello Elaina, we are so sorry for your loss. She will be missed. Please, let us know if there is anything you need."

I turned and was surprised to see my neighbor and her husband. They could see me! They were talking to me; therefore I must be real! I am back! I am truly back! They must be confused, my grandmother had already passed on, and they were acting as if it was the day of her funeral. Hmmm, what was going on?

I thanked the couple and wandered down the hall. My feet led me while my head went blank. I saw more friends and family members congregated outside in the halls. Another wake was going on and people were everywhere. And onward I walked. Just around the corner I spied my room, where my family and friends had viewed me.

I stopped at the threshold and shuddered with revulsion. Determination prompted me further into the room. Over to my right, I saw a line formed that led straight to my grieving parents. I got in line behind some distant cousins. Time snaked by and finally it was my turn. My

Father reached for his handkerchief, I bent down to my mother. She grabbed me and held me close.

"Elaina, what are we going to do without your sister? It's not fair. It's just not fair that she should die so young." My mother blathered.

Goosebumps covered my arms and the hair on the back of my neck stood up. And then I smelled a familiar scent. I stood to see Zane embrace my Father. Zane, he looked the same as earlier. Was this movie in reverse?

"Elaina, love, how are you doing?" he asked.

"How am I?" I responded. Good question, I wondered myself.

I must have said what I was thinking, because my mother's head glanced up and I saw her heart broken face a washed with tears. I wanted to spare her that pain twice in one day. How cruel. I sent a prayer up that she would be spared. An invisible force brushed up beside my mother and I knew her Guardian Angel was here.

I turned and looked back at Zane and he had walked over, to the head of the casket. I went to stand beside him. He put his arm around me and pulled me close. Lying there in my favorite suit with her hair piled on top and that life-like make-up job Aunt Ida and Cousin Ella-Claire gushed on and on about was my sister Eileen. Oh, my God, HE did it, I had been replaced! A smirk broke out on my face, one that didn't escape Zane's notice.

"What on Earth could you possibly find so funny about the death of your sister?" He asked in an angry hushed tone.

Not missing a beat, I looked up into the pained eyes of my lover and stood up on my toes, and whispered into his ear, "Maybe nothing on Earth, but I know the Sun is shining and the Devil is whining because another one of his minions has gotten her due!" I spun on my heels and turned my back on my sisters' corpse and my lover's stunned face.

Later at the Pearly Gates Cemetery, Zane kept his distance and was the last to stand over Eileen's grave. I had secreted myself behind a neighboring headstone and listened as he grieved. He knelt down beside her freshly filled grave,

"Eileen, this was not supposed to happen. It was not supposed to be *you*. What made you take her car? You knew I had had the brake line cut. I just can't understand why you were in *her* car. We had it all planned. Why did you go against the plan? Damn you! I needed that money to get into the Senate. You promised me!"

Six feet below, Eileen was screaming, "I'm here Zane! I'm HERE! SAVE ME!"

Three feet away, still hidden, I reached down into my pocket and withdrew a tape recorder. I neither wondered, nor worried where it had come from, but I was relieved to see it rolling. I started to rise, when the wind began to howl.

I looked up over the headstone and saw a woman approaching. She was cloaked in a dark hooded robe. In her hand was a long ancient looking athame, the hilt encrusted with rubies. I sat back down and cowered. In my drop to the ground, I upset the recorder and knocked off the stop button.

The woman appeared beside Zane and pulled back her hood. Her androgynous features were masked with hatred. She plunged the knife in a downward arc and drove it deep into Zane's chest. I froze in horror, as I watched the man, I had loved, shudder and die. The woman looked familiar, and yet, she was no one I knew.

The woman stood and walked over to where I hid, too terrified to move. The air around me became hot and I felt stifled. She moved with a predator's grace stalking her next prey. My pulse raced as she came to stop inches from my face. I could smell her breath, a scent so foul I tried to turn my face away from her. Her hand snaked out and grabbed my chin.

"Elaaaiinnnaaa" the woman hissed.

I tried to pull myself from her grasp and stood transfixed and watched terrified. Her fingers elongated and transformed into fiery red talons her nails tipped in black. The hood she had removed completely from her head and red curls tumbled free. This creatures' appearance shifted from moments ago. The androgynous being was a beautiful siren in face with the body of a snake and yet she had arms and talons. Her image and my mind were at war to comprehend what stood before me.

I felt the ground beneath my feet rise up to greet me as started to faint; the She-Creature reached out and caught me. She pulled me close to her body and whispered into my ears,

"Elaina, a s-s-soul for immortality and your s-s-sister promis-s-sed me your s-s-soul if I would grant her immortality. The Other s-s-stole you from me, thus further denying me a s-s-soul. I will have my s-s-soul and I will have my vengeance."

I felt her heated breath on my cheeks and smelled her putrid breath and knew this was not the boy, who had said he was GOD…this was something else. Inside, my soul was screaming for Aria's protection and God's grace for my sister's soul. The creature placed one of her talons on my cheek and ripped open the flesh from my face. She dipped her black tipped talon into my blood and hissed.

"I will empty the bones for you tonight, and dine I will on Zane's soul, tomorrow I will come to empty the bones of YOU and your tainted soul, I will add to my collection. Sleep now little Angel protected Elaina. The Other's statement "It is finished" is so overrated…it was finished when Eve took and ate the apple I offered her.

Dark Light

The Lost Changeling
by
Jana Boskey

Elita Ray woke up with a start. She sat up too quickly making her head spin as if she had a hangover. Groaning, she put her hands against her temples, and tried to get her bearings. She could see nothing around her. The darkness that surrounded her was thick and oppressive, granting her vision of nothing except it's night colored air.

"Hello?" she whispered into the air and strained to hear an answer. Elita heard shuffling to her right. "Is someone there?"

"Not for long," a deep, scratchy voice answered back before a scream sounded through the space, echoing in Elita's pounding head. Elita felt her eyes widen as she listened to the screech and felt her stomach turn and the scream was cut off by a gurgling sound. She put her palm to her mouth to stop her own yells.

Looking around she noticed that her eyes were adjusting to the dark, though only just a little. Elita saw a vague outline of what appeared to be a door illuminated by a stretch of light. Determined to get to it she got up, she took only a few steps before her legs gave out from under her, sending her to her knees. Biting her lip, she forced the cry in her throat to recede. Wherever she was, she did not want them to know she was awake.

Dark Light

Elita got up once more, feeling the agony burning through her legs with each broken step she made. After what seemed like hours the small light was only an arm's length away. Tears of happiness pooled in her eyes as she reached her hand out to grab the door. Just as her fingertips brushed the aged wood the door swung open, blinding her. Squealing, she pushed her fists into her eyes to stop the pain.

"Oh good," she heard a voice say in a softly lilting voice belonging to some accent she couldn't pinpoint, "you're awake. The King will be pleased."

Before Elita could even recover from being blinded she felt smooth hands roughly grab her shoulders and pull her out of the room. "Careful!" the man snapped at her as they walked. Elita stumbled every few steps but the unknown man always caught her by the arms, and righted her on her feet, mumbling in a language she couldn't understand.

"Please," she sobbed, "my legs...they hurt so bad."

Elita turned to look at him for the first time through misting eyes. She heard herself gasp as she caught sight of his face, even through her blurry vision she could tell how beautiful he was. The man had long black hair, as long as her own, which reached the middle of her back. It was straight, and looked as fine and soft as silk. His skin was alabaster; it almost glowed under the soft lighting of the hall they were walking down.

The man turned and looked at her with eyes that were so pale of a blue they were almost white. They were as startling as they were striking. Elita noticed how sharp his cheekbones were, and the shape of his eyes was almost

92

cat like as they tilted up towards his eyebrows. Wanting to see his face in more detail she started blinking her eyes to clear out tears. Elita wiped at her eyes gently, rubbing away the last bit of fog. When she looked at him again there was still a mist around him, as light as it was it still obscured him. She felt her eyebrows bunch together and her lips turn down into a deep frown. He gave her a dark smile, "That's the Fog you're seeing. Don't bother trying to clear your eyes, it won't work. You aren't ready to see us yet, Elita."

"How do you know my name?" she asked quickly. She took a wobbly step away from him, her brown eyes wary. "Who are you?"

The man laughed a horrible, grating laugh that sounded like glass shattering, "Everyone knows your name, my lady," he answered, dodging the last question.

"Why?"

He put up his finger and waggled it, "Save your questions for the King, he's more likely to give you an answer than I am. Now, come mortal," he held out his hand for her, his expression impatient.

Elita regarded him with reservation, her gaze on his hand. She thought he had beautiful hands; the fingers were long and tapered, the skin smooth. She wondered what his flesh would feel like on hers. Hesitantly, she reached out to him and gently touched his palm. Elita bit back a gasp as she felt his hand, which was as cold as ice. She shivered as she grasped it with her own, "You're so cold," she whispered.

He flashed a quick, twisted smile that was gone so fast Elita questioned whether or not she even saw it. "We must make haste, my lady, the King will not be happy if I bring you to him late." Her escort walked up to her and before she had a chance to protest swung her into his arms, and carried her bridal style down the hall.

Shocked, she looked at him through narrowed eyes, "Do you have any manners at all?"

He shot her a dark look. Elita felt herself slipping as his hold on her loosened, she grasped desperately at his neck, her nails sinking into the frigid skin. "I can always let you fall,"

"No! Please, I'm sorry!" Elita pleaded as the hand that was supporting her top half let go completely; she fell back at the waist. Her torso dangled, her head narrowly missed hitting the stone floor while he had a firm grip on her legs, not allowing her to fall completely. Elita screamed and her high-pitched voice reverberated off the walls. She struggled to pull herself up, but her sweaty palms wouldn't let her keep her grip. "God, PLEASE!" she screeched.

Elita hung there for a few more seconds before she felt her body swing back slightly before catapulting up, the man's arm snaking back around her shoulders.

She grabbed the fabric of his shirt tightly as she tried to get her breathing under control, and quell the desire to punch him in his pretty little face. Elita could feel his body shake slightly in silent laughter. She shot her head over to glare at him, "You're not funny, you ass."

At her insult he threw his head back and laughed, a rich sound the made Elita want to smile, but it also sent shivers down her spine. There was an edge to it, something that was almost sinister that lurked on the fringes of his laughter.

Biting her lip she turned her head and stared at the wall, noticing for the first time that they were made of ice, casting a distorted reflection of the two of them as the unknown man walked. Though the image was blurry she could see her pale blond hair was ratted and tangled, messily gathered up into a bun that was starting to come loose. She knew that her light brown eyes were wide with distress, the whites tinged pink from exhaustion and lack of sleep. Her caramel colored skin was flushed, the skin of her face streaked with mascara trails, her lipstick faded and smeared. Underneath her pant legs on her jeans her calves were decorated with bruises that throbbed. A cut ran across her collarbone, staining the fabric of her pale, rose-colored shirt, which was covered in dirt and ripped across her midsection.

What happened last night?

Elita wasn't aware that she even spoke out loud until she heard the man carrying her ask, "What?"

Looking away from her reflection she gave him a questioning look, "Excuse me?"

He let out an exasperated sigh, "You mumbled a question, which I assumed was for me, so I asked 'what' because I didn't hear you."

"Oh, I was just thinking out loud, I suppose."

He shrugged, "Suit yourself,"

"Can I ask you a question?" she asked before she lost her nerve.

"You just did," he answered in a flat voice, his tone suggesting he didn't want to be asked anything.

"You know what I meant,"

"Do I, now?"

"YES!" she nearly yelled as she struggled to keep her anger in check, but she decided to rephrase, just in case he tried to pull the same thing again. "Can I ask another question after I ask this one?"

He answered her question with one of his own, "Didn't I tell you? No more questions!"

Elita puffed out her cheeks in exasperation. "Am I not allowed to know anything?"

The side of his mouth quirked up again, "Not just yet," he said vaguely.

Crossing her arms tightly over her chest she worked her jaw for a few moments before speaking again. "Can I at least know your name?"

Elita felt the man stiffen underneath her slightly, his grip around her legs and shoulders tightened. "My lady," he almost sneered the word, "if you could forgive me, I cannot give you my name. I can give you something to call me by, if that would please you." His voice was tense, the words clipped.

She bristled at his tone, her hands clenching into fists. "How about I give you a name?" she asked through clenched teeth.

"If that is what you wish."

"Bastard."

He stopped abruptly, gaping at her. "What did you just call me?"

Elita gave an innocent look, "You said I could give you a name, sir. So I gave a name that suited your personality."

The man suddenly threw Elita from his arms, sending her crashing into the wall, her head smacking against the icy surface with a meaty sound. Her breath left her, quickly and painfully, on the moment impact. She heard the sickening crack as a few ribs broke, agony shooting through her back and chest. Small cracks splintered their way up the height of the wall, racing their way to the ceiling. Elita landed in a heap on the ground, her hand twisting awkwardly beneath her. A few chunks ice broke off the wall and fell on her, their sharp edges digging into her exposed skin.

All Elita could do was lay there in shock, her mouth open, gulping down the breaths that she lost a few second earlier. She tried to speak but her vocal chords seemed frozen, words stuck in her throat forming a lump that was making it hard to swallow. She could feel warm liquid trickle down her arms, she knew without looking that it was blood. The acrid, copper smell assaulted her nose and a metallic taste tainted her mouth making her want to gag. She heard the sounds of footsteps nearing her and she braced herself for another blow.

"My King told me to bring you to him alive. He said nothing about damaged." Elita could hear the smile in his voice as he spoke. Her stomach dropped as she heard the amusement he was taking from seeing her bloodied and broken.

Any fight that Elita had in her dissipated at that moment, leaving her vulnerable, her will crushed. She closed her eyes, accepting that death would soon come, and praying that it would be quick. Elita felt arms pull her onto her back and she bit the inside of her cheek to keep from crying out as her battered shoulders hit the ground. Her eyes flew open as she gasped when she felt the shards of ice that were embedded deep in flesh being pulled free. With each piece of ice that got extracted she felt herself slipping away, her vision dimmed little by little, blackening at the edges. As the last fragment exited her skin she first felt relief that overrode the sharp pain, and then she felt nothing at all.

Elita awoke to the sound of muffled voices speaking near her, the words garbled and slurred together. She caught a few words, king, queen, awake, death, rule, waiting, but nothing that could be put together to make a sentence, let alone make sense. When she attempted to move her body she felt white-hot pain lance through her body, causing her to scream.

"Elita?" a melodic voice asked from over her shoulder, "Are you all right?"

"Why did she cry out, Siaryl?" a deep voice demanded.

"I apologize, my King," Elita's eyes flew open at that sentence. *So this is whom that man kept referring to.* "I swore that I gave her enough herbs to stave off the pain, shall I give her more?"

Footsteps made their way around the bed she was laying on, getting closer until Elita was met with the most gorgeous man she had ever laid her eyes on. The King was beautiful. He had long, wavy white blond hair that grazed his collarbone. His bones jutted out from his face in a grotesque, yet lovely way, somehow only enhancing his beauty. His eyes were the same clear blue of the man who had hurt her, they titled at the same angle, making him appear catlike. The King's skin was milky, the texture as smooth as marble. Elita had a strange urge to touch his face to see if it was a creamy as it looked.

He knelt down next to the bed, bringing himself eye level with her. His stare was piercing, scrutinizing as he raked his gaze over her body, making her feel strangely naked despite her clothes. Elita held her breath as he lightly touched the skin on her forehead and neck, his cold fingers dancing across her heated flesh. She felt her stomach contract with each touch, heat slowly building within her. She sucked in her breath sharply when he grazed the sensitive skin above her breast. A fierce need washed over her then, a desperate longing to be held by this man. To feel his hands on every inch of her body, to feel their bare skin touching, melting together until they became one. Elita's breaths came in shallow pants, her cheeks flooded with blood at the images she had racing through her mind.

The stranger's eyes widened in concern, "My love? Are you in pain?" He cupped her cheek as he spoke, his pale eyes softening.

Not trusting her voice she nodded her head, the pain had ebbed seconds after it erupted. Against her better judgment leaned into his palm, somehow feeling safer than she had all this time.

A smile curved onto his full lips as he stood up. Panic flitted through her as he retreated. She reached for him, "Please don't leave me," she breathed, her outstretched hand shaking, moisture pooling in her eyes. Just as her tears began to fall the King bent down and kissed them before they hit her cheeks. Her heart swelled at his actions, the tender care he took when he kissed her.

"Do not cry, my Elita, I will return to you soon. There are a few things I must take care of first so I can devote all my time to you." His deep, sensual voice sent shivers through her.

"Promise?"

He kissed her on the temple before answering, "Cross my heart,"

Elita closed her eyes, savoring the lingering feel of his lips on her skin. "Hurry back to me."

The King stepped back, and bowed deeply to her, "As you wish, my Queen." He turned on his heel and walked towards the door, before leaving he looked back and said, "Take care of her, Siaryl, or you will regret it." In one smooth motion he opened the door, stepped out and then close it behind him.

Elita felt shaky without the King in the room with her. She struggled to pull herself up into a sitting position, resting heavily on the headboard she wiped a slight sheen of sweat from her brow before turning to look at the other man named Siaryl.

He looked a lot like the King, he had the same shade of blond hair, but his was longer, it was knotted into a braid that fell over one shoulder. The same angular face, yet it was slightly less pronounced, and the same pale blue eyes. He was much like a younger version of the King.

"Your name is Siaryl, sir?" she asked.

He bowed to her, "Yes, my lady, I am here to take care of you until my King returns. Anything you need, I'll get it for you."

She looked down at her tattered, and bloody clothes, she didn't even want to know how her face and hair looked.

Sheepishly she looked back at Siaryl, "Actually...sir, if it isn't too much trouble, would I be able to have a change of clothes, and maybe a bath? If not, that's fine, I can deal without one."

He looked up at her with a small smile, "I'll send for a maiden to come and give you a bath, and we'll have our seamstress make something for you."

She shook her head, she shouldn't ask for someone to make her clothing. "No, no, that's alright, I don't want anyone to go to any trouble for me. I'll just wear these."

"But my lady, there is no trouble in this at all. We've been awaiting your return for so long, especially the King, we're more than happy to attend to you. I'll go and fetch a maiden for you."

Before Elita could ask what he meant Siaryl walked briskly out of the room. Sighing, she leaned back against the headboard and looked around the room she was in. She gripped the silk sheets of the bed she was placed on. The headboard and frame were made of a dark cherry wood; the mattress was soft, allowing her to sink in slightly. It cradled her body with the smooth material that was the color of pearls. The whole thing seemed too modern for her surroundings, an underground labyrinth with halls made of earth and ice, and carpets made of grass, leaves and flowers. Torches of fire, and seemingly homemade candles on wooden platforms lighted the rooms. The doors were constructed of wood of a dark red, almost black color, like old blood. They glistened softly under the light of the fire that always seemed to be flickering nearby.

She heard a soft knock on the door, "Come in," she told them. Elita watched as the door creaked open so show two beautiful girls walk in carrying a large basin. They looked like opposites in a way, one had white blond hair much like her own, and the other had matte black hair. Though they both had the same pale skin, and piercing blue eyes. They smiled at her in unison before setting down the basin near the bed and bowing to her.

The one with the blond hair spoke first, "Hello my lady, we have been informed you would fancy a bath?"

"I do, but if it's too much trouble, I don't mind not having one."

The raven-haired girl looked at her in confusion, "Why would this be too much trouble, my lady?"

Elita gave her a look, "Do you usually bathe other girls? Is this normal for you?"

She smiled at Elita, transforming her inhumanly beautiful face to that of an angel. "Not usually, but we've been waiting for you for so long, so it's no trouble, my lady, truly."

She gazed at the girl for a few more seconds, studying her face. "Why does everyone keep saying that?"

The dark haired girl opened her mouth but was cut off by the blond, "No more chit chat, we must draw her bath."

"But I-"

She held up her hand, "My lady, please, once we get you in the water I promise we'll answer all the questions we are allowed to."

It took the maidens a full twenty minutes to coax Elita into the basin. The moment she sat down in the water she assaulted them with questions.

"First, may I know your names?"

"I am Bryony and my sister, the blond, is Bryna."

"You have very beautiful names," Elita mused.

"Thank you, my lady," they said in unison.

"Okay, next, why is it that everyone is calling me 'lady'? And what do you mean that you've been waiting for me?"

A short pause followed her question. Elita looked back and saw they were staring at each other. "What's wrong?"

Bryna looked at her, "Well, it's just that, my lady, there are some questions we aren't allowed to answer. We're not sure if we're supposed to tell you the answer to those."

"Why?"

Bryony sighed, "The King, my la-" she stopped when Elita gave her a pointed stare, "Elita, he wishes for you to remember on your own. He gave us all specific orders to not give anything away."

"No offense, but how would he know if you told me, if I said that I remembered on my own?"

The sisters exchanged dubious stares, their full lips curving into secret smiles. "If anyone asks, you didn't hear it from us," they explained together.

Elita smiled gratefully, leaning back against the warm metal.

"Do you like myths and legends, Elita?" Bryna asked.

"Yeah, actually, I'm getting my college degree in Mythology, a useless degree, but it's what I enjoy."

"What do you know about the Fair Folk?"

"Fair Folk? Oh, you mean faeries. Well, sadly, not much. I know they aren't like Tinker Bell, that's for sure. There are two Courts, right? The Seemie...Searie?"

Bryony laughed, "Seelie, and Unseelie," she provided.

"Yes! That's it. The Seelie is the light and the Unseelie is the dark. The Seelie Court is known mainly as the Summer Court, ruled by fae of light, and summer, while the Unseelie is the Winter court, ruled by fae of darkness, winter and ice, correct?"

"Very good. Now have you ever heard of a changeling?"

Elita closed her eyes, thinking back as the girl washed her gently, removing the dried blood and dirt, careful not to touch any of her wounds. "Um, isn't that when a human child is switched with a faery child?"

Bryna clapped, "Yes! See, Bryony, we barely have to tell her anything."

"Very true, Bryna. Now Elita, about 40 years ago was the last time the fae had used a changeling, and not just any changeling. This faerie was a rare one; she was born with a mother of the light Court and a father of the dark Court. She was coveted and desired by both side, a war broke out over who would get this child. Until one night they decided to spirit her away from the Courts, and switch her with a human child. It was decided that the first child she would bear would go to the fathers Court, and her second would go to the mothers Court when they turn 22."

A cold shiver ran down Elita's spine when she heard that age. *I turned 22 last night.* Bryony's words were drowned out by the rushing blood that pounded in her ears.

It can't be me, she told herself, *there's no way. It's just a story, a myth. Nothing to be scared of.* Something seemed to be pricking at the back of her mind, a memory of something long forgotten. Bits of images flashed in front of her eyes of her mother, with hair the color of moonlight, eyes warm and brown as cinnamon. Another image of her mother crying, clutching her father tightly, whispering to him she couldn't say good-bye to someone yet. It was too soon.

"Elita?" a voice snapped her out of her reverie. Shaking her head, she swung her head to meet the concerned eyes of Bryna.

"I'm sorry, what?"

"You looked as if you were a million miles away just then, are you remembering something?"

"I think I am, but I'm not sure. I saw my mother, she was crying, telling my dad that is was too soon to say goodbye. But goodbye to who? Why goodbye? Why too soon?"

"Elita, tell me, have you noticed something about most of the people you've seen here?"

Elita scrunched her brows together, confusion rolling through her. "What do you mean?"

"Have you noticed any similarities? At all."

"Now that you mention it," she began, thinking back, "almost everyone I've met has that pale blond hair, like mine, or just a few shades darker. And those blue eyes. Those piercing blue eyes."

Bryna smiled, "That's right," she grabbed at her hair, holding it up, "this hair color is a dominant trait for our people, along with the eyes. They will show up, no matter how diluted our bloodline is."

"Wait, wait, wait. What do you mean, 'our people'?" Elita turned around in the bathtub, so she didn't have her back to them anymore. She hugged he knees to her chest, trying to get as far from them as she can. "Who are you two? Really?"
"Elita...you're...we are...Elita, your mom was the changeling. You're half fae." Bryony told her.

Elita stared at Bryony for a few minutes, her mouth working, trying to form words but was unable to. Her mind raced, picking and pulling through her memories, trying to find any evidence that what Bryony told her was wrong. But every memory she called on seemed to fade and become fuzzy, always coming back to her mother telling her father that she can't say goodbye, but now she can hear the exact words she spoke.

"David, I can't let her go, I just can't," her mother sobbed into his shoulder. "I can't let Elita go."

Her dad hugged her mom tightly, "I'm sorry Maeve, and I wish we didn't have to. But you know what Nickolai would do if we didn't give him Elita. He would kill us all." He set his hand on her swollen belly, "I know you'll have to give Madison away too one day, but we'll have our son, who is growing inside of you now. We'll never have to give him away. Ever. I know it's never going to take away the pain of having to let our 2 daughters go, but just remember we'll always have him." He bent down and kissed her stomach, "I can only hope it's enough to keep the guilt away."

Elita let out a gasp, and clutched at her naked chest. She set her head down on her knees, taking deep, shuddering breaths. "No," she cried, "NO. This can't be!"

"Elita, I'm so sorry. This is why we didn't want to tell you. The King is going to be furious with us for making you sad. He's the only one who can take away your pain."

She looked up at Bryna sharply, "What do you mean by that?" she snapped.

Bryna took a step back, her eyes looking sad and hurt. "I-I just mean that, he loves you. He's been waiting for you for 50 years, to fill the void he's felt all these years. You complete him, and he completes you."

Elita's anger died as quickly as it ignited. Somehow, in some part of her soul she knew that Bryna was speaking the truth. When she thought it him it felt as if her shattered soul seemed to repair itself, her blood pumped stronger, she felt...whole.

"I'm sor-" she was cut off by a knock on the door. Sighing she yelled for them to come in.

"Oh! My lady, I'm so sorry!" she heard Siaryl's voice say. "I didn't know you were still bathing. I will come back later."

"No, no, it's quite alright. Come on in, you can't see anything."

The sister let out a nervous giggle at her bold remark. She smiled at them and turned her head to glance at Siaryl. "What can I do you for?"

He stared at her for a few moments, his eyes confused. Elita could almost hear the gears in his working, trying to figure out what her question meant. So he just held up a bundle of fabric and pointed to it with his free hand.

"Oh! My clothes. Bryna, would you mind getting that for me and showing Siaryl out?"

"As you wish, El-my lady," she corrected herself as she remembered that Siaryl was still in the room. Elita watched as she took the dress from him and walked him to the door.

"Bryony, could you help me up?"

Bryony gave a shy smile and grasped her outstretched hands, pulling her up gently and guiding her out of the basin. "I hope you'll forgive us, my lady, for our behavior. We should never have told you, it wasn't our place."

Elita held up her hand, "Nothing to apologize for. I asked you to tell me, I'll take full responsibility for when the King comes back to my room for my knowledge."

"If I may be so bold, my lady, but you are taking this a lot better than the King thought you would."

Elita let out a laugh and she began to walk towards the bed, "Trust me, I'm a wreck on the inside, but I remembered something about faeries."

"What's that?" Bryna asked.

"You are incapable of lying. So I know that all this is true, and that it is true that the King loves me. For some reason, that just seems enough for me tonight. I can't make any promises of how I'm going to be tomorrow, or even the next day. But for this moment, I'm...well," she looked at both of them and smiled, "I'm okay."

Bryna smiled back, "Well, that makes me happy, my lady. I mean, Elita," her smile broadened. "Now, shall we help you into the gown?"

Elita's gaze went down to the dress. The skirt was made of layers of deep purple taffeta, the ends just grazing the grass floor. The bodice was a tightly fitting silk, with a deep neckline and draped sleeves. Stitched flowers decorated the entire dress, forming an unknown pattern. Amethyst jewels adorned the collar of the gown, glittered softly under the candlelight.

"Don't you think this is a bit...fancy for me?" she stuttered out.

The sisters looked at each other, then back to her. "Fancy? Elita, you do know who you are, right?" When she gave them a blank stare, Bryna elaborated, "You're the Queen of the Unseelie Court. There is nothing too fancy, or too good for you."

Elita felt her jaw drop slightly, and a blush creep onto her cheeks. "Wow," she whispered.

Bryony gave her a supportive smile, "It is a bit much to comprehend. When we dress you would you like us to leave you, so you can be alone?"

"Is the King back?"

She winked, "He's just waiting for you."

"Then yes, but send him in immediately."

They both bowed, "Of course, my Queen."

Elita was pacing her room, her hands tugging at the snug fabric of her gown. Her heart was pounding so hard against her chest she half expected it to tear through the skin and bone. Putting a hand on her chest, she stood in front of the floor length mirror and stared at her reflection, attempting to slow her breathing.

Her white blond hair was curling softly around her face and down her back, the same color as Nickolai's, Siaryl's and Bryna's, the dominant hair color of her people. The fae. Elita waited for the break down to come, for her to crumble into a ball and cry, but even after fifteen minutes of staring at her reflection nothing came. *How can I be handling this so well? I mean look at me!*

Her face was flushed with excitement, her cheeks rosy, her toffee brown eyes sparkling. The dress fit to perfection, it hugged every curve, showing off her voluptuous figure. Elita had never seen herself look this beautiful before, she could hardly recognize herself. *I'm...I look almost happy. What is wrong with me?*

She ran her fingertips over her temple, where Nickolai kissed her. The skin still tingled from his touch. Elita jumped as she heard a knock at her door. Swinging away from the mirror she faced the door, her hands roughly smoothing down her dress and her hair. "C-come in!" she squeaked, her hands shaking.

The dark, cherry wood door opened slowly until it was open as wide as it could go. Nickolai stood before her, his blue eyes raking over her with a hungry gaze. Elita blushed, trying to pull up the neckline that exposed her ample bosom. Before she could even blink he was standing in front of her, his cold hands on her own, stopping her motion. "Don't cover yourself up, my love, I want to see every inch of you," his voice was sensual as he spoke. Elita felt her breath hitch in her throat. A deep-seated desire burned hotly through her, warming her body.

She slowly dropped her hands, exposing her bust. Nickolai's eyes roamed over her chest, lingering on the exposed skin. Licking his lips he dipped his head down and planted a kiss on her collarbone. Elita let her head fall back, a sigh escaping her throat.

His lips explored her neck, tasting every inch of skin before traveling lower to her chest, where he left kisses on the tops of her breasts, sending shivers of pleasure down Elita's spine. Pulling back he put a hand on the back of her head, pushing it up until they were nose to nose. His cool breath mingled with her own, raising goosebumps over her body.

"You have no idea how long I've waited for you, my Queen," he whispered to her. "I almost thought you would never come to me, I don't know wh-" Elita stopped his words by placing a finger on his lips.

"I don't want to talk, not right now," she told him her voice sad.

Nickolai's brow furrowed, his eyes concerned, he pulled her finger away and asked, "What happened, Elita? Did someone hurt you?" When she shook her head, he let out a sort of growl, "Then what happened? Tell me who has made you sad, and I swear I will peel their skin off and make you a rug out of it."

Horrified, Elita took a step back from him, "Would you honestly do that?" she asked, bile rising up in her throat.

"If someone hurt you, yes, I would," he answered quickly, his tone deadly serious.

He's from the dark Court, Elita, of course he would.

"I will never allow someone to hurt you,"

"What about the man that threw me into the wall? Did you do that to him?"

He shook his head, "No, his sentence has yet to be decided. Is that what you wish to happen to him, my Queen?"

"No!" she yelled, "No one deserves that!"

Nickolai looked confused by her words, "My Queen, he could've killed you. Attacking a member of our own..." he stopped in the middle of tirade, his jaw slack as he looked at her with wide eyes. "I mean, attacking another person is just wrong."

Elita smiled wanly at him, "Nickolai, I know who I am."

His eyes darkened in anger, "Who told you? I bet it was those damned twins. I'll have their heads for this."

"Nickolai!" Elita gaped at him, appalled. "Don't you dare hurt them, Nickolai, or I swear to you I will walk out of here and never come back."

"You wouldn't dare."

She raised an eyebrow at him and put her hands on her hips, "Want to test that theory?"

They glared at each other, the air between them crackling with electricity. Nickolai was the first one to look away, "Fine," he mumbled. Elita smiled in triumph for a few moments, savoring her victory.

"Did they tell you everything?" Nickolai asked, his voice tight.

She shook her head, "Not really. They told me a bit about the Courts, and what a changeling is, then they told me the story about my mom. I think I knew it then, but I didn't want to believe it. Not until they told me that my mom was the changeling, then I remembered something from a few years ago. My mom was pregnant with my brother, and she was telling my dad she didn't want to say goodbye to me" Elita's voice cracked, her heart was heavy as she relived the memory again. "She's going to be so sad when I don't come home," Elita covered her face with her hands, "God, why does she have to get hurt like this?" "Elita, I'm...I'm so sorry for the pain this is going to cause you and your parents. If it helps at all, I was only a boy when she was sent away as a changeling, so I had no say in what they did to her."

Elita pulled her hands away to look at Nickolai, "Then why is it that you've been waiting for me if you didn't even know my mom?"

Nickolai took a deep breath before he explained, "It was destined that the first daughter born from Maeve would be blooded to the next King of the Unseelie Court. And the second daughter born would be blooded to the next King of the Seelie Court."

"Blooded?"

He gave a small smile, "Think of it as being soul mates. At birth our people are blooded to another, whether they are born yet or not. They aren't complete until they find that person, it's as if a piece of them is missing. They search everywhere to fill the void, every relationship they try to get into fails for some reason or another, making the hole in them wider and wider, until all together they get consumed by grief and lose all hope." Nickolai's voice was somber, his eyes misty and faraway.

Elita knew all too well those feelings, since she herself had felt those for 22 years. Never knowing when the ache in her heart would stop, when her soul would finally feel whole again. "Is that how you felt without me, Nickolai?" she whispered.

"Every day of my life, Elita."

She stopped breathing as she saw the raw pain in his haunted eyes. They looked as if he had seen years of sadness, completely devoid of happiness and hope.

"I'm sorry," she told him.

Nickolai shook his head, "Never apologize to me for this, you have done nothing to wrong me, Elita. It is I who should be apologizing to you."

She cocked her head, "For what?"

He barked out a laugh, "For what? Well let's see, you woke up in a dank cell, heard the sounds of someone being put to death and got thrown into a wall. Should I not apologize for that?"

"Since it doesn't matter right now, then no."

"It doesn't matter that I did all that to you?"

"No, because you didn't do anything to me. That man put me in a cell, he killed that person and he threw me into a wall."

"But I allowed all that to happen, I should've had you sent to my room, where none of that would have happened to you."

Elita sighed, "Alright, fine. I accept your apology, are you happy?" she began to drum her fingers on her hip in annoyance.

"No," he answered.

She threw her hands up in exasperation, "Why!"

"Because you're not," he said simply. He took a few steps towards her until he was mere inches away, his pale blue eyes seared into hers as he spoke, "Why are you unhappy?"

Elita tried to look away from him, but the way he was looking at her, the protectiveness radiating from him, she couldn't bring herself to do it. She'd never had a man genuinely care about what she was feeling; they'd only said what she wanted to hear so they could get her into bed. And every time she fell for it like a fool, playing into their lies, their pseudo concern, forcing herself to believe they cared. But with Nickolai, he seems to actually care about how she's feeling. His distress for her when he thought she had been hurt, the protectiveness that seems to be radiating out of him. It all just seems too good to be true, no man has ever cared for her.

"This isn't real," she murmured, "you can't care about me. You don't even know me. You just can't."

He took her face between his frigid hands, a fire igniting behind his irises. "You better listen to me Elita, and listen well. I may have never met you before today, but I do care about you. My soul has yearned for you for years, to have you in my arms, to hold you, to finally become whole again. All these years that I have been blooded with you, but couldn't be with you, were like hell. I could watch you from afar, but could never approach you. I watched as you grew from a lovely young girl, into the beautiful woman you are today. I may not have been there for you when you wept, or when you got hurt, but I promise that if you let me, I will be there for you for every day of forever. I will never let anyone hurt you, I will never let you cry out of sadness, I will heal every wound you have endure and will ever endure. Never say I don't care about you ever again. I may be the King of the Unseelie Court, but that does not mean I am incapable of loving."

"You aren't saying that you-"

"Yes, I am. I love you, Elita. I loved you back then, I love you right now. I always have, and I promise I always will."

Elita struggled to breathe as he told her he loved her. Her legs felt as if they would give away at any moment, she reached up and gripped his shirt, her nails digging into the fabric, to steady herself. Her breath came out in short bursts, her chest shuddering, trying to draw in oxygen. She was about to tell him she knew he was lying when she remembered what she said earlier; faeries can't lie. Lifting her shaking hand she set it on his cheek, feeling cool skin, as she looked into his eyes.

"Don't break my heart, Nickolai, I can't handle much more pain before I am broken beyond repair," she breathed.

Nickolai caressed the top of her cheek with thumb, his expression sincere, "I would never hurt you, Elita, and those who have hurt you in the past are going to realize later in life that they let go of the most perfect woman anyone could ask for."

Tears flooded down Elita's face at his words, her heart beating so loudly she swore he could hear it. "Kiss me, Nickolai. Make me forget the past."

He dipped his head down and captured her lips with his own. Elita heard herself moan at the taste of him, it was like snow and fire. Her entire body became alive, reacting to each touch, eliciting shivers from her. She reached up and tangled her hands into his hair, marveling at how soft it was.

Nickolai traced the tip of his tongue along the shape of her lips, asking for entrance. Elita gladly opened her mouth, allowing their tongues to dance together. He deepened the kiss, exploring every inch of her mouth as she explored him - he tasted of ice and passion. Nickolai snaked an arm around her waist, pressing her into him. Elita could feel his muscles beneath his thin shirt, hard and toned. She pulled her hands out of his hair and she tugged at his shirt until she ripped it up the middle. Elita splayed her hands across his abs, feeling them contract and shudder beneath her touch. She let her hands roam over his torso, not leaving any section of skin untouched.

Reaching around to his back she trailed the tip of her nail lightly down his spine, smiling when she felt him shiver. Elita pulled back from his slightly to look into his translucent eyes, she felt fire burn within her as they locked gazes, staring at each other with such passion. Nickolai bent down and scooped her up into his arms, never breaking their eye contact. He laid her on the silken sheets gently; he hiked up the skirt of her dress so he could lie between her legs. Elita's skin sizzled as he put his entire weight atop her. Her head spun as she felt every inch of his body on hers. She wrapped her arm around his neck and pulled him down to her.

She kissed him lightly on the jaw, trailing kisses along neck, nipping at the skin every few kisses. Bringing her face back to his she grabbed his bottom lip between her teeth, nibbling and pulling gently at it. Elita heard a deep groan rumble in his chest, she felt his hand tighten around

117

her as he traced the outline of her waist and hip and further down where he cupped her backside, squeezing it roughly. Elita let out a gasp and arched her back, eliminating the little space that was left between them. She pressed her lips into his fiercely and wrapped her legs around his narrow waist, delighting in the feel of him on every inch of her body.

She could feel herself getting lost in him, in his kisses and touches. She had never felt anything like this in her life. Elita had never felt this whole in her entire life, or this happy. With each kiss she felt her wounds repair themselves, each scar start to fade little by little. Nothing seemed to matter then, not that she would never see her family again, or that the Seelie Court would take her sister in a few short years, or even that her mother would lose another daughter to the fae. All that mattered was the moment she was in now, with Nickolai. She waited 22 years to find him and she was never going to let go, she was going to hold on to him with both hands. Elita had finally learned the true reason for existing, to love and be loved, for there is truly nothing better.

A Full Wolf Moon
by
L.D. Ricard

Unknowingly being watched, the pack ran gracefully following their leader. The snow was deep in places, but the full moon shining down made everything beautiful. The creature watching them felt the hunger rising in itself. As they hit the property line they stood as one...on two legs. Looking towards their leader, they went to dress and have dinner. No kill tonight. The run had been purely for fun. As they went into the house, Pauli, a green eyed, redheaded beauty, noticed someone was missing.

"Jonas, where is Michael?" She asked the leader.

"I don't know. Maybe he came back in early. I'll go up to your room and check."

At that time they heard screams coming from the forest. They sounded so inhuman; they couldn't tell what it was. Pauli made a move to for the door. Jonas grabbed her arm.

"No, not tonight. We'll go as a pack tomorrow. We have no clue what's out there.

"But Michael could be out there injured or worse." He was her mate.

"I know sweetheart, but I can't risk the pack for one. I thought I caught a strange odor of death, but really didn't give it much thought."

119

"Jonas, we are twenty five strong. What could be out there that could touch us?"

"We will see in the morning what there is to see. That is my final word on the matter. Now little one, go get something to eat and get some rest." With that Jonas turned and walked into his study. Glad she couldn't see the worry on his face.

Jonas sat at his desk thinking. Maybe it hadn't been such a good idea to bring the pack to Ontario for the reunion. They could have met at his ranch in Montana. They had many times before. He thought a change of scenery would be good for everyone and being the dead of winter, this place had been cheap to rent. He had heard stories of course. Of a creature who thrived here in the winters. The Cree were full of Folklore and Legends. Hell even in Montana he'd heard some. Well nothing to do about it until the morning. With a sigh, he turned off his desk lamp and went up to bed.

The morning dawned with a sun so bright it was blinding with the snow. Jonas had ten of his pack with him. The others had no clue what was going on and he could see no point of alarming them. Pauli of course was right by his side. They would be cross-country skiing. He wanted no chance of being spotted by others out skiing or by low flying planes. They were a motley crew in their wolf forms, belonging to no breed of wolf known to science.

They headed out in the direction he and Pauli had heard the screams coming from. Steven looked ready to kick ass. He was a hot head at best, which made his human job as a bouncer at a club in New York perfect for him. They all looked grim faced as they skied through the woods. Michael hadn't returned last night and for him to leave Pauli was unthinkable.

About a mile from the main house, they found Michael. Or what was left of him. In human form he was six foot six. As a wolf he was magnificent. A very large black wolf with ice blue eyes. A gift from his Celtic roots. There wasn't much left of him and most of him had been devoured. Pauli fell to her knees, making a keening wail that broke the hearts of the others. Wolves mate for life and for Pauli there would never be another. Jonas assigned Steven and a pack member to clean up the remains. He gently led Pauli and the rest away.

About and hour later Jonas came down stairs after sedating Pauli and putting her to bed. The others were in the den wanting answers. He wasn't sure how to explain. Steven stepped over to him and asked the question everyone was thinking.

"Jonas, what could have done that to Michael? As a wolf he weighed at least two hundred and fifty pounds and was in fine physical shape."

"Please everyone sit. I've given this a lot of thought since last night. The Cree have a legend about a creature. It has many names, depending on the tribe. Most commonly it is known as a Wiliko. The Algonquin call it a Windigo. It's a solitary cannibalistic spirit. The stories vary, so it's hard to know what's fact or fiction. Some say it can take on human form to get its prey. Others say it can blend in so you can't see it. About the only thing they agree on is that every time it feeds it gets bigger. Supposedly it lies dormant for periods of time."

Steven, ever the hot head fisted his hands, "If you knew this how could you bring us here? To risk even any of the pack?"

"They supposedly live in Montana as well. We've never had any problems there. I wasn't sure they even existed. I should have known better, after all we don't exist either."

Mona, the smallest and ever the peacemaker of the pack, stepped in between the two men. She laid a hand on each of their chests. "Gentleman, what's done is done. We can't bring Michael back. Now do we leave or stay and try to bring down this creature?"

"I've given this some thought," Jonas wondered how they would react to his decision. "I think the oldest of us should stay. The newest and youngest should go to the Montana ranch. If we don't succeed in killing this creature and it gets us, the pack would go on."

There was some muttering around the room. It was clear that what Jonas said made sense, but even so, all wanted revenge on the creature. Always thinking and never one to question Jonas, Mona spoke up. "Who would lead the Montana pack?"

"I've given that a great deal of thought as well. I honestly think you should Mona. You keep your cool in tough situations and those who leave will obey you. If anything happens to me, you could always take a vote if you don't want to be leader."

"I will do my best to hold everything together and I know you'll come back to us."

In a few short hours all but seven had left. No amount of pleading could get Pauli to leave. She wanted her revenge or would die trying. All that remained was Jonas, Steven, Margo, Allen, Tanner and of course Pauli. Jonas ordered them all to get some rest. They would head out as soon as the moon was up. Jonas went back to the den to do more research on the Wiliko. He had a bad feeling they were going to need all the help they could get. By the time the moon had started to rise he had what you could loosely call a handbook on fighting Wilikos.

As they wouldn't be hunting for food they feasted before hand. Jonas gave them a short version of what he learned.

"As I said this is a cannibal, so even in wolf form it's going to know we're human. There's so much has been lost through the years and different tribes have different versions. Another thing they all they seem to agree on is this thing stinks. I noticed a foul smell last night, but didn't give it much thought." He silently wondered if he had if Michael would still be alive.

"When out there keep your noses going at all times. Look for something in your perpetual vision. That's another way it can get you, supposedly. If we run into a human take a good sniff. And we stay together at all times." This last statement was directed at Steven and they all knew it.

"Ok, let's head out. Remember everything I said."

They changed into wolf form. In their world most people don't even know they're wolves until they are in their twenties. The older wolves could sense one and try to stay close when they have their first change. It wasn't something they could control and you just can't walk up to someone and say, "Just to let you know your going to become a wolf sometime in the next few months." They'd run like hell from you. So you watch and wait.

They ran cautiously through the forest and fields. As they past the spot where they found Michael, they all noticed no tracks other than Michaels. It gave them a moment's pause as to how they were going to track something that didn't leave tracks. They would have to rely on their noses.

As they ran side by side a horrible smell reached them. It had to be the Wiliko. They turned to the smell. Steven tried to pass Jonas and was snarled at. Jonas didn't want any heroics and Steven always thought he should lead the pack.

They came to a small clearing where the smell was very strong. It smelled like a three-day road kill in ninety-degree weather. They all stood very still. They knew something was there but couldn't sense where. Suddenly out of the corner of his eye Steven spotted a movement. He didn't turn his head and watched, as a very large creature seemed to appear. None of the others seemed to notice. It was tall with its skin pulled tautly across its bone to the point of emaciation. What lips it had were bloody and its teeth were pointed fangs. The creature's eyes glowed an eerie red.

Just as Steven was thinking he could take down this sickly looking thing, Allen took a step toward it. Steven knew Allen didn't see it. Before he could growl out a warning, the thing was on Allen. Now they all could see it. Allen never had a prayer. The Wiliko had him by the scruff of his neck and with one swipe of its razor sharp claws, had Allen's internal organs falling on to the snow. At first stunned, the pack froze. Then leaped into action. Steven was quickly knocked back and out. Tanner tried to get behind it for an attack, but the creature seemed to be everywhere at once. Pauli managed to get a good grip on the arm not holding Allen off the ground. The creature was defending his kill and was not going to part with it. Pauli's grip gave the rest of the pack a chance to move in. She was fighting on pure rage and wanted to avenge Michael. The others knew if they got out of there alive it would be a miracle. They needed a better game plan. Suddenly it shook Pauli off and sent her crashing into Margo. They both went down. With its arm free, it was a force to be reckoned with. It slashed out and took Tanner out of the fight. He was going to need stitches and he was damn lucky he still had a throat left. A little bit more and his jugular would have been severed. Jonas retreated; he had a gash that ran from his shoulder to his flank. He also would need to be stitched.

Only the two females had come out of this unscathed for the most part. Margo thought she might have a few cracked or bruised ribs from the impact with Pauli. Pauli had a growing lump forming on her head and was seeing double. It was with total dismay the pack watched the creature carry off Allen. They wondered if they would ever find what would be left of the body.

It was a very broken and downtrodden group that arrived back at the house. Margo had nurses training that could patch and stitch everyone up. After showers and being doctored up they all met in the den.

Jonas poured everyone a brandy. Margo glared at him, but he felt they needed it. They all could now see how the creature had taken out Michael. He normally ran at the back of the pack as second in command. He had probably scented the Wiliko and went off to see what it was. They all were somber and sore.

Jonas waited until everyone had taken a drink then spoke. "We now know what we're up against. I'm sorry about Allen, but there was nothing we could do. Steven I saw you tense up right before it grabbed Allen. What did you see?"

Steven looked up, tears in his eyes, "I saw what you all saw. Just out of the corner of my eye. If I tried to look at it straight on it disappeared. I thought I could take its emaciated ass. I couldn't believe that was what killed Michael. How are we going to stop it? Is there anything in your research that tells you how?"

Jonas stared at his glass, "Fire…maybe… it's all I've found. We rest up a few days and go after it again. This time, some in wolf form and some human. Steven, you're going in wolf form. You spotted it first, so you'll know what to look for. Tanner, you're banned from going out there. With your throat injury your in no shape for another fight."

Tanner just looked at his feet with tears in his eyes. "I want to hurt that damn thing. For Pauli, Michael and for Allen. I know your right, but it doesn't hurt any less."

Jonas could feel his pain, "I know and we will get it. Pauli and I are going in human form. We're the only two that can shoot bows with any accuracy. If we can find it again we're going to fry its ass."

"Flaming arrows?" Pauli looked shaken at the thought. "The only problem I have with that is none of us saw the damn thing until it had Allen. Are we going to have to sacrifice another to get it?"

Jonas looked grim, "We know when we smell it, and it's in the immediate area. That may give us an advantage, how ever small. Look I don't want to lose anymore of the pack. We just can't leave that thing running around out there. The summer people are safe. It thrives in the cold. We'll just have to do what we can." He looked around at his beat up pack

None of the pack wanted to give up. They all wanted pay back. Now that it had hurt them all in one way or another, they wanted blood. They gave it three days before trying again. Jonas informed them if the tales were true, it would be hunting already.

It was a somber group that left at dusk. Tanner watched from the front window, saying a silent prayer for their safety. He hated the fact he couldn't be with them, but a small part of him was glad. The Wiliko had scared him to the bone. They had looked for two days for Allen's remains. Someday someone would come across a wolf skeleton and wonder how it died. Contrary to what Hollywood portrayed, when they died they stayed in what ever form they were in.

They stuck close together. They had to move slower than normal because of Jonas and Pauli being in human form. Maybe it was for the best. Less chance of it getting jump on them. Pauli looked like a warrior. Her and Jonas both had arrows notched and ready. Each of the arrows tip was wrapped with gas soaked rags.

Two hours into the search they started to get whiffs of odor. It was hard to pin point it. It almost seemed as if the creature was circling them. Staying far enough away to keep an eye on them. If Jonas was right, it was probably hungry already.

Suddenly Margo stiffened up. She had caught a slight shift of movement to her left. She looked and it was gone. As soon as she looked forward again she could see it again. The stench it carried with it was getting stronger. She went up to Jonas and bumped him with her shoulder. He looked down and she motioned with her nose in the direction she had seen it. He stood stock still, trying to glimpse it. The smell was closer and he feared he might lose another before they could act.

All at once all hell broke loose. Steven had also spotted it and tried to warn Pauli. She was busy trying to get her arrow lit. Her hands were shaking too bad. She kept dropping the lighter and now it had snow in it. Steven stepped between her and the glimmer of the creature. Jonas was having better luck. He was waiting for the Wiliko to make its move. No doubt they would lose another in order to end this.

Steven figured the only way to make it show itself fully was to make the first move. Jonas was down on one knee, waiting to light his arrow. Steven bunched his muscles and leapt in the general direction of the creature. Pauli screamed and ran to Jonas for a light. Steven had hit his mark and now the Wiliko was visible to them. Now they had another problem. Margo had joined the fight and only managed to outrage the creature even more. She had her teeth sunk into its leg. The monster had it's teeth sunk into Stevens shoulder and was trying to slice him to ribbons. With one back hand with those claws it managed to slice Mona's head nearly off.

Pauli was screaming at Jonas, "I can't get a clear shot off with out risking Steven.

Jonas was trying to move to a better position, "Steven! Drop down if you can. Get hell out of the way!"

Steven managed to shake loose and drop. Just as soon as he was out of the way Jonas and Pauli let fly. Their arrows flew true and both connected with the Wiliko. His screams were unworldly as it caught fire and burned. The remaining members of the pack watched in horror. They stood and watched until there was nothing left but a smoldering body.

Jonas spoke first, "We'll come back later and bury Margo. If what the legends say is true we need to scatter what's left of that around."

Pauli looked at the gruesome sight, "Are you trying to say it could come back to life?"

"I don't know, but I'm not taking any chances. Let's go get Steven cleaned up. Tanner and I will come back out here."

Leaving Steven in Pauli's hands, Jonas and Tanner headed back out an hour later. Tanner was unusually quiet. Jonas figured it was due to his own injuries. Once the grisly job was done they headed back.

Jonas couldn't handle Tanner's silence any longer. "Ok out with it, what's bugging you?"

"Mona called while you were out doing battle. She decided to do more research on the Wiliko. It seems you can survive being scratched by it. But some of the legends say if you are bitten that you will turn into one." He looked at Jonas with sad eyes, "I was thinking about how badly it bit Steven."

Jonas was about to reply when they heard Pauli screaming from the house. They broke into a run. They reached the front of the house in time to see Steven heading into the forest out the back. They ran in the house to find Pauli ripped to shreds. They looked at each other. Both thinking the same thing…he knew about the ranch in Montana. Also, they knew how to kill him. He wouldn't be easy. Jonas went to phone and warn her. It wasn't over yet. They had to get to Montana before it did and they didn't know how fast it could travel. Somehow it had to end. Jonas felt in his gut it was going to be a long fight…let the battle begin.

His First Snow
by
Linna Drehmel

On the world of Zahomla all celebrated this special winter season, mortals as well as immortals. The winter moon alignment was tonight. It was the one night of the year where the moon of the Master, the Lord and the Guide all came together to share their life giving light with the mortal world. Mortals and immortals called this night the night of the Lord alike.

One emissary from each of the moons had been sent down, one by the Master and one by the Guide to the planet of the mortals to find a gift for the Lord. A third emissary had been sent from the moon of the Lord to find a gift as well. Caelan was the one chosen from the moon of the Lord to go. It was his first time to the planet since he had become an emissary. He had been told by many of his fellow emissaries that he had to stand in a snowfall. They told him it was an experience unlike anything he had when he was mortal.

Caelan was excited as he began to descend to the planet through clouds that he knew held snow. He pushed through the cold feathery clouds and felt the soft tickle of the crystalline flakes of beauty touch his skin as he slowly descended to a small hill just outside a city, and sank into the snow up to his knees.

He laughed in wonder at the sensation of the cold that surrounded his legs. The feeling of his legs encased in snow would have been uncomfortable, even painful while he was mortal, but now as an emissary the feeling only filled him with delight.

Using only the merest bit of his power he extended his wings of light and gracefully rose above the snow so he could walk just on top of the drifts. He loved the sound of the snow as it crunched under his feet. He laughed once again keeping his wings out so he could stay above the drift and kick the snow and watched with glee as the snow fell in chunks around him. He reached down he scooped up a handful of snow, quickly formed a ball in his hands and lobbed it at a tree hitting it strait on.

"Ha!" Caelan laughed to himself, "I was not that good of a shot when I was mortal."

What a fantastic sight this young emissary was, as he played in the snow like a small child with laughter in his dark brown eyes. His dark hair stood out in sharp contrast on the white snow, his wings of light caught each tiny diamond flake causing it to gleam in the dark of this special night.

Caelan was so caught up in the sensations of his first snowfall as an emissary that he forgot his mission, until he looked through the cloudy sky and saw how close the moons were to the alignment.

"The gift!" he gasped out loud.

He fully extended his wings and quickly sped through the cold winter air toward the city not knowing where to find a gift that would be fitting for his Lord. Caelan searched the quiet city streets looking, listening for

132

anything a song or a sight that he could capture with his power and carry back to the Lords moon in time.

Caelan began to panic and chided himself for spending so much time playing in the snow, until he heard a sound that caused him to feel cold. A cold that had nothing to do with the snow filled air; it was the sound of fear and pain.

Caelan forgot his panic over finding a gift as he raced to the sound. His duty as an emissary of the Lord was to protect the lives of mortals from beings of darkness. Help and protect was first in his thoughts as he flew around the side of the Masters sanctuary. Caelan saw one such loathsome being attacking two young clerics as they tried to enter the sanctuary. One cleric was on the ground as the other was trying to wrestle a knife away from the creature.

"Stop!" Caelan cried as he sped through the air pushing all of his power into his wings. "Cleric look out," he called out his warning allowing the young man to duck in time as Caelan barreled strait into the dark beast, lifting it off the other cleric, who lay bleeding in the snow. "You cannot have them beast, they are clerics in the Master's service!" Caelan declared angrily as he slammed the dark beast against the wall of the sanctuary.

The dark beast was weakened by Caelan's attack, but still had strength enough to hiss in laughter "I have already taken one."

"You cannot have the unalloyed soul of a cleric!" Caelan avowed as he began to glow brighter. The beast squealed in pain from the light but managed to say with menace in its voice, "I will have their wretched souls yet, but for now I have at least taken that one's life so he will no longer be able to serve the Three."

"You cannot have him!" The emissary yelled again as the light that emanated from him intensified to the point that the beast fought just to get away from it, but Caelan held firm to the dark beast, until the vile monster imploded, overcome by the emissary's pure light.

Once the beast had vanished, Caelan descended as lightly as the countless snowflakes around him to the ground next to the two clerics.

"Emissary help Autreo please, I think he is dying." The young man pleads desperately.

"What is your name cleric?" Caelan asked softly.

"I am Kriess cleric in service of the Master. Autreo is cleric in the service of the Lord." He said through his tears.

Caelan knelt next to Kriess in the snow and put a comforting hand on the young man's shoulder using his power to bring comfort to the distressed young cleric. "Be at peace Kriess we are all one in our service to the Three."

"But please Emissary can you help Autreo?" Kriess begged urgently.

"I am sorry but Autreo has passed into light."

The young cleric bowed his head in grief as his hot tears fell to the ground melting the cold snow.

"Kriess you must go into the Masters sanctuary where it is safe and tell the Vercovo of the sanctuary what has happened," Caelan instructed him.

"But what about Autreo's body?" Kriess sobbed, "I can't leave him out here."

"Be at ease Kriess, I will care for him. Autreo's election is made sure."

Kriess looked up quickly when he heard this, knowing full well what it meant. "He is going to be a…" He stopped not daring to speak it.

"Yes, his soul is pure." Caelan confirmed what the young man was going to say. "Now go be safe and at peace, for it is the Lord's night."

Kriess got slowly to his feet and with melancholy in his voice said, "Thank you Emissary, blessed night of the Lord." Kriess looked sadly back at his friend for just a moment, and then crossed into the safety of the Masters sanctuary closing the heavy door behind him.

As Caelan knelt on the cold ground he was enveloped in the quiet of the winter night. He looked at the poor soul that lay on the ground where his precious life was taken before his time. Caelan knew what he needed to do, but this meant that he would have to use most all of his power and would not be able to find the gift he had been sent after, but that didn't matter. Caelan would do his duty as an emissary of the Lord even if it meant that he would return to the moon of the Lord empty handed.

Caelan focused almost all of his power on his hands and placed one brightly glowing hand on Autreo's forehead and one on his chest releasing the powerful light into the lifeless body. He then called Autreo's soul back. Using his power, Caelan eternally sealed the young cleric soul and body together.

Feeling drained of his power Caelan took his hands from the young man as Autreo opened his eyes with a gasp of surprise.

"What has happened?" Autreo asked as he sat up looking down at his clothing that was now as white as the snow that fell around him.

"You passed into light and will soon be an Emissary of the Lord." Caelan explained simply.

"But how? Where is Kriess?" Autreo questioned him. "Who are you?"

"I too am an Emissary of the Lord. My name is Caelan and it is time for us to return to the moon of the Lord." Caelan said as he stood up, fully extended his wings and held out his hand. "Come, the moons have aligned." The young man who would soon be an emissary stood up, took Caelan's hand and the two of them ascended into the snow filled night sky. The journey that the two of them made on the night of the Lord would have seemed to take an eternity to a mortal, but for two immortals it happened very fast.

The two of them burst through the clouds and were pulled by the light of the three moons that had aligned as one to the presence of The Master, The Lord and The Guide.

Caelan stood silently in the glorious presence of the Three, watching as the other two emissaries presented the Lord with their magnificent gifts, and saw the happiness it brought to all of the Three. But Caelan didn't know what he was going to say as he walked sadly empty handed before the Lord.

"My Master, Lord, and Guide," He formally addressed the Three with a shaky voice. "I am sorry to tell you I have no gift."

"Please, tell us why," Was the Lord's soothing voice.

Caelan bowed his head in shame, "I was enjoying my first snow fall and thought of your gift." He began. "I flew quickly to the city looking for what would be a gift for you Lord, but I heard a fight. Two clerics were attacked by a dark beast, I did my best to save them but one was killed." He said as he gestured to Autreo. "He was a good cleric in your service Lord with a pure soul, I used my power to raise him so he could be an emissary in the service of the Three."

Upon hearing this The Lord arose from his seat and descended the steps with a smile on his glorious face. The Lord approached Autreo and said, "My son." As he folded him in an embrace and passed his hands over the young man's back then drew his hands out, as he did so two magnificent wings of light emerged from Autreo's back. "Welcome home Emissary."

The Lord then turned to Caelan and then enfolded him in a tight embrace that filled him with the power of light that he had been drained of when he raised Autreo.

"I am sorry I failed you Lord," Caelan whispered in shame as tears fell from his eyes.

The Lord released Caelan and stood back looking at him with a dazzling smile, "You did not fail my son. You have brought me the best gift of all, for the worth of a soul is great in my sight."

Dark Light

Dementria's Task
by
Amanda R. Browning

<u>Chapter 1</u>

The portal room of the Academy of Infernal Avocation was crowded with the demon students and their families, the instructors, and the two massive hellhounds guarding the portal. Today was a graduation of sorts for thirteen fledgling demon students. Each student had just completed the academic portion of their demonic studies, and the time for their final test had arrived. They would all begin their Proving today, as soon as they stepped through the portal and onto Earth. During the Proving, each fledgling demon would be given temporary full reign of their powers in order to complete their individual assignments. The air in the room was heavy with nerves and desperation; to fail this test was *not* an option.

Dementria waited along with her classmates. Her tall, slim body shifted anxiously. Her five foot nine frame allowed her a decent view over the shorter occupants here. Her violet eyes looked around the room restlessly, trying to remember every detail to recall while she was in the unfamiliar Earth dimension. The walls, floor, and vaulted ceiling were made from smooth black marble. The polish was so intense that the room was reflected in the glasslike surface. There were intricate designs made of interlocking demonic symbols ringing the edge of the portal in an arch, and the portal itself looked like shimmering purple water, lit from behind. The edges of the portal looked like black ink had been dumped into the incandescent lilac fluid. Black tendrils spread out from the fringes, writhing against each other like snakes. The two gigantic hellhounds stood to the sides of the portal, black fur gleaming in the light from the torches mounted on the wall. The hound closest to Dementria swiveled its glowing red eyes and focused on her. She quickly looked away, knowing better than to challenge the dominance of a hellhound, and her long black hair slid forward to cover her face. After a moment, she glanced up, appreciating the sight and smell of the deadly nightshade sprigs in the black vases on the wall, above and behind the hellhounds.

Dementria was nervous and scared about the mission she was to complete. Her power was the ability to alter the reality of her target to cause insanity. Dementria fed on the energy given off by a broken psyche. She could easily get this energy from an asylum, but she had to earn the right. As a fledgling demon, she currently had only partial use of her powers, and therefore did not need to feed on human energy to survive yet. For her initiation, she was assigned a mentally sound person, and she was to take that sane person and turn them into a demented lunatic. If she were successful, she would have a career finding humans who were already unstable and pushing them over the edge. However, if she failed, she would be stripped of all but the most basic demonic powers and forced to work in the slave dens. The slave dens were a nightmare, even to a demon. They were slums built in one of the more depressing sections of hell and there, the best she could hope for was to become a whore. The alternatives were much less pleasant to imagine.

Continuing to try to memorize this moment, Dementria looked around her at the other people in the room. Her parents were closest to her. Her father was tall and terrifying in his demon form, while her mother looked small and demure in her human form next to him. It was an odd contrast, and Dementria had to smile fondly at them. They were good parents. They treated each other and her well. She wasn't sure she would say they *loved* each other, but as much as demons *can* love, they did. They were fond of each other, at least. Grinning again at her mother, Dementria turned and ran into her best friend, Averia.

"Oops, sorry Tria. I'm just so excited and nervous! This is it, if we do well, we will land the important, respected positions. I am *SO* not meant to work in the slave dens. It's dirty and hot, and there are *never* any attractive men, or women for that matter." Averia said, finishing with a lewd wink.

Averia, and the twelve other students, were all in their human disguises. They had been forced to maintain them constantly for the entire school year, in preparation for their quests on Earth. Averia was five foot six inches of walking sex. Her long straight blonde hair had blue streaks that accented her cerulean blue eyes. Her body was literally built for sin, and her aura oozed sexual energy.

Tria laughed, "I certainly don't have to worry about you failing. As a Succubus, all you have to do is get laid and steal the sexual energy from whatever human is lucky enough to be chosen by you. Pssshh, not even an evil demon talent, Avery. So sad." She said with mock disapproval. Tria loved to tease her friend, not all demons were pure evil, but one's malice was like a mark of respect in hell.

Avery smiled wickedly, "Oh, honey, you know I have all kinds of evil up here." She tapped her temple, "I just haven't had a chance to let it out yet. You will be fine, Tria. No one knows how to mess with a mind like you. You will have that human raving mad in no time at all. Not as fast as I will meet my quota, but still fast, I'm sure." Avery said with a teasing laugh.

"You're right. I know what I'm doing. Breaking one puny human mind should be no trouble at all for me. Besides, there is no way in heaven I'm working in the slave dens!" Dementria said, her moment of uncertainty gone. "Now, where is Lelia? We won't see each other until we come back; I want to tell her bye. Although, as a dream thief, I guess she could always come see me."

"Let's go find her. She's tiny, but the bright red hair should make her easy to spot. We can split up and circle the room, meet back here in ten minutes. The portal will open soon." Lelia was the third member of their trio. All three women had known each other since birth, and remained close as they grew over the last twenty-five years.

Tria nodded and turned away from Avery, scanning the crowd for the short mass of curly red hair and green eyes that her friend possessed in human form. Lelia was a dream thief demon. She was able to enter and control the dreams of humans, and she fed from their dreamed reactions to the worlds she created. Lelia had been given several emotions that she was to create and steal from human victims. Lelia's human body was just over five feet tall, and sported some healthy curves. Tria found her by the wall opposite the portal, flirting with full-demon older brother of one of their classmates.

Tria tapped her on the shoulder, and said, "I see where you've been. "With a wink, she glanced at the demon Lelia had been flirting with, "I'm sorry, we are about to leave and I need to say goodbye."

The girls made their way across the crowded room to meet Avery. They wanted to say a private goodbye before they bid their parents farewell and stepped across dimensions to earn their powers. Lelia was the first to speak, "You two better let me in your dreams! I can be the go between for all of us. We will all be on the same continent, but I doubt we will end up together. At least we don't have to find places to live; the Council took care of that for us." Lelia rambled nervously.

Avery smiled widely, "Have no doubt, little one, they will be the crappiest places they could find. And that's crappy by hell standards, my dear." She laughed, and several heads turned at the sensual sound. "You are welcome to walk my dreams whenever you like, but I take no responsibility for whatever depravity you may find there." Averia declared with a wink.

Tria looked at her friends, "I'll miss these talks of ours, you know. Avery, you won't be there with a dirty comment when I need one-"

"That's what she said." Avery interrupted. At their blank stares she continued, "Well, humans find it funny anyway."

"And you, Lelia, I know I will need your calm deviousness and you won't be there. You two better meet your quotas, because I don't even want to *visit* the slave dens." Tria stated.

"We will, I think we are all too stubborn to be slaves." Lelia replied.

"I have sex for *my* pleasure. I'd be a terrible whore." Avery said.

"And we all know *I* would go crazy if I was stuck there." Tria added.

Tria's mother tapped her on the shoulder and all the girls turned to see their parents had gathered together and come for a last goodbye. A glance at the portal showed the color deepening and the light within the liquid surface glowing brighter; it was almost time to go. The girls said goodbye to their parents and lined up with their classmates to go earn their futures.

Tria watched Leila and Averia go ahead of her. When it was her turn, Tria looked back at her parents, gave a small wave, and stepped through the portal. The slick tendrils of dark energy powering the portal caressed her. She had a strong coppery taste in her mouth and the hairs all over her body began standing on end. But the sensation quickly faded and was replaced with much more unpleasant feelings. She felt like she had been dunked in ice water, and then electrified. Her whole body felt as if it had been skewered by a thousand needles and she felt the world spin around her. After a few agonizing moments, the world righted itself and the pain faded away. Tria cautiously opened her eyes and look around her.

She was clearly not in hell any longer. There were trees on either side of her and no houses in the immediate area. Tria appeared to be next to an empty road outside of a city. She could see the lights in the distance, and having no better option, she began walking toward the only civilization in sight. She was to wait for her demonic contact to find her and brief her on the details of her mission as well as show her the living quarters she had been given.

Tria's walk was uneventful; she'd scared a pair of raccoons, but that was it. She spent most of the time studying the night sky, so very different from the one she knew. She made her way to the edge of the woods she'd arrived in, and saw the city about a mile ahead of her. There was a sign next to the road here that said, "Welcome to Evansville, Indiana! Please enjoy your stay!"

Tria had no idea how her contact would find her, but she continued walking, wondering about the human whose mind she would soon destroy.

Chapter 2

Tria had no idea where to go to meet her contact. She was lost and alone in this world. She wandered through the streets, looking for something to catch her interest. After several minutes of exploring, she found a park and decided to sit for a while and watch the humans. Tria found that she enjoyed watching them, as there was such variety! Some seemed driven and in a rush to get where they were going, and some were relaxed as if they had no plans to move at all anytime soon. Tria felt lost without an immediate objective, she'd been training her entire life for this, but had never really learned to sit idly.

As a demon, she had been trained to use her powers since she was old enough to understand. Tria's power was different than most demons' powers. Her ability to cause insanity worked on any species, even other demons. When she began training to use her abilities, her powers were bound so that she could only use them on assigned targets. Only the Demon Council had the authority to choose her victims. Tria didn't particularly like the restriction, but she did understand the reason for it.

For lack of anything more productive to do, she studied the humans and their behaviors. After about an hour, a tall man approached Tria from the shadows. "Dementria?" A rough, gravelly voice asked.

"Yes, that would be me. I assume you are my contact? I am glad you found me; I was not told where to go. I'm ready to hear the details of my mission." Tria responded eagerly.

"I am. Follow me." He said briskly before he turned and walked away. Tria followed quickly behind.

"What is your name?" She asked.

"Pfadfinder' but you may call me Thad" He said with an accent that I knew from my studies.

"That is German for 'pathfinder' isn't it?" I asked, curious if my memory was correct. German was a popular language among demons because the guttural sounds lent themselves well to demon tongues.

As they walked, they stepped into the pool of light cast by a streetlight and Tria was able to see him better. He was very tall, towering over her five foot nine inch frame. His shoulders were broad and muscled and his hair was a light ash blonde. He turned to face her at her question, surprise widening his light blue eyes. "Indeed, it is. My parents knew what I would be, and wanted me to have a fitting name."

The pair continued walking at a brisk pace, until Thad led her into a dingy, depressing apartment building. Tria followed him up two flights of stairs and into the apartment he opened. Thad handed her the keys as she walked through. Avery had been right; this was a crappy apartment, even by hell standards. The bare light bulbs illuminated the paint that peeled from the walls and the ceiling that was stained and sagging. The floor creaked uneasily under their weight, and the air smelled of fear and desperation. Though she was a demon, Tria enjoyed her material comforts and she hoped she would be able to complete this mission quickly.

They sat down at the dilapidated kitchen table and Thad turned to her and said, "This will be your living quarters during your quest. You have one month to complete your task." Thad stood and grabbed a file from the counter. "Everything you need to know to find your target is in this folder. I must be leaving now, but should you be truly lost, I will know and arrive to lead you back to your path. Know this, I expect you to succeed, Dementria. I will not take kindly to failure." Without another word, Thad handed Tria the folder and left, quietly closing the door behind him.

Tria set the file on the table and opened it. Inside was just one sheet of information. Well, they were certainly going to make her work for it:

<u>Proving Assignment for Dementria Azanon</u>
Target name: Sabine Brise
Age 21
5' 7"
Brown hair
Brown eyes
Single
Student at USI
Lives in dorm, no roommate
Studying meteorology

"Seriously?" Tria thought. *"This is all I get? How am I supposed to know who she is, there must be at least a hundred medium tall, brown haired, brown eyed girls living on campus!! Aggghhh! Well, Tria, you better get to work. This apartment smells bad and the sooner you get home the better."*

Looking around the dingy apartment, Tria tried to think of what she could do to make it more comfortable. Her powers could change reality for her victims, but she had never tried to use them for her own benefit. This seemed like an opportune time to test the theory, anyway. Closing her eyes, Tria focused her mind, concentrating on the way she wanted the room to look. When she opened her eyes, her vision was filled with bright reds, yellows, and oranges. It had worked! Tria spun around happily, and then circled the room touching everything. She knew it was not real, and yet that did not hamper her enjoyment. Swiftly reimagining the rest of the rooms, Tria smiled at the new apartment before her. She tried to relax, anxiously passing the time until the next day when she could begin her search.

Tria changed her clothes with a thought. That part was a handy little skill every demon possessed. Demons were taught from childhood how to perfect and maintain their human glamours. The glamour spell included clothing, and was an old magic imbedded into her demon blood. Because her kind fed on the emotional energies of humans, they must be able to seamlessly blend in and not be remembered.

Dressed to emulate the females she'd seen in the park earlier, in a hoodie and jeans, Tria left the apartment and headed toward the college campus. She went to the geology department, hoping to pose as a student and possibly meet Sabine. The building wasn't terribly busy and Tria easily charmed her way into one of the classes. There were about thirty students present, six of which were women who fit her target's description. Tria chose a seat near the back, next to a slim brunette. As she sat, the woman turned and when violet eyes met brown eyes, Tria jerked in shock. She wasn't sure how she knew, but she did; this was Sabine. Tria hadn't wanted to force a meeting so soon. She'd wanted an opportunity to study Sabine first.

Tria realized that she was still staring and muttered a quick hello. Sabine smiled shyly and turned her attention to the teacher at the front of the room. Tria wanted to observe her quarry directly, but to do so this close to her would set off every mental alarm the human possessed. Tria settled for occasional sidelong glances, composing a flawless mental image to be used later. Her hair was thick and glossy, a bright mahogany color, and her eyes were a beautiful dark chocolate brown that seemed to have hidden depths. Sabine took meticulous notes and appeared to be absorbed in the lecture. She also had the habit of tapping her pen when she wasn't writing.

When the class was over, Tria watched Sabine leave and followed the girl's scent at a discreet pace. Tria followed her to the rest of her classes and back to her dorm. Knowing what a typical day was like for Sabine, Tria was now compelled to see what the woman did on a typical night. Sitting in the hall waiting for her to come out the door was hardly an option, but there was a tall tree outside that should offer both a view of Sabine's window and the dorm door.

Tria managed to make it up the tree unseen and hid herself among the foliage. Through the window, Tria watched Sabine finish her homework and curl up on the bed with a book. She memorized the way Sabine held her book, the angle she tilted her head, even the way she held her drink. To find the weak links in the girl's mind would require intense observation. Satisfied that Sabine was not going anywhere tonight, Tria returned to her apartment and got some rest.

Every day for a week, Tria kept up the same routine. She knew Sabine's class schedule now, and sat in the back of every class, watching her. She memorized her facial expressions and mannerisms; now Tria was confident she could emulate her successfully. She decided it was time to force an actual meeting between the two of them. Tria needed to move to the next phase of her plan.

Chapter 3

As the lecture ended and students began to gather their things and leave, Tria watched Sabine. When the brunette stood and left the classroom, Tria followed shortly behind. Sabine headed to the campus coffee bar, as she had every day this week. Tria stepped into a shadowed alley and glamoured a different outfit for herself, wanting to impress Sabine. She now wore black tailored pants and a violet silk blouse that matched her eyes. Satisfied with her appearance, Tria entered the coffee shop and inhaled deeply the scent of coffee. Sabine was in line, waiting to place her order and Tria approached her and purposely bumped into the human girl, stabbing the brunette in the shoulder with the pencil she conveniently held in her hand.

"Oh, excuse me. I'm so sorry." Tria said, lending a musical lilt to her voice.

Sabine rubbed her injury and turned around to see who had assaulted her. The beautiful woman who'd bumped into her stunned her. *Real* people weren't that perfect, were they? "Don't worry, I will be fine. It barely broke the skin." Sabine stammered, inexplicably nervous. She couldn't figure out her reaction to this woman. She wasn't attracted to the stranger, yet her body was tingling with awareness. Sabine thought she would have felt even plainer next to this exquisite creature, but she felt infinitely more alluring. The stares of the men in the room rested on the two women, and Sabine reveled in the unfamiliar attention.

The woman laughed guiltily and said, "Nonsense, I can see the blood seeping through your shirt. Please, at least let me buy your drink. It is the very least I can do after injuring you so."

Sabine didn't feel that injured, but she did feel compelled to snatch at any excuse to spend more time with this mysterious woman. "Um, sure. That would be nice." She told the woman what she wanted and excused herself to find a table for the two of them. Tria joined her a few moments later, bearing two steaming cups of frothy caffeinated goodness.

Handing Sabine her cup, Tria said, "Again, I am so very sorry for tripping and stabbing you. Are you sure you don't need a doctor?"

The sincere concern on the stranger's face made Sabine flush. "Really, it's nothing, Miss...."

"Oh! Please forgive my dreadful manners! My name is Tria Azanon."

"And I am Sabine Brise. It is a pleasure to meet you. Azanon, that is a unique name, where are you from?" Sabine asked.

"You are correct, my homeland is far from here." Tria said evasively. Looking at the book Sabine had set on the table, the demon changed the subject swiftly. "Is that a meteorology text? I've always found the field fascinating!"

Sabine blushed again and replied, "Yes, it is. I've been obsessed with the sky since I was a little girl. I want to know how the weather works. Eventually I want to find a way to improve the early warning system. My aunt and uncle were killed by a tornado a few years ago. With a better warning, they may have stood a chance." Sabine's eyes shone with her passion for the subject, and the admiring stares increased as her inner beauty began to show.

"Clearly you harbor hidden depths, Sabine. I have to be going now, but I'd love to meet you for coffee and conversation again, sans pencil next time, I swear." Tria said with a disarming smile.

Sabine eagerly accepted. She mostly kept to herself, and didn't have many friends. This vibrant, glamorous woman wanted to be her friend. There was no way she was going to deny herself this chance to break out of her shell. They made plans to meet the next day. Sabine headed off to her dorm room and Tria made her way back to her apartment to revise her plan for the coming day.

Tria spent the night in the tree outside Sabine's window, utilizing one of her more useful powers. She was able to enter Sabine's mind and view her memories. While she could not change what Sabine remembered, she could change *how* Sabine remembered it. Finding several memories of Sabine uneventfully walking home alone at night, Tria altered the memory so the girl would remember running home in terror from an unknown menace. Changing as many memories as she deemed safe at this stage in the plan, Tria planted the seeds for paranoia and fear in Sabine's mind. Satisfied with her work for the night, Tria went back to her apartment and began to practice her 'Sabine' glamour.

The next day, Sabine dressed carefully and headed off to class. She tried to focus on her lectures, but all day she felt as if she were being watched and couldn't concentrate. Finally, the end of her last class arrived, and Sabine hurried to the coffee shop to meet Tria. Sabine was eager to see if the enigmatic woman was as fascinating today as she had been the day before.

When Sabine arrived, Tria was already seated at the same table they'd had yesterday, with two steaming cups resting on the tabletop. The two women chatted and gossiped for two hours, then parted ways, planning to go shopping the next day. After Sabine left the coffee shop, she decided to walk for a while on the path next to the river. She was wandering aimlessly when she caught sight of a familiar woman ahead of her. Sabine was shocked, she could have been staring at her twin, and they were even wearing the same clothes. She blinked and the woman was still there, talking to a tall, handsome man. Sabine saw her look alike flirting with the man and she crept closer to see if the resemblance was as close as it seemed to be. Hiding behind a tree, she got near enough to see the woman's face clearly, and it was like looking into a mirror. The woman had the same facial expressions Sabine knew crossed her own visage, her hand motions and body language were the same too.

Deciding to talk to this strange woman, Sabine slipped from her hiding place and circled the tree. She only lost sight of the strange woman for a moment, but when she rounded the tree no one was there. Sabine spun around, but the woman was nowhere in sight. Confused and unsettled, Sabine decided to return to her room. She ran the incident over and over in her mind, but was unable to make any sense of it. Had it been real? If it was real, how had it been possible? Sabine grabbed a quick dinner from the supplies she kept in the dorm kitchen and returned to her room. She intended to go to bed early and face the next day well rested and with a sound mind.

Changed into comfortable pajamas, Sabine curled up in her bed and almost instantly fell asleep. At first her dreams were random and disjointed, but that changed once she settled into a deeper level of sleep. Tria watched Sabine sleep from the tree outside the window. She was going to use another of her powers on Sabine. Tria had the power to control the dreams of her target. Unlike her friend, Lelia, who could control the dreams of any human. Tria had a very specific set of dreams that she planned to plant in Sabine's subconscious mind. When she felt Sabine slip into a deep sleep, Tria focused on the girl's mind, sending dark tendrils of thought to her, taking over the dream she was currently having.

I woke with a start from a dream I could not remember. Glancing around the room, I saw it was 3 in the morning. I listened again for the sound that had awakened me and heard steps shuffling and a strange scraping sound in the hallway. Standing up, I saw that my dorm door was open, though I was certain I had shut and locked it. The lights in the hall seemed different, dimmer and flickering. I heard the shuffling steps and scraping get closer and I peeked my head out the door to see who was approaching. I couldn't see very well, so I stepped into the hallway and came face to face with myself. The other me was standing there, wearing the same pajamas, but she was covered in blood and carried a wicked looking knife that she was trailing along the wall, making the scraping noise I'd heard. The other me raised her knife and turned it toward me. As she plunged the blade down, I screamed and-

155

Sabine woke with a start, tangled in her sheets and covered in cold sweat. What a horrible dream. Sabine wanted to get a glass of cold water, to cool her parched throat and to help clear the disturbing dream from her mind. She got out of bed and stumbled tiredly in the direction of the sink. She kicked something with her left foot as she walked, and Sabine flipped on her desk lamp to see what it had been. The light reflected off the long, sharp blade of the knife on her dorm room floor. There were several drops of what Sabine sincerely hoped was not blood on both the blade and the floor. Sabine dropped the knife in shock and ran to the door. It was still locked. How had the knife gotten into her room? She didn't remember going anywhere since crawling into bed. The dream tugged at her, as did the memory of the woman near the river today. Sabine didn't know what it all meant, but she was too terrified to either leave the room or go back to sleep. She curled up on her bed with her meteorology text and read until it was time to get ready for class.

Chapter 4

Sabine drifted through all her classes in a distracted haze. When she met Tria to go shopping, she wasn't able to hide the fact that she was bothered by something.

"Sabine, what is wrong? You seem to be terribly upset." Tria asked, showing such sweet concern.

"It's nothing, really. I had a nightmare last night and I can't seem to shake the feeling of doom it left me with. I couldn't go back to sleep and I'm kind of tired now as well." Sabine answered, not mentioning the knife she'd found *after* she had awakened, the knife that had disappeared this morning.

"Oh, you poor dear. That's awful," said Tria. "What you need is a nice cup of tea and a good nap. A good cup of tea can fix many problems, I've heard."

"That does sound nice. Ok, I think I will go home and try to get some rest. Thanks, Tria. You've been so wonderful and supportive, and we only just met!"

"The pleasure is all mine, Sabine. You are a delightful girl!" The smile Tria gave her seemed a little off to Sabine. She couldn't pinpoint why, but it just wasn't right. Chalking it up to her exhaustion, Sabine waved and headed back to her dorm.

On the way, she glimpsed her twin again, this time talking to a group of college age girls outside a movie theatre across the street. The other woman again wore the same clothes and looked and acted exactly like Sabine. Losing sight of the woman as she struggled to cross the busy street, Sabine finally regained sight of the sidewalk in front of the theatre. It was deserted. There were no college girls and no Sabine look-alike. She shook her head and wondered if she was getting sick or having hallucinations. Surely seeing oneself walking around town doing things that one had absolutely no memory of was not normal.

Suddenly desperate to get to her room, Sabine ran blindly through the streets until she slammed her door behind her and decisively locked it. She threw herself down on her bed, dropping her shopping bags on the floor as she walked. Exhaustion and stress crept over her, drawing her into a deep sleep filled with strange flashes of memories that had her flinching in terror even in her dreams.

She woke a few hours later, feeling even more exhausted than she had before. The world seemed different to her. The colors just slightly off, and things didn't feel quite real. Sabine wondered if she was dreaming, but a quick pinch convinced her that she was indeed awake. It was just now early evening, so she went off to find something for dinner. Then she returned to her room to do her homework for the day.

Exhaustion settled around her like a fog, making it difficult to concentrate on the report she was reading. Deciding to take a break and hopefully catch a dream free nap, Sabine lay down on her bed and pulled the covers up to her neck. Sleep overtook her almost immediately, at first gentle and relaxing, but quickly shifting to a more sinister scene.

I heard my feet hit the pavement in time with the heartbeat that pounded through my veins. My only thought was sheer, gut wrenching terror; I had to get away from whatever was chasing me. I didn't know what I was running from, but I knew if I were caught, I would lose something I desperately needed. Security, sanity, whatever, it didn't matter. All that mattered was putting distance between myself and the thing chasing me. I ran as fast I could, my legs burning with the unusual effort. I stumbled on a lose rock and fell, only sparing a split second glance behind me as I threw myself from the ground and continued running full speed. I could hear footsteps quickly approaching behind me, but could spare no concentration to look back. My foot caught on some unseen item and I went down again, tangled with whatever had caught me. A wave a pure terror washed through me as I realized that I could not get up right away. I was losing any distance I had gained and that thing was going to get me. I struggled with the object wrapped around my foot and scanned the area around me for my pursuer. I felt a presence behind me, and though I desperately wanted not to, I turned and looked to see what I was so afraid of. I screamed in horror as I came face to face with myself. Only I had never looked quite like that! Where my eyes should have shown color, there was only in infinite, flat black. Thick ruby tears of blood cascaded from the bottomless pits of the eyes and dripped down onto the white dress my twin wore. She reached toward me, and as she placed a palm against my cheek, I released a blood-curdling scream.

Sabine woke with a start, bolting out of bed and running for the mirror over the sink. The urgency to see her own brown eyes looking back at her was overwhelming. When Sabine glanced in the mirror, her breath released in a whoosh of relief, the face staring back at her was normal. She bent to splash cold water on her face and grabbed a towel to dry herself. She glanced back into the mirror and shrieked in shock and terror. The eyes reflected in the mirror were not the deep brown she had been expecting. They were twin inky vortexes and the pale skin underneath was streaked with bloody tears.

Sabine closed her eyes tightly, cutting off the disturbing image. *It's not real, Sabine. Get a hold of yourself. It's not real. It's not real....* Tria smiled to herself as she watched Sabine mouth the mantra, trying to convince herself she hadn't really seen what she'd seen. She felt the pitiful resistance Sabine's mind put up against her powers and had to admire the human girl for trying. Deciding to let her think it was just imagination, Tria lifted the hallucination a moment before Sabine opened her eyes.

When she cracked her eyelids open to peek at the mirror, Sabine was infinitely grateful to see her normal face reflected back at her. She couldn't shake the feeling of terror, though. Something was happening to her, and she didn't understand any of it. Needing something to distract her, Sabine turned her TV on and watched the news.

"The bodies of two Evansville residents were found in their home today. The victims' names have not been released yet, but the police did say that both were the victims of brutal homicide. The coroner places the time of death around midnight, two days ago. Both people were stabbed, but no murder weapon has been recovered. Police say—"

Sabine was consumed by a vivid memory of the dream she'd had two nights ago: walking into the hall and seeing herself covered in blood and brandishing a wicked looking bloody knife. *"Did I do that? Is it even possible? There was no blood on me the next morning, but I saw the knife lying bloody on my floor. But the knife was gone the next morning too. Nothing makes any sense. I am so confused and scared. Am I losing my mind? But crazy people don't know they are crazy, do they?"*

Satisfied with the night's work, Tria descended the tree and made her way back to her apartment, leaving Sabine to doubt her sanity unobserved.

The next morning, as Sabine made her way to the dining hall, she was jumpy and paranoid. Certain that someone was going to attack her, or that she would attack someone, she violently shied away from anyone who even tried to smile at her. Keeping her gaze riveted to the ground in front of her, Sabine continued walking, afraid to stop for any length of time. She made it to the dining hall and choked down a quick breakfast, knowing she would need her strength to figure out what was happening to her. She disposed of her trash and left the room, intending to go back to her dorm because she did not have class today.

Sabine felt a little surer of herself after getting a meal and some energy. She allowed herself to look around, and was immediately sorry for her decision. Across the lawn, stood her doppelganger. This time she was alone and, though she couldn't be sure, something looked different about her. As usual, she was wearing the same clothes Sabine wore, but it seemed as if her eyes were flickering. The distance made it difficult to be certain, but it looked like the woman's eyes would be bright and normal, and then for a moment, they would go dark and empty. Sabine walked a few steps closer, intent on talking to her mysterious twin.

When she was close enough to see clearly, but still far enough to run, Sabine stopped and opened her mouth to speak to the strange woman. At that moment, she turned to face Sabine directly and Sabine knew why she looked different today. Her eyes were indeed flashing. They were normal brown eyes one second, and they would be the flat black pits with the bloody tears the next, and then back again. "Who *are* you? Why are you doing this to me? *What* are you doing to me?" Sabine asked desperately.

161

With a deep, guttural voice that Sabine was certain she had never uttered before, her crazy eyed clone said, "You. I am you." The black eyes had stopped changing back to normal and the dark, endless stare bored into Sabine.

"No, it's not possible. *I'm* me! What the hell is going on?" She shouted. The doppelganger disappeared and Sabine was left standing alone on the campus lawn, with students giving her strange looks and trying to avoid her. She stumbled blindly in the direction of her dorm, flinching away from everyone she passed. Sabine saw students pass by her, staring and when she looked back, their faces changed, going bloody and corpselike. She was running in terror by the time she reached her dorm. She flew up the stairs and into her room, slamming and locking the door behind her. Then she crumpled to floor and curled herself into a ball on the floor and wept desperately.

Chapter 5

Sabine cried herself into an exhausted sleep, right there on the floor of her room. She didn't dream, and when she awoke stiffly a few hours later, she felt a little saner, but not much. The memories of the dream and this afternoon on the lawn were still with her, consuming her thoughts. Deciding to research mental illness, Sabine went to her laptop and opened Google.

She searched for mental illness and was stunned by the number of results. She chose the link for a popular medical website and found the list of symptoms for schizophrenia. She had several of the symptoms, especially the hallucinations and feeling of paranoia. Sabine didn't want to believe it. If she was actually going crazy, she *couldn't* be aware of it. So she had to still be sane. But if she wasn't going insane, what the hell was happening? The only explanation that made any sense at all was insanity! *How's that for irony?* Sabine thought.

Realizing that she would find no satisfying answers, Sabine got up and called her parents. She wanted to be reassured that she was not alone right now. That she still had something normal in her life. The phone rang four times and the machine clicked on.

"Hi, you've reached the Brise residence! Sabine is off to college, and Byron and Nicolette are currently backpacking through Europe right now. Please leave a message and we will get back to you as soon as possible."

She waited for the beep and opened her mouth to speak, intending to say that she loved and missed them and hoped they had fun, but she actually said, *"Backpacking through Europe!!!!* How could you not tell me you were leaving the fucking country? How is that responsible parenting? What if I had died, Mom? Or if someone kidnapped me, Dad? How much fun would your spontaneous little trip be then?" Sabine screamed into the phone. As quickly as the rage fueling her tantrum had come, it was replaced with deep sorrow and fear. "I feel so alone right now. Something is happening and I don't understand it. I don't know how to stop it. I'm worried that I'm doing things I don't remember, and I am seeing things that aren't there. I'm so scared, please help me." Sabine's breath hitched and she began to sob uncontrollably. It took her a moment to remember to close the cell phone and end the message. She sobbed until she again fell asleep, her dreams restless and terrifying. She did not dream of the strange woman claiming to be her, and for that she would have willingly taken a thousand nightmares.

Sabine woke the next day and dressed for class. She was determined to try to stick to her routine. Maybe it would help her feel a little more normal. Sabine nearly screamed and bolted back into her room when she opened the door, seeing her neighbor, Jean, down the hall, standing there with a slashed throat and blood covering the white t shirt and jeans she wore. Sabine slammed her eyes shut and forced herself to calm down. She opened her eyes again, and Jean was standing there, but her white shirt was clean and she was not harmed at all.

Jean was watching Sabine's strange behavior, so Sabine smiled and gave an awkward wave before she hurried down the hall and out of the building. Once outside, Sabine took a few deep breaths and looked at the sky that normally calmed her. Today it seemed ominous and offered her no solace. The dark clouds seemed to roll over themselves like waves, barreling down on her. Sabine gasped and wrenched her gaze from the sky. She moved toward her first class, delighted when the first people she saw looked completely normal.

She kept walking, not having any more crazy visions and starting to feel better. That's when she heard the voice.

"Kill. You know you want to. I see it in you. The darkness, the rage, it's all there. Festering away at your soul, clawing itself out. Take that knife in your hand and kill."

Sabine looked down to see herself clutching the same knife she'd found in her dorm, its blade crusted with dried blood. She screamed and dropped the knife, running toward the geology department and class, hoping to lose herself in the lecture and drown out the voice. Sabine needed to pretend that everything was all right. If nothing else, she could sit quietly and close her eyes so she wouldn't see these horrible hallucinations.

She chose a seat in the back of the classroom, with no one near her. Sitting down, Sabine got out her notebook and pen and waited for the teacher to start lecturing. She zoned out and stopped paying attention, just letting the teacher's voice wash over her and lull her into a trancelike state. Tria smiled from the seat she occupied a few rows away from Sabine. Now was the perfect time to start the waking dreams she had planned.

The teacher droned on and on and I couldn't concentrate on what he was saying. I felt an unfamiliar anger growing in the pit of my belly. It seemed to radiate out through me until my entire body tingled with rage. I wanted to kill something. To watch the life leave the eyes of another sentient being.

I heard the voice again, "Yes, Sabine! Let it out! Give in to your dark desires. The knife, you have it. That teacher, he never liked you. Always thought you were a pathetic little mouse who was scared of her own shadow. Stand up now, and show him you are not afraid!"

I felt the heavy knife in my hand and the rage boiled over. I stood and took a few steps toward the front of the room, the knife behind my back when the teacher looked up at me.

"Sabine? Is everything alright?" Sabine shook her head and realized that she had been dreaming. This room was different; the colors different, the lights brighter, and there were more students here. She also realized that she had actually stood and taken a few steps toward her teacher. Shock overwhelmed her, and her face lost all its color.

"I'm not feeling well. I'm going back to my room." Sabine said before gathering her things and quickly dashing from the room. She collapsed into a stall in a nearby ladies room and wept bitterly. What was happening to her? Nothing made any sense at all.

She dried her eyes and rested her head against the wall of the stall. Sabine closed her eyes for a moment, trying to summon the will to walk to her room, chancing the hallucinations she would likely have on the way.

I was walking home and could not fight the feelings of dread and horror that overcame me as I reached my dorm hall. I looked down that hall and everything seemed normal at first glance. I looked again; sure that something was horribly wrong. There! The doorjamb of Jean's dorm room had a strange dark smear across it. I know it wasn't there this morning. I got closer, wanting to investigate. As I neared the door, I could see that it was open and the smear seemed to be a sticky red handprint. I looked in the doorway and screamed before lunging to check for a pulse. Jean lay in a crumpled heap just inside the door, her lifeless face frozen in a mask of terror; blood drenched her slender body and formed a drying pool on the floor. I stood and ran into the room to call for help when I saw Jean's roommate sprawled across her bed, her throat slashed and blood drying everywhere. I stood there in shock, unable to comprehend the awful truth before me. Then my mind stared flashing with pictures, flashing quickly to play out a scene. I saw myself knock on the door, and when Jean answered, I stabbed her multiple times. She tried to stop me, but I was relentless. I pushed her hand out of the way and continued to ram the blade into her stomach. She grabbed for the doorjamb, but her blood-slicked fingers could not find purchase. When she dropped to the floor in a lifeless heap, I saw myself in the mirror on the wall and my eyes were the fathomless black pools I had seen on the evil vision. The bloody tears streaked down my death pale face and I smiled, wickedly and with no remorse. Then I continued into the room to take care of the roommate, my rage and desire to kill again taking over my body. She saw the bloody knife and me and she started to scream.

Sabine jerked awake and struggled to control her breathing. She picked up her bag and ran from the ladies room and back to her dorm, refusing to look up from the ground. She arrived at the dorm hall breathless and nearly fainted when she saw the dark smudge on Jean's doorjamb. She didn't stop to examine further, Sabine thrust the unlocked door open, surprising both girls with the intrusion. Sabine was flooded with relief when she saw them alive. "Oh thank God, you're not dead! I didn't kill you!"

Jean looked confused and a little frightened. "Of course we aren't dead and you didn't kill us. What the fuck are you talking about, Sabine?"

Her roommate just looked angry, "This is not a funny joke, Sabine. Get out!"

Sabine turned and ran from the room in embarrassment, slamming and locking her door behind her. Safely back in her room, Sabine pulled out her cell phone and called the local hospital. She asked to speak to someone in the psychiatric department. When a nurse answered her call, she outlined the last few days and asked what she should do. The nurse said she should come in and talk to one of the doctors, immediately. Sabine decided that she would rather be crazy than some psychotic murderer and left for the hospital right away, stopping only to pack a small bag with essentials.

Chapter 6

Tria was delighted with her progress. This pathetic human was proving easier to break than she'd thought. Sabine was on her way now to the hospital; she had finally accepted that she was not of sound mind any longer. Tria thought the murderous daydreams had been a nice touch. But she hadn't quite anticipated the reaction Sabine had experienced. Clearly the threat of turning evil was worse than the threat of going insane. That would be the key to pushing the girl over the edge into madness. And Tria planned to take full advantage of it. Sabine teetered on the edge of insanity already, and tonight, Tria planned to finish her task.

Sabine checked herself in and the doctor talked to her at length, listening to everything she had to say. Completely baffled by the conflicting information he got from her. She was clearly showing signs of advanced schizophrenia, but she was aware of the mood swings and fugue states. She acknowledged that she was having hallucinations and hearing voices that were not real. The doctor had never encountered anyone this far gone down the road to madness that was still capable of lucidity like this. He wanted to keep her for observation, and Sabine readily agreed, not wanting to be alone tonight.

The doctor gave her some paperwork to fill out and they found her a room. The doctor did not want to give her any medication yet, so she sat in her room filling out paperwork and trying not to fall asleep. Sabine turned on the TV for ambient noise and despite her efforts, was soon asleep.

I was in a black marble room. The vaulted ceiling, walls and floor were polished to a glasslike shine and my image was reflected, as were the torches mounted on the wall. I turned around and saw a strange looking arch. The symbols etched around it were unfamiliar to me, but I could sense a dark energy emanating from them. The center of the arch looked like a shimmering purple liquid, somehow backlit, with odd black tendrils reaching inward from the edges, writhing together. I heard footsteps behind me and turned again.

A man was approaching me, a very terrifying man. He stood nearly ten feet tall, with deep red, scaly looking skin. His muscles bunched and rippled as he walked. He wore only a tight pair of black pants, the fabric leaving nothing to the imagination. His face was all sharp angles hard lines, with black hair and black eyes. The black horns protruding from his forehead shocked me. The eyes reminded me of my vision woman, and I wondered how they were related. He smiled cruelly at me, revealing rotted, jagged teeth. "Sabine, are you ready for hell?" he said, his guttural voice grating on my nerves.

Hell? But I didn't do anything, I thought. "Who are you? What are you? Why would I be going to hell? I haven't done anything!" I protested.

"You will. You're going to kill soon. There is a fount of evil and darkness within you. Already you dream of releasing your evil. I can feel your hold on it weakening, soon it will claw its way to the surface, and you will be mine."

"Yours? Who and what the fuck are you?" I shouted.

"I am the demon who owns your soul. No one can save you now, you belong to me." He said smugly.

"That isn't possible. I didn't sell my soul, and I sure as hell didn't give it away. How could you possibly own it?" I asked, confused.

He laughed wickedly. "Ah, little human. It was not truly yours to give in the first place. Everyone has forsaken you. I bought your soul from your Guardian."

"My Guardian?" I asked, still confused and terrified.

"Yes, your guardian angel. He said you were boring. Although, admittedly, he is not a particularly good angel or he would never have made the deal. Not any more though, my pet. You already had darkness hidden within yourself and my influence has amplified it nicely."

"So, I'm not going insane?" I asked, trying to make sense of what he'd said. While refusing to think of the angel and the God who had apparently turned me aside.

"No, pet, you are going evil." He handed me a strange looking knife. The handle in the center looked like old bone and the blades that curved outward from both sides of the handle looked like demon horns. The blade just felt evil. I could feel the dark purpose it expected to be used for.

Sabine woke with a start when a nurse walked into her room to check on her. She asked for a glass of water and sat up in her bed. This last dream had deeply disturbed her.

She was turning evil? Her? Sure, she had a temper she'd always been afraid to show, and she sometimes had some pretty morbid thoughts, but demon serving, murdering, God forsaken *evil?*

Tria sat in the unoccupied room next to Sabine's. She tuned into the girl's recent memories and decided that this was the perfect time to complete the plan. Sabine was already at the hospital. They would care for her when her mind snapped. Waiting for an opportune moment, Tria watched the nurse check on Sabine.

The nurse returned with the water and left Sabine alone. She tried to settle back into sleep, but that was not an option. She couldn't focus on the television either. She fidgeted in bed for about an hour when she heard footsteps outside the door. Tria assumed her Sabine glamour and opened the door. Sabine's breath caught when she saw herself walk calmly into the room. Sabine pinched her arm to be certain she wasn't dreaming. Her dark clone thankfully did not have the black, bloody eyes this time.

"What is happening? What do you want from me?" Sabine asked desperately.

"I need you to go insane." The doppelganger replied simply.

"But I'm you, you're me! Why?" Sabine stuttered, stunned.

Tria resumed her own human form and said smugly, "You're not me actually."

Sabine's mind reeled with confusion and betrayal. Tria had been her friend! Sabine felt her mind teeter more precariously on the edge of madness. "What are you?"

Tria smiled without humor, "I am a demon. I am able to cause insanity and I feed off the energy released by your broken psyche. Everything you have seen or felt for the last two weeks was carefully crafted by me to loosen you from your sanity. I even left you the ability to recognize you were losing your mind. All the visions and the dreams and the voices, that was me."

Sabine felt her tenuous hold on sanity quickly slipping away and forced one last question past her lips, "But why, why would you do this to me? Why destroy my life?"

The smile Tria gave her was full of malice. There was no trace of the friend she'd made over coffee. Tria's image flickered between her perfect human visage and her grotesque demon form. The demon form seemed to shift and change, becoming whatever would disturb Sabine most at that moment. "To see if I could." Tria said without emotion, as if destroying Sabine's life meant less than nothing to her.

The sudden knowledge of the horrible truth was just too much for Sabine. Though she tried to fight it, she was powerless to stand against the weight of all the mental torment she'd received. She felt the balance shift and the last few fine threads of mind tethering her to sanity snapped free. Suddenly all the fear was gone. She didn't have to be afraid anymore, she didn't have to care. She felt separate from her body, as if she were watching from the outside. Sabine was aware of a terrible, screeching sound around her and halfheartedly realized that she was screaming.

A team of nurses swept into the room, trying to calm her. They restrained her hands because she was tearing out her hair and scratching her skin. Quickly and effectively they forced her on to her bed and injected her with fast acting medication. Tria, dressed as a nurse, bent down and whispered, "Shhh, Sabine. Everything will be all right. Sleep now."

Sabine's eyes were drifting closed when she saw Tria walk through the wall, surrounded by black streaked violet light. Then the medication took over and Sabine sank gratefully into oblivion.

Dark Light

Blood and Soil
by
William Greer

"Veronika, the spring is here." Lena sang quietly as the sun's shadows crawled across the wall. She had not heard that song in years, because of its singers' 'Jewish blood.' Hardly a good reason to deprive the world of beautiful music, but it was doubtful the Nazis would ever learn that all blood tasted more or less the same. At the moment, the radio offered one of Joseph Goebbels' latest speeches. The Propaganda Minister called Churchill a gutless criminal and declared imminent victory over Stalin's Bolshevik dystopia; strident words which only reminded Lena that the radio in Berlin played more music than the broadcasts available to settlers in the East. Rural farmlands afforded greater privacy, though. So living space was not without its trade-offs.

She lay on the settee, safe from sun's reach, but could still see out the window. About sixty feet from the house, a gnomish Pole labored over a patch of tomato plants. His audacity to work shirtless made Lena scowl. Even at a distance, she saw ragged tufts of hair creeping out from under his armpits, and greasy, glistening sweat on his hirsute back. If she'd felt like slathering herself with zinc oxide and lugging her parasol out into the dirty, late afternoon, she would have tracked down Ernst or Peter, who'd make sure the cow regretted his immodesty.

A car appeared on the road, glinting chrome leading a charge of swirling dust. When it turned onto the driveway winding up to the farmhouse, Lena donned her sunglasses and sat up. Being so close to the sun's path made her wince. A few seconds of direct exposure could turn her skin bright pink, drawing fat white blisters soon afterward. Before long, it would start broiling her insides. She squinted at the flag waving above the car's fender and dropped back onto the settee, sighing. It was the SS. She needed to put on her shoes and jot on some make up.

Lena rubbed her lips together, smoothing out her lipstick as she closed the drapes. She crossed the living room and checked herself in a mirror. Good enough. She turned off the radio, and was starting to heat some water in the kitchen when there was a knock at the door. "Just a moment!" she piped. Lena positioned herself behind the door as she opened it, keeping away from the sun but still visible to her guest. The SS officer at her door had sharp brown eyes, a small nose, and not much of a chin. Judging by the tabs on his collar, he was fairly high ranking. He was also Gestapo, which made Lena take a slow breath through closed teeth.

With a polite nod, he said "Good day, Frau Memminger. I am Major Kübler. May I come in?"

Lena coquettishly tilted her head to one side. "Of course, Major. To what do I owe the pleasure?"

He strode into the living room and slowly turned his head, taking in the décor: the Swastika'd throw pillow, a framed poster advertising a past airplane race, photographs from Lena's days as a night club singer. Kübler leaned over the table next to the sofa and picked up a picture of Lena and a man holding hands inside a church. "This is your husband?"

"Why, yes." She smiled. Kübler studied the picture closely. Ferdinand, the man holding Lena's hand, looked like he was stifling searing gas pain, which he'd insisted did not look unnatural. Lena gestured to the kitchen and told the Major "I was about to have some coffee. Would you like some?"

Kübler waved his hand. "That won't be necessary, thank you."

"Well, just let me tend to the stove." She turned on her heel and went to the kitchen.

"Your husband," he called after her. "Is he here?"

Lena turned off the gas stove looked at the clock on the wall. Almost ninety minutes before sunset. Ferdinand wouldn't be up until then, which was good. What did Kübler want? What if he got pushy about talking to Ferdi? With the Gestapo in the living room, Lena was not anxious to go down to the cellar and rouse him. Anxious, she tapped her teeth with a fingernail, until the smell of wool and tobacco warned her that Kübler was coming down the hall. She turned around just before he came through the doorway.

"Well." Kübler folded his hands over his stomach. "Is he here?"

"Yes." Lena nodded. "But he's asleep."

"Asleep?" Kübler raised his eyebrows. "What does he do?"

"He's a philologist."

"Hmmm." Kübler pursed his lips. "Like Nietzsche?"

Smiling, Lena leaned against the stove. "Yes. He's doing independent research and prefers to work at night."

"So he's writing a book? A good one, I hope." Kübler chuckled, and then made the same slow scan he'd done in the living room. His nostrils twitched. "And you?" He turned toward her. "You keep odd hours as well? I hear that during the day, there is not as much coming and going as there is with other homes in the area."

"The farm stays very busy during the day," Lena said. "But I try to overlap my schedule with my husband's preferred hours." She unfurled her cutest smile. "It's all a girl can do." With her sapphire eyes and lambent blonde hair, most Nazis treated Lena like racial royalty, but Kübler just stroked his chin. Lena pushed herself upright from the stove. "I beg your pardon, Major. But is there something I can help you with?"

The SS man let out a short, apologetic sigh. "Yes. There have been some disappearances, and I am tasked with finding their source."

Lena frowned. "I've heard. Dreadful, isn't it? But it's only Poles, right?"

"So far, yes," said Kübler. "But their families have started complaining to the Gestapo because they think we are arresting them. Apparently, none of the missing had caused any trouble." A slight laugh waddled in his throat. "Now some German families have started to worry. They're afraid that a mutiny is in the offing." He held out his hands. "So you can see this is a bit of a problem."

178

Lena nodded. "Well, I run the farm overall, while Ferdi works on his book. Our two overseers, Ernst and Peter, take care of the day-to-day. You could talk to them if..."

"We have," Kübler interrupted. "Oddly enough, they claimed they weren't aware of any disappearances." He gestured toward Lena. "You wouldn't know if any of your laborers have disappeared?"

Slowly, Lena blinked. "To be truthful, I don't keep very good track of them. They all kind of look the same." She unspooled a flimsy laugh.

Kübler took a cigarette from his breast pocket. As he lit it, Lena walked to the kitchen table and stood a couple of feet away from him. She raised her eyebrow. "May I have one, Major?" Kübler obliged, and lit it for her. She took a long drag, leaning her hip against the back of a chair. "So, what are the Poles saying about this?"

"Some of them just think we're lying." He shrugged. "Others think there's a monster. If so, I guess it likes cheap meat." Kübler snickered.

Lena's eyes narrowed a little, and she forced a laugh. The kitchen floor was tiled. She could rip Kübler apart and clean up the mess well before sundown. Not without ruining her dress, but she could just order another one. But with the Gestapo already worried about her and Ferdinand's nighttime poaching, she did not want to know who would come looking for Kübler if he went missing.

Kübler's eyes drifted to the shuttered window above the stove. "You and Herr Memminger don't have children?"

"Not yet," Lena said.

Kübler thinned his lips. "This land is here to further our race. Without children, was it difficult for you to acquire a plot?"

"We're lucky, I guess. Ferdi knew some people." Acquiring the land had been expensive, but not difficult, thanks to Ferdinand's centuries-old investment portfolio.

"My wife is carrying our third child." He looked at her intently. "You are planning on having children, though?"

"Yes," Lena chirped. "As soon as Ferdi finishes his book."

"Well." Kübler stubbed his cigarette in an ashtray on the kitchen table. "I must be going. I would love to talk to your husband about his book sometime. I studied a little philology at the University."

Nodding, Lena walked him to the front door. "I'll be sure to tell him. Maybe you could stop by tomorrow night for dinner. Will you be free by eight o'clock?"

Kübler turned in the open doorway. "Yes, that would be splendid."

Lena smiled. "Until then, Major."

"Until then, Frau Memminger." He made another polite nod, and strode down the walkway. When Lena shut the door, she pressed her back against it and let out a long breath.

***

"Wake up, Ferdinand." Lena stood atop the cellar stairs, ringed by a corona of electric light. The stink of carrion dusted with lime prickled her nose. Ferdinand stirred from his repose on the dirt floor, near the bottom of

180

the stairs. A sticky, brownish-red muck caked his mouth and stained his shirt. Since settling in the East, he'd seemed to have forgotten the utility of a bed. Lena said "Ferdinand, get yourself together and meet me in the living room. We have a problem." He looked up at her, holding an arm above his eyes. A bottle of vodka was nestled in his other arm. Next to him, lay a man with grayed temples and a gaping coagulated throat wound. It was a miracle that Kübler hadn't demanded to see the cellar.

Twenty minutes later, a freshly scrubbed Ferdinand joined Lena on the sofa. He'd also changed into a rumpled, but clean, set of clothes. Lena lit a cigarette. "A man from the Gestapo, Major Kübler, stopped by today."

One of Ferdinand's shoulders flicked, his face impassive, but Lena sensed his restraint.

"He was asking about all the disappearances," she said.

Ferdinand folded his hands over his stomach. "So…" The word came out in a meandering hiss. "They are suspicious of us?" Lena nodded. Ferdinand shook his head, dismay weaving through his brow. "That's odd." He leaned back into the sofa. "I always figured the Poles would come after us first."

Lena laughed. "And just how far do you think a mob of peasants wielding torches and pitchforks could go before they were shot down by the SS?"

"Fair point," said Ferdinand. "But this is a real problem, isn't it?"

"Yes." Lena tapped her cigarette over an ashtray on the coffee table. "And Major Kübler is coming over to dinner tomorrow night."

"Uh." Ferdinand's mouth hung open. "Why? You let him?"

"I invited him. I didn't want him to think I was trying to get rid of him."

"We have a lime pit full of bodies in our cellar. You should want to be rid of him."

Lena tapped the couch next to his knee. "I have a plan."

"A plan that involves this Major Kübler coming back into our house?"

Lena raised a hand. "We'll take precautions." Smiling, she gently patted his cheek. "And you'll just have to pretend that you love me."

***

Kübler arrived precisely at eight p.m. the next evening, firmly grasping Ferdinand's hand as he came through door. Lena and Ferdinand led the Major to the living room, where he declined an aperitif. Ferdinand drank two, but successfully navigated Kübler's probing questions about philology and his alleged book.

Before long, they moved to the dining room where Kübler complemented Lena's cooking: lamb, cooked rare with rosemary and boiled, seasoned potatoes. They chatted about the war, agreeing that America's newfound belligerence made little, if any, difference. Kübler boasted about his family. Gunther, his oldest, recently earned a sports badge in the Hitler Youth, and his youngest, Hannelore, was a precocious reader. A third was on the way, which they would name either Dolphus or Gudrun.

Near the end of his meal, Kübler said, "Some more Poles have gone missing. A ten-year-old boy and his parents."

Ferdinand stared at his plate, while Lena covered her mouth. "Oh my," she said.

"Yes." Kübler made a terse nod. "Last night." He took another bite of lamb and chewed it with leisure, eyebrows slightly raised. After swallowing, he said, "We are worried that something very dangerous is in our midst." He sipped some water. "What were you two doing last night? You were safe, I hope."

Ferdinand rubbed between his eye and the bridge of his nose. "I was parsing Xenophon."

Lena swallowed a bite of lamb. "I reviewed some recipes for tonight and washed our good table cloth."

Kübler wiped his mouth with a cloth napkin. "That must have left you free for most of today then?"

"There's always a lot to prepare for good company," said Lena. She rose from her chair. "Now if you'll excuse me, I have a surprise." A moment later, she placed a dusty bottle of seventy-year-old Bavarian wine on the table.

Kübler exhaled appreciatively as she poured the thick red liquid into three glasses. "Well," he said, "I've been declining your offers of spirits all night. I wouldn't want to appear rude." Kübler swirled a glass under his nose and took a slow, but modest, sip. He asked Lena "Are you Bavarian?"

Lena smiled. "I grew up in Munich."

Kübler's eyes widened. "Were you there during Hitler's *Putsch*?"

"I was just a girl, but I remember a spectacular energy charged the air, like something amazing was about to happen. The SA often marched past my school in their smart, brown uniforms, singing the *Horst-Wessel-Lied*. My spine still tingles when I think of it."

Kübler leaned back and gazed at the ceiling, glass in hand. He sighed. "Phenomenal." After another sip, he said, "You two are such fine people. Why don't you have children?"

"I'm sorry, Major," said Lena. "I wasn't wholly honest with you yesterday." She reached over and clasped Ferdinand's hand.

Kübler's eyes hardened. He put the glass on the table. "Oh dear." He smiled. "What did you do?"

Ferdinand ran a nervous finger across his upper lip. Lena took a sip of wine. "We're not waiting for Ferdinand to finish his book." She beamed at her ersatz husband. "We say that because we keep trying, but I haven't been able to get pregnant. We have no idea what's wrong."

Kübler nodded, pressing his lips together.

Lena swept an arm into the air. "So this farm, what we grow, is our contribution to the Reich. We donate half our produce to the Army."

"I see." Kübler rested his chin in the crook of his hand. "That is too bad, but I understand." He looked at his watch. "This has been a lovely meal, but I must be going." On the way to the front door, he said, "I do not wish to intrude, but I know a doctor who specializes in fertility problems. He's in Potsdam, but he still might be able to help. I'll stop by tomorrow with his address." He shook their hands and strolled into the night.

184

***

Ferdinand paced the floor of the kitchen. "If Kübler comes back as late as tomorrow morning, we'll be lucky. You shouldn't have invited him to dinner."

Lena sat at the kitchen table, her feet propped on a chair. A wine bottle filled with blood sat next to her elbow. "He won't be back tonight, but when does, I'm not sure he'll be so polite."

"Why didn't he just insist on searching the house in the first place? I'm not complaining, but this whole..." Ferdinand raised his arms and waggled his hands. "Game of his— it's annoying."

Lena settled further in her seat and took a sip of blood, trying to wash away the hollow swell in her stomach. Human food tasted good enough, but was as nourishing as candy.

"For someone like Kübler," she said, "It is all about wits. He wants to catch us in a lie." When she was a nightclub singer in Berlin— before her rebirth, and long before she'd met Ferdinand— one of her suitors had been in the Gestapo. He'd lacked Kübler's patient subtlety, but Lena saw first-hand how such men enjoyed tormenting others with unapologetic authority.

She took another sip, closing her eyes as the thick, coppery liquid glazed the inside of her throat. "We couldn't charm him away. So now..." She rose from the table. "You'll be happy staying in the cellar for a few days, right?"

Ferdinand nodded.

Stopping at the back door, she said. "Do want a cot down there? You don't have to sleep in the dirt, you know."

Ferdinand gulped from a bottle of Polish vodka he'd taken from the pantry. "My ancestors owned this land during the age of Frederick the Great." His lip curled. "Long before the Treaty of Versailles." He took another great gulp of vodka. "This soil gives me better rest than the finest down pillow."

Lena rolled her eyes. "Suit yourself." She stepped out the back door and into a wide, furrowed field.

Ferdinand's histrionics were not lost on her. For centuries, this farm had been Prussian, until Britain and France corralled it into an ad hoc Polish state. It was natural that Germany retook the land when the war started. Most human politics had ceased to concern Lena, but land was something she still understood. People needed a place to call home, to stake a claim to something greater whenever possible. Lena recognized how Hitler had tapped these desires among the German people, but the Nazis' racial hierarchy still seemed petty to her. Small varieties not withstanding, all humans were livestock. Kübler may have been a smarter breed of cow, but his confidence flirted with hubris. He needed to know his place.

At the edge of the plot sat a low, stone-walled shed. A brick fire pit smoldered next to it. That morning, after upbraiding Ernst and Peter for their hapless response to the Gestapo's questions, Lena had ordered them to secretly burn the remains from the basement.

Lena scuffed her foot on the floor of the shed, clearing a small depression with the toe of her shoe. She leaned over and opened a trap door. Below, in a dark bunker, something scuttled and hissed. She checked her hair, making sure nothing was too loose or easy to grab, and dropped feet-first through the hole as if dipping into a deep swimming pool.

The boy came at Lena as soon as she landed. Little fangs showed dull white in the soupy black air. His little blue eyes flared with an angry, predatory glow. She reached out and clutched his shirt collar. Small, hard fists pummeled her forearm, and hurt more than she cared to admit. "Shhh," she said. His chin jabbed into the base of her thumb. He was trying to bite her. The boy was a fast learner; she had to admire that. "Shhh," she said again. She spun him around and pulled his shoulders back against her stomach, pressing his forehead with an open palm so he couldn't bite her other arm. In his ear, she whispered "Sprechen Sie Deutsch?" He stopped fighting and looked up, bewildered. He was too young, and too Slavic, for most Germans to address him with anything but the informal 'du.'

The boy tried to nod. "Yes."

Lena stroked his hair. "What is your name?"

Quietly, he said "Nemec."

Lena turned the boy around and knelt in front of him. "You were kidnapped by the Nazis. They wanted you for labor in Germany, but you're safe now."

"Where are my mom and dad?" Tears snaked down his dirty cheeks.

"I'm sorry." Lena glanced at the floor. "They are dead."

Rage blazed in the boy's eyes. His legs wobbled.

Lena shook him by the shoulders. "Do you want revenge?"

"Yes." The word rode from Nemec's mouth atop a taut breath.

"The Nazi who killed your parents and put you in this cellar is named Major Kübler."

"Where does he live?" He shouted. "Tell me!"

Lena reached in her pocket and pulled out the napkin Kübler had used at dinner. "I don't know, but this is his scent."

He took the white square of cloth from her hands and pressed it over the lower half of his face. He inhaled deeply. The way that the napkin and his scruffy, birch-brown hair framed his bright eyes almost made Lena laugh. Under the cloth, she saw him frown. In a muffled voice, he asked "How can I find him with this?"

Lena smiled. "Haven't you noticed how things are different?" She raised her nose toward the ceiling of the bunker. "How all the smells of the world blend together but are distinct at the same time?" The boy pulled the napkin from his face. He tilted his head, confused. Lena repeated herself in a mix of Polish and German.

"I feel different but…" Nemec shook his head.

Lena touched his cheek. "Sometimes, something so bad can happen to someone that their pain gives them enough strength to right the wrong. It happened to me. The Nazis killed my sister." She wondered where her sister really was, but only for an instant.

Nemec's mouth twisted downward. "But you live on this farm. You're German."

"I am German," Lena said. "But I am not a Nazi."

Clouds of emotion swirled behind Nemec's eyes. After a long pause he said "I can really find this man by his scent?"

"Yes, and you are strong enough to kill him when you do." Lena stood up and put a hand on the boy's shoulder. "But you only have until sunrise. When dawn approaches, you must go and lie down in an open field so the angels can heal your grief."

"Thank you!" Nemec wrapped his arms around Lena's waist and pressed his ear beneath her breasts.

She patted his head. "God speed, child."
Nemec skittered up a small ladder beneath the trapdoor, and was gone.

***

The next day, Lena emerged from her bedroom shortly past one p.m. She was pulling a bottle of blood out of the pantry when there was a knock on the kitchen door. Hair mussed by sleep, clad in a robe and nightgown, she grumbled and put the bottle back in place. Another knock rattled the door. When she cracked it open, Peter stood at the doorstep. Anxiety strained his gangly features, and sweat soaked the neck and armpits of his shirt. His cap drooped from his hands, which were clasped at his chest.

Lena lowered her eyebrows. "What is it?"

"I'm sorry to interrupt you, Frau Memminger," he said. "But none of the laborers showed up today. The SS is gathering Poles in all the nearby villages."

Lena beckoned him inside. Peter gingerly stepped into the kitchen and looked around. "Please sit," she said. "Do you want some water?"

Peter sat at the kitchen table. "Yes, thank you."

Lena filled a glass at the sink and Peter drank half of it in a single tip. A small burp escaped him. "I'm sorry." Lena shrugged and sat across from him.

"This morning," said Peter, "the wife of a Gestapo officer and their two children were found murdered. They were ripped apart."

"Really?" Lena smiled. "And what about the Gestapo officer?"

"Apparently, he survived," Peter said.

Something cold stretched inside Lena's throat. Then she glanced up at nothing in particular and decided she probably had nothing to worry about.

"I don't know much," Peter continued. "Someone from the next farm came by and told me what she'd heard." He took another gulp of water. "Since sunrise, Ernst and I have been doing all we can to keep this place running. We won't be done for a while." He shook his head as if to settle his thoughts back in place. "Anyway, the SS is executing two hundred Poles in the area. Fifty for each of the Germans who were killed last night."

Lena frowned. "I thought there were only three."

"The wife was eight months pregnant. They're counting the unborn child." Peter looked down at the table for several long, silent seconds, the color draining from his face. He looked back up and said, "This is because of yesterday, isn't it? The bodies you asked us to burn. Did you attack the Major's family?" Before Lena could reply, he scooted back in his chair and raised his hands. "I'm sorry. I just need to know if Ernst and I will be safe."

Lena propped her cheek on one hand. "You will be safe."

Sheepishly, he said "It might be a good idea to leave; find some place else."

Lena smiled. "We're fine here. Major Kübler and the Gestapo clearly have other things to worry about now."

Peter finished his water and mustered a wavering "Very well." Lena showed him out and locked the door.

She spent the rest of the afternoon listening to the radio and watching the day's shadows crawl across the living room. A new victory in Russia had occasioned a pounding litany of military marches. In the distance, just beneath the music, Lena heard a slow, steady cadence of rifle shots. She declined to count them, focusing instead on the brazen oaths of the *Panzerlied:* "If our fate calls upon us, then our tank will be an honorable grave." She switched off the radio and went to fetch some blood from the pantry. Lena was standing barefoot on the tile floor, bottle tilted to her lips, when she was startled by a loud thud at the front door. She turned toward the sound, a small splash of blood spilling down her chin. The hinges whimpered, and heavy feet clunked inside the house. Lena put the bottle on the stove and hid beside the doorway. Deliberate, leaden footsteps plodded down the hall toward the kitchen. Then they stopped, only to resume a few, grating seconds later. A horrible stench penetrated Lena's nostrils, stinging her eyes and nettling the back of her throat. Garlic.

In a soundless fraction of a second, she reached up and took an iron skillet from a hook on the wall behind her. Hands wrapped tight around the handle, Lena raised the skillet above her shoulder, poised to implode the intruder's face. Her knees quivered, as the garlic stink grew stronger.

A tiny, sarcastic voice inside her wondered if she could just as easily drive the stranger away with a cascade of puke.

A hairy arm stuck through the doorway, wielding a large, wooden cross. Lena would have laughed if she weren't wracked with nausea. Her elbows tensed, and she shifted her weight back on one heel.

One.

More.

Bang! The back door flew open. Lena whipped around and saw a man leveling a pistol at her head. A gunshot roared through the kitchen, and a harsh metal clang lanced her ears. The skillet quaked in her hands, forcing her to let it clatter to the floor.

With another roar of the pistol, a molten rod of pain bore into her cheek, just below her left eye. Half blind, she flailed her arms, groping for balance. The first intruder sprang through the doorway and closed on her, looping a string of garlic around her neck. He punched Lena in the stomach. She collapsed, landing ass-first on the floor. On impact, a fetid gruel of blood and ruminated lamb gushed from her mouth onto her chest. Her eyes burned as if they were soaked with a mix of chlorine and piss. Lena cried out stuttering blubber.

A foot struck her ribs. Rough hands grabbed her ankles, pulling her flat on her back. The same heavy foot pinned her stomach. She choked on another well of vomit, until it spilled from the corners of her mouth and into her ears. The foot pressed harder. Eyes wide, Lena looked up at her attacker.

It was the Pole she'd seen two days ago, working without a shirt. Except now, he was not very gnomish. Up close, he stood almost six feet tall, with broad shoulders that he'd ringed with his own necklace of garlic. He had a sharp nose, slim eyebrows and deep, brown eyes that radiated hatred and disgust. Through bared teeth, he spoke to her in a mix of German and Polish. "Nemec, my nephew. The Nazis threw his smoldering head into the market square before they forced half our village onto trucks and drove them to a pit outside town." Lena glanced over to his accomplice, who drew a wooden stake from a satchel and laid it neatly on the floor next to a hammer and a meat cleaver.

The man pushed his foot deeper into her stomach and pointed at her with a long, calloused finger. "You killed Nemec's family! You corrupted him! *You* are responsible for the others who disappeared!" Lena narrowed her eyes, and he spat on her forehead. "The Nazis are barely human, but you are an abomination!"

His accomplice hovered over her, stake in one hand, hammer in the other. He pressed the sharp wood into her left breast and raised his other arm. Drawing a deep breath, Lena screamed. "Ferdi!!!" The man with the hammer flinched, his grip on the stake faltering.

A pall of cheap vodka drenched the air as the cellar door disintegrated in a rain of splinters. Her attackers jerked their heads toward the noise. The man let go of the stake, and Lena saw his upraised arm bend like a reed in a squall. He screamed. From behind him, Ferdinand plunged the hammer into his outstretched jaw. Spatters of blood and teeth arced through the air as Ferdinand raised the hammer again. The next blow landed in the man's eye. His corpse tumbled backward onto the floor.

With the speed of a humming bird's wing, Ferdinand yanked the garlic string from Lena's neck and flung it toward the back door of the house. He wheeled on the other man, who stood slack jawed, his foot still pressed into Lena's stomach. A second string of garlic flew across the room. Ferdinand plucked the man from the ground and pinned him against the wall. The Pole howled as Ferdinand bit into his throat, shaking his head like a hungry dog.

Lena crawled to the corpse on the floor. She collapsed across its shoulder, extended her fangs, and bit desperately into its neck. Blood dappled her tongue. Pressing its chest, she forced a beat from its dead heart. The blood welled into a thick stream. As Lena drank, her nausea evaporated, tears cleansing the rawness from her eyes. With another draught her wound began to close, urging the bullet to the surface like an errant wisdom tooth. Above her, the remaining Pole's screams trailed into silence, and she looked up at Ferdinand. He dropped the fresh corpse to the floor and wiped his mouth on his sleeve.

"With all that noise," she croaked, "why didn't you come sooner?"

He looked back and shrugged. "I assumed you'd take care of it on your own."

***

Ferdinand stared through the windshield of his car as a glittering black cone of pavement scrolled beneath the headlights. He hadn't spoken since before they'd left the farm when, in a colorless voice, he'd told Lena to pack her things. Occasionally, Lena looked over at him from the passenger seat, where she sat with a towel pressed against her cheek, but he just ignored her. After almost two hours of silence, he finally cleared his throat and said, "I must say that in hindsight our partnership was not a sound decision."

Softly, Lena said, "I'm sorry."

He glanced over at her, the headlights of an oncoming truck casting dark half-moons under his eyes. "You lack patience."

She nodded. A plangent ache beat through her cheek. The bullet had squeezed out a couple of hours ago, leaving a slimy abscess that would last at least another day. "It just seemed to me," she said, "that if…"

Ferdinand raised his hand and shook his head. "No." After a moment of silence, he said "I'll let you stay in my apartment in Berlin until you can make your own arrangements."

"Are you going back to the farm?" Lena asked.

A long, low sigh seeped out of him, like air leaving a tire. "Eventually. I'll have to figure out when it's safe, but that will take a while." He returned his gaze to the road. Lena felt a hot twinge in her stomach. She opened her mouth, and then closed it again, choosing instead to turn the dials on the radio until she heard music. Then she leaned back and watched the night's shadows skate across the roof of the car.

Dark Light

The Darkon Prophecy
by
Linna Drehmel

Wilhelm felt the blood, salty and sweet gliding sensually down his throat. He hated it even though he craved it, needed it. This was not the life that he would have chosen. It was forced on him, on his wedding night. His bride Louisa, whom he had known for years before they were married, was secretly a Darkon one. But how was he to know, he was never allowed to touch her while they were courting. After all no one truly knows who is Darkon and who is not.

The one night in a young man's life that should have been sweet turned ugly as his new bride confessed what she was as she made him like her. He tried to fight her off, but she had the amplified strength of a Darkon and soon over powered him. He struggled, pinned under her as sharp crystalline fangs descended from her upper jaw.

"I love you Wilhelm, I have waited so long for this." Louisa whispered softly. He screamed in pain as she sank her fangs into his neck and began to drain his life away. The darkness of death quickly began to claim him. Wilhelm welcomed it. This was a world that he no longer understood or wanted to be a part of.

Just before the blackness completely consumed his thoughts he felt something hot and salty begin to burn his lips as it dripped into his partly open mouth. It was her blood. Louisa was making him a Darkon one like her. His mind, his human soul screamed no, but his body did not want to die.

Once enough of Louisa's blood had given him back a measure of strength, he reached out and grabbed her bleeding wrist and began to suck the blood out of her hungrily.

She groaned with pleasure at the feeling of his lips on her wrist, but pulled her arm back from him, "Not too much my love, it only takes a little to crystallize your heart." Louisa said with passion in her voice as she leaned down to kiss him, but he pushed her off from him as an excruciating pain began to lace though his chest.

"What have you done to me?" Wilhelm gasped in agony.

I have made you like me, so we can be together always." She told him with an innocent look in her large brown eyes. "You were a latent Darkon, Wilhelm. We have been waiting for you to change on your own, but when you did not the council told me to change you."

"What are you talking about Louisa? I am a human. I have human parents!" His face contorted with agony as well as indignation.

"Wilhelm, be calm. You have to listen to me." She begged him.

"But...PAIN!" He cried through clinched teeth gripping his chest.

"I am sorry Wilhelm that cannot be helped. It is a part of the Darkoning process. Your heart is turning from weak flesh to eternal crystal." Louisa said her voice as smooth as silk as she put her arms around his shoulders. "We all have to go through it, be still and it will not hurt so much."

"Don't touch me!" He screamed shoving her away from him with more strength than he knew he had causing her to fly across the room and then hitting a wall.

"Wilhelm, please listen! I have so much to tell you." Louisa said as she got quickly to her feet.

The pain of changing to Darkon dissipated quickly and Wilhelm jumped with surprising agility to his own feet, but the pain of betrayal burned within him as he whipped around and fled the room by jumping through the open window into the warm summer night.

"Wilhelm! Come back." Louisa cried arriving at the window a moment too late.

He landed easily on his feet, where he should have been grievously injured or even killed jumping from a window of that height.

Wilhelm began to run, to where he was going he did not know. He only hoped to out run the pain that he felt as his soul was ripped from him by the sound of Louisa screaming his name from the window. He ran fast and hard from the sound of his new wife's voice. A part of him wanted to turn and run back to her but he shut that feeling out. She betrayed him, lied to him. Why didn't she tell him what she was? He would have loved her anyway.

There was another feeling that drove him forward into the forest. It was an uncontrollable hunger. "I will not kill!" He screamed to the cloud covered sky. But the hunger in his new crystalline heart told him differently as he ran onward.

He stopped with the grace of a predator when he heard the rustle of an animal walking through the woods. It was not just the sound but also the hot and salty smell of the creature's blood. His soul cried no, but his body flew at the animal almost of its own accord. He grasped the large feline in his strong arms almost crushing it. Wilhelm cried out in pain when he felt his own crystalline fangs descend out of his upper jaw, and then his soul cried out in pain when he sank his fangs in and took the creature's lifeblood from it.

He dropped the forest cat's lifeless body to the ground hating himself, but feeling his body and senses grow stronger.

Wilhelm forgot his pain and self-loathing and was lost in the enchantment of experiencing the summer night in a new way. He looked into the darkness with sharpened eyes and could see the smallest insect crawling over a tree limb that had fallen to the ground. He could see the small flicker of light that was its life essence. Wilhelm looked to the dark and cloudy night sky and enjoyed the sight of a phoenix. The amazing bird like creature left a trail of light behind as it soared powerfully through the air.

He could also hear the smallest whisper of sound. The young Darkon turned his head to the sound of a small rodent chewing on its stolen meal. He relished the sound that came from the direction of the sea that was many days journey off. There was the soft rushing sound as waves broke over the sandy beach that soothed his tormented soul. Wilhelm could also hear the delightful sound of the large sea leviathans calling out to each other from far under the water.

There was a sudden and much closer sound that caught his ear; it was the sound of fear. A child nearby was crying out for help. Without even knowing why he raced toward the sound. It was just a feeling or an instinct in his newly crystallized heart that compelled him. He needed to protect that child.

Wilhelm blazed past trees and rocks so fast that they were all just a blur to him. He was focused solely on moving as fast as he could toward the growing sound of fear. He was also able to pick up a new sound that was growing. It was the sickening sound of skin shifting over muscle and bone. This could only mean one thing. Whoever this crying child might be was being attacked by a boser'traum.

***

Gottlieb watched with eyes that pierced the darkness as his new von'ehe son sped past him with the strength of a new Darkon into the woods. He felt the burning pain of betrayal that emanated from Wilhelm. Gottlieb felt badly for him and how confusing all this must be.

Wilhelm only knew what most humans on their world did: there was an ancient clan of Darkons that they had always shared the world with, but no one truly knew who belonged to the ancient clan. One could not tell a Darkon from a human. Some humans feared them. Some wanted to be them. Gottlieb knew from the feelings that poured from his von'ehe son that Wilhelm was one that feared the Darkons.

The Darkons lived under a strict code of secrecy. They were not to tell anyone who they were for the human's own protection. But on rare occasion a Darkon would marry a human out of love and so they could gain the immunities that humans have from the giant white sun. However, such a marriage was only done with express permission from the Darkon Council.

The Darkon Council had many such strict rules about feasting on human blood and changing full blood humans to Darkon. Such a thing was only done in times of war with the boser'traum. The human must volunteer of their free will and must never be completely drained. The human also had the choice to be made a Darkon when it was over, because the humans on their planet were theirs to protect not to exploit.

But Wilhelm was not like most humans. He in fact was not human at all. He never was. Although he did not know it, Wilhelm had latent Darkon blood, but never transmuted as most latent Darkons do when they become adolescents. The council of Darkons instructed Louisa to change Wilhelm on their wedding night.

Wilhelm did not know any of this. All he knew was that his marriage to Louisa had been decided when he was but a small boy, and that he spent most of his childhood getting to know her. Even though the Council felt sure that Wilhelm was not just a latent Darkon but was also the one that was promised to ride the races of the boser'traum. Louisa and her family were still forbidden from telling him who they were. The council wanted to see if he would transmute on his own, but when he didn't Louisa was given sanction to change him after they were married. Once

Louisa had changed him she was supposed to explain everything and then bring him to the Council, but Wilhelm fled before she had the chance.

Gottlieb needed Wilhelm to come back, not only could he hear his daughter Louisa's crystalline heart shattering, but all the people on this planet needed him. Gottlieb knew that Wilhelm was the one that had been chosen to stop the boser'traum. The boser'traum are an evil race of shape shifting soul takers, who only used humans to fulfill their lustful need for life essence that they get by consuming the dreams of humans, and then in a most violent manner kills the human by drain them of blood. This fight between the boser'traum and the other three races had been foreseen many centuries ago. Gottlieb knew in his own crystalline heart that Wilhelm was the one foretold to stop the boser'traum.

"Strong human soul not knowing his crystalline heart will have the strength to free races three: Human, Darkon, Mond'tier from death in dreams." Gottlieb muttered the prophecy to himself as he started to race through the wood after his von'ehe son. Wilhelm must choose to embrace his Darkon blood and follow his now crystalline heart so he can save the three races from death in dreams.

Gottlieb felt fear stab at him when he heard Wilhelm cry out in pain that he would not kill. He knew what this meant. Wilhelm now felt the hunger of a newly transmuted Darkon.

Gottlieb began to run harder, he had to reach Wilhelm before his von'ehe son's hunger took over and Wilhelm hurt or killed a human. He heard Wilhelm cry out in pain again and he picked up his pace to the point that if one could see him it would appear that he was flying across the ground.

The Darkon man could feel his crystal heart slam against his ribs as he ran but not from the physical exertion but from fear. He hoped that that Wilhelm had not harmed anyone. If he had the Council would not be very forgiving and might order Wilhelm's exile or even his death. He could not let this happen; Gottlieb knew deep in his soul that Wilhelm was the one.

He stopped short at the smell of a fresh kill. He looked wildly around him for the victim and found the large forest cat lying lifeless at his feet. He heaved a sigh of relief, but his relief was short lived as his sensitive hearing clearly picked up the sounds of a struggle as well as the sound of a boser'traum changing shape.

Gottlieb began to run again, fear propelling him forward. Now his fear was for the safety of his von'ehe son. He had to get there to help Wilhelm. Only a few Darkons have ever taken on a boser'traum alone and lived to tell about it.

***

The scene that Wilhelm came upon was horrifying. The boser'traum had a small girl child by the shoulders, and was slowly changing shape. Wilhelm could hear a disgusting stretching and sucking sound as its ears were elongating and its face began to take on the look of a muzzle.

If Wilhelm didn't know any different he would have thought that it was a Mond'tier that was attacking the child.

But the clouds covered both moons, Mond'tier didn't attack human children and he could also see the dark light that emanated from the creature. He could see the creature begin to suck the pure light essence from the child through its hands.

"Come with me Aalina, it is alright." It said with a voice that sounded soothing and feminine.

"No, you are not my mother." Aalina screamed.

"Of course I am, Aalina my madchen." It said trying to calm the child so it could feed.

"No you are not." She cried, "Help me." Aalina begged as she spotted Wilhelm's rapid approach.

Without a word Wilhelm plowed straight into the vile creature, yanking it away from the child. The sheer force of Wilhelm's attack lifted the boser'traum off its feet as Wilhelm slammed it against a tree.

"What are you?" The creature gasped in pain, having been taken by surprise. "Your body is Darkon but your soul tastes human."

"You will keep your filthy hands off me and off that child." Wilhelm told it, ignoring the boser'traum's question.

"I guess it doesn't matter what you are, your soul is strong and sweet. I will drink your soul, whatever you are boy. And then I will drink up her little wild soul, and fest on her lovely blood." The boser'traum hissed in its multi-toned voice as it arms and legs quickly elongated and coiled around Wilhelm beginning to crush him like a giant serpent. The boser'traum them placed its hands on Wilhelm's back trying to suck the dreams from his still human soul.

"I said keep your filthy hands off from me."
Wilhelm gasped as he struggled for air, while the creature
shifted its muscle and bones to become more serpent-like,
trying to crush him.

"Oh but your soul tastes so sweet. Once I drink up
your soul then I will feast on your fragrant blood." It
taunted him with glee. "Then once I have cast your
worthless empty corpse aside. I will take my time drinking
up all that child has to offer."

At hearing this Wilhelm felt a burning ignite in his
newly crystal heart. He could not let this thing harm that
child, and he struggled with all his might trying to free his
arms as his fangs descended from his jaw. Wilhelm quickly
sank his sharp crystal fangs into the creatures shoulder
causing it to scream in pain and loosen its grip on Wilhelm
just enough.

Wilhelm took advantage of its loosened grip and
hurriedly pushed his hands up between himself and the
creature. Then spun around putting his back to the tree and
shoved it with all his might dislodging the creature from
him.

The boser'traum was not able to stop Wilhelm from
pushing it off but was able to anticipate the fall to the
ground and quickly rearrange it frame so it could land
harmlessly on the ground in a cat like form. It then swiftly
pounced at the young man with a feral growl.

Wilhelm did his best to fend off the now cat like
creature that knocked him into the tree. It took all his
strength as a Darkon to keep the beasts snapping jaws and
clawing hands away from him.

"Wilhelm the only way to paralyze it is to puncture the gland at the base of its skull. That is the only place that they are truly vulnerable." Gottlieb called to his von'ehe son as he quickly approached the fighting pair.

"Father...I can't." He gasped as he struggled with the vile creature trying to keep it from ripping him to shreds.

"Yes you can my von'ehe son; you are so much more than you know. You must embrace the strength in your new heart." Gottlieb said as he rushed to the crying child, to see if she was all right.

"That's right boy," The boser'traum hisses as its voice becoming deeper and its body changing shape once again, becoming bigger and shoving him with great strength against the tree at his back. "You can't fight me, you can't fight any of us. I am happy your von'ehe father is here, his insignificant soul is hardly worth taking but his Darkon blood will make me strong."

Wilhelm struggled with the beasts shifting shape. He tried to keep it from pinning his arm. His instinct was to push the boser'traum away from him, but he reached for the strength in is crystal heart and let it flow into his whole being. "I will not let you take my soul or anyone else's." Wilhelm vowed as he reached out and startled the boser'traum by pulling the creature to him and wrapped his arms crushingly around it.

This took it by surprise as it was still changing shape. The boser'traum expected Wilhelm to push it away, but Wilhelm managed to pin its arms down so it could not move as it intended to.

Wilhelm saw this and took advantage of this moment of weakness and stretched his neck as far as he could so he could sink his fangs into the base of its skull like Gottlieb advised him. He could taste the vile fluids spill from the punctured gland and spat it out as the boser'traum squealed in pain, "I can't breathe, I can't move."

Wilhelm let go of the creature and it fell to the ground heaving and panting weakened and unable to shift its appearance, "What are you?" It cried.

"He is the Darkon One." Gottlieb answered it as he swung the small girl child into his arms, "You only have short time to live before your shifting gland is completely empty and you are utterly paralyzed, you best go while you can and tell your people to get off my planet. Tell them that the foretold Darkon One is here and he will destroy you all if you hurt anyone else on our planet or the Mond'tier planet." Gottlieb warned as the now pathetic looking creature whimper and slowly got to its feet and slunk away into the trees.

"Father, I am what?" Wilhelm asked as he wiped the remainder of the shifting fluid from his mouth.

"You are the one that was prophesied centuries ago, a human soul and a Darkon heart that will save all the races from death in dreams." Gottlieb explained to him. "Your instinct was to protect and to save both me and this child."

"I could not let that thing take a human child's life. I only did what anyone on this planet would have done."

"Wilhelm, my son. Take a closer look at this child." Gottlieb advised him.

Obediently Wilhelm crossed the short distance to where Gottlieb stood protectively holding the child. He looked closely and saw a beautiful little face with creamy skin and a head of glossy black hair, and then looked into her eyes and gasped. "She is a Mond'tier."

"Yes son, this fulfills the prophecy. You will protect and save us all." He told Wilhelm with confidence.

"But who does she belong to? What do we do with her?" Wilhelm asked trying to grasp the idea that he was the promised savior of the three races.

"Ask her." Gottlieb told him simply.

"What is your name child?" Wilhelm asked her.

"My name is Aalina." She answered him.

"Where is your family Aalina?"

"It killed them, I tried to run but it caught me." She told Wilhelm as tears began to fall from her yellow almond shaped eyes. "I kept hoping that one of the moons would show so I could shift into a wolf and fight it off and save my family but there was no moon. I thought it was going to kill me too but you came and saved me."

Wilhelm reached out to wipe the tears from her sweet little face. "We will protect you until we can find your family and get you back to your planet."

"That thing killed all my family," The child cried. "I don't have any left."

"Then you will be my madchen." Gottlieb spoke up and hugged the child close. "Wilhelm will be your von'ehe brother. We will all be your family and we will protect you."

Aalina began to cry with relief and hugged Gottlieb back, he looked over her head and addressed Wilhelm,

"Come, let's get her back to the house so she can rest, you need to see your wife and I need to speak to the Council."

At the mention of his wife, Wilhelm felt his new crystal hear leap painfully in his chest. "I left her, will she forgive me?" He asked with painful worry in his voice.

"I cannot speak for my daughter but we shall see, let's go." Gottlieb said as he took off running with his new Mond'tier daughter held securely in his arms.

Wilhelm only stood for a moment trying to absorb everything that had happened this night, and then began to run. The only thing that mattered to him as he ran was getting back to the woman he loves. Louisa and her family had kept this secret from him but he no longer cared. It didn't matter to him. He knew that when he ran out on her. He hoped she would forgive him as he rapidly approached the house. And without a word to Gottlieb he gracefully jumped and landed on the window ledge that he so recently escaped from.

"Louisa," He called as he entered the room looking for her.

The soft sound of her weeping caught his ear but he did not see her. "Louisa where are you?" He asked as he searched the room for her, finally finding her huddled on the floor between the wall and the bed still wearing her traditional blue wedding gown.

"You left me." She said her voice filled with pain.

"I know I am sorry." He said as he knelt down beside her. "I didn't know. I didn't understand who I was."

"I was going to tell you, but you didn't give me a chance." She said accusingly as she looked up at him.

"I am so sorry Louisa. I can only hope that you will forgive me." He said as he gently put his arms around her. "But something happened to me when I was out there tonight, and I understand who I am now."

"You do?" she asked with hope in her eyes.

"Yes, but what matters to me right now is whether or not you will forgive me for leaving you, and hope that you still love me."

Louisa reached up and wrapped her arms lovingly around his neck. "I do." She said.

Wilhelm sighed with relief as he hugged her tightly. He then leaned down and gently kissed his wife, finally beginning the sweetness of his wedding night.

Dark Light

The Faery Hunt
by
Alexia Purdy

"Grab your gear; we're almost ready to go," Jay hollered out to me. He was dressing in full hunting gear, cargo pants, black shirt with knives sheathed across his chest. A quiver stuffed full of arrows crisscrossed the belt of knives, making him look like a black ops soldier. Groaning, I pulled myself up into the back of the truck, grabbing my hunting gear that matched his and snugly strapped it on. "Oh come on, I was heading towards the mall to hang out with my girls. What's going on that you guys had to screech on over here and interrupt my perfect evening?"

Jay tossed a bow at me and snickered, "I think this is much more important than shopping for shoes. "

I glared at my brother, wishing I could give him a slap. He never cared for anything but the hunt. Sighing, I was glad I remembered to wear decent shoes, I had learned long ago that a hunt can happen at any time and it was better being ready than sorry.

"Heads up!" Craig yelled out from the cab of the truck. A flashlight went sailing out the window and barely missed my head. Catching it, I cursed him under my breath.

Dark Light

"You could have killed me, moron!" Stuffing the
flashlight into my belt, I pulled the truck door open and
plopped on the seat, glaring at my older brother Craig.

"Sorry Pudge, didn't mean to almost take your head
off. Just helping you prime your lightning fast reflexes.
It's gonna be a doozy tonight!" He stuffed a flashlight of
his own into his jacket and hopped out. I did the same,
slamming the truck door and scurrying towards the back to
find him and Jay scoping out the woods.

"Hey, don't I get a say in the game plan? This isn't
a 'boys only' club." I sighed, turning to scan the darkening
woods before us. A trail on our left led deeper into the
trees, disappearing from the road after the first turn. It
looked scary, and the pit of my stomach agreed. Shaking
off the dread, I followed my brothers into the forest, letting
the truck disappear behind us in the thick of the woods.
"You sure there were sightings in these woods? I don't see
any tracks yet." I knelt down to study the dirt, looking for
any disturbances. The twigs and dead leaves cluttered the
forest floor and made it difficult to pinpoint any tracks. I
studied it intensively until a small splash of dirt across
some sapling leaves betrayed our prey.

"This way," I said, confident that I had discovered a
track. No way were they getting away from us this time.

We tracked them for about an hour, as the dusk
sucked the daylight away. The trees rustled in the cool
evening breeze and made it hard to hear any movement
around us. As the night approached, the lights became
clearer, marking the faeries in the distance.

"Faery lights," whispered Jay, motioning towards
the darkness beyond. In the distance, firefly-like glowing

orbs reflected back towards us. I sucked in my breath, steadying my bow as I swept my flashlight back and forth, counting the lights. Faery lights were the retinal reflections of the woodland faery tribes that haunted the woods around the city. They had caused a number of disappearances lately, thus keeping us hunting them regularly.

My brothers were on full alert, guns and arrows pointed and readied towards the flashing targets. They watched us approach, not wavering in their positions. Their confidence made the hairs on my neck stand on end; these were not so easily spooked like the others we've encountered.

"Amy, take the left flank, I'll take the ones on the right, Jay you're center point man. Don't spread out too much, stay together." Craig said intently, stepping carefully towards his right as they expanded their perimeter.

"Now!" Jay gave the command as he had many times before. Craig and I followed with a cascade of arrows flying into the darkness, hitting the glowing targets around us.

The infernal screams that followed were deafening. The carnal wailing all around us swallowed even the loud roar of the wind through the tree canopy. I wanted to fall to the ground and hold my hands over my ears to muffle the screeching. This band was louder and madder than any we had extinguished before.

We continued to hit them with arrows and bullets as Craig shot some down with his handgun. I reloaded as fast as I could but realized that the mass of dark faeries had taken a different stance and began to bum rush right at us. *Crap!*

I pulled out a hunting knife from my belt, just in time to slash one across the chest and butt another in the head with the bow. Their bright green blood splashed across my face and arms as their veiny skins burst open under my blade.

Their hair was made of twisted twigs and thistles while their skin was green like an emerald forest in spring with veins like leaves that spread across their bodies like emblazoned tattoos. They wore moss and long grasses woven into capes and pants. Their eyes glowed a yellow of cat's eyes, reflecting the moonlight like feral orbs. They fought us bravely, falling in piles as our weapons got the best of them. Iron arrows and bullets decimated their numbers efficiently.

Their sheer numbers pushed me farther from my brothers as they too spread apart to keep up with the rampage. Sweat gathered on my brows as my heart jumped in my chest. If we don't end this soon, we will be no match against them.

As if they heard my thoughts, the attack slowed, more warriors came to stand around me as my ammo ran out. The ceasing of gunfire let me know that Craig too had run out. Panic seared through me like lightning, threatening to burst my chest open. I held my knife out, dropping the now useless bow to the ground.

In a flash, one faery grabbed the hand holding the knife, squeezing hard enough for me to yelp out and drop it. He moved in a blur as he twisted my arm painfully around my back and held it tight. Unable to break free, he shoved me forward, deeper into the forest and away from the calls of my brothers. The pain in my arm seared through me, making my eyes tear up as I stumbled under his impatient shoving. When we approached a clearing, he shoved me down to the floor where I struggled to get back on my feet, rocks and mulch scraping my hands. Looking up, my eyes rested on another faery that stood staring down at me intently.

"Let me go!" I yelled. The still face remained unmoving, boring down into mine. I tried my best to look away; knowing that to stare back into the bright yellow glow of faery eyes was to become a prisoner of Faerie itself. I pulled my gaze away, tears spilling down my cheeks as I stared at the ground.

"Please, don't hurt my brothers. I'll go with you, but please, don't hurt them. Let them go." My voice quivered as my body shook, exhaustion and terror crawled over me, threatening to collapse the last bit of strength left inside me. Looking back up, I waited, studying his features, which were similar to the rest of their kind. The only difference was a twisted crown of wood and vines sitting on his head. His eyes glared at me, seemingly sucking my soul out into them as the world swam around me. I could hear but a whisper in my head as he agreed with my terms. Reaching out, he touched my cheek. A blazing burn ran from his touch down my neck and set my body writhing in pain. It seared through my bones like a raging inferno until a moment later when it receded slowly. Lying on the ground, I blinked back into consciousness. Slowly getting up, I stood and stared at the woodland Faery king. He nodded, turning back towards the forest and motioning me to follow. Glancing down at my hands, I realized the same leafy green texture of their own now tattooed my skin.

Reaching up, I touched the twisted twigs and vines that now was my hair and felt the mossy softness of the soft grassy dress that replaced my cargo pants and shirt. Gulping, I watched the faeries retreat behind their king. I turned and saw my brother Jay tied to a tree, watching in terror.

"Oh, Amy, no, don't go with them, no, no, no." His head bled a deep scarlet where he had sustained a hit. Craig lay on the ground near him, knocked out but breathing.

Relieved to see them alive, as the king had promised, I smiled to my brother, whispering *I love you guys* into his mind. Turning away and ignoring his pleading, I walked with the procession of retreating faeries and knew I would never see my brothers again.

Breakdown
by
Bonnie Bernard

It was easy to see her hair, so that's what he noticed first. Cobalt blue strands, flashing against the scorching sun and catching the desert breeze. Then he got closer and saw her hat. Oversized and cowboy. The boots caught his gaze next. White and sexy against those tight, black pants. But the cropped t-shirt got him most. Red, with black letters:

667...One Step Beyond Ordinary Evil.

She stood alone in the sizzling center of Nevada-nowhere, a purple backpack propped against her knee and her hitching thumb extended. He slowed. Then he stopped. That's when he saw the red gem glistening in her belly button, and the matching one in her nose. There was eyebrow jewelry too, and tattoos. An angel on her left bicep and a devil on the right. From a distance, the ink-work had looked like mud, or maybe car grease. She stood by a red, 1964 International truck with its hood popped, so the grease would have made sense, but upon seeing her up close, the tattoos did too.

He shut down the Harley's engine, motioned toward the International. "Your old beast broke down, huh?"

Dark Light

She raised the pierced eyebrow, making its red gem twinkle against late afternoon sunlight. "No, my spaceship caught fire and crash-landed about a mile from here."

He looked down at his gas tank, hoping the red on his face could be blamed on sunburn.

She stuffed the backpack over her left shoulder. "So, you gonna give me a ride, or not?"

"I don't have an extra helmet."

She shrugged.

"Want mine?" he pointed at it.

She shrugged again. He took it off and gave it to her, hoping the cops would spare him a ticket when he relayed the Good Samaritan story.

"Sorry about the sticker," he pointed to the helmet's left side. "It's supposed to be funny, but most girls don't see it that way."

She read it, smirked. "Good one." Then she put on the helmet. He grinned, because it was always nice to meet up with one of the few girls who got the joke.

"I'm Ryan." He offered his hand for her to shake. She smirked again and straddled the bike.

"I'm hungry. Know any place that has Chinese?"

"I know we're about fifteen miles out of a place that probably does." He started the engine and off they went; two perfect strangers riding into the sunset at the end of a scorching summer day. He was exhausted from riding and she was cute as hell in the helmet that read: *10% of women are battered, but I still like to eat mine plain.*

They wound up at a dive motel behind the town's only Chinese restaurant. Every time they opened the room's door, stale air blew in, and so did the stink of rancid

220

frying oil and sweltering asphalt. After a romp in the bed between sheets that felt like sandpaper, he took his phone and walked to the Chinese place for a number 3 and broccoli beef. While he was gone, she showered and slipped into a short black skirt with a matching skinny camisole. By the time he returned from his errand, the contents of her backpack were scattered about the motel room floor. He observed several changes of clothes, all of them stimulating. She didn't seem to own a stitch of underwear.

They ate with chopsticks, watched an old WWII movie and she asked questions he couldn't answer like, "What was Hitler's middle name?" She leaned against the headboard and watched the TV with an intensity he'd never seen before in a woman when it came to war movies.

Dessert was fortune cookies and another romp, but this time it was on the dresser. He decided it was maybe a good idea to never again set down his burger and fries on motel furniture.

"Prepare for tomorrow, today." She chuckled. "What's your fortune say?"

"A change of head begins with a change of heart." He smiled at her and winked.

She smiled back. "Ready for round three?"

***

Spikes of morning sunlight pushed through an opening between the curtains. He groaned, stretched, and pushed the sheets down with his feet. Her itty-bitty clothes, big cowboy hat, and purple backpack were gone. He'd never been with a blue-haired girl before and figured he never would again, so for a moment, melancholy crept into his consciousness. But by the time he smacked the key-card on the dresser and shut the door behind him, his thoughts were on what to do next. He'd only lied a little bit. The bike didn't break down and he wasn't two hundred miles from home, which meant he had an hour to kill before riding home to his wife in Reno. He'd never done this before, was unlikely to ever do it again, and decided admitting to it would cause irreparable damage to an otherwise stable marriage. So he relaxed in the sticky, beige vinyl seat at the "Pancake House and BBQ Grill", slurping black coffee and shoveling in scrambled eggs with bacon. Outside the plate glass window, a truck from "A and B Towing" crawled by. A red, 64 International was chained under the front bumper, like a fish on a hook. Good, he thought. She's got it under control. Though he knew nothing about her, including her last name (her first name was Shawna…or was it Samantha?) he thought those deviant tattoos and unexpected piercings covered over a real sweet girl. Lucky for her she'd met up with him. Nevada wasn't generally known for its savory types. He set down the coffee cup and rubbed his temples. His head ached a bit, even though there had barely been any alcohol involved last night.

Shawna - or was it Shelly this time around? - she could hardly keep track anymore, sprinted like wildfire across the desert, to a nearby hill. Tucked behind it, a small craft waited. It looked like a common glider plane, but it wasn't, and the team would arrive soon to repair the burned out engine. Then she'd be on her way. The broken down truck had just been a lucky break. Some old guy came back this morning to have it carted off. It had sure made her look authentic, though. And the boss would be pleased to hear she'd scored another human incubator. His head should be aching right about now and when the birth process kicked in sometime tomorrow morning, all he'd know would be a sudden urge for mass murder followed by suicide by fire…it was best to leave no trace of the vessel.

Bryan - or was it Ryan? - had been her fortieth incubator. She was kicking ass over the rest of the crew, who jealously insisted she was cheating. She wasn't. She just wanted to earn special recognition and privilege when the blue planet became all theirs.

Dark Light

Ouija'ust Wanted To Have Fun
by
Dominique Goodall

None of us could have been expected to realize that we were making a mistake. We were young and it wasn't exactly like we knew what we were doing when we all sat around in a group, our fingers touching a glass in the middle of a board. Someone screamed when the glass moved, though I had my mind set on the fact that it couldn't be happening, not really. When the glass moved to the letters I, C, A and N – even I had to start panicking. There wasn't any reason for one of us to scare anyone else...we were just young and trying to have fun.

When I heard Krystal scream, I followed suit. She was my sister as well as my best friend – and if she was scared well...that meant there was a reason to. She was sat to my right and Sara to my left, while Tony and Edward were sat across from us. It had been Edward's idea to come to the old abandoned De'Morte house and do an Ouija board. We had all agreed with him, buoyed up with false bravado and stolen gulps of cider. Krystal had been the only one of us to complain, but I had urged and blackmailed her into coming along, not wanting to be left alone with Tony and Edward.

I heard crying from in front of me when the glass moved again to the letters S, E, E and then paused, as though taking a breath. I tried to remove my finger, but couldn't, though my hesitation seemed to urge whatever was directing the glass onwards, giving it energy to complete what was being spelt out. Y, O and U completed the selection of words with the glass going to the middle of the board, no longer touching any other letters. This paused us for a moment, before we actually realized that this could only have left us with only one thought on our minds, that someone, or something had clearly just had us spelling out 'I can see you.' The fact that Tony was crying scared me. He was the leader of our group. The reckless one, the one we ran to when we couldn't do something dangerous - here he was sniffling and crying like he had just watched someone he loved die.

When a door slammed, we all jumped out of our skins, and I wasn't the only one to scream, at least one of the others screamed with me. My heart was thumping, was all I could hear before doors began to slam open and shut without a wind to cause them, making us all jump, cringe, cry or as I did – scream until our throats were hoarse. A silence fell suddenly, before the glass started to move without us even touching it, the movement catching our eyes and drawing our heads down in horrified fascination. Words formed where before we'd had to piece together the letters into small sentences. 'I will find you. I will get you. I will take you. You are mine.'

Krystal was whimpering beside me at this point – and I definitely wasn't telling her to shut up, especially not when I felt like joining her. All I could do was put my arm over her shoulders, and cuddle against her, she may have been the older sister, but I was definitely the braver one of us, the one most likely to go along with what Tony said or urged us to do. I sat there, cuddling Krystal against myself before jumping when Sara spoke.

"I've heard that you can use salt to protect from things like this. Did anyone else think to bring any? I only have a few little sachets." When we all wordlessly shook our heads, she huffed before sighing, and closed her eyes, putting on her thinking face – that she was angry was something she liked to make very clear.

Edward was the next to speak, and the sound of his voice had Sara snapping her eyes open.

"My sister told me that white candles are meant to bring only good spirits in. I thought she was joking, but I do have a candle in my bag. I could only find one, but it's white. I don't know if that'll help?" I sat there myself, trying to rake through the chaos that was my memory. I was so sure that I remembered something, but Tony speaking ruined it for me, made me forget what was planning on my mind and lingering on the top of my tongue.

"Sage is what we need. I have a little in my pocket. I didn't want to come without something…just in case."

I sat there, feeling like an idiot until I heard Krystal clear her throat and look at me. It was only when I returned her gaze that she spoke with a gentle smile that made me relax just a little.

"There are prayers you can say, to help drive away bad presences and to ensure protection. I know them, and can coach Dominique in them while we prepare. Surely we can all use what we have to do something?"

When I looked at her, she smiled briefly, though we both cringed as the glass scraped against the board and drew our attention back to it. 'Your plans are fruitless. Nothing will get rid of me. You are mine. Mine! You are mine to devour. Only mine to scare and scar and feast and feed on.' Whatever was controlling the glass was certainly not benign in nature.

After the glass stopped moving, everyone started arguing around me. I could feel the pressure in the air gathering above me, making me cringe just a little as everyone's words ran together on a never ending reel of film. Harsh voices and mean faces ran in front of my eyes.

"My salt will do the job!"

"No, a candle, we don't need stupid salt to do anything!"

"Will you just burn the sage?! That's what Google told me to do!" I was shocked when my sister stood up, Krystal didn't normally force her opinion on anyone, but here she was, just doing that!

"I'm sure the prayers would keep us safe, so we can get out of this house!" The argument carried on, rolling and rocking back and forth like we were on a boat, in stormy seas, leaving me getting more and more tense until I sat up and just screamed, letting lose all the frustration, fear and anger I was feeling in that moment.

"Everyone, can't you just stop?! Just stop it! Please! We can't all fight like this. We're going to end up doing what that thing wants us to!"

When my voice finished ringing through the room, everyone went silent, turning to look at me with shock in their eyes. I'd never ever been this loud before, because

228

although I was brave, I didn't shout scream or rage at anyone normally. Edward went quiet first, sticking his hands in his jacket pocket and nodded silently at me when my eyes hit his face. One by one everyone else nodded, and I stepped forward into the guise of leader. Tony was too shaken to be the fearless leader we needed him to be, so who else could have done it?

"Sara, get the salt please. Edward, Tony. You need to get the candle and sage. I have a plan. If you come here Krystal, then I can learn what you meant by these prayers."

The glass was sliding sluggishly back and forth between the letters H and A repeatedly, a clearly mocking tone that was lacking in energy as we redirected our fear and focus elsewhere. When Edward lit the white candle, and then started to burn the sage smudge stick, the glass faltered in its movements, now moving to the word NO on the right-hand side of the board. Again and again it moved towards that word, and the snippet of what I remembered was suddenly hooked on a sweeping, search line. I left Krystal beginning to recite a prayer to the Goddess (something stronger to us than the prayers to God and Jesus, as we are a pagan family) and Sara making a thin, but complete circle of salt around the table.

I put my finger on the glass, and began a battle of wills. Mine must have been stronger as I moved the glass to the word Goodbye, hopefully sending whatever spirit had tormented and frightened us away from the space we were purifying and back to whatever hellhole it had come from. I didn't leave it there; I grabbed the glass and threw it out of our circle, listening to the satisfying smash of glass and then the sudden silence that came over the house. It was peaceful now, no longer haunted with malignant and evil beings of anyone's imagination.

We began to recite the prayer, our voices reaching out in shocking crescendo, the words almost sung, and the magical pitch of the invocation unmistakable.

"I am a witch of ancient lore,
I petition these trees, and forest floor.
Converge myself upon this site,
spider weaving, power and might.
Air and Fire, Water and Earth,
aid in my quest, I call you forth.
Aradia, Aradia, I intone,
thrice the power you have shone.
Open my spiral of strength and sorcery,
encompass the soul, you have granted me.
Pentacle of old, stones of deep,
protection around, assistance I seek.
Marry my veins, to this Earth,
Cernunno's I summon you forth.
Steel needles and pins,
red blood of sins.
Buried deep in clandestine dusk,
liquid Venus, scent of musk.
Hear my words from Moon to Moon;
Cite the Lord & Lady's Rune
By the law of three times three,
so mote it be...."

We recited this at the top of our lungs until we walked out the front door, our voices now hoarse though we were triumphant at escaping the house behind us. We collapsed against the door, laughing – only for laughs to turn to screams when something thumped loudly. We did what anyone would do, that day. We ran, ran and never turned back to look for what had made that noise.

We never looked back after that, never went back to the De'Morte house – though we heard that it had tried to be knocked down, only to be back the next day as though nothing was wrong. The house and the spirit it had housed. I like to think we grew up that day, but that night also symbolized the breaking point of our little group – me and Krystal found a coven to join, training us to be better in the service of our Goddess and God than we were. Tony changed too, becoming withdrawn and almost appearing haunted after the events of that night.

Edward and Sara started going out, and became the golden couple of our school – but despite our differences, every time something happened in the De'Morte house – our eyes would meet and we would shiver in remembered fear and panic at the way what had happened had twisted us so savagely that even Krystal and I argued when she suggested going back to the house and making sure that the spirit was to rest. I didn't care, and fortunately – she listened to me...this time.

We were even more grateful that we never went back there when we opened up the newspaper one day, to the small headline that made tears roll down our cheeks.

Local Boy, 19, hangs himself outside the De'Morte house. Tony Maggorio was found hanging outside, from the large tree that overshadows the property. Foul play is not

231

believed to have happened. More will come when the
autopsy reports are in.

We both knew why, it was two years after we had done that fateful Ouija board, but it was poor Tony who had paid the price for our childishness.

Ghost Reapers
by
Rebecca Gober

"Excuse me, Miss!" A young man calls out from a booth in the back.

Realizing he's calling to me, I set down the maple syrup container I was filling, wipe my hands on my wrinkled apron and head over to his table.

"Yes, may I help you?" I ask not looking up from my notepad. Eye contact is not really my thing. Too many emotions can be received through a simple gaze. Nearing the end of my double shift, I've just about hit my pain quota for the day and my meds are already wearing off.

"Oh *yes* you can." He says in a flirtatious tone that hints of a man who is used to getting his way.

I roll my eyes. My head is down, focused on my notepad so he doesn't notice. It's not uncommon for me to get hit on by men based purely on my outward appearance. If they saw what was inside me though, the shell of a girl that I once could have been, who screams inwardly in torment; they would turn and flee from me. People, they don't look deep, so I just brush off the wasted advances knowing that they can offer me nothing.

I clear my throat waiting for him to give me a real answer.

"Well then, can I have a menu please?" He asks amused.

Great he's one of *those* guys who like a challenge. Without responding to him I grab a menu from the booth behind me and hand it to him continuing to avoid eye contact as to not encourage him in anyway.

I stand there trying to be patient while I wait for him to make his drink order. He whistles while he reads the selection.

To make a point I start tapping my foot in annoyance only to realize that the front part of my shoe is breaking apart from the sole. *Just great!* Unlike the average nineteen year old, a pair of shoes is the last thing I want to spend my money on. An unnecessary expenditure for such a thing cuts into my savings, which means I will have to wait another month for my procedure.

A month is excruciatingly long when all you think of and all that you feel is pain. I have been so wracked with pain that it has become a part of me; it has become who I am. Since my seventh birthday it has been there, taunting me, prickling every edge of my soul. There is a way to turn it off. Ghosting is the medical term for the procedure. A permanent fix that turns off all human emotions and feelings; it's rarely recommended except to those with the most extreme *gifts*.

A *gift*; what a ludicrous name for this plague that thrashes my very soul. The doctors confirmed that my circumstance qualifies me for the procedure but it comes with a hefty price tag. I have been saving up for it ever since I can remember. Employed in some shape or form since I was ten, I have saved nearly all of my income in anticipation of getting rid of this agony that has haunted my life.

The man clears his throat and finally gives an answer. "I would like coffee and a slice of blueberry pie please."

"Okay, may I have your MediCard?" I ask. That's when I make the mistake of looking up and into his eyes. I vaguely hear the clank of my pen hitting the ground right before I'm caught up in it. A feeling of utter tranquility washes over me in intense waves. It rushes steadily over me, hypnotizing me by some great force while I stare into this stranger's crystal clear green eyes. A small voice from within me tells me to stop staring, that I'm being rude, but I ignore it. Instead I continue swimming in the feeling of peace that these steadfast eyes bestow upon me.

His voice stirs me from my hypnotic state. He hands me his MediCard.

I hesitate a moment because to grab his card from him would mean I'd have to look down, away from the emerald city that lies deep within those eyes. His eyebrows rise a bit in question.

Being caught in the act of staring should make me blush, but nothing embarrasses me. I do on the other hand need all of the tips I can get, so I'd better stop staring and get back to work. I have to forcefully blink my eyes to sever the connection. The instant my eyes retreat from his, I feel it, the icy cold loss of serenity.

Shaking my head to clear the cobwebs, I quickly brush off the strange connection I just had and grab his MediCard. I scan it with my tablet and wait for a response. It beeps a minute later with a conditional approval. I show my tablet's screen to him saying, "You may have a slice of blueberry pie and black coffee. You do not have a caloric allotment left today for cream or sugar. Is this okay or would you like to revise your order?"

The insurance companies control the government these days, which means that our every action is being medically tallied and controlled in order to reduce medical treatment costs. The MediCard monitors our weekly exercise regime and our daily caloric allotment. It's just another way our government controls our lives.

He raises one eyebrow and gives me a sly boyish smile. He is a rather stunning young man. Not that I care much about physical appearances but this man's black hair provides a striking contrast to the bright color of his green eyes. He winks and says, "Black coffee it is then. Thank you, Austin."

I'm not sure why, but I get flustered when he says my name. Perhaps it's the way my name lingered on his lips, as if he knew me intimately. I look down at my chest for the reminder that my name is engraved on my nametag. Two can play at that game I think to myself. "You are welcome, Chance." I say boldly after reading his name on his MediCard.

A jolt is sent through my system when I go to hand him back his card accidentally making contact with his hand in the process. I gasp as the intense feeling cycles through my blood stream. I'm not sure how to describe the sensation other than euphoric. I realize that my hand is still making contact with his but I can't seem to pull it away due to some unseen magnetic force holding it steadfast. I look up into his eyes and a dizzying sensation washes over me. A second later I find myself floating in the air, weightlessly carried like a feather through the cafe and out the front door into the cold night. Icy snowflakes melt on my warm cheeks. I don't feel cold though, only warmth. Relishing in the carefree ethereal feeling I close my eyes and allow myself to enjoy this moment. I can't possibly process what is happening or causing this; all I know is that for the first time in my life, I feel no pain. I don't even feel that dull ache that is still residually left after I take my meds for the day. This must be what it feels like to ghost I think to myself.

"Austin, you need to open your eyes now." Chance says in a hushed but urgent tone. I shake my head 'no'. I'm swimming in elation and I can't bear to pull myself out.

"Yes, you need to open them now." He says again, more urgently this time.

I don't listen to him and a moment later I'm jolted awake and lying alone on the snow covered ground. I open my mouth to scream out in agony but I'm rolling in a pain so deep that my brain can't process it fast enough to even make my vocal chords work. My eyes are open now but the pain is so intense that I feel as if I'm blinded by it and all I can see is darkness. The arctic cold air blasts at my exposed skin and sends prickling goose bumps across my bare arms. I vaguely hear my name being called over and over again.

"Austin, look at me. Look at me Austin!" Chase is yelling in my ear now. This time he touches me slightly dulling the pain. He uses his hands to guide my head upwards to meet his eyes. "Look at me Austin." He says again.

I comply and will my eyes to focus on his. Like the lens of a camera going into focus I see into Chance's eyes. With it comes the peace I had felt earlier in the cafe. I take a deep breath and exhale it slowly as the excruciating pain subsides. "What was that...I mean this?" I ask groggily.

"I don't have time to explain it. They are coming now and I must go. You need to get back inside the cafe now." He says urgently.

"But..." I start to say but am cut off by the shrill sound of a scream not too far away.

"I will come back for you. I promise." He says helping me to my feet. He brushes my hair away from my face and gives me a gentle guiding push towards the cafe door.

I look back when I reach the door to see him still standing there, yet he's poised to run. "Now." He says demandingly.

Although I don't want to, I turn and go inside. Once I'm safely in the doors I look out the window to find him gone. Emptiness settles into me with his absence, which is strange since I had never met Chance before. I don't have time to dwell on it when I see *them*. To the naked eye they look like average people, but I know better. The two men walking down the empty street are Ghost Reapers. I know because I have seen men like them before, a long time ago.

I still remember that night that they came for my parents. It was my seventh birthday. I had just blown out the candles when we heard the first scream. It sounded like our housekeeper, Lucia.

My father grabbed my hand and told me gravely, "The time has come."

"No daddy." I remember saying as tears started flowing down my cheeks.

"Yes honey. You must go, remember the plan. We love you, but you must go now." He said sadly. He kissed me on my forehead.

My mom bent down and gave me the strongest hug she could muster. I could feel her arms shake. I knew she was scared. "I love you." She said her eyes pooled with tears.

They pushed me out the back door and into the night. Ever since I could remember, my parents would practice the plan. I was to run through the forest and loose myself inside the city. They told me that a time would come when they would need to leave me. My mother was on the run from some very bad people. She had a gift that they wanted and since she chose not to join them, they sent the Ghost Reapers to hunt her.

Reapers have a horrific *gift*; they take. Most Reapers control their abilities and avoid physical contact, which commences the taking. If uncontrolled a Reaper can take everything of value within a human including thoughts, emotions and memories. The process is said to be excruciating and can leave the human severely damaged or brain dead. A Ghost Reaper is a Reaper who underwent the ghosting procedure. With their emotions and feelings turned off, they are easy to control and often used by the government or other evil factions.

I never knew what my mother's gift was or why it was so wanted. I didn't understand much of anything my parents did back then.

Although I had rehearsed the escape plan over and over again with my parents, executing it was a different story. At first I hid just within the confines of the forest. When I saw the Ghost Reapers through the kitchen window I froze unable to avert my gaze. It wasn't until I heard my mother scream that I finally turned to run. I was so scared that night that I ended up taking the wrong path and tumbled off a shallow cliff.

The doctors had said I laid there for two days in the forest unconscious. I had fallen fifteen feet and broken or fractured over sixty bones in my body. I spent two months in the hospital. I pretended to have amnesia. My fingerprints didn't match any of those on file so I was labeled a Jane Doe.

I ended up in foster care. That was where I first found out what my *gift* was. The doctors said I was a Receiver. Similar to the average receiving device, my *gift* allows me to receive emotional signals or waves from those around me. Because of my personal physical and emotional pain, my body tends to receive heightened signals of the same accord from those around me. Which in short means that when those around me suffer from pain or anguish, I do as well. I spent much of my childhood in and out of hospitals and moving from home to home because of my *gift*. I was often immobilized by pain and it took many tests and trials for them to find a combination of medicines that could dull the pain and allow me to function semi-normally.

What I never truly understood was how my *gift* never sparked when my parents were alive.

I'm brought back to present when Mel, one of the servers calls my name from the back. I look back through the window and see that the Ghost Reapers are gone, then turn and head towards the back of the cafe. On my way, I look around and notice that the world hadn't stopped like I felt it had. Everyone is still going on with their eating or working without a hitch. Nobody seems to have noticed my dramatic exit or the crazed Ghost Reapers roaming the streets outside.

I head over to Mel, the server who called my name. "Yes?" I respond.

"Are you feeling better?" She asks. Her face doesn't show concern, so I can only assume that she chalked up my exit outside as one of the many dizzy spells I get when my pain gets too intense.

"Yes, sorry about that." I say.

"Why don't you go on home then." She says looking at the clock. "There's only an hour left on your shift anyhow and it's pretty slow in here."
I normally would balk at even losing one hour worth of wages, but tonight I agree without complaint. In the back of my mind I secretly hope that if I head out now, I might run into Chance.

***

Walking to work the next morning I chide myself for feeling disappointed that I didn't run into Chance last night. I have one major rule in my life that protects me. I don't allow myself to care about other people. Being close to someone means I have to feel too much and I can't afford any more pain in my life. I also receive stronger signals when I touch people, so I try to avoid all physical contact when possible.

I wonder what Chance's gift is. Whatever it is, it must be one of the few good ones left. I find myself yearning to touch him again and to get lost in the serenity it brings. *Stop it Austin!* I chide myself. I do not need to get mixed up with Chance; after all, if the Ghost Reapers are after him, he must be running from something awful.

My eight hour shift goes by mindlessly fast at the cafe. I found myself watching for Chance even against my better judgment. He didn't show up. When the clock strikes ten in the evening, I pull off my apron; throw on my coat and head out the door into the chilly night. My body aches and groans from the long shift and the usual pain I receive from those around me. I can feel the medicine begin to wear off and I hope to make it home quickly as to avoid any additional reception of signals from passersby's.

I step up my pace when I turn on the street of my residence. I live in an extremely small efficiency. The building is rather run down but the walls are thick with concrete, which blocks signals from the other tenants in the. That's all I can ask for these days.

I enter the building and head up the stairs towards my flat but stop midway when I see a shadowed figure standing near my door. It's not uncommon to see a petty thief in my building. I don't usually worry much about them though since I don't own anything of value. Even still, my heart picks up it's pace knowing there is a stranger nearby. I quietly reach my hand into my purse to grab out a can of pepper spray that I carry just in case. Clutching it in my hand, I cautiously continue to ascend the stairs. When I reach the top of the steps the stranger steps into the light. A rush of relief swooshes through me as I stare at Chance in wonderment.

"What are you doing here?" I ask.

"I promised I would come back." He says then looks down at my hand and continues, "Whoa, I can leave if you would like me to."

I look down at the pepper spray that I'm clutching. I quickly put it away in my purse then look back up towards him purposefully avoiding eye contact. Not that I don't want to experience that elated feeling again, but I need some answers first. "How do you know where I live Chance?"

"I followed you home last night." He says shamelessly.

"You...You what?" I ask caught off guard. *Why would he follow me home?*

"I wanted to make sure you were safe. I didn't think that they saw you with me but I had to make sure." He says.

"The Ghost Reapers?" I whisper questioningly.

His eyes open wide in surprise. "You know what they are?"

I nod in answer.

"How?" He asks.

"I don't really want to talk about it." I look away from him when I sense that he's trying to make eye contact with me.

"Anyhow, I'm safe. You see it for yourself so you may go now." I say brashly. On one hand I hope he will go and on the other, I hope he will stay. It's a lonely life that I live and having a meaningful conversation with someone is a rarity in my world.

"Yes, you are safe for now. I should leave, but I don't want to." He says the last part as if he's trying to convince himself otherwise.

I dare to look up and into his eyes. It overcomes me again, the feeling of peace and tranquility. I savor in it as one would savor the warm sun on a cold day.

He looks down breaking our connection. "Do you mind if we go inside?" He asks.

I should say no, but everything inside me says yes. "Okay." I step around him, careful not to make contact with him, and unlock my door.

Once we are both inside Chance goes right to making himself comfortable by taking a seat on my couch. It's odd looking at him sitting there. I've never actually seen anyone sit on my couch. Actually, I've never had anyone in my apartment except for the building's maintenance supervisor for the occasional repair. Something about the way he stares at me feels extremely intimate.

He runs his hands through his hair and asks, "So how long have you been a Receiver?"

"Excuse me?" Most of us who have *gifts* don't vocally advertise it; so to hear him say what I am out loud strikes a chord that puts me at instant unease.

"Come on Austin. I know what you are. I don't see why you are trying to hide it from me. You already know that I have a gift as well. You can trust me."

"I don't *know* you Chance and I don't trust anyone. Since you know what my gift is, I think you should tell me what yours is." I stand in front of him with my hands on my hips trying to look dominant.

"I don't think you really want to know what my gift is." Chance looks down at his hands.

Something about his posture and the way he says it hints of loneliness. Perhaps he and I may be more alike than I had originally thought. I relax my stance and decide to take a seat on the couch. I sit on the opposite side allowing the middle cushion to act as a barrier between us. It's not that I don't want to be close to him, because I do. In fact, I want too badly to be close to him, to touch him. That feeling I get is like a drug and I feel that the line to addiction is way too thin. I can't afford something so menial as dependence. No, I need to keep my distance, but that doesn't mean I can't find out what it is that causes that feeling. "I do want to know." I say urging him.

He looks up at me, catching my eyes and pulling me into that safe place that only he can seem to take me to. "Shield."

I shoot up off my couch like a rocket. Breaking eye contact with him sends sharp needles of pain shooting through my head. I use my fingers to massage my temples. Although I have my back to him, I can feel his stare. *A freaking Shield!* In my living room too, this is so not good. I should have known this whole time what he was! He's a Shield and Shields block gifts. That's what that feeling is, the absence of pain! My body doesn't understand what it's like to be without it so that explains the intense euphoric sensation I get from him.

"Do you even know the danger you put me in by being here? Do you even care? I can't believe you are a freaking Shield!" I wheel around and gasp when I find that he's standing only a foot from me. So close, that I can feel it radiating off of him, that blissful peace. If I just reach my hand out I can take some of it for myself. No! I ball my hands into fists to keep myself from reaching out to him.

"You don't think I know? Do you think a day goes by that I'm not reminded of what I am or what I run from? I didn't choose this gift! I wish it never were! I made a mistake in coming here. I don't know why I did. It was just...the feeling I got when you touched me. It was like coming home. I know it sounds absolutely absurd, but the instant you touched me, I felt like I had known you forever. I've never felt this before for anyone. I don't even allow anyone close enough to give it a chance." He runs his hands through his hair frustrated and continues. "Now, I'm just rambling on. I will leave. I'm sorry Austin" The look in his eyes is so sincere that I believe him.

I almost feel bad for Chance, but I can't afford to worry about it. I have to protect myself and as we speak I could be in danger. If word got out that I had a Shield in my home, I would be hunted just the same. I've heard stories of people being tortured in an attempt to extract information about a Shield's whereabouts. Shields are not allowed to exist outside of the Government. When you are labeled with the gift of shielding you are instantly forced to join into the militia forces. There is no choice; they are forced to serve. It is such a rare gift that only one in a million are said to have it. The Government knows the necessity of owning a Shield during wartime.

A shiver runs through me when I think of Chance being thought of as a belonging, not a man who has a choice. "How are you even here? I mean, how did you get away?"

"My mom chose to give birth at home with a midwife instead of going to the hospital. She had bad experiences with hospitals. She was a Receiver like you and the pain signals inside the hospital were too intense for her to handle. She said that she felt it the instant she held me in her arms when I was born. Many Shields do not show signs of their gift until later in life. My mom said that my gift must be exceptionally strong. My parents chose to hide me, knowing the fate that was bestowed on their only son. They paid off the midwife so that my birth was not documented." He pauses and takes a deep breath, moisture filling his eyes. "When I was fourteen, a neighbor realized what was going on. They turned us in. My parents tried to run with me, we survived for two years. When I was sixteen they found us. My parents forced me to run away, but I saw what happened. The Ghost Reapers came for them. They took everything from them trying to reap through their memories to find a hint of where I was. I wanted to go back and help them, but my mom made me promise that I would not allow their sacrifice to be for nothing by giving myself up. I never break my promises." He says the last part boldly.

Before I can catch myself, I find myself reaching out to touch him. It's unlike me, but I want to comfort him, perhaps since nobody was ever there to comfort me. I place my hand over his and it begins. I take in shallow breaths as I let the feeling run through me. This time I know what to expect, so I fight to maintain control and not pass out like some lightweight who had her first shot of Russian vodka. I look down at my hand that is still touching his and relish in the absence of pain. I look up into his eyes and see something there. I'm not sure what it is, but it's like hunger or need. When he leans into me and nears his lips to mine, I back away instantly freezing up in shock. *Is he trying to kiss me?* I've never been kissed before. I mean, I've seen people kiss, but I've never experienced one. I've never let anyone close enough to me to even try.

"I'm sorry Austin, I overstepped." He backs away looking concerned, like he hurt me.

I look down at my hand and see that I'm still holding on to his. I don't want to let it go. There is an irrevocable voice in the back of my head that is saying that I should never let it go. My heartbeat is racing and something feels strange within my stomach. It's like a fluttering inside that won't stop. I hold onto it with my empty hand hoping that if I hold my stomach tight enough the feeling will ease. It's not a bad feeling, but since I've never experienced it before, I feel vulnerable. I look up with confused eyes at Chance wondering if something is wrong with me. His emerald eyes look confused at first but then a look of knowing crosses them.

He rests his empty hand on my cheek then leans forward ever so slowly and places his lips upon mine. The feeling of the kiss runs boldly through my veins and I'm swept up in everything that is Chance. He pulls me closer to him kissing me harder now. I turn my mind off and allow myself to be, to enjoy for once in my life. To not care about the consequences or the outcome. It isn't until he pulls away that the thoughts flood my mind.

The first lame thought that seeps in is, did I do it right? I mean, I've never kissed a guy before, was it enjoyable for him? I instantly admonish myself for thinking such childish thoughts. The dilemma here is that he is a Shield. The worst thing of all is that something inside me tells me that I don't care. That I would gladly run away with this man if it meant that I could kiss him like that forever.

Chance can tell that I'm confused so he says gently, "I'm sorry Austin. I should have given you more time. I tried to...I just couldn't help it. I will go now." He breaks contact with me, which sends an icy shock through my body. Then he turns to head towards the door.

"Wait!" I yell a little too loudly.

He turns around and a look of encouragement flashes in his emerald eyes. "Will you come back?" I ask.

"Only if you want me to." He says with a look of hope on his face.

I nod my head.

"Then I will." He comes back up to me and places a tender kiss on my forehead, then heads out my door.

I find it hard to sleep tonight. My brain ramped up like a racecar. *What are you thinking Austin?* This is not like me. My life is about self-preservation. But what am I trying to preserve anyhow? My only goal has been to save enough to get the ghosting procedure. But now, this man comes along and throws my plans for a loop. I feel when I'm with him. For once in my life, I feel what it is like to be myself when I'm with him. I don't feel anyone else, or anything else. They don't exist. He shields me from it all.

Before I finally fall asleep a realization pops into my mind. My mother was a shield! That was why she was hunted and why I never received when we were together. It makes sense now. The only question now, is do I want to be like my father? I wish I could ask him if it were worth it. Running in fear with my mother, was it worth it?

***

I don't see Chance for the next two days. I look for him, against my better judgment. I wait for him to show up at the cafe or at my home, but he doesn't come. Tonight I've finally made the decision to stop looking for him. Why should I? I haven't depended on another human being since my parents were murdered. I don't need anyone. I don't need Chance. I try to convince myself of my last declaration.

Dark Light

There is a brisk chill in the air tonight. It's the kind
that you can feel deep down in your bones. The icy cold
intensifies the pains that radiate through my body. I pull my
coat tighter around me and pick up the pace. I dislike
working the graveyard shift at the cafe and having to walk
home in the middle of the dead night. I couldn't turn away
the offer for overtime pay. I'm so close to having enough
money. By my estimate I should have enough by the end of
the month to pay for the ghosting procedure in full. My
stomach tightens in knots thinking of it. I never had a doubt
in my mind that I wanted this until Chance had to come
along. Ghosting turns it all off, I will basically just be.
Some people continue to have slight emotions, but other
than that you just exist with no highs, no lows, no feeling.
Which for me means no pain. On the other hand it also
means that I will never feel those strange fluttering
sensations in my stomach that I experienced when Chance
kissed me. I will never again have a desire to reach out and
touch him...or anyone. Why did he have to come along and
make me doubt?

When I reach my street I jog the rest of the way to
my building door. Yanking it open I rush inside burring
from the cold. It's not that much warmer in the hallway but
at least the icy wind is not battering my body.

I head up the stairs to my flat but it isn't until I get
to the landing that I sense that something's off. My door is
ajar. I know I closed and locked it today when I left.
Perhaps it's Chance! Maybe he came back. I allow myself
to feel an ounce of excitement about seeing him again.

I push the door open further. *No!* Someone has been
in my home. My few sparse belongings are thrown about
around the room. The sofa that Chance and I had sat on just
the other day is turned on its side. The cushions sliced open
with stuffing spilling out.

A crash in the bedroom makes the hairs on the back
of my neck stand up on high alert. The instincts my parents

ingrained in me for seven years sets in. I don't wait to see who or what is still in my house. I turn on my heel and flee not sparing a look back. I push through the door of the building and back out into the frozen silent night. I planned my escape route the day I signed the lease for my flat. Following the path I memorized, I run down the back alley and out onto the street that leads into the city center. My plan was to lose myself in the giant city and to take advantage of the fact that nobody looks or notices anything, making it easy to disappear. I hadn't accounted for it to be in the dead of the night when the streets are deserted.

When I turn onto Fifty-second Street I hear it. It's the sound of a second pair of running feet pattering against the pavement less than a block away. I dare to look back briefly and see that it's one of them, a Ghost Reaper! My heart starts pounding through my chest more from fear than from physical exertion. My brain starts running rampant trying to find a way out of this. The way I see it is that I have to lose it at the next turn and I have to lose it quick. The Ghost Reaper seems to be about matched with my speed so at least it's not gaining on me, yet. My eyes start darting from side to side as we come up on a few intersections. I make my choice and gear up to take the sharp turn.

When I get up to the corner I turn sharply and then dart down the street running with all that I have. I make it to another intersection and turn quickly allowing a slight glance behind me. It hadn't turned the corner yet. I picked a good street that has many alleys intersecting. Behind me on another street I hear a shrill scream in the dead of the night.

With fear running ice cold through my veins, I continue to run up the alley as fast as I can towards a busier street that can provide more shelter and places for me to hide. When I turn on it I take the opportunity to hide in the alcove of an apartment building catching my breath.

Straining my ears I try to listen for the sound of running feet. I hear nothing. Except for a revving engine. *A car!* I should have known! Ghost Reapers don't normally travel alone, they usually travel in packs. I turn around and try to open the door to the apartment building but it's locked. No time, the engine is roaring louder! I dart out into the street and high tail it down another alley. The sound of the screeching tires rings out in my ears. The alley is thrust into light when the lights of the car hit it. I look back. The car is in the alley, headlights screaming towards me.

I try to run faster, if only I were a Lifter and could take flight! Tears spring to my eyes as I see how far away the mouth of the alley is. I'm not going to make it! This is it. I think of the sound of my mother's scream. Will it hurt when the Ghost Reapers take from me?

The car is so close to me that if I stopped right now, it would run right over me. I would rather die at the hand of a car than at the hand of a Ghost Reaper. I stop as suddenly as I started and turn around blinded by the oncoming lights. I close my eyes bracing myself to be hit. Bracing myself for the end of this life. Tears stream freely down my face. I had thought many times about my death and whether it would bring relief or not, relief from this pain.

Nothing comes, no pain, nothing. I open my eyes and find that the car has come to a halt. Why didn't it hit me? It takes me a moment to realize that this means I can run, I turn around and start off. I can't run nearly as fast as before because my legs are shaking so hard I feel as though they may give out below me.

A car door slams. No! I will never outrun this one!

"Austin!" I hear my name called out in the night from the direction of the car.

Chance! It's Chance! He came back for me! I turn around and run to him, tears of relief soaking my face. I run right into his arms gripping him tight.

"You are shaking. It's going to be okay Austin, I promise." He says holding me safe and secure. He repetitively runs his hand soothingly over the back of my head.

I don't say anything, I can't. I just take. I just receive all that he can give me. His strength, his comfort and the serenity he provides by shielding it all.

"Okay, we need to go now, we are not safe here." He says pulling away from me just a little. He takes my hand and guides me to the car. I climb inside reluctant to let go of his hand. "It's okay Austin." He says when he lets go of my hand then runs around and gets in to the drivers seat. He quickly picks up my hand again and doesn't let it go, not even when he shifts the gears, he just moves my hand with his, working the car as we start driving.

We don't make it out of the alley though; a car stops blocking us in. Chance lets go of my hand and shifts the gear into reverse. He stealthily maneuvers the car in reverse all the way back to the entrance of the alley only to be blocked in by another car.

"No!" Chance yells along with a whole sleuth of other expletives. A Ghost Reaper gets out of the car and starts heading towards us. He's huge, looming about six feet tall and coming up towards the driver side door.

"Stay in the car, do you understand Austin?" He looks at me his face contorted with anger aimed at the situation, not me.

I nod my head quickly all the while my heart is pounding ferociously.

"Lock the doors," he says as he steps out of the car and slams the door.

It takes a lot to get my shaking hand to press the lock button. I turn around looking through the rear window as Chance goes up to the Ghost Reaper. The Ghost Reaper puts his hand out as if he will suck Chance's life force from him without even touching him. Then a look of confusion crosses his face.

"You idiot!" I hear yelled from far off. I look through the front windshield and see another Ghost Reaper all the way at the other side of the alley. This one looks a lot shorter. He yells out, "He's the Shield."

Chance takes the opportunity during the distraction to jump the bigger Ghost Reaper knocking him to the ground. I can't see what's going on but when I turn back around I see that the shorter Ghost Reaper has started running to back up his partner.

Chance seems like a strong guy, but I don't know how he will hold up if it's two against one. I start looking through the glove compartment for anything that I can use as a weapon. No dice. I guess if there were a weapon, Chance would probably have it on him. The shorter ghost reaper has already made it a quarter of the distance of the alley.

I have to think quickly. I jump over into the drivers seat. The keys are still in the ignition and the car is on. I try to recall my one lesson on using a stick that I learned in one of the foster homes. I throw my foot down on the gas and then double up on the clutch putting it into first. The car stalls out. *Crap!* I shakily turn the key over restarting the engine. I try it again. This time I make it into second and red line it towards my intended target. I'm less than a few yards away when the shorter Ghost Reaper pulls out a gun! As he aims it at me, I slide down in the seat and gun it as hard as I can towards him. I hear the shot crash through the windshield. It didn't hit me but the sound nearly deafens my ears. I sit up just in time to see the Ghost Reaper a few feet ahead aiming at me again, ready to take another shot. I punch the clutch and knock it into third. I let out a piercing scream as the car rams into the Ghost Reaper sending it sprawling up over my hood and into my windshield. Blood splatters across the glass. It's still moving! I slam on the breaks sending the Ghost Reaper plummeting back down to the floor of the alley.

I shift the car into reverse trying to cleverly maneuver back to where Chance was. The sound of the metal screeching against the alley wall tells me that I'm not as nearly skilled as Chance is at driving in reverse. When I see Chance cringing in my rear-view mirror I slam on the breaks. He triumphantly walks up to the driver's side and I gladly move back to where I belong, the passenger seat.

"Wow." Chance says jokingly to me.

I shrug my shoulders but inside I'm delighted to see that he's safe.

"Buckle up now!" He says, staring furiously ahead of him as he lurches the car forward.
I buckle up and look ahead. The shorter Ghost Reaper is standing again, but is hunched forward severely injured. Never the less he has his gun deadlocked on Chance.

"Down!" Chance yells.

I comply and sink down in my seat as far as the seat belt will allow.

He stomps on the gas sending the car shooting faster than I managed to make it go. Another gunshot rings out, this one shatters the windshield sending small glass crystals across the dashboard and onto us.

I look up just in time to look right into the Ghost Reapers eyes. Even from this distance I can see that there is nothing there. No humanity, no remorse, nothing. How could I have ever thought about having that ghosting procedure done? Sure I wouldn't be a Reaper, but to have all humanity stripped away. What is worth that?

The Ghost Reaper continues to stare at me even when Chance plows into him sending him up and over the back of the car.

Knowing it's over I close my eyes, only to see the image of that dead stare looking back at me. Bile rises up into my throat and I barely find the control to keep from vomiting all over Chance's car.

"Hold on!" Chance says as we reach the mouth of the alley that's blocked in by the dead Ghost Reaper's car. He crashes into it, and the loud thrash of metal on metal rings off in the night. The car is pushed out of the way enough for us to pass. With no more Ghost Reapers in sight, Chance grabs a hold of my hand and drives us out of the city and into the night. The cold air beats down on us through the broken windshield, but it doesn't matter.

***

I hadn't realized until we pulled into the self-storage a few miles outside of the city that Chance had been hit. Blood soaked his white shirt and bled into the car seat. Guilt pounds at me when I realize that he was injured this whole drive and hadn't complained once. When we pull up to a garage sized storage locker I rip out of the passenger side and around to him. He grunts in pain as he gets out. I pull up his shirt being careful when I get to the part where the bullet hit. It went straight through, a clean shot through the fleshy part of his left arm. I sigh in relief knowing that it's only a minor injury and that he will be okay.

"Do you have a first aid kit?" I ask.

"Of course. A man on the run is always prepared." He pulls out a key from his pocket and opens up the garage door revealing a shiny new truck loaded with supplies. He opens the door and rifles through a backpack sitting on the floorboard of the passenger side. He pulls out a first aid kit. I open it and start dressing his wound.

When I finish putting the bandage on, my hand lingers there on his chest feeling his heartbeat. My breathing hitches, being acutely aware of the close proximity of our bodies. I can feel his breath hitting my neck. When I look up at him I feel his heartbeat speed up and mine follows suit. This time when he leans down and places his lips on mine, I don't freeze up. I melt into him, allowing myself to enjoy this new feeling that heightens all of my senses. I could kiss Chance for hours and bask in this peaceful serenity that his gift brings me.

When Chance pulls away, I do my best to mask my disappointment.

"I'm sorry Austin, but we need to put as many miles between us and this city as we can. It won't be long until they track this storage room back to me. We need to be long gone before then." He says.

"Okay," I say fluttering my eyelashes up at him trying my best attempt at flirting. It seems like I'm trying new things all of the time lately. Kissing, flirting, running over evil Ghost Reapers, I guess it's all well in a day's work.

Chance looks at me and gives me a sexy smile. My eyelash fluttering must have worked. He leans down as if he wants to give me another kiss, but plants a quick peck on the bridge of my nose and turns to get into the truck.

I feel my cheeks flush with heat and I raise my fingertips up to feel them. So this must be what it feels like to blush. I follow Chance's lead and hop into the passenger seat of the truck. I steel a stare at the side mirror and see the red pleasantly coloring my cheeks. I guess that's another first.

***

I must have fallen asleep sometime after Chance switched vehicles.

Yawning I stretch out and open my eyes which are instantly blinded by the midday sun. When I get the sleep out of them and my vision adjusts I look over to see Chance smiling in the drivers seat.

"Good morning sunshine." He says steeling a look at me out of the corner of his eyes.

I look down and notice that he's still holding my hand. He has barely let it go since we switched cars. He must have held onto it the whole night. No wonder I slept so well. "Good morning to you too." I say, and then look out of the windows at the surroundings. I gasp in surprise. We are winding along next to a glossy river, surrounded by looming mountains on both sides. "I have never seen the mountains before!" I say in wonder. It's true. In fact, I haven't seen much of anything in my life, only the brick and mortar city. Covered in snow as far as the eye can see and dotted with glorious pine trees, I can see why mountains are described as majestic.

"Well, I can show you many things you have never seen before Austin. That is, if you will allow me to." He says.

He's a Shield. I know what it would mean to be with him, running for the rest of our lives. I finally understand my parents and why they did what they did. Why they ran...for freedom, for love. I look over at Chance, my heart fluttering with this feeling that I have yet to explore. I realize as I look down at our hands interlocked together that we are two puzzle pieces in a mad world, meant to fit together. No matter the consequences. For once, I feel hope, painless undying hope. I smile for the first time in years and say, "Yes, I would like that."

Death Becomes Him
by
M.R. Murphy

<u>Chapter One</u>

You never know how long you have to live or if you've lived a life worth dying for until the day comes that you are no more.

***

The image of her eyes wide in horror, the crimson splatter of cooling blood clashing against her soft ivory skin as the sound of utter heartbreak and fear screamed from her glossy lips, rang like church bells in my mind.

Darkness edged around the outside as my body shivered in the sweltering summer night air. I don't remember when she pulled me into her arms, or when the tears soaked my cheeks from her weeping, but the scent of gunpowder mixed with her Burberry perfume lingered until I couldn't see through the haze anymore.

It wasn't until I woke up what I thought was hours later that I realized that I would never again hold Alyssa in my arms, never again feel her warm body pressed against me as she professed her undying love to me. Poor, sweet Alyssa, how I loved to tease her about those freckles that danced across her cheeks, and soak in the stormy seas of her blue eyes.

I still walk up and caress her face and run my hands through the tangles of her auburn hair, but there isn't any reaction to my touch. No smiles coated in love, no more words to whisper. But then that wasn't true. I told her everyday how much I love her and that I can't live without her. But living I am not, not since that hot July night. I am dead, well living impaired more like it. I didn't find my way up to the pearly gates, and I sure as hell didn't see any bright white light except that of the butt of the gun going off in a flash. To think I had never before considered that ghosts were real, and here I am, one of the perpetual spirits bound to roam the earth. Though it has some perks. I still miss the way Alyssa's lips tasted after drinking her Guinness or the feel of her slender body curled into mine for safe keeping as we slept at night.

She was, no, she is my world, and every day since I woke up like this, I haven't left her side.

***

Three months ago I thought I had the world figured out, knew what my next step was. Yet I didn't see my death coming into play. It was our second anniversary, and I had planned on making it the most memorable night possible.

We had started out at our favorite little Italian joint, Piccola's. The glistening of her eyes as she slipped the glass of wine to her ruby lips and sipped the burgundy liquid, god she screamed sensuality. My heart tripped over itself every time I stared into her eyes, and the box in my pocket burned to come out and say hello. But I was waiting for just the right moment.

Waiting until we walked down by the pier, her favorite place to visit, it funny the things we remember about the little moments. It was at that very pier where I first met her, leaning against the rail; her delicate hand propped up her chin. Her auburn hair shimmered in the midday sun as tendrils danced behind her in the summer breeze while she stared off into forever. She looked like an angel, peaceful and beautiful. I fell in love that very moment.

The walk from Piccola's to the park had been filled with ideas about the future and where we were heading. The night sky was littered with stars and a full amber moon, burning so brightly that you would swear it should be daytime. Even with all the midnight sun's illumination, I didn't see the group of men standing under the covered bridge we were about to cross. Cross but never reach the other-side.

I held Alyssa's hand tightly in mine, the feel of her slender fingers weaved between mine were a small comfort to keep me from full-on sprinting to the pier and whipping out the tiny black box. The smell of the tide lingered all around us, but I only noticed her sweet perfume. Leaning into her neck, the warm pulse that thrummed beneath the supple patch of skin under her ear was beating wildly. She hid her emotions well within her soft smile and perfect up do, so gracious even when in the thick of things.

Inhaling her deeply, I was momentarily distracted by my body's reaction. Too distracted to notice that her hand had tightened around mine and her hair was standing on edge.

"I-I think we should go back." She murmured, slowing her walk. "Please, Jason….let's go back."

"But I thought you wanted to go to the pier? You love it here." Pulling her close, I could feel the small trembles radiating down her arms. Guess in hindsight, I should've picked her up and ran for it. I was just too damn stubborn to give up on my plans.

Dismissing the odd uncertainty in the air, I wrapped my arms around her, and pressed a kiss to her lips, promising her it would all be okay. God, how wrong could one person be.

I didn't see the first male come at us, barely heard his footsteps, but damn if I didn't feel the hard crack of wood against my head. The steamy rush from fresh blood that covered the back of my skull didn't compare to the rattling around inside. Reaching behind to blindly inspect the damage, I could barely focus to see another man come from the shadows.

The bellowing of her screams went through me like lightening bolts as I spun around to find her pinned against the wall by another man. The sickening way he sneered at her, licking his lips and grinding himself against her shaking body. Fear plastered tears in her eyes as she tried to push her assailant off her.

"Alyssa!" Her name screamed past my lips as I lunge for the bastard clutching her. Rage seared through every vein in my body, coiled every muscle as I fought back against the hammering in my head.

The next hit bounced off my back as I crashed into Alyssa's capture. Knocking him off her and falling to the cobblestone covered ground. His grunts echoed off the stone walls as he hissed out curses between my punches. My fists coiled tighter as the fury rose higher.

"Jason Look out!" she screamed behind me, before another cracking sound silenced her cries.

I tried to reach her; I tried to fight off the two men that tackle me back down to the ground. Each taking turns with Louisville sluggers. Her angelic face twisted in anguish as the last man ripped at her cloths, laughing at her rolling sobs. I couldn't stop them,.....couldn't save her, my failures would devastate her for the rest of her life. What a fool I had been. If I had just listened to her, left when she wanted to, sweet Alyssa could've been spared this.

The sting of the bullet that penetrated my back knocked the last of my breath out, as I spun around to see the gloating crooked smiles of out assailants. I didn't know these men who attacked us, but their faces I could never forget and didn't plan to.

Chapter 2

It seemed as though hours had passed before she found her way to me. My body beaten and twisted, my lungs that burned for air, were only blood filled the sacs as I aged against the cold cobblestone ground. Her face, covered in splatters of my blood mixing with streaks of runny mascara clouded my vision. I could've sworn she was wearing a halo as she pulled my shoulders into her lap, covered by torn reminisce of her dress. "Are you ok?" I said weakly, reaching to touch her swollen cheek.

"I'm—I'm so sorry sweetheart." The words felt heavier than a ton of bricks with weight of this guilt.

"Shhh, don't talk. It's all right baby. It's going to be all right. Just hang on. I've called 9-1-1; they should be here any minute." Her shaky voice struggled to stay strong as she sucked in a hard breath. Even filled with tears, she had never looked more beautiful. The reflection of my swollen face, and cut up lip and brow in her eyes didn't seem to matter anymore.

"I...love...you...Alys..." The pain burning inside my body cut off all thoughts as the crushing wave overwhelmed me. Darkness crept in around the edges and her sobs began to silence as I fought to stay with her. Fighting was useless, my mind started to detach from my body, the last sense that still worked was my sense of smell, as I inhaled her sweet perfume.

Drifting off into the vast blackness, I wasn't sure where I would end up. Though I wasn't a complete sinner, I sure as hell wasn't any kind of saint. Her sobs rumbled through my body as the void of death welcomed me into its cold embrace. I tried to hang on her voice, her warmth, to her scent, but I couldn't fight it. Even as I screamed at myself for being weak, and giving up, my body just refused to listen and spark back to life.

All I knew, all that I loved was taken away from me as I passed through void of time and space. I wasn't exactly sure where I would end up, so believe me when I say, ending up as a specter freaked me the hell out. Waking up in our bed, my arm wrapped around her, I honestly thought it had all been a bad dream. Until she climbed out of bed, tears staining her cheeks and sleep deprived eyes. I remember asking her why she was upset. She didn't answer, didn't even acknowledge me.

I climbed out of bed to comfort her, but my hands couldn't pull her close, she didn't even flinch when I pressed my lips to her cheek.

"Why? Dammit! Why? Why did you have to take him!" she sobbed, crumbling to the floor, the shirt I wore the night before clutched tightly in her hands.

"Baby, I'm right here," As if my words could sooth her, looking down on her dresser, it was then that I saw what had caused her tears to erupt again. The pamphlet from a funeral, *my* funeral, dated three months earlier. "Oh shit."

It was not one of my finer moments. The translucent reflection in the mirror barely outlined my body as shock shot through my veins. "What the hell is happening to me?"

The answer I was seeking didn't come clear as a billboard for me to read. No instead it was a whisper in my ear. "You're dead, but you can't leave yet." The voice called out.

"What do you mean I can't leave yet? What the hell am I then? A ghost." Scoffing at the idea it sounded ridiculous, but what else could I go by.

"Yes." I still couldn't make out if it was a male of female voice, but I guess it didn't really matter either.

"So why am I here then, what's my purpose?" I demanded, not really sure if I wanted to a reply. Eyeing the room, I couldn't see anything or anyone other than my sweet Alyssa, scrunched down in a ball, sobbing into the last shirt I wore before we left that day. The scent of her tears assailed me as I crouched down next to her. My fingers ached to touch the curve of her cheek, and wipe away those hot salty tears, but they passed through me like air.

A chill in the air shivered the room, as I turned to look for the source. No window had been open, yet a strange shadow hung in the corner of the early morning hours.

"You need to protect her," The voice spoke in the same whispered hush as before. "She's in grave danger. The men that killed you now seek her out."

"What! Where are they? I'll kill them for what they did to her." Anger boiled deep within, as I searched for a face in the dark shadow. "Where can I find them?" I demanded. I couldn't hide the rage that burned me to my core.

"They watch her from afar. You'll find them. But killing them won't get you into Heaven."

"I don't care about getting into Heaven or saving my soul or any of that shit. I won't let them hurt her again, damn it! Look at her for Crissake! Even a blind man could tell that she's not functioning. This isn't the Alyssa I know." The tick in my jaw started to ache as I ground my molars together. None of that religious crap mattered to me. Saving Alyssa and getting my revenge were my only priorities. "You want me to save her, than let me do it *my way*. We clear."

"As you wish, Jason." It didn't take long to realize when the shadow had left, but I still couldn't believe what was happening.

"I'm a friggin' ghost. Holy shit…Alyssa was right." Looking back down to her, my first reaction was to pull her close and carry her back to bed, soothe away her hurt and wipe away her tears, but there was no way for me to do that. Not this time.

The sorrow that poured off her could drown a city, and there wasn't a damn thing I could do about it. Anger clashed with guilt as I watched her curl tighter into herself. I won't let those bastards get away with what they had done to her, to me. I had more than a lifetime to spare and tracking down each one of those scumbags would be more then just a mission, no more like my pleasure. There was no way I would let anyone of them live to breath the same air as Alyssa. And tonight I would prove that being a ghost had its perks too.

Now if I could just get a handle on the basics.

Chapter 3

"Shit!" If it were possible to sweat, I'd swear I would be pouring buckets right now. For hours I tried to solidify my hand to grasp the hammer on the floor. Hell even a penny, but the closest I came was moving it a few inches across the floor.

Alyssa had been moving numbly from room to room, staring for long moments at all the pictures that littered the shelves. "Happy Birthday Jas..." She murmured, stroking the picture from our last vacation together.

No wonder why she couldn't function. Hell I would've been twenty-seven today. She always loved to surprise me with little presents and her most naughty lingerie. Who was I to stop her? She looked friggin' amazing, dancing around in leather and lace. Not today though. She wore her grey yoga pants that she had obviously been in for a few days and stretched out tank top, her hair was tied back in a sloppy mess of a ponytail. Shaking my head, she didn't resemble the beautiful woman she truly was.

She carried a sliver of pinkish-silver scar that curled around the line of her hair on her forehead, down her temple. That little reminder of what those bastards did to her was enough to light the fuel to my fire and make me focus on the mission at hand.

My heart sank as I watched her make a cup of tea, without any care of how much tealeaves she used or honey she poured. Her ordeal and my death had caused this. Once vivacious, she was reduced to a shell of a woman.

I had to find them, those who did this to her, find them and make them pay with every ounce of breath in their pathetic deviant bodies. I could feel all the rage fuel into balls in my hands as I lunged for the hammer once again. The hard feel of the wooden handle cupped in my fist didn't register until I lifted it up off the floor and sent it skimming across the area rug. The soft thud barely rippled in the air as I glanced back to Alyssa, waiting to see if she heard it too.

The expressionless look in her haunted pale blue eyes barely lifted to notice as she set her cup of tea down on the side table and sank into my favorite recliner. Why hadn't I noticed before how frail she looked, how pale and withdrawn she seemed.

I had to get her attention, somehow let her know that she wasn't alone. I couldn't miss the fact that she hugged my shirt, sniffing what little scent of mine had lingered on it. I had no more thought about being by her side, and then I was there. "How the hell?" looking back to where I was just standing, I was seriously hoping that this wasn't just a freak accident. Thinking about where the doorway was, I seemed to flash there in a blink of an eye, then back next to Alyssa's side. "Cool." It didn't take much to wonder if it would be possible to move objects with the same conviction.

I looked around for a moment until I found the perfect object to practice on. I envisioned it shaking at first before falling off the mantel. The tremor that quickly erupted before my mental command that carried out was subtle. The crash of the picture frame and shattering of glass snapped her head up, breaking Alyssa from her numbed out state.

At first she looked blankly at the broke frame, until she realized which one it was. Launching herself to the floor, the crunch of broken glass under her knees didn't seem to faze her as much as the image that had been marred by the broken glass.

As much as it broke my heart to watch her stare into the image of a better time, when life waited for us to make our plans on that sandy beach in Aruba, I learned a lesson that when I was alive, I could never imagine happening. Trying to physically move an object took an explosion of anger, while moving objects and myself came from my mind. Guess all my ideas of the living impaired are blown to pieces.

Marveling in my new talents, I didn't notice when the soft vibrations of Alyssa phone buzzed on the coffee table. Slowly she pulled it to her ear, and answered with a shaky hello.

"Sure, Clare, I'll be there within the hour. I'm sorry you're not feeling well. Just hang in there; I'll be there soon sweetie," That was always my Alyssa, willing to help out whenever she could, even at her own expense. I was so close I could smell her sweet nature perfume and yet I was a lifetime away from her kiss. "Yup, bye."

She looked back down at the mess then at the picture in her hand. The longing and sorrow in her eyes misting over with fresh tears hit me like a wrecking ball to the nuts. I hated to see her like this, hated knowing that there wasn't anything I could do to save her from all this.

All I could do was save her from the men that now watched her and silently threatened her life. The men that wanted to finish the job they had started three months earlier. Payback would be my sole mission from here on out. That I would promise Alyssa, protect her from whoever or whatever came her way.

But first, there was something I needed to see before my protection detail started. The sprays of the water sounded from the bathroom, as Alyssa shut the door closed. Odd, she never did that before. Shrugging it off, I followed in after her, not like she would notice me watching her as hot soap suds sluiced down her body. Not that she minded much when I was living. She's always been a natural beauty, with long auburn hair and pale blue eyes, with curves that would make the Venus de Milo weep. I might be living impaired, but I'm not blind.

Chapter 4

The walk to the bakery didn't prove eventful as passersby stalked off to whatever was so important to them.

Alyssa, plastered on a smile that screamed painful, still she had always been polite to her customers. She opened Sex on a Stick Bakery a year ago and business had been good. So I wasn't surprised to see the little café packed. She twirled around the kitchen serving up pastries and coffees effortlessly. Her black and pink apron was covered in fresh flour as she passed a young couple their box of cake balls.

The day seemed to fly by as I watched her from the window. I could've sworn she had looked right at me when the calm of customers had left her idle for a few minutes. Her beautiful eyes stared into mine, yet she didn't see me. Couldn't see me, but I felt her eyes staring right at me, as a small smirk that pulled at the corner of her lip almost gave me some hope that she knew I was there. As quickly as that hope came, it left when she turned away from our invisible connection to attend to her counters.

When the last of the customers left I sidled up to her, smelled the flour that covered her clothes, and the warmth that radiated from her skin. Slowly she walked around and cleaned the place from top to bottom.
I knew why she was stalling on returning home, she hated being alone, and it had always been her fear. Somehow she managed to find something else to do until the place was so spotless that you could eat off the floors.

"Alyssa, please…you need to get some rest," I heard myself saying, as I brush my knuckles across the soft curve of her sallow cheek. "Please sweetheart, get some sleep. I'm with you, I'll always be with you."

"Jason…" her eyes snapped around the room looking for…me. Clutching her heart like it was breaking all over again. Cupping her cheek, the way she nuzzled into my palm and closed the dark rings of her eyes, made me want to jump out of my skin and kiss her senseless.

"I'm right beside you sweetheart, right here touching you. Can you hear me?" God I wanted her to hear me, to realize that I'm standing next to her.

The sadness that painted her face returned when she pulled away. "Crissake Jason, I need you. I can't make it through this life without you." Circling her arms around her waist, she looked seconds away from shattering.
Hot fresh tears pricked her eyes as she stormed back into the kitchen. The crashing sound of metal screamed through the air.

"Alyssa!" I ran back just in time to see her shaking, surrounded by pots and baking sheets scattered about the floor and the shelving unit toppled over. "Holy shit!" Was my only reaction, I hadn't seen this side of her, a side where she snapped and came unglued. Sinking down next to her, with her head in her hands as sobs rocked her body I did the only thing I could think of. I held her. True she didn't know I was, but I couldn't be completely convinced otherwise. As my hand brushed over hers, it was a moment I swear would last me a lifetime. She looked right at me and smiled.

"Jason..." she whispered. "I love you." It wasn't my imagination. She was seeing me, feeling me touch her skin.
"I love you too, sweetheart." I wanted to say more, but the words were stuck in my throat. Lame I know.

The recognition in her eyes as she blinked away another onslaught of tears stunned me like a taser. She tried to reach for me, but her hand caught only cool air.

Shaking her head, she shot up to her feet and angrily picked up the shelving and started to load it up with all the tumbled kitchenware. "Great, you're going crazy. Nice. First you lose him, and now you lose your flipping mind."

But she had seen me, she heard me, so why couldn't she still see me? What had changed? I couldn't bare this reality, one I couldn't be with the one I love, doomed to roam the earth, waiting for her to die just to be with her again.

The pounding in my skull tripled the second she walked out of the door and locked up shop. Something felt off. My vision blurred as I stormed after her, what the hell was going on? Could ghosts have strokes?

She had made her way across the street and around the corner building when I realized who was following her. It was them. Slapping myself back into focus, I ran after them. If blood still coursed through my body it would've been boiling by now.

They were my prey and I their hunter and if it took me until Hell froze over, I will get the revenge that is deserved.

I didn't have to think to hard about where they were before I just appeared there. The retched stench of booze scented the air as the one who pulled the trigger on me, now pointed his finger at the back of her head, motioning to do the same.

Flashes of that night came back like a battering ram slamming them into my head. My hands started to shake as I crashed down on the dumpster, sending the wheeled menace sailing down the alleyway towards them, clipping one the tall lanky male hard in the back. The howl of pain that erupted from his lips did little to distract me. I was far from done though. They couldn't see me, but I couldn't resist the urge to send broken bottles flying towards the two remaining males. It was time to have some fun.

Bottle after bottle, they crashed and shattered against their faces shattering into millions of brown and green pieces, sending them running for cover. As the last bottle flew, I turned to see dumpster guy finally got to his feet; I sent him the same gift and coupled it with a hub cap to sheer off the grimy Yankees hat right off his head.

Looking back down the city street, I couldn't find her and my hope was that I saved her from what these three had planned, if only for tonight. But it wasn't all bad news, as I felt a renewed sense of power sear through me, like electric energy renewed every synapsis throughout the ghostly form. Now if I could only get Alyssa to see me again, then I'll admit that it was a decent day.

Chapter 5

Frustration rode me hard every time I tried to make her hear me or see me. But it was useless. At least while she was awake. I found her dreams to be a little more conducive to talk to her. Each night I curl up next to her as she drifts asleep and during the moment when your mind slips past waking into deep sleep, that's where I come to her.

The first few times she broke down and cried, especially once I told her why I was here. Every night I met her in the same clearing we used to visit when we were camping in the White Mountains.

Dark Light

The soft amber flecks from the fire's light glisten against her ivory skin as she curled into my arms to keep warm. We'd talk for hours, well more like what felt like hours since dreams have no definition of time as we plan out our life together. I lean down to inhale her sweet jasmine scent and realize every time that it *was* just a dream and I seem to have no sense of smell.

Every time I hold her close, it feels like the first time and that nervous twist in my gut seems to churn until she places her hand over mine and whispers my name. The lithe way she says it makes the aching in my um, manly parts start to twitch. I can't even think about reality when we are here like this. If I couldn't be with her in the flesh, then her dreams would have to do. It's a bitter pill to swallow, but it's better then nothing.

I never thought of myself as an envious person, it seemed like such a wasted emotion, but now I would give anything to trade places with some poor sap for just an hour. Just to feel her body pressed against mine, as I stroke her cheek and kiss her gently. But it wasn't to remain as each new dawn broke up our imperfect happiness.
It had been a few weeks since I last saw those males follow her home, and I had hoped that they wouldn't return. Each day I stayed with her as she made her way to work, and watched her as she served fresh muffins and scones to her customers. Even covered in powered sugar and coffee stains, she was still the most beautiful woman I had ever seen.

Every day she got up and went about her daily routine numbly, far from the Alyssa I held and kissed each night. I tried to warn her of the dangers that lurked in the shadows, but she dismissed it once her beautiful pale blue eyes popped open in the morning, searching in vain for me. Going about her routine with the same rogue awareness, there was just no life in her eyes. Her smiles were heartbreaking, the way danced across her face and light up any room. But there weren't any more smiles for the world to see. She combed through her long autumn hair, and tied in up in a sloppy bun and carelessly threw on a pair of her dark jeans a tee shirt with the Bakery's logo in it.

My heart ached watching her doing this, missing the smell of cinnamon and sugar on her clothes at the end of the day, and flour in the sweet crevasse of her breasts from making her treats from scratch. There wasn't a day since opening the bakery that Alyssa didn't smile. Not until that day.

Shaking my head at what has become of her; I can't help but feel the weight of regret all over again. She didn't bother to make the bed or fuss in the mirror to put on make-up. She walked numbly down the hallway into the kitchen, careful to not look at the pictures hung on the walls and perched on the side table of better times.

The heaviness in the air thickened at she stared at the calendar on the fridge. Hot tears pricked her eyes as I followed her gaze to see what she was looking at. You know when they say "In moments of shock, everything seems to move in slow motion", they weren't kidding.

It had been four months to the day since that night. Four months since I palmed the small velvet box, with knots in my stomach as I paced the room trying out my proposal to my reflection in the hallway mirror. It seemed like a lifetime ago.

I followed behind her as she walked towards the hallway closet. Her hands shook as she reached for the doorknob. She looked like an angel as she lowered her head and inhaled deeply. Whatever she was afraid to see behind the door had caused pricks of tears to trickle down her cheeks. It felt like an eternity until she opened the door.

I couldn't see anything out of ordinary as I peered over her shoulder. Slowly she crouched down; I could see the flush of her cheeks pink up as she held her breath. Pulling free a white plastic bag, sudden realization hit me like a tons of bricks. "Damn you! Why did you leave me here like this? I miss you so much Jas…" tears streamed down her skin as she pulled free the blood soaked clothes I was last in. The dried-on brown stains of my blood covered nearly every inch of cloth. My stomach roiled as I gazed down at her curling into my shirt.

All I wanted to do was rip it free from her grasp and burn the damn thing. Wrap my arms around her and kiss away her tears until all her fears disappeared. Acid covered my throat thickly as I bit back a growl. Vengeance kicked my nuts with renewed vigor as I watched her clutch the last reminisce of me close to her chest.

She tried to stand, bringing my clothes up with her, only to stumble back into the closet on the way up. *Thump!* The soft bounce of a small black velvet box falling from my pants pocket echoed in the tiny room. Her watery gaze scoured to find the source of the sound, blinking back tears as she bent over, searching with her free hand.

"Oh shit, the ring!" My heart flipped and lightening shot through my veins like electric currents as I watched her expression turn from despair to shock.

Peeling back the lid, the sound her of gasp mimicked the pounding from her chest. My clothes littered the floor as her hand covered the perfect "O" of her lips. Staring at the glittering diamond even in low light, the radiant sparkle dazzled with a spectrum of a rainbow. Her favorite emerald cut with baguettes traipsing down the sides tucked in platinum gold.

It should've already graced her dainty fingers, but fate decided otherwise. I wrapped my fingers around her hand, and knelt down on one knee. I knew it wasn't fair to ask her to love me forever, Hell it's not like she knew I was there anyways. But I did just that.

"Alyssa, my love I'm sorry I didn't ask you this sooner. But time is all I have now, even though it's too late for us. I promise to love you for all eternity. I'll give you my heart and soul to keep if you would do me the extraordinary honor of becoming my wife."

"Yes!" she whispered. "I'll marry you." Her eyes lit up with that same devotion and love she had always shone me. Still in disbelief, had she heard me ask her? Was it even possible? I wanted so badly to slip the ring on her finger and kiss her senselessly. Biting back a curse I watched in awe as she slide it onto her finger. It looked exquisite, like it was meant solely for her, designed by heaven just for her.

"I would walk to the ends of the Earth just to be with you again Jas. I love you."

Chapter 6

As the day passed I watched my angel with her tennis match of emotions, struggling to go five minutes between happiness and on the verge of tears. When Cara, her employee asked about the ring, Alyssa quickly tucked her hand close to her chest and blushed, admitting the truth of her find.

It only took moments for the tears to flow before she angrily wiped them away. Sucking in a deep breath, Alyssa did what knew best to do. Bottling up her emotions and storing them for a private breakdown after hours. As the day waned and the final few customers left, Alyssa let Cara off early to be alone, the quiet seemed to comfort her where as I couldn't.

Guilt assailed me, washing over my like a tsunami before the tingling in my head turned to a jackhammer on steel. She meandered through the storefront, making sure everything was clean and just right, when I caught sight of shadows lurking across the street.

Clicking off the lights and locking the door, Alyssa stepped out into the night, with a cool wind catching her hair in its loving caress lifting her auburn tendrils towards the sky. I followed her and waiting for her predators to stalk her as the pounding in my head had become a warning beacon of their proximity. I always figured when you were dead, you just didn't feel anything. Man, I'm so dead wrong!

My anger boiled in me as I glared at the first of the three males step out from the alleyway. The stink of their putrid intentions littered the air. "Run Alyssa!" I screamed with every ounce of my being. She must've heard me or realized something was off because as she glanced behind her, her pale blue eyes lit up in fear and she took off before a second warning could be issued.

"That's my girl!" She didn't disappoint that much was true. Her instincts were spot on, now if only I had listened to her that fateful night. I wouldn't be stalking her predators in my ghostly form like some pathetic excuse for a poltergeist.

My heart kicked up a notch when I saw the last two males launch out of the blackened alleyway in pursuit of her. Snarls were fresh on their greasy lips as they laughed with malicious depravity. It didn't take a psychic to see what they were planning. I guessed it had been too much to ask for with the beer bottle assault a few weeks earlier that they would stay away. Tonight they were out for blood. Her blood and I'd damn my own soul if I let them succeed. I could hear her heart thundering in her chest as she kicked off the pavement in a dead run. Her breath sawed in and out of her lungs as she braved a glance behind her. I tried to fuel up enough energy to toss another dumpster in the way of the males, but I wasn't fast enough this time.

Crashing hubcaps and metal lids across the brick walls to distract wasn't working either. She barely made it two full blocks when the first male crashed into her, sending them both to the ground in a victorious grunt. The glint in his devious eyes ignited my fury, as I watched her fight him off, kicking and punching with everything she had. I sent whatever I could flying after him, shattering more bottles against his back, until I saw that Alyssa had been cut in the aftermath. Small scratches of blood seeped from shallow wounds on her face and neck as she struggled for freedom.

"Shit!" He had her pinned when the other two males finally showed up minutes later. Panting and out of breath, but cheering for their catch nonetheless.

"Get her inside," The Male-in-charge ordered. "In here, it's empty. No one will disturb us this time. Right my pet?" he sneered, licking his lips.

I lunged for him as Alyssa hawked a wad of spit in his face. I barely made a stir as I passed through him, cursing as my lack of connection. Tears pricked at her glistening eyes, but she refused to shed a single one when the males grabbed and pulled her callously into the dark empty building.

"Fucking pathetic sacks of shit! You think you'll get away with this? I survived you once before. You won't break me now." Her chortled laugh echoed into the vacant space where only moonbeams cut through dingy windows.

"Now, now my pet. Don't think we'll be that kind again," He crooked smirk curled as he eyed her up and down. "No this time you'll get the full treatment."

Elbowing his friend, fear settled into my stomach when I saw the dull sheen of a bowie knife shoved in waistband of his jeans.

Frantically I searched around the room for anything to hurl at them. Aside from dust and piss covered blankets, nothing was left inside. "God damn it! You can't let her die! What the fuck!" Desperation ruled my every dead breath as I threw useless punches at the scum molesting her.

"Why her! Answer me....why Alyssa?" I didn't really expect to hear an answer; I mean I hadn't believed in ghosts until I became one, so why would God or anyone else answer me?

"She is meant to serve a higher purpose." The whisper of a voice called out. Searching for the source, it only took a moment to see a tall, lean male with wings extending out behind him standing across the room. The look of concern etched across his bronze skin.

"Why her, tell me!" I demanded. Pounding my silent footsteps towards him, his blonde hair perfectly hung down his shoulders like he was the Master mold of male models. "I won't let her die!" the growl that rattled through my chest seemed to vibrate off the concrete walls.

His brows dipped low over freakishly yellow eyes, challenging me with that stare. "Then go and save her if you can."

I turned only to see the glint of a silver blade slice across the strained indent of her dainty throat. "NO!" I lunged for the males, something deep inside me pulled out a savage vengeance as I pulled the blade free from her attacker and slammed it down through his back, piercing his lung. It didn't take me a second to yank it free and launch after the two males pinning her arms to the grimy floor.

Maybe I couldn't destroy these males by my own brand of torture, but I sure as crap on a cracker wasn't about to let them live for what they had done to my sweet Alyssa. I sliced the lanky one first, gifting him with a permanent ear-to-ear grin. Crimson rivulets flowed effortless from the wound as he cupped it in sheer panic. The second male watched in abject horror as he tried to back away cautiously looking for the shadow that stalked them now. He swung at the air, and had I been mortal I suppose he might have come close to hitting me.

With a fierce growl I unleashed all I had inside of me, my fury and rage that boiled deep within my heart and I stabbed him in the chest. The sharp hiss of air escaping from the wound wasn't enough to appease my anger. I struck him again and again, as blood sprayed into the cool night air. He struggled to get away, losing that battle quickly with every ounce of blood that flowed freely to the floor. But he wasn't who I really wanted to take my revenge out on. No. I wanted their leader, fucktard number one who I stabbed in the back first.

His useless moan as he tried to climb to his feet made the hairs on the back of my neck stand up in excitement as I turned to stalked him once again. The cool blade settled comfortably in the palm of my transparent hand. I could feel the curl of my lips peeling back the closer I stepped to him. The sad strangled cries from Alyssa's lips pulled my gaze to her deathly form as she reached out for me.

She mouthed my name, covered in blood with a trickle of tear running down the side her head. The aching in my heart pounded as I faced off with him, the reason she was lying on a dirty nasty floor dying. I wanted to save her, would give up my soul to, but nothing I did could. Instead I turned my sights back on him, scared as hell as I focused all my energy to become visible.

"Ho—ly H-e-ll!" he struggled to say between raspy airy breaths. His eyes grew large as I raised the knife over my head and crouched down low, taunting him with future. "Y-ou-r d-ead" He mouthed.

"You're right. I am." I didn't hesitate, slamming my fist full of blade down into his heart over and over again. The rage inside grew psychotic as I plunged the knife into him again and again. If this is what justice felt like, then I didn't want to be wrong.

I would've sliced and diced more if it hadn't been for the sound of her gurgled sputtering coughs. I spun around quickly to see her pulling herself in her final moments towards me. Dropping the knife, I hurried to her side, kneeling to the floor as I smoothed the back of my hand over her bruised cheek. "I love you so much, Alyssa. Please hand on baby. Don't die on me. Not now. It's not your time."

Her lips moved to say my name, but no words would speckle the air in her lithe voice. Tears flooded my eyes as I stared down into the stilling blue pools of hers.

"I told you, she has a role to play, this..." motion around the blood soaked room, the Angel peered back down to me. "...was meant to happen earlier. You weren't meant to die in the tunnel that night. She was. You just delayed the inevitable."

"What the hell do you mean?" I snapped. Surely he couldn't be saying what I thought he was saying. Alyssa...was she meant to die? No fucking way. She had too big of a heart, she was loved by so many. It's not her time. This wasn't the place. "Dammit! She can't die!"

"I do believe she's about to pass as we speak." I followed his eyes back down to her sweet face. Her eyes, even dulling from life saw me. I curled my arms around her body, pulling her into my chest.

"I'll let you two have a moment. Oh and your welcome."

"What? Welcome for what?"

"She can see you and feel you now." His smirk was just so damned arrogant as he turned to walk away. But I couldn't help to notice that I was in fact holding her close. I could smell the metallic scent of blood mixed with her natural sugary sweetness. I could feel the warmth of her blood as it cooled on my skin.

"Alyssa, please stay with here. Don't die." I begged her, for what little good did. The tears in her eyes dried up and she reached for me, cupping my cheek. I couldn't help but notice the deep shadows under her eyes as she leaned in and pressed her lips to mine. It had felt like centuries had passed since I felt warmth of her kiss. Yet here was lay, dying in my arms. Not fucking fair.

Her lips fell away a moment later as her head lolled back. The last of her escaping breath vanished from her body. It had happened, she died. Not old in the comfort of her bed, no. Here in this shithole building by the hands of a sadistic street-rat. My life and death had ended the moment she passed. I had no reason to exist anymore. Everything that I had loved had just vanished from this world, all that I was, now was gone. Closing my eyes to this new reality I couldn't bare the idea of leaving her body alone to rot. I found her cell scattered on the floor and attempted to text Cara.

I was pretty damned amazed to find out that working electronics when you're dead is a cinch with a strategic mind trick. Punching in the location of Alyssa's body, I hoped at least she could have a proper burial surrounded by all those who've loved her.

My heart that once beat solely for her, now shattered into a million pieces as I held her in my arms.

Chapter 7

As expected, Cara saw her lifeless body and called the police. It didn't take long to for the final decision of homicide, though the detectives were a bit stumped as to the deaths of the three attackers. Oh well, not my problem. Alyssa's sister had swiftly arranged the funeral. I knew it was ridiculous to attend, but I wasn't ready to say good-bye. I hadn't seen that golden Angel since the night Alyssa died, but something tells me it wasn't the last time I would see him.

The air felt crisper than normal, as I watched everyone huddle down into their pea coats and jackets. The pastor went on and on about the life that had been lost and loved very much. I wanted so badly to scream at the top of my lungs and say, "It's a fucking travesty! She wasn't ready to die." Still he yammered on and said his vocal praise to the old mighty one above.

Barking out a laugh, I guess it's a good thing mortals can't hear ghosts. As I looked out over the rest of the cemetery something odd stood out against the grey headstones and colorless sky. Coppery auburn tendrils dancing carefree in the cold breeze like a halo of dark fire inviting me to follow. "What the?" Using my nifty mind travel trick, I came up close and very personal in a blink of an eye.

Dark Light

Sucking back a gasp, I couldn't fathom what I was
seeing! She was resplendent in flowing white gauze gown,
like a Greek princess. "Alyssa." I whispered, afraid if I
spoke to loudly that everyone would turn around and mob
her. "How can it…." I couldn't believe what I was seeing,
her here in the flesh. "be I was there, when you….died."
Her beautiful smile fell when she stared into my eyes.
"But how? I saw you, when they…I held you…God I'm so
confused." Her lithe voice hitched as she cupped my cheek.
Tears trickled from her piercing blue eyes, vibrant and
intoxicating. I was completely mesmerized by her gaze,
trapped like a dumb animal in a cage.

"Shhh-Shhh, its ok I'm here now. I'm not going to
let anything happen to you." Thumbing away her tears, the
sparkle that I had thought dead renewed to life as she stared
lovingly into my eyes. "I thought I had lost you."

"I prayed that I would find you in heaven, I couldn't
bare living when you weren't! Oh Jason, I died the day they
took you from me. Nothing made sense anymore. I—I
couldn't.."

"It's ok, everything will be ok. Well I mean, just
because we're living impaired doesn't mean we can't still
have fun." Tossing her a wink, her smile lit up once again
just in time for me to lay a kiss down on those luscious
pink jewels. "God, I've missed you so damn much. I've
slept next to you for months and you had no idea I was
even there."

"So you're the reason I always felt a cold draft
going up my shirt." Cocking a copper brow at me, she had
me busted.

"Can you blame a guy? I mean it was just a little feeling..." a slow burning growl erupted from my chest as I pulled her closer. "I'd like to continue that feeling, if it's alright with you?"

"Ah hem, as much as a dead porno would be so enthralling, I'd prefer it just the same if you two would wait until I leave." The yellow gaze of the Angel pegged me hard in his stare. Fricking irritating.

"What the hell do you want?" I probably didn't have the right to go all 'I am man protecting my woman so step the hell off bitch' but I wasn't taking any chances either.

"I told you, she...has a purpose, notice the nice set of feathers sprouting from her back?" my eyes zeroed in to find what he was suggesting. And sure as shit, wings were emerging from her shoulder blades. She didn't even flinch as they grew freely, expanding in front of me like it was second nature. "You on the other hand, don't' fit our normal molds. So what to do with you now?"

"You won't take her away from me again. You can just go fuck yourself if you plan on trying." Damn I sounded like I had a set of steel balls. Popping out my chest, her dainty hand came to rest lightly, easing my stress without a second thought.

Arching a perfectly golden man-groomed brow, his smirk widen as he saw the effect Alyssa had on me. "See, I told you she has a purpose. She's simply amazing."

"Back off asshole." The snarl in my threat didn't stop there as images of ripping his perfect head off from his perfect body and shoving it straight up his I presume perfect anal orbit had that same sadistic appeal to it as had killing our murderers.

"Easy Jas....He's of no concern to you and I. Jas...Jason...look at me." She grabbed my face between the warmth of her palms and held my gaze. "I love you. I will always love you. Here, now in this place, wherever this place may be, we can be together, forever."

God, she always had that way with me, no one could press the chill button and calm me right the hell down like she could. The soft gentle love in her eyes swirled with desire as she stroked the line of my jaw tenderly.

"I have a job for you, that is, if you can brake away from *our* Angel for a few hours." I didn't care for the way he said "Ours" like she was public property or something. In fact it grated on my nerves and I secretly promised to punch him the hell out the first chance I got.

"She is not 'Ours', she is mine. Got that, and what kind of job are you talking about?"

"Well since you're not Angel material, and you've seem to acquire some interesting skills, the Boss thinks you might come in handy. We need someone of your special talents to handle delivering a message from time to time. Today being one of those times. I promise you'll be back soon and then you can do whatever it is that you humans do."

"Jas, what is he talking about?" her eyes searched mine for answers, but shame shadowed anything I had to offer as an answer.

"I did some things, when you were alive babe. I-I killed those bastards that murdered us! I had too."

"What? How? I don't understand. Jason, how could you? You're a ghost?"

"Don't remind me. I don't know, somehow I manage to summon up some kind of crazy energy and figured out how to move things."

Her eyes fell as I continued on explaining in detail about the weeks leading up to her death. Sadness and confusion danced across her face as she listened with silent resolve to understand. "And that's pretty much it. So here we are, and now.." turning back to face our golden boy, I pegged him hard with a questioning glare. "you want me to and I quote 'deliver a message'? to whom?"

"I'll give you all the details on the way."

"Well if it's so important then why can't you deliver the message?" throwing up the air quotations just to be an ass, I'm so going to have fun pissing him off for all eternity.

"Because, jackass, I'm an Angel. We don't do brainless minion work. That's for you useless primitive human types, like you." He shot back. Good so he can dish it too. This might be the beginning of a beautiful battle of the wills.

"Alright Captain obvious, then let's get the show on the road, or do you need to primp some more before he go? Powder your nose maybe?"

"Jason!" slapping my chest, the playful smile that I had missed so dearly had finally returned to her beautiful face.

"And you…." Pulling her close to me, I wasn't about to let her go, not yet. "I asked you once if you would marry me, and you replied yes. Is that your final answer or would you like to choice the fifty-fifty?"

"Oh my god, you really did ask me! I thought I was just hearing things. Yes! Yes, I want to marry you!" Her lips found mind before I could reply some witty wisecrack. Crushing down into the delicious feel of her kiss as I sink lower into her sweet mouth, ah death is good. I got the woman, and now a killer career, what more could I ask for?

Dark Light

Dark Fairy Reflection
by
S.J. Thomas

22nd April

Dear Miss Cooke

It is with deepest regret that I must inform you of the death of your Aunt Miss Pamela Shale.

She died on April 6th and as her sole surviving heir her estate is left to you.

I would be grateful if you would contact me at your earliest convenience to discuss the terms of the will and to undertake the necessary arrangements.

I remain yours respectfully.

P.R. Wynstrong

Wynstrong, Herbert and Smith Lawyers

Poor Aunt Shale.

She was my Aunt on my mother's side and though she was my only family I hadn't seen her in years. I tried to muster the appropriate degree of sadness but it was hard to elicit strong emotions over someone I barely knew.

Harder still was not feeling a measure of excitement over what I might have inherited. As a struggling artist, money is not something I see a lot of, and so the prospect of some ready cash was appealing to say the least.

I phoned the lawyer and fixed an appointment for two days time. No point in delaying.

24th April

My Aunt had lived out in the country in a small village called Yelton so I had to hire a car to get there. Boy was it worth it.

Not only had I been left a tidy sum, I was also now the owner of a bone fide historic country cottage that my Aunt's lawyer Mr. Wynstrong informed me was over one hundred years old.

Mr. Wynstrong was all impartial politeness and cold efficiency, striking the required balance between commiseration and congratulation. The only thing that struck me as odd was his reaction when I asked how my Aunt had died.

He seemed reluctant to talk about the cause of death but eventually admitted that her heart had given out on her. Not so surprising for a woman in her late seventy's but there was something odd about his manner and expression.

He was even more reluctant to admit that my Aunt had died in the cottage. As if that would disturb me, but it didn't, not really. Let's face it, how many houses that old wouldn't have seen some death over the years?

Knowing I wasn't going to get any more out of him I let it drop but decided I would see what I could find out after I moved in. I left with a set of keys and a bundle of paperwork.

28th April

First sight of my new house. A picture perfect country cottage complete with low stone wall and picket gate surrounding a rambling garden just starting to run riot with new growth.

I parked up and walked down the path, not quite believing all this was now mine. A heavy oak front door with rusty hinges, which I had to shove to open, greeted me. The door opened with a creak and sunlight flooded the hall, catching the dust motes dancing in the air.

The cottage had a traditional two up, two down layout with the hall running down the middle. As I glanced around the living room and kitchen, I saw piles of books, old pictures and ornaments. A lifetime expressed in a seemingly random collection of objects and images.

Sadly I could also see that my Aunt had not been able to take care of the place. Dust lay heavy on the furniture and the walls were scuffed and faded with heavy cobwebs collecting in the corners.

What caught my eye the most though was a large antique mirror hanging at the end of the hall. The frame was carved oak and the glass was broken, a large crack running down the middle. The carvings were beautifully ornate; trees, leaves and vines and for a few minutes I stared at it fascinated.

As I looked I also began to make out the barest hint of faces and bodies, lithe sensuous figures dancing through the trees and vines. The more I looked the more images I could see and I decided that I would get the glass fixed.

1st May

Lots of sorting and dusting had unearthed some unusual and disturbing things about my Aunt.

She'd apparently had an interest in folklore and fairy tales and had collected many books on the subject. Sadly towards the end she had also become delusional.

In her bedroom I found her journal and a pile of particularly antique looking books on fairies and mythical creatures. Books so old they were bound in leather, the archaic language hard to understand, and the print so faded I could barely make out the words.

One book in particularly drew me. It looked far older than the other books but despite its obvious age it was shocking in its graphic illustrations. Illustrations of strange fairy like creatures engaged in orgies, killings and bloody rituals. Males and females writhing together in wild abandon. Brutal battles where the losers were torn to pieces by animals. Sickening sacrifices of children, their hearts cut out of their chests while they screamed.

Horrific images of dark creatures that bore no resemblance to the tales of fairies I grew up with as a child.

My Aunt seemed to have become obsessed with the stories though because her journal was full of references to these dark fairies. She wrote about noises and whispers in the night, vivid dreams, and reflections in the mirror.

The more I read the more sinister her delusions seemed to have become. To the point where she believed something, or someone, was after her.

2nd May

After I found the journal I went into the village to ask if anyone had noticed my Aunt's behavior, and if so, why they hadn't helped her or called social services.

The village shopkeeper was reluctant to talk but I kept on and eventually she caved. She confirmed that a few weeks before she died my Aunt had become reclusive, never leaving the cottage, and reacting violently to anyone who tried to help.

I asked her if she knew what had happened when my Aunt died and after much hesitation she admitted that it was quite a few days before her body was found.

Found in front of the mirror at the end of the hall. The mirror I had just had repaired.

She could not offer any more details and I returned home, feeling an unexpected sense of relief when I saw the cottage.

As I opened the door and stepped into the hall, the mirror caught my reflection, and for a second it looked like someone was standing right beside me. I couldn't see any features but I got an impression of someone tall and dark.

I jumped, spinning round, but of course there was no one there and when I looked back there was just my reflection in the mirror, my eyes big and wide, and my skin pale. I looked into the living room and kitchen but was alone.

I shut the door and put down my bags then stepped up to the mirror, my hand reaching out to touch the glass. My gaze moved to the frame, the carved figures somehow seeming more distinct. As if they were choosing to show themselves.

"Don't be so silly Abbey" I muttered under my breath. As I stepped away I felt foolish for letting my imagination run wild.

Clearly my Aunt's journal was getting to me.

3rd May

Last night when I was lying in bed I swore I heard noises in the house. Like footsteps moving along the hall, pacing. With my heart beating a wild rhythm in my chest I made myself get up and check, but there was no one there and the doors and windows were all securely locked.

I went back to bed but lay awake for ages, my heart still racing, a cold chill running up my spine, but eventually tiredness won and I fell asleep.
And dreamed.

In my dream I woke up, aware of someone in the room standing over me. For some reason I couldn't see the person clearly but I got the same impression I had when I saw, or thought I saw, the reflection in the mirror. A male.

Tall and dark. Looking down at me with a frightening intensity.

I bolted up, meaning to scramble away, but something made me stop. His voice maybe; like a command ringing in my mind.

I looked up at him, fear and anxiety knotting my stomach, and he slowly leant towards me. Helpless I fell back against the bed while he came ever closer, unsure what would happen, unsure what I wanted to happen.

He stopped just inches from me and I felt the pull of his eyes. Silver, swirling. Like pools of liquid I could drown in.

He paused for the briefest moment, a second or a lifetime I couldn't tell you, and then pressed his lips to mine. The barest softest brush of his skin against my lips and my whole body ignited in a blazing fire. I shuddered and gasped, waking from the dream as the most intense orgasm of my life ripped through me.

My body throbbed, my blood roaring in my veins, and I moaned with abandon as my body locked in an undeniable climax. A climax that left me quivering and breathless against the pillows, spent.

As I lay there stunned I knew I should run, should get out of the house, but exhaustion took me and I did not wake till the sun was piercing though the window.

6th May

I am so scared. I think my Aunt was right. Someone is here and he wants me like he wanted her.

Since the day I came back from the village, since the night I had the dream, I keep seeing him in the mirror. Nothing more than a reflection out of the corner of my eye but every time I see more of him.

I know he has black shoulder length hair and pale skin. I know his body is strong and muscled. A scar runs across his cheek and there is a tattoo of a tree on his shoulder.

I don't know who he is but every time I see him his expression becomes more and more consuming. Like he wants to devour me.

I sit in the living room, reading through my Aunt's journal and books, and what I am seeing ties up with what she wrote about. Slowly I decipher references to dark realms and the beings that inhabit them. Dark fairies that need living souls to survive, who crave and desire mortals. Creatures not of our world but who can come through to ours via pools, ancient sites ... and mirrors made of the heart wood of the earth.

Like the mirror in the hall.

The mirror my Aunt died in front of. The mirror that was broken as if something, or someone, had tried to come through.

I look up at the mirror through the doorway and again I see him. The barest flash of his image but he is staring straight at me, his hands pressed against the glass. Terror grips me and I run for the front door but as I reach for the handle a suffocating panic takes hold of me. A panic so strong I can barely breathe. Gasping I drop to the floor. I turn around, looking straight at the mirror, but I see nothing. Forcing my breathing to slow I turn my head to the side and relax my gaze. After a few seconds he appears again, his image growing larger as if he is walking towards the glass. Again he presses his hands to the mirror; again his gaze is locked on me.

Slowly I stand and move down the hall, my back pressed to the wall. He follows my movement until I stop in the doorway to the living room, my hands gripping the frame so hard my knuckles turn white.

Still I see him in the mirror, a hungry desperation in his expression, and I suddenly understand. The mirror is a doorway. And this man wants to come through. This dark creature that came for my Aunt and is now here for me.

Suddenly his image bends, as if the glass has flexed under the pressure of his hands. A scream builds in my throat as I run for the stairs, not daring to look back.

15th May

I cannot leave. I am scared but I cannot leave. I hear footsteps and whispers at night. I see him in the mirror, always watching me. At night I dream. A heavy feeling of dread wraps itself around me like a blanket and I know something dark and terrible is coming for me but I am held here.

At first I was held by fear; a paralyzing panic bringing me to the floor whenever I tried to leave the cottage. Now though I am held by something else; an inexplicable compulsion to see him again.

For days I have poured over the books. For days I have walked back and forth in front of the mirror desperate to see him.

I cannot leave. Like my Aunt before me I am trapped.

19ᵗʰ May

I know who he is now.

Nazeil, king of the dark fairies, a fearsome warrior who took over the fairy realm with blood and fire. A being that chooses mortal women, taking them to his world for his dark pleasures, feeding on their souls to enhance his powers. A being who delivers desire and death in the same breath.

He chose my Aunt but she was too weak to survive and now he wants me. I see him closer every day and god help me I crave him.

I remember how the mere touch of his lips in my dreams makes my body erupt in reality and I want more. He is hard and cruel, without mercy or compassion, but the feel of his gaze on my body sends liquid heat through my veins.

Lust and damnation blaze in his silver eyes and I want to taste it, want to lose myself in him. Want his strong hands on my body; want him inside me, consuming me, possessing me.

And I know from his dark gaze that he wants me too.

I know I don't have much time left now. Every day the glass bends a little more and soon he will break through. And I won't want to run from him.

He will come for me and take me heart, body and soul and I will be forever his. Trapped in the mirror.

Dark Light

Yelton Gazette – Saturday 12th June

Police forced entry into Lavender Cottage on Wednesday 9th June after reports that Miss Abigail Cooke, the young woman who had recently moved in, had not been seen for some days. Miss Cooke was not found in the house and police were not able to find any trace of her or any leads as to her whereabouts. An officer on the scene reports that they found an unusual collection of old books on folk law, together with a journal belonging to Miss Cooke's deceased Aunt, Miss Pamela Shale. The journal seems to confirm local rumors that Miss Shale had suffered some sort of mental episode prior to her death. Apart from the books the only other unusual thing officers found was a broken mirror hanging at the end of the hall, the glass completely smashed.

Dark Light

Spider Whisperer
by
Lisa Goldman

"Jeesh!" I groaned, swatting another spider from crawling on my leg. "How do you people live like this?" I stopped walking, searching the ground for more of the devils as Melanie, my sister, drudged onward through the overgrown path of knee high weeds and thick bramble. A backpack filled with garbage bags and cleaning supplies was slung to her back.

"You used to be one of these people." Melanie slowed her swift pace and glanced over her shoulder. She sighed. "So what was it this time? An ant?"

"Ha, ha." She knew I hated spiders, bugs, anything that resembled the blood-sucking, pinching, crawly, hairy, winged, multiple-legged insects of the world. I couldn't escape them in their entirety, but it was the main reason I left this trivial country life as soon as I graduated high school—hoping never to come back—for a high rise in the city where fewer chances for the little critters existed.

Melanie tilted her head, her way of telling me she waited for a reasonable explanation. "I know what you're thinking, but this one was huge. A spider. You didn't see it, and they seem to keep getting bigger."

She made her way back the overgrown path and gave me a stern look. She wanted proof of this gargantuan spider. I pointed to the wiggling legged creature that fell next to my pumps. She bent down, hand extending. I gasped. "You're not going to touch it, are you?"

Not only did she touch it, but she picked it up and balanced it on her thumb inches from my face. "This little guy. He can't be any bigger than that ant I mentioned."

"That's because his legs are all curled up now. You should have seen him pawing up my pant leg."

She gave me a wry look, glancing up and down at my improper outfit. After two days of relentless arguing, she had talked me into coming with her to sort and clean Dad's old shed. Although she offered to loan me a pair of jean overalls, like the pair she wore now, I refused. Disgust had filled my mind at the image of me in such an unflattering, repulsive outfit. Of course, since she remained in this drab one traffic light farmer's town, the clothing looked just fine for someone like her. I never told her of my adamant dislike for her clothes and instead rejected them politely, saying, "I'm sure I can find something in my suitcase to wear." My options, however, were limited. But I put on the most casual outfit I brought, pair of sleek black pants, a periwinkle-colored, silk, tunic top, and my favorite black pumps. Unfortunately or purposely—I couldn't be sure which—she neglected to mention the despair and hazards of the trail and the shed where I would ultimately be working in over the next few hours.

Glancing at our destination and back again, I nervously pulled at the ends of my shirt. I debated on offering her money to get out from venturing further across this wild landscape.

She must have seen the skeptical look in my eyes because she puffed out a sharp breath, making her long ash blonde bangs sway. Then she flicked the spider off her thumb, grabbed my elbow, and said, "Come on. You're not backing out on me now. We're almost there."

I yanked my arm away. "I'm reconsidering. You know I'm not cut out for this kind of work. Can't we just hire someone to haul the junk away that's in the shed and bulldoze the rest of it?"

She chuckled with uncertainty, but her eyes were scornful in half shut slits. "Honestly Mia, you've put this off for two years. You rarely call home. You never visit. If Brant hadn't been in that unfortunate—but thankfully nonlife threatening—car accident, I doubt we would have seen you for another two years."

Brant, I mentally spat. He and Melanie had been married for a little over three years and if she hadn't called me with terror mixed with sobs, I wouldn't have set foot in Hillsdale. Generally, I liked Brant. He made my sister laugh and I could see the enduring love between them, but at this moment, surrounded by the untamed wilderness, a tiny part of me held a grudge against him for bringing me back to this awful place. I plastered on a smile and said truthfully, "I'm glad Brant will make a full recovery." She nodded with a worn, tired grimace that I had seen her wearing too often since I arrived in town.

As if another thought crossed her mind, she gestured over her shoulder down the path that we were heading on. "We need to go through Dad's things. There might be something important."

I eyed the dilapidated shed. It was surrounded by oak, maple, and popular trees, their leaves weaving a canopy of green while their limbs where knotting and twisting like oversized gnarled fingers. When I was seven, Dad had painted the shed an uplifting lemon yellow, but over the years, the cheerful color faded and chipped, leaving four walls of mostly gray weathered, warped wood. The only notable color was the shiny green ivy that crept along the right side, spread across the double doors, and completely covered the metal handles.

A grasshopper leaped from the corner of my eye. I shivered as a new thought crossed my mind. *What if the ivy or some other dark shadowy area were the home—the nest—for those creepy crawling creatures? There's bound to be more of them.*

"Do I need to remind you," Melanie said, interrupting my observations, "that Brant and I are selling the house? It's too big of a property for us to maintain plus the upkeep of our own house. This may need a little work, but it's a good home." She paused as though remembering. When she continued, her tone was filled with sorrow. "Dad wanted you to come back and live in it."

"He never said that."

"He said it to me just before he died." Her words came out sternly and she sighed, trying to calm her voice. "He thought—we all thought—you'd come home." We've had this conversation a hundred times. There wasn't anything she could say to change my mind, but now that house was going up on the market soon, I felt as thought she needed to hear my decision again.

Softly, but persuasively, I said, "My home is in Manhattan. I don't belong here. I never have."

"You haven't given it a chance. You made up your mind when you were a very young and never looked back."

"Melanie, what do you want me to say?"

Her pale eyebrows knitted together. She held up her hand, stopping me from uttering another word. "Forget it. Let's just go see what's in that shed and then you can go on with you busy life in the big city, forgetting about Hillsdale, forgetting about Dad, your home, and about me."

"That's not true. I can't forget about you. You're my sister; my only sibling. I love you."

For a few long seconds, she stared at me with one raised doubtful eyebrow. Her lips pressed together making a thin line of pale pink.

I opened my mouth to protest to her hostility, but she tugged on both straps of the backpack, shifting it higher on her shoulders, then turned on her heels and marched down the overgrown path, forcing prickly branches and tall grass out of her way.

***

When I caught up to Melanie, she had the backpack unzipped at her feet and was squatting over it. Her hands rummaged swiftly and intently through its contents. I leaned forward slightly trying to get a better look at what she was looking for when without a glance or any other indications she whipped out a pair of gardening gloves, pea green with alternating blue and orange flowers. They sailed through the air toward me. I stumbled awkwardly trying to catch them without falling onto the most likely—*ewww*—insect infested ground. I snatched one between my ring and pinky fingers while the other plummeted down. I retrieved the second one, eyeful for any gruesome, little critters. Thankfully, I didn't see any and donned on the gloves.

By the time I readied myself for the next task, Melanie had zipped up the backpack and put on her own pair of gloves. She tossed the bag behind her, glowered at me, and then ripped into the ivy that covered the door.

Although the air was pleasantly warm for this mid-June morning, I could feel the coldness from that look. I knew the only way she would believe that I still loved her and that my choice in living in the city had nothing to do with her was to actively participate in this God-awful job. I took a deep breath, stepped forward, and torn at the ivy too. Once the ivy was gone which now looked like leafy green snakes circling around my feet, I turned the doorknob. It turned but something prohibited the door from opening. From the curvature of the gray worn wood, I suspected the elements of time shifted something. Under normal circumstances, I would have called the building maintenance supervisor. But this was far from normal. I was at a loss and looked to Melanie for help. "It won't budge."

Her lips pursed thoughtfully. "Let me give it a try." With her knee bent, she braced her foot in the middle of the wall to give her extra leverage as she pulled the doorknob. The top corner split open just enough that I could see briefly inside the shed, but the bottom stayed securely wedged.

Looking beyond Melanie's profile, I noticed a fallen tree branch, its scarce leaves withered and brown as though it had been detached from the tree for a while. I pointed toward it. "Do you think we could use that to wedge it in like a crowbar?"

Her eyes followed the path that I gestured to. She smiled. "Little sis', I think you might actually have a good idea there."

"I come up with them once in awhile," I muttered, a smirk of gratitude spreading across my face.

With knees high, she trampled the tall grass and retrieved the branch. Together we torn off small limbs and crumbled leaves until we were left with a crooked four-foot long branch.

While she yanked at the door in the same interesting position, I shoved our makeshift crowbar into the crack near the top. After a minute a pushing and pulling, I heard a thunderous sound and the door snapped open. My heels slipped in the intertwining vines, my arms flailing wildly through the air as I flopped through branches and weeds to the earth. Melanie stumbled as well, but with the handle still grasped tightly in her hand, she managed to stay upright.

Winded with wide eyes, she darted over to me. "Oh my gosh, Mia are you okay?"

I cursed then looked down and laughed incredulously. My beautiful silk shirt was ripped over my left shoulder, but other than a light graze over several spots going down the same arm, I seemed to be fine. "No worries."

At that precise moment, something tickled my foot. I glanced down and saw a stinkbug crawling over my skin. I flicked it off, screamed, and jumped to my feet. "This place is infested!"

"Don't be so melodramatic." Melanie picked a leave out of my hair. "They're just little bugs. I'm sure it's more scared of you than you are of it."

"I wouldn't be so sure about that," I muttered, self-consciously checking myself for any more of the repulsive bugs.

Melanie laughed at my grumpiness and turned her attention to the contents inside the shed. Standing on my tiptoes, I peered over her shoulder. Shovels, rakes, a jagged saw, pots in various shapes and sizes stacked haphazardly on a long shelf, and other gardening paraphernalia lined the far wall. On my right, a motorless reel lawn mower looked as though it beckoned for some TLC after a long thirty-year hibernation. Dust mites danced in the suns rays from the one tiny window along the same wall as well as coming from the unexpected hole in the ceiling that was roughly the size of my fist. Cheap plastic lawn chairs were tossed drunkenly in the middle of shed and to my left, carbon box after carbon box were stacked from floor to ceiling, forming a new kind of wall. All these things were covered by a thick layer of dust. And like a bad omen, large cobwebs seemed to be in every nook and cranny.

I grimaced. "When was the last time you've been in here?"

"I haven't." She cleared her throat as though it was suddenly dry. "At least not since Dad died."

Despite my fears, I didn't want to argue with
Melanie again and with a growing anxiety, I wanted to get
this over as soon as possible. I inhaled a sharp breath and
asked, "Okay where do we start?"

"I suggest we take out all of the chairs except for
two in case we want to sit and then disregard anything else
that isn't deemed necessary. That way we can go through
these boxes and see if Dad left us anything that you might
want to keep."

I highly doubt it, I thought miserably but plastered
on a fake smile.

Over then next hour, we searched, sorted, and
cleaned. We moved all the chairs but two outside. The
lawn mover came next. I tested it on the overgrown grass,
but it didn't even dent the wildness. We scanned the
gardening wall, tossing old seeds, worn rusted hand trowels
and shovels, and dull pruning shears into one of the many
garbage bags from the backpack. Melanie found a broom
in the back corner and stirred up so much dust I started
sneezing and had to leave until she finished.

By the time we were about to start on the boxes, I
was famished. Melanie hadn't suggested lunch, and I
decided not to interrupt our pace. *The sooner we finish, the
better,* I reminded myself.

She handed me the first box and went to retrieve
another for herself. "Do you want to take a break soon?"

I shrugged not that she could see me since her back
was still toward me. "I'm fine. I'd rather just get this
done."

"First, I can't get you to come into the shed, now I can't get you to leave. You know, it may take the rest of the day to finish going through all of this."

My reply came in the form of a nervous laugh as I set my box on the floor, the wooden boards groaning beneath it. I teetered on the edge of one of the plastic chairs and pulled the tape off the box. Melanie placed her box near mine and pulled her chair closer. I exchanged a look with her while my hand moved around the flaps of the box. Something small and thread-like tickled my wrist. The hair at the base of neck stood up on end. I looked down seeing nothing unusual. I pressed the boxes sides open when two black spiders the size of a half dollar with fat bodies and long legs crawled out. I screamed and sprang to my feet, the chair tumbling on the floor behind me with a thud.

Melanie jumped to her feet. "What is it?"

With one hand trembling and clamped over my mouth from shrieking louder, the other pointed at the box. I gulped and stuttered, "S-spid-der. Two spiders."

"Is this another one of your ant sized spiders?" Her voice was tinged in mockery.

Adrenaline kicked in, and I darted for a long handled shovel, holding it defensively over my shoulder. "No, these were bigger. This time you need to believe me." I shook the shovel. "But don't worry, I'm not giving in." My eyes darted back and forth searching for the critters.

One of them scampered across the floor and headed to the crevice under the shelf that held the gardening pots in the back of the room. I slammed the shovel down, narrowing missing the dreadful spider. It moved under the shelf before I reached it. I threw down the shovel and started taking the pots off the shelf.

"What are you doing?" Melanie asked.

"What does it look like? I'm moving the shelf."

"But it's probably long gone, having found another hole to crawl out of."

My eyes squinted into tiny frowning smiles. "If there's any chance its still in here..." My voice trailed off and I shivered, before continuing, "I can't work with those things in here! So you can either help me, or you can just stand there."

She rubbed her palms down the front of her overalls as though delaying but then joined me in my mission. "Spiders actually do good. They eat mosquitoes and beetles that damage flowers or vegetable plants."

"Don't care." I barely paused taking the pots off to glare at my sister.

When we each grabbed the last of the pots and set them aside, she picked up the shovel and I positioned myself to move the shelf. "You ready? You're not going to back down are you with all those thoughts in how great spiders are?"

"I didn't say they're great only that they..."

Her words were cut short when I slid the shelf away from the wall with a grinding noise and a long black leg slid out the front side of the shelf. The spider's body and remainder legs followed swiftly. I gasped. This wasn't the same half dollar sized spider I had seen moments ago. No, this spider was the size of a Chihuahua. Its legs looked like tent poles against a solid furry body. Fangs twitched as it glided toward my sister. Her face blanched, her muscles frozen in horrid. "Run!" I shrieked.

My single panicked word must have shook and cracked her icy shell because before the monstrous spider put one creepy leg on her, she lifted the shovel high, building momentum, and slammed it down. It bounced back up. She thrust it over her shoulder again. Her arms swung the shovel like a golf club and hit the spider on the side, sailing it into the back corner. It shook its head like shaking off a daze then rolled back on all eight legs readying itself to charge again. I exchanged a nervous look with Melanie.

"Now we run!" she said. She tossed the shovel with a loud clang, grabbed my wrist, and yanked me toward the door.

Spiders with varying hues of black or browns in equally different sizes—yet none as large as the one we enraged—scurried from every crevice and shadow on the floor. They spilled out of corners and down the sides of the boxes. Hundreds of spiders converging on us. As we crossed the threshold side-by-side, one slid down a single silky thread coming dangerously close to my head. I ducked as we entered into the bright sunlight.

We ran through the overgrown terrain not stopping until we reached the car in front of the house. Glancing back, I discovered the spiders didn't advance on us and seemed to be nowhere in sight, but that didn't stop Melanie from jamming the keys in the ignition and peeling out of the gravel driveway.

"What the hell was that?" I asked breathlessly.

"I don't know. I've never seen spiders congregate like that. And that big one...I should have pulverized him. How does a spider push a shovel back like it was made of rubber? How do you explain that?"

"I don't know." I shook my head, my racing heart starting to slow. "I don't just know."

"Well, I'm not going back there—at least not like this."

"And you think I am? I never wanted to go there in the first place."

She inhaled a sharp breath and let it out slowly. "But we need to see what's in the boxes." Her voice sounded calmer, more rational. "Dad might have left something important."

"What do you suggest, an exterminator?"

"No," she snapped. "We can't kill them."

My mouth dropped. After almost becoming a human-sized fly, subjected to the spider's predator advancements, how could she defend those creatures?

As though she knew what I thought, she gave me a forced smile. "I'm not going back in there with those spiders." She shivered. "I didn't change my mind on that, but I still think spiders are good bugs."

"Then what do you suggest?"

"You're going to think this sounds nuts but there's a lady who lives in town. Her name is Madame Josephina. I've only heard about her work, but she's authentic." Melanie paused, giving me a sideways glance, as though making sure I was listening. "She's...um...that's to say...it may sound weird, but she's a spider whisperer."

"A what?" I gasped, thinking I heard her wrong.

"A spider whisperer. She can communicate with spiders, any arachnids. She can get rid of the spiders without harming them."

I shook my head incredulously, but when I opened my mouth, I remembered the irritation and doubt Melanie had toward our relationship. I didn't want to anger her again. I wasn't convinced a spider whisperer could help, but for my sister's sake, I decided to give Madame Josephina a try. "Okay where do we find this spider whisperer?"

***

MADAME JOSEPHINA, SPIDER WHISPERER, the sign read in bold capital letter on the glass door on the middle of High Street. Although Melanie knew roughly where Madame Josephina's place of business was located, she had driven passed the door three times before we parked the car and decided to search for it on foot. The door was hard to locate because it was tucked in an alcove between the bookstore and a bakery that specialized in gourmet breads.

I pushed the buzzer, shifting uneasily on one heel to the other. Melanie stood beside me peering anxiously through the glass door at the ascending stairs.

"Do you think she will come out to Dad's property today?" Melanie asked.

"I don't know," I said honestly. "I hope so. I'm not sure how many more days I can get off work before my boss gives me hell."

The corners of Melanie's mouth fell and then her lips pressed into a thin line. She didn't say the words, but from that scorn look, I could tell she wasn't happy about me leaving again. She claimed she needed closure on Dad's estate, but I suspected it was more than that. She missed us—missed our sisterly bond. We had been close once—nearly an inseparable pair—but we both changed and grew apart. It had only been a few years since I left town but it felt like eons ago.

I stared at her profile as she stretched her hand in front of me and pressed the buzzer again. Two blonde braids fell on either of her ears and ended at her shoulders. Her sky blue eyes squinted through the glass door, the freckles that dotted her tiny nose and high cheekbones shifting with the slight movement. With my dark hair and dark eyes, we couldn't have looked more different. Yet, she was my sister—the only family I had left. At that moment, I wanted to reach out and hug her for all the birthdays and holidays and togetherness I'd missed.

When I extended my arm to embrace her, she jumped back, saying, "I think Madame Josephina is coming."

I snatched my hand back, and the door opened where a tall, almost six foot, slender woman appeared. She wore black boots and a long-sleeved black dress that ended below her knees. Around the scooped neck line and flowing cuffs were delicate woven silver threads that reminded me of the spider webs back at the shed. Her golden eyes peered down on us.

I cleared my throat. "Um...Madame Josephina? We're looking for Madame Josephina, the spider whisperer. Are you her?"

"I am she." She curled her long bony finger at us, a silver spider ring twinkling at me like a bad dream.

"Follow me." Not waiting for our reply or knowing if we would follow, she ascended up the wooden stairs, her boots making the slightest of whispers.

We were near the top when she continued, "*They* don't like me to do business down there." Her voice was smooth and velvety, her motions precise and graceful. She pushed aside a door of glistening copper beads and gestured for Melanie and me to enter. The mostly tan room that she led us to was a living room which yielded little light, not that there wasn't windows because two lined the far wall and another was on my left, but all were covered by long camel-colored drapes. A variety of greenery broke up the tan monochromatic color scheme, making it look alive and earthy.

While the center of the room featured a cozy couch and love seat, nestled on opposite sides of a simple wooden coffee table, the focal point seemed to be the wall on my right behind the sofa. Rows of terrariums in all shapes and sizes were situated in an elaborated shelving unit that spanned from the floor to the ceiling.

My eyes darted away immediately. A spider whisperer could only have one type of creature—the eight-legged variety—in those terrariums, and if I caught sight of any of them, I didn't think I could calmly and rationally talk to Madame Josephina.

Madame Josephina glided over to the sofa and seated herself at the edge of the middle cushion with her ankles crossed and her hands clasped around her knee. Melanie and I sat across from her on the love seat. As if Madame Josephina had expected us, three tall dew covered glasses were in the middle of the coffee table.

Melanie gave me a sideways glance then spoke to Madame Josephina. "My name is Melanie Walker and this is my sister, Mia Cooper. We had hoped you could help us. You see, we were cleaning out our father's shed..."

Madame Josephina held up a hand interrupting my sister. "Sadly, I've heard what happened at you father's house." Melancholy tinged her soft words, but her eyes contradicted them, zeroing in on me condemningly. My hands fisted at my sides. I didn't know what I had done to have to desire her callousness, but after a moment, I mentally shrugged it off, believing I was still jumpy from my encounter with the spiders.

"Then you've heard about the attack?" Melanie asked.

"Indeed." Her eyes met mine again.

That's twice. I shoved my fisted hands under my thighs trying to not to show my irritation. Putting on my sweetest fake smile, I asked, "We just left our father's home. It happened only a short while ago. How did you hear about it so quickly?"

She gestured to the dewy glasses of water as an offering. Wanting nothing more than answers and to rid the critters from the shed, I shook my head, but my sister picked up her glass and took a sip. Madame Josephina turned slightly to face the terrariums. Her finger extended and a large brown spider the size of a baseball crawled across the back of the sofa and onto her hand. Carefully, as though holding a precise gem, she cupped the spider and faced us again. "They, the spiders, told me of the mutilation—the assassination."

My shoulders tensed, and I slid further back in my chair to create more distance between the spider and me. "What mutilation? What assassination?"

"The killing of their brethren by you." Her jaw jutted toward me while she gently stroked the spider as though she petted a dog. "They hear your words. They know the abomination you hold against them. They see when you kill one of their own. Their whispers spread like a breeze in the wind. I know what you have done and their retaliation and why you have come."

"Mia didn't know what she was doing," Melanie said. I didn't need my sisters defending me and glared at her, but she continued as though she needed to sooth the obvious tension in the room. "Her fears compelled her to do awful, unimaginable things to these animals. I am sorry for that, but you need to understand, they need to understand, the shed is—was—our father's. He's dead now. But it has the last parts of him in it. We need to finish what we started. We need the shed back. Will you speak with the spiders that are in there, make them understand? "

I kept my mouth shut, digging my fingernails into my palms under my thighs. Madam Josephina continued to stoke the spider, her eyes closed as though considering. An entire minute passed before any of us spoke.

Madame Josephina set the spider back on the outside edge of a terrarium. "Thank you, Jasper," she said to the spider. It scurried up the side and crawled inside. Madame Josephina turned back to us. "I have asked Jasper his opinion in the matter. That is, if I should help you or not. He doesn't believe Mia feels remorse for her wrongdoings."

"My wrongdoings!" I snapped, standing. "So what, I killed a spider or two that was crawling on me, invading my personal body." I grabbed Melanie's arm and yanked her to her feet and said to Madame Josephina, "Look lady, we came to you for help to rid those spiders, so we can go through what belongs to us. If you aren't going to help then I'm sure the friendly exterminator down the road will." Feeling too overwhelmed to wait for a reply, I headed to the steps with my sister in tow behind me.

"Wait," Madame Josephina hollered. "I don't want you to call the exterminator. I'll talk with them."

"You'll make them understand. I want them out. All of them and for that matter any that are residing on the entire property—the house and the land too."

"You can't mean that?" Melanie shot me an appalled expression.

I squinted, casting daggers that told her I wasn't backing down.

Madame Josephina's smooth face blanched. "Do you know what you're asking?"

"I do."

"But you're going to upset the balance of nature. I'm sure with my help; you and the spiders can coexist together in harmony."

Only a split second of indecision crossed my mind. I had left this town to get away from the overwhelming amount of bugs and highly doubted ridding one property of spiders would really mess Mother Nature. I shook my head. "I want them out. If not, I'm calling the exterminator."

Before she had a chance to try and change my mind, I added, "So what time can we expect you?"

Madame Josephina sighed, her shoulders slouching in defeat. "Two o'clock. Does that work for you?"

I nodded approvingly and gave her the address. She walked us down the steps, but before she closed the door behind us, she said, "Melanie, you seem to be the voice of reason. It's not too late. I still think you and the spiders can coexist. Don't take them away in their entirety. Talk to Mia."

Melanie smiled weakly. "I'll try."

***

Melanie and I ate lunch at Hoagie World where she kept her word to Madame Josephina. On a number of instances, she reiterated the good qualities of spiders while justifying their need in nature. She also explained that her intentions were to never rid them of the property, only of the shed and that was just while they go through Dad's things.

Each time she tried, I countered by shaking my head and saying, "No, I want them out. Every one of them and especially that big one." The image of the dog-sized spider with legs the length of tent poles crawling toward my sister sent shivers up my spine.

By the time we pulled in the driveway of Dad's house, I was more adamant than ever that all of the spiders had to go. Madame Josephina's car—a black hearse with her name and job title painted the side—was parked in the driveway but when I looked in the windows, she wasn't in it.

Melanie shrugged. "She must be around back already."

I nodded and followed Melanie to the back of the house when she stopped abruptly in front of me. The muscles in her back tensed. Slowly, I peered around her and gasped.

The shed was fifty yards away tucked under the canopy of trees surrounded by the tall grass and bramble, but I could still see Madame Josephina as though we were much closer. She sat on a plastic chair near the doorway of the shed with her back toward us. Her ankles were crossed and her hands were rested softy on her knees. She seemed to be relaxed, yet spiders in different hues of black and brown in all kinds of size surrounded her from every angle. The largest, the dog sized spider, was centered in front of her, nodding its head as though it understood.

Melanie and I exchanged nervous glances but did not advance on Madame Josephina and the army of spiders. Time ticked by excruciatingly slow. Finally, the spiders directly in front of Madame Josephina moved backwards allowing her to stand and turn toward us. "Have you come to a decision?" she asked us.

My sister intertwined her hand with mine. She said, "We may not be completely in agreement, but I must accede with Mia. We want all the spiders to evacuate."

Madame Josephina nodded. "Very well. I suggest you step back and caution you not to move. They have agreed to your conditions, but request that you do not interfere while I relocate them."

"We won't." Melanie squeezed my hand.

I simply nodded unsure my voice would work properly.

Like the parting of the Red Sea for Moses, Madame Josephina opened her arms wide and hesitantly stepped forward. She nodded to her left and then to her right as the spiders made way for her to move through the overgrown path. As she gracefully ambled forward, the spiders marched behind her, holding their heads high. I felt like we were the spectators for a Memorial Day parade, honoring the brave soldiers from our country, except these weren't men and women dressed in uniforms. Heck, they weren't even human.

When Madame Josephina passed us, taking slow precise steps, she glanced at us disapprovingly and warned, "Don't move. I will be back as quickly as I can once they are loaded in my car."

Following her orders, my body stayed rigid, as did Melanie's.

Spiders crept down the walls of the house and came from the both sides of the yard. They converged in the on-going processional, the smaller legged ones moving twice as fast to keep up with the strides of the larger spiders.

"My God," Melanie breathed softly. "There must be hundreds, possibly thousands, of them."

"Yeah," I whispered, clutching Melanie's hand as though it was my lifeline. "I'm going to need lots and lots of therapy after this."

She giggled hauntingly.

Thirty long minutes later, Madame Josephina strolled toward us. Her arms held the large dog-sized spider I had seen from the shed. She stroked its head. "They are loaded in the car," she announced. "You may move freely now."

"But not all of them," I pointed out, not moving from my spot.

Madame Josephina looked down at her pet then back up at me. "Yes, I guess that is true. But I assure you, all are loaded except Maximo. He insisted on coming back to greet you. He wants to give you a message."

Melanie's face paled, but she mustered up a weak smile. "What is it? What do you need to say Maximo?"

Tucking in a long black leg that slipped out from her arm, Madame Josephina said, "Maximo thinks his size frightens you both, but really he is a big softy." She nuzzled her cheek near his furry face.

"The message," I glowered impatiently.

She lowered the spider and protectively cradled him again. "He says the answers you seek are in the shed—the bottom box furthest back in the shed."

My eyes narrowed. "What answers? I don't know what he's talking about."

Madame Josephina glanced back down at the spider, her eyes searching him as though holding a private conversation. When she looked back up, she said, "Look for the box with a big red 'X.' It holds your answers."

"What answers?" Melanie tried this time.

"The answers Mia seeks. Now I must go. They grow restless crowded together like they are in the car." She turned and disappeared around the corner of the house. Although she told us we could move neither Melanie nor I had until we hear the roar of the hearse's engine and the crunching of its tires on the gravel driveway.

We let out audible breaths. Then Melanie started for the shed. I quickly followed after her. "What do you think Maximo is talking about?" I asked, pushed bramble out of my way.

"I don't know. You really aren't seeking answers to a question?"

"Not that I'm aware of. If you remember, I didn't even want to come to this shed."

"Hmm... I guess we know which box we need to start with."

We pushed the boxes that we had left abruptly to the side and began lifting and shifting the top boxes off until we reached the box with the red "X". We centered the box between us and exchanged an anxious look.

"Ready?" Melanie asked.

I inhaled a sharp breath. The last box I had opened caused a spiral of terrifying events in the past few hours. I didn't know what could possibly be in the box and how it would answer questions, but the curiosity won over my lingering fears. I nodded to my sister. "Open the box."

She yanked the tape off and pulled down the flaps. "It's only a bunch of camping gear," Melanie announced. I leaned down further and searched through the contents with her. There were two Barbie sleeping bags, a green tent, metal campfire forks, a couple of lanterns, and one doll that was smudge in a layer of grim.

She continued, "I didn't even know Dad kept this stuff. What do you think it means?"

I shrugged. "The doll was mine, but most of it really means nothing." I examined the doll holding it by the very edge of it tattered dress, trying not to touch too much of the filth. I laid it aside. "Let's see what's in the other boxes."

***

By the time we sorted through most of the boxes, the sun had moved across the sky and was directly above the tree line. We had come across some peculiar things, but none like the lost treasures of the box that Maximo pointed us too. I couldn't keep its contents and the memories that it brought out of my mind. As a young girl, Mom would often set up the tent in the backyard during the summer months. One particular memory had been pushed far back in my mind, but now I could see Mom's excited face clearly. It was lit up in a way that told me she had something fun planned. I was playing with my doll in the playroom at the front of the house, when Melanie and Mom bounded in.

"Mom said we could set up the tent. Were going to campout in the back yard," Melanie shrieked.

"Can Stacey come to?" I asked.

Mom scooped me up in her arms and spun me in a circle. "Sure you and your doll can both come."

That evening, Mom went on a scavenger hunt finding grasshoppers, beetles, earwigs, and spiders to show Melanie and me. They crawled on our hands and up our arms. Their light touch tickled my skin and I giggled. We put them in canning jars with holes in the lids. At dusk, we caught more bugs—fireflies. It had been a joyous occasion except for the few times that Mom clutched her stomach as though it hurt. In my nearly five-year-old, high pitched voice, I asked, "Mama, are you sick? Do you need to lie down?"

"I'll be fine, honey." She tousled my hair. "This is yours and your sister's night. I don't want to ruin it." When the sun finally settled behind the horizon, we let all the bugs go and cooked s'mores over a campfire. I sat in my lawn chair, eating my snack, and stared up to the stars. They shone brightly since no clouds covered them. Mom pulled up a seat next to me. I asked, "Do you think I will ever be able to look down on earth from up there?"

"You want to be an astronaut?"

I nodded. "That or a doctor for bugs."

Mom laughed, but her amusement quickly faded as she pointed to the stars, "I don't know if you will ever be able to go up there your lifetime, but I hope all your dreams come true." She paused as though considering her words. "And if they don't, you can always look down on earth from heaven. I know my grandpapa is looking down on us now, just as his father before him is too. Do you understand?"

"Yes mama. People who die go to heaven."

She looked down at me and smiled.

Mom died that following autumn. Cancer.

A teardrop trailed down my cheek. I didn't want Melanie to see my anguish and stepped outside of the shed. The stars were slowly emerging, but the sky still shone in pinks and oranges. My eyes scanned the backyard. Although overgrown grass and bramble covered the area where the tent and fire pit had been, its image was burning in my mind.

Melanie came up beside and when she saw my expression, she asked, "What wrong?"

I told her my last camping memory and what Mom had said about looking down from heaven.

"So you think she is watching us now?" Melanie asked. Her tone was agreeable as though it was what she believed.

"I do." I paused, coming to a new conclusion that I never thought I would have. "And Melanie, I think ... I think I want something else."

"What's that?"

"I want to come home—to this home."

"What about New York?"

"It's not home. It never was." I paused letting her consider my revelation before continuing, "I know you and Brandt can't afford to keep your house and this one, but this is my house too. I don't want you to sell it. I'll do whatever you ask. Pay you for your half of the inheritance. Just don't sell it."

Tears welled in her eyes. She stretched out her hand and embraced me in a hug. "It's about time. Welcome home little sis."

We held each other for a long moment. When we broke apart, she slapped a hand on her neck and groaned, "Mosquito."

I chuckled, "I guess we need to bring the spiders back."

She moaned then laughed too.

***

Three months past before I finalized my affairs in New York and found a closer job, and two days after I moved back home, I got up the nerve to visit Madame Josephina again. I greatly misjudged her and the spiders and felt as though I needed to thank her. I stood in front of her door, alone and trying to decide how to phrase my words when she came down the steps and opened the door.

"I've been expecting you." She turned and headed up the steps.

My mouth dropped. *How did she know?* Then I remembered how the whispers from spiders spread to her the first time Melanie and I came. Despite not seeing any spiders today, I had no doubt hidden spiders overheard my conversion with Melanie and conveyed my intensions.

It felt like déjà vu as I sat in the same spot on the love seat. Madame Josephina wore a similar black dress and was across from me stroking Maximo, who had clambered out from the greenery. She assured me that the rest of the spiders from the shed were released deep in the forest, but that didn't stop me from gazing at the others, creeping along in their terrarium habitats, their beady eyes peering at me. I shivered. I may not have the fearless actions of a five year old, but I thought I'd come a long way over the months, reading about spiders and accepting them as a valuable part of nature. I inhaled a sharp breath. "Do you know why I came?"

"I've heard the whispers, but I'd like to hear it from you. I believe Maximo does too."

I began by telling her the story of camping in my backyard with my mother and sister. Then I admitted that part of my hatred and fears towards bugs and consequently, the same part of me that wanted to escape Hillsdale was because my mother died.

"It's only natural that you miss your mother."

"I was young and maybe I'm still learning, but I needed things to fall out like they had. I needed to see what was in that box to remember the joy my mother brought. Not repress anything that I associated with her as I had on the day you came to the shed."

"It takes a strong person to overcome their fears. Fears and prejudices go hand in hand. You never took the time to understand the arachnid, to know their importance. Every living thing has a purpose and to bring unjust harm to another creature, whether human, animal or even an eight legged spider was wrong."

I nodded agreeably.

"There are times, the food cycle for instance, that death is immanent for others survival, but I believe you are regretful."

"Regretful, but thankful," I corrected.

She smiled faintly. "Yes, Maximo accepts your shortcomings and apology."

I hadn't exactly apologized to the dog-sized spider, but the thought crossed my mind.

"Would you like to stay for coffee?" she asked.

"No. I promised Melody I'd stop over. Her husband, Brant, is being release from his final physical therapy. They're having a celebration."

"I understand. Please give them my best."

Madame Josephina walked me down to the door, but before I left, I asked, "How do you do it?"

"What's that my dear?"

"Talk to the spiders. Do you have a psychic link?"

A dark wicked curl crossed her lips. "It's simple. I'm Madame Josephina, Ancient Mother of all Arachnids."

The irises in her eyes shimmed with silver. Maximo scampered out of her arms and up the stairs, stopping at the top. She grabbed her stomach and hunched over as though a sudden painful cramp clawed at her from the inside. Concerned, I extended my hand. Before I touched her shoulder, the muscles over her back rippled. I yelped and jumped back. She crumpled to the floor. Her black dress melted into her body replaced by fuzz. Sickening sounds of bones and sinew snapping registered to my ears. I couldn't understand what was happening. Then each arm and leg grew thinner, shifting, until it finally broke into two identical parts—totaling eight long legs. She pushed up on her legs, lifting her body and head to the full height she was as a human. Her fangs twitched at me for a few long mocking seconds. She was the Mother of all Arachnids. I bit my lip from screaming. My body was engulfed in frozen terror. She turned, scampered up the steps, and disappeared from my sight.

Slowly let myself out the door. When my feet hit the sidewalk, I began to run, my heart pounding at her horrific image burned in my mind. *My God*, I thought. *She's a shapeshifter. The Ancient Mother of all Arachnids. What kind of town had I agreed to move back to?*

The Kiss
by
Jenny Phillips

I pushed my way through the sea of swaying bodies. The dance floor was packed more than normal, though I was far from a regular…yet. The sweaty, dark and overcrowded dance club had been the source of my escape from reality for the last month. My latest and nowhere close to greatest foster home was conveniently located only a few blocks away. The current techno beat was numbing my brain exactly the way I liked. I didn't care much for the music, or company for that matter, but I could get lost in the crowd. And it helped that the bouncer never took the time to actually look at the fake ID I flashed at him. Yes, I could hide here without standing out or having my foster parents breathing down my neck. The elderly couple meant well, but they were suffocating me. Luckily I was now only a few hours away from my eighteenth birthday and headed for the real world. I had a job and only needed a place of my own, and that was hard to come by when you weren't yet a legal adult. But tomorrow that would change and I would start the apartment hunt. The Whitcomb's had agreed to let me stay in their home until I could get something lined up.

My usual dark corner was taken in the club and I set out for a new shadow to lurk in. The music changed to a faster beat sending the crowd into a frenzy. I shifted my path to the outside of the dance floor and examined the occupant of my corner. I expected to find a couple groping each other in the cover of darkness. Instead a man geared in all black stared back at me. His eyes watched me cross in front of him and I shuddered unexpectedly, the intensity of his stare was intimidating. I quickly turned my back on the stranger and searched for the next secluded spot.

I found it across the room, another corner, situated in between the bathroom and the entrance. I soaked in the free time, people watching, leisurely sipping on a mojito but never daring to leave the comfort of my shelter.

I ignored a couple of attempts to get me to dance. An older guy was distastefully bold and asked if I'd like to join him in the bathroom. I rolled my eyes accordingly and ignored his insults at my rejection. My red hair always attracted unwanted attention. My full lips naturally turned down into a pout that apparently signaled damsel in distress. At least that's what I'd been told by countless sleazy pick-up lines. I let the refreshing mint roll across my tongue and imagined that within a few more weeks I could be in my own apartment, no more annoying foster parents or perverted foster "siblings". A place of my own. Clothes that couldn't be stolen, food I actually enjoyed, privacy. Ahhh.

A rude bump jolted me out of my daydream. I opened my mouth to protest but was abruptly slammed into the concrete wall behind me. The dance floor had started to spill over in my direction. There were shouts and screams followed by more forceful shoving. The commotion seemed to be a fight that had now consumed half the occupants on the dance floor. The lights flicked on and the DJ announced that the club was shutting down for the night. I thought they were overreacting slightly, it was a bar fight not a riot. However I realized more bodyguards were rushing in to help disperse the fight. Bodyguards were wrestling people to the ground, but just as quickly more people were joining in to meet the new wave of guards. This had definitely gotten out of hand I could hear the shrill police sirens in the distance.

With a fake ID in my pocket I decided it was time to disappear. The desire to get out of the mess outweighed my disappointment at my much anticipated leisure time. The night air was shocking after the stifling heat of the club; the fresh air filled my lungs and stung my eyes. It hadn't felt unbearably cold when I'd entered the club but somehow it had managed to drop in the short amount of time I was in the building. I desperately wished I would've brought a jacket and tugged my long sleeves down over my bare hands.

I caught a quick glance of the guy that had taken my corner, he seemed to be searching the crowd for someone and I knew I hadn't ever seen him at the club before. Must've been meeting someone there, I should get my corner back next week I noted. His eyes fell on me again and narrowed. Had he been searching for me?

I started out for home and tried to ignore the nagging feeling in my stomach that told me not to turn my back on this guy. What could he possibly want from me? I'd never seen him before. My breath sent little puffs of white into the chilly night. The thud of shoes behind me sent a little chill up the back of my neck but I didn't dare allow myself to look over my shoulder. Instead I focused on getting around the corner and into the light of some downtown shops.

Once the light spilled across the sidewalk I relaxed slightly in the orange glow.

"Ella." I heard a deep voice call from behind, I stiffened back up immediately.

The guy was only a block behind me. I fought the urge to run and decided it would be easier to just get the confrontation over now.

"What do you want from me?"

He continued to walk closer, not answering me.

I tried again, "Do I know you? How do you know my name?"

He was only a couple yards away now and I could see him consult his watch in the moonlight.

"Wanna grab a coffee?"

"Seriously?" I asked exasperated.

"I'd like to talk, and maybe you could warm up." He shrugged but still seemed to be in a hurry.

"I really shouldn't, I need to get home." I stifled a shiver and pivoted on my heel.

"You and I both know your foster parents aren't going to realize you're even gone."

This stopped me midstride. It should have scared me. It should have sent me screaming into the nearest shop, which I realized ironically was a coffee shop. But somehow it didn't, if this guy knew something about me, then he probably had other opportunities to hurt me, if that was his goal. If he intended to rape or kill me, would he have taken the time to research me? Wouldn't he have grabbed the first girl on the street? What could a coffee in a well-lit shop hurt?

I eyed him skeptically and chewed my lip. I finally shrugged and opened the door to the coffee shop. I motioned for him to follow me. The warm smell of roasted coffee mixed with sweet French vanilla and hazelnuts filled my nose. Despite the odd scenario I inhaled deeply and placed my order for a large macchiato. Mystery man ordered a plain black coffee and followed me to a table by the front window.

The light did wonders for him. He no longer seemed menacing but surprisingly normal. He could've been any guy from a number of my classes. His blond hair was short and he had dimples that were visible even without a smile. His green eyes however, did not fit his pleasant face, they were guarded and sad.

Once we were seated he held his hands up, "See? Harmless." He joked.

I didn't relax.

"So how do you know my name?"

"Right to the point," He smiled coyly, "I like that." He took a sip of his coffee. "Ella, I've been watching you for some time, well-*we've* been watching you." He corrected.

The fact that he knew my name had already eluded to that piece of news, what I wanted to know was why. He continued, "I am part of an Order, and we help girls like you."

I shook my head slowly, indicating he had completely lost me, "Girls like me…orphans?"

"Succubi." He corrected.

"I'm sorry, what?" An internal war raged, one half wanted to get up and leave the table immediately. The other and clearly the winner, wanted to humor this stranger with sad eyes.

He rubbed his hands over his face, "This is never the easy part." He cleared his throat. "You are a Succubus. Known by many different names throughout history, Succubi suck souls or energy depending on what you believe in. A sort of vampire you could say, only instead of blood they suck the life force of another human being."

"Ha. Well I've heard enough for one night." I rose quickly, eyeing my quickest exit and wondering if I could make it home without this guy bothering me.

"No, I'm serious. Ella you need to listen to me." He put his hand on my arm, I flinched but couldn't bring myself to leave. Again there was something holding me there, maybe the seriousness in his eyes. "I'm here to help you. The Order is here to help girls like you make the transition as easily as possible. There *are* others like you."

I didn't take my eyes off of him but slowly sat back down, he retracted his hand.

"Unfortunately with Succubi, many are orphaned, seeking guidance."

"Why is that?" I asked.

"Well, the way it works is that Succubi can live immortally as long as they continue to feed off the souls of others. This damns them to a life of solitude I'm afraid." He clasped his hands together and laid them on the table. "Obviously an intimate relationship would only result in death for the partner."

"But what about the…" I wasn't quite comfortable using the word Succubus, or Succubi, was that right? "The Mother? What happens to them?"

"Ah," He trained his eyes on his folded hands. "There are hunters of Succubi, individuals seeking the power of others. It is said that if you kill a Succubi in a certain manner you are able to taste their immortality."

"Certain manner?"

"Sacrifice."

"Oh." I chewed on my bottom lip. "So most Succubi have been eliminated by these hunters?"

"I don't know about most, but a lot. There are Succubi who choose to live a normal life."

"How is that?"

"Succubi only keep their immortality by sucking souls, others can live a normal, if shortened, human life by not draining others of their essence. Simply abstaining from what they are."

"And how do you do that? Be a Succubi? Suck souls, whatever."

A shadow seemed to pass over his face, "Oh, well through intimate contact," When he saw my blank expression he added, "like kissing."

"Hmm, so why are you just now telling me this if you've been following me for a while?"

"You will transition on your eighteenth birthday."

"That's tomorrow."

"I know." He took another sip of his coffee, mine remained untouched.

"Does it kill them?"

He nodded solemnly.

"So I'll never be able to kiss someone I care about without killing them?"

He pursed his lips, "That's right."

I should've have been walking out the door, rolling my eyes and continuing on with my life. But somehow I knew that what I was hearing was right, some deep-rooted knowledge that what this stranger said was the truth. I felt tears stinging my eyes. I had always felt different, and lately that part of me felt more and more alert.

"How do you plan on helping?"

The guy took a deep breath. He seemed relieved as if he were prepared to argue his point, not to have me accept it so willingly.

"I can take you to be with others, we can all help you, together."

I had to admit, it sounded great. Not the soul sucking part, but being surrounded by others like myself. Not that I really knew what "like myself" meant at this point, but I guess just the concept of being surrounded by people that care.

"So how did you know about me?"

"Um," his forehead scrunched while he seemed to struggle for an answer. "We're each assigned a Succubi to... to help, you know, transition." For the first time he seemed uncomfortable, jumpy even.

"But who-"

"Should we head out?" He stood and pitched his coffee into a nearby can.

"I...guess." I answered uncertainly. I couldn't decide if he was genuinely in a hurry to get going or if he was avoiding my question. I followed suit and decided to take my drink with me. At least it would give me something to do with my hands. I shrugged and headed back out into the cold air.

"I don't even know your name?" I spoke up.

After another pause, "Mark."

"How far are we going?" I pressed with another question.

"Are you cold?"

"Freezing. Do you mind if I stop by my house to grab a jacket-"

Mark caught my elbow hard, I spun around surprised and dropped my coffee. His hardened face quickly disappeared and he pulled his hand back. He now rubbed his hand absently, as if he were trying to scrub off germs he'd contracted from touching me.

"It's just that it's in the opposite direction, and I know they're waiting for us." He ran his hands through his hair roughly, the impatience creeping into his voice. "We'll be there in as much time as it would take for you to go home and get your jacket." He tried to come across normal, but it was too late. The warning flags had went up and regardless of how bad I may have wanted to have people to talk to, I had come this far on my own. I was used to being alone. Trust was not something that came easily to me, no matter how enticing or promising it was.

"Fine." I said attempting to hide my own irritation. I didn't want to tip him off that I had grown suspicious. I decided it would be best to keep him talking. Hopefully I could distract him enough that I could slip away in a crowd or a better-lit area.

"So are you like me?"

"No!" He snapped, disgust thick in his voice. In this one word I knew that Mark, if that was even his real name was full of shit. He could not be here to help someone that filled him with such revulsion. I couldn't let him know that I was on to him. If I ran, he would. He would catch me I was sure of it. So I forced myself to act calm and curious.

"Are there male Succubi?"

"Incubus." His patience was thinning. "Men are Incubi."

"You said earlier that you are each assigned a Succubus...who assigns you?"

"I...uh, it's kind of confidential."

"Okay." I said slowly, "How do *they* find us?"

"A Tracker can detect Succubi-like by their energy surges. Your energy reads different than someone mortal." He was far from calm and collected now, the initial façade giving way to irritation.

"Mortal, so I'm not really human?"

"Well technically you're half. Your mother needed to procreate with a human."

The sarcasm was hard to fight down. "You mean there are no purebred Succubi?" I couldn't quite seem to hide it completely in my voice.

"No." His sense of humor, or lack of, was very evident in his own voice.

We passed closed shops, their windows dark and lonely. I knew from experience that this part of town was pretty desolate this time of night, but I allowed myself a small amount of hope to filter in because two blocks over there was a popular night club. It was also an exclusive nightclub that would have customers waiting in line and possibly an enormous bouncer checking ID. I silently prayed that we would continue in that direction without any detours. If I could just get into an area to make a run for it, preferably with lots of people to conceal me, I would be okay. Worst-case scenario, I could always yell and make a commotion that would alert people to my distress.

The next block we remained quiet. My abductor, could I call him that? Technically he wasn't forcing me, I was willingly following him. There was no doubt in my mind that he would restrain me if I attempted to run…yes, I would consider him my abductor. I tested him by changing my speed, if I slowed down, he slowed down. If I sped up, he quickened his own pace. Yep, no doubt he would pursue me if I ran.

I could feel the tension radiating off of him. He seemed eager to reach our destination and if I had to bet, it was more to be rid of me than anything. He didn't seem to enjoy this assignment.

Luckily we did not turn off; we seemed to be heading in the same direction as the nightclub. I tried to remain patient, though the urge to flee danger was now trying to claw its way out. My natural instinct was combating my own reason. I shoved my inner war down to the pit of my stomach and forced myself to focus on something else. I watched Mark instead. I reached up to scratch my nose and he flinched. I knew he was all too aware of my movements. There could be no hesitation when I ran. I would have to act immediately and not look back.

We were coming to the intersection I'd been waiting for. My palms were sweaty and I could feel my heart pounding in anticipation. I hoped my adrenaline would be enough to carry me as far away that Mark would not be able to catch up.

We stepped onto the intersecting street. It was significantly brighter than our previous path and this warmed me inside, if only a little. But my optimistic celebration was abruptly cut short when I realized we were not headed right, toward the club, but instead Mark was leading me straight. I had to pay that much more attention for the precise moment to run. Too soon and he would catch me before I could ever reach the line of clubbers. Too late and I would never get a chance to test my escape plan. I waited until we were about to disappear onto the adjacent street. Mark had almost reached the corner building when I made my move. To say I hauled ass was putting it lightly. My lungs were burning, my legs were already protesting, I could feel sweat beading on my forehead. I had the element of surprise but he was not far behind.

I ran the length of the club and once I had reached the farthest corner of the building I pushed through the line of people, instead of rounding the corner and putting more distance between us, I hooked a hard left. I stayed between the exterior wall of the building and the line of people standing in line. A few noticed me and protested but I pushed on, using the crowd to camouflage myself.

A young girl probably only a couple of years older than myself watched me curiously. I put my finger to my lips and pointed at Mark as he passed. I held my breath praying that he would continue around the corner and give me more time to run. Unfortunately he was smarter than I gave him credit for and as he started back toward the entrance he watched the faces in the line closely. The blond girl turned and faced Mark obstructing his view of me. She was covering me.

I held my breath, willing my heart to slow down. The girl finally turned back, she jerked her head sharply and I understood that she was signaling a clear coast. I stood shakily and gave her a thankful smile. I wasn't sure which way Mark had gone but I figured heading toward my house was the best option. I crossed the street so that I would have more cover in the shadows of the buildings. I set myself at a jog so I wouldn't wear out too fast, I wanted to steadily put myself as far from the direction Mark had intended.

In the pale bluish light from the moon this side of town was eerily abandoned. No late night grocery stores, laundry mats or restaurants.

Nothing.

Well, nothing but the thump of my shoes on the sidewalk. It was a gradual incline making my run back harder than the initial trip. I knew I could only be a few blocks away from the club I had visited earlier and allowed myself to slow down. I couldn't believe the mess I had almost gotten into. My brain too stunned from the closeness of disaster to even contemplate the new information.

Tomorrow my world would change, I would be a Succubi. I wasn't even sure what that meant, how it worked. I couldn't hold any truth to what Mark said. How could I discern what was fact and what was being used to cloud my trust. I caught myself chewing my nails down to nubs and thrust my hands into the pocket of my jeans. The moment I became vulnerable, with my hands restrained in my pockets, he hit me. He threw his weight at me from the hidden alley tackling me to the ground. I hit hard and felt my hipbone hit the concrete. Mark wrapped his hand in my hair and my skull crashed into the sidewalk.

For a split second the world went white. A blinding white flashed, the world slowly seeped back in and I fought the waves of nausea. I didn't have time to allow myself to be sick, though my stomach begged and pleaded to empty its contents. I sucked in air and bit my lip to keep from getting sick.

I screamed for help and thrashed wildly while he held me to the ground.

He spat into my ear, "No one will hear you."

I screamed again and he slammed my head into the ground again. I felt like my head would shatter. No matter how hard I tried to look strong I couldn't control the tears escaping, an involuntary reaction to the pain. He yanked at my hair pulling me to my feet.

"You *will* come with me, whatever I have to do to get you there, got it?" He shook me by the hair.

I sobbed in answer and he shoved me forward back toward the club. I would not become his victim. I had to make another move. I would fight the whole way. I promised myself that much. The throbbing behind my eyes made it hard to focus but I knew I would have to make a move soon, the farther I let him get me toward his destination the further my chance of escape became. If I struck soon I could possibly surprise him.

I seized the moment and stomped his foot, it wasn't as excruciating as say slamming his head into the sidewalk but he hadn't seen it coming. I took the opportunity to add further insult and rammed my knee into his groin. His hold on my hair slipped and I made my move. His hand never fully let go of my locks and I grit my teeth as the hair ripped from my scalp.

I felt myself release from his grip and ran as hard as I could. I could hear his steps and knew for the second time that night he was right behind me. I zigzagged down a couple of alleys and though my lungs burned I ran faster because my life depended on it. Like earlier, I could not spare a glance behind me. I had to always assume he was right on my heels.

A building to my right caught my attention and after sneaking a second peek I noticed why. The abandoned building had a door that had a considerable sized crack in it. I wasn't quite sure I would be able to squeeze through the opening but I wouldn't be able to outrun him all night. I would have to make a move, why not now?

At the last possible moment I hurled myself at the door, I crashed into it, taking another second off of my time. I stuck one leg through, then the other, and then wriggled my body through. My head was last and I could see that Mark was not as close behind me as I originally thought. I quickly pulled my head through and threw myself up against the wall to make sure he would not be able to see me when he passed.

I heard his footsteps just as my back hit the cool brick. I held my breath, my heart hammered in my chest. It felt so loud in my ears that I was convinced Mark could hear it. For the moment though I was safe, I heard his footsteps pass and took inventory of my surroundings. It looked like an old bookstore or library. The dust was thick and covers rested across what I assumed were bookshelves. They stood like ghosts in the pale moonlight. A tremble ran through me as I thought about childhood fears of ghosts and monsters under the bed. Now here I was running from something far scarier and so much more real. I would give anything to go back to those nights of comforting myself from non-existent threats.

I had to keep moving, I couldn't chance Mark popping his head in while I stood unguarded and plainly visible. I crossed the room and into a dark entry, I felt my way along the wall and moved with it until I hit a staircase. I felt for the banister in the dark and guided my hand along it delicately. I had no idea how long this place sat rotting and in the dark I couldn't tell the extent of the disrepair. After what I imagined had to be several floors of stairs a sound from below stopped me, I stood frozen, scared to let out a breath.

Another sound jolted me to attention, an unmistakable blow to wood. The sound of it splintering forced my heavy legs to move. I hoped the sound of Mark knocking his way through the front door would drown out my flight up the stairs. I moved as stealthily as I was capable of and reached a landing by the time the strikes stopped. I knew he had gotten through and I would have to keep moving or find an excellent hiding spot. The moon illuminated the floor through a wall of windows to my right, the left grew progressively darker. I ventured to the left knowing it would provide better cover from Mark. But a door seemed out of place among the wood and antique feel of the building, a steel door with a push bar. In the dim light I could just make out the exit sign that hung uselessly above it.

My heart fluttered at the idea of an exit and I didn't allow myself the chance to wonder where it could possibly lead to, or worse, where it might not lead. I winced as the hinges creaked from years of desertion. I had to assume

Mark heard and hastened my pace. The door led into a concrete room lit by a small window. It was another staircase, it obviously led back down to the floor I had originally entered but also up to what I had to assume was the roof. I couldn't risk going back downstairs and running into Mark. There was a chance he had heard the door open though and was already on his way up, giving me the chance to escape back the way I had come. But what if he hadn't? What if I ran into him on my way? It seemed too risky, too much of a bargain. I had to chance the roof, maybe a neighboring rooftop would be close enough to jump across, or there would be a fire escape…the roof seemed to provide the possibility of more options.
I dug my nails into the palms of my hands and cautiously took the stairs up to the roof. Unfortunately the door had been locked by a thick chain and padlocked. I felt tears threaten my eyes, disappointment, fear and frustration burned at them. For one split moment I felt resignation creep in, but the stronger part of me refused to go down like this. I searched the dark, felt along the walls, and yanked the door in desperation. It only budged enough to let the cool, crisp night air in to tease me. I fought the urge to scream for help, though panic was rising I couldn't just hand myself over to Mark. I had to keep fighting. I couldn't

be that pathetic girl I had laughed at in so many predictable movies.

I had finally argued with myself enough to resign heading back down the stairs. But felt a sharp metal box along the brick wall. A fire hose complete with ax, just like the movies. I sent a silent prayer up to the heavens as I discovered the glass had already been knocked out, or never existed judging by the lack of shards on the ground below. I removed the ax and found I had to use both hands to bear the weight. It was far heavier than I imagined. The first blow to the padlock didn't budge it, neither did the second or third. I recoiled with every blow, surely Mark would come running. I hoped the steel door leading into the staircase would be enough to mute the sound of me battling the padlock. After finally knocking the lock open I pushed through the door only to discover Mark had found his own way up to the roof. He was waiting by the door with a smug grin that I was beginning to despise.

He landed a punch to my jaw but luckily in the last hour I had learned to take a hit. I swallowed down the cry that had worked its way up and launched myself at him. This was clearly not what he had expected, he had probably assumed I would go down after the punch or run the other way. I managed to knock him to the ground. I pushed myself up and kicked him hard in the head before running to the edge of the rooftop. I slowed down once I reached the low wall that bordered the roof. This side dropped off to an alley below, no fire escape, and no buildings within reach. I spun to check on Mark but he was already on me.

For a brief moment we were locked in a battle for life, I was dangerously close to the edge. In the end, he won the fight. I toppled over the edge.

But some measure of luck was on my side, I managed to fall feet first and my hands gripped the wall in a last minute attempt at survival. Mark loomed above me grinning.

"It's a shame." He said gruffly while his nose poured blood from my kick. He smiled and his mouth filled with red liquid. "I didn't want to kill you."

I wanted to answer, I wanted to land another kick to his nose, but instead I dangled from the side of a building gasping as I tried desperately to get some sort of foothold.

"Well, I guess that's a lie," He spat the words like venom, "I mean in the end you're going to die either way but I really wanted to get you to the Order. Then they would kill you. Sacrifice you more accurately. You see why it is important for me you get you there? If you die now it's for nothing, a waste. I can't allow you to become one of *them*, a disgusting parasite that thrives off of others. I won't allow you to turn anyone into a shadow."

"Wh-Wha-What?" I managed to get out breathlessly.

"When you take a life, what's left, becomes a shadow, some*thing* unable to enter the afterlife without a soul, unable to walk the earth without a body. And after sucking the energy out of someone, your energy burns a little brighter. Yes it keeps you young and healthy and potentially immortal, but with every life you attract the shadows. The brighter you burn, the more drawn they are to you, like moths to a flame."

My eyes caught a nearby building harboring a gigantic illuminated clock. It distracted me long enough for Mark to make his move. He bent down unexpectedly and pried my fingers from the building. I started screaming in protest but he gripped my fingers and began to pull.

"Look, you don't understand. I have to bring you back or they'll kill me."

I had my elbows on the building, my feet rested on a groove I was unable to reach just moments ago.

My voice felt scratchy from fatigue, "It's you or me then, one of us has to die."

"Yes." He said it as if he were relieved that I finally understood what he was trying to explain, "And I'm the Tracker." He said pointedly, "It's as much of a curse on me, as what you are."

He began to pull my wrists up but I leaned forward and whispered into his ear, "And I know something you don't."

He pulled back and looked pensive for a moment. I brought my face to his once more, "It's midnight." And before he had a chance to realize the implications, I brought my lips to his. Generations of the curse guided me, while I heard bells toll in the background. I felt Mark's hands dig in to my wrists. The only sign I was doing something right. The rest of him was placid, complacent even. His head tilted to give me access. I knew once his body went slack that I had succeeded.

I never got to see the look of surprise he must have expressed once he finally realized that midnight meant I was officially eighteen and now a Succubus. Instead his face looked peaceful. I hauled myself up over the wall and sat for a moment next to Mark's body. I struggled momentarily wondering what to do with him.

I eventually decided on leaving his remains, this building sat untouched for quite a while judging by the thickness of the dust. Aside from the smashed in door, most people would probably continue to walk by never noticing. I would piece together as much of the door as I could on my way out. Even if they had something linking me to this man, I would be long gone by morning.

Whatever Order was waiting for Mark tonight will be disappointed. Tonight, they will continue waiting with no reward at the end. I know this is not the end of my story, quite the opposite now that I know who, or what I am. My story is just beginning. I will never return to my foster home to collect my things, not that I had much anyway. Better for them to think I'm dead. The least amount of trails I leave the better. I know others will come for me, hunt me. But I will not give them the satisfaction of being easy pretty. No I am a natural predator and I will do everything I can to stay alive.

I worried about what I would become, about how much of Mark's opinion of Succubi was true. But I could have all the dark magic in the world inside me and still not be as sinister as Mark or the people he worked for. I didn't wish to inflict harm on others, I would do what I had to survive, but I wouldn't go out intentionally luring in bait to be sacrificed. That was unthinkable.

Maybe it was best that I had been brought up the way I had. I had seen both good and bad people in this world. I could only think that would help me, guide me in this transition and my looming struggle to discern right from wrong. I would continue to look for others like me, someone that could help answer questions.

But tonight I had to get moving. I could feel the shadows moving in. I knew Mark had not lied about that. I could see them dancing at the edges of my vision. Waiting. The Succubus in me had been born and I would never be the same…though that may not be a bad thing.

Goddess of Death
by
John Hansen

Liam never liked demons, not only because they possessed his younger sister and nearly killed her, or because they were in the process of chasing him throughout New York City. He hated demons because they were vile, repulsive creatures that, frankly, disgusted him. They weren't very attractive-looking and were extremely unpleasant to be around in the first place, but after they possessed his sister, Liam's hatred of demons only intensified.

Admittedly, it wasn't too difficult for the demons to get a hold of his sister because there wasn't much security provided in their house. Liam did not like the term "illegal" but after his parents died nearly two years ago (their bodies were found on a deserted beach with strange claw marks in them), he and his younger sister – after avoiding a foster home – moved to a desolate part of town alone. Liam wasn't technically old enough to be a legal guardian for he was only sixteen but he and his younger sister, Ashley, made out well enough. Liam cared for her, fed her from the income he received from his accounting job and neither of them complained. The two dropped out of school as it was not a necessity and Liam forged a fake ID that stated he was 21 – he was tall and mature enough for this to be believable – and then got offered an accounting job. They lived happily enough in the small, rundown shack of a home for several months. It wasn't a spectacular life, but Liam and his sister had each other. And that was all that mattered, that is, until Liam returned from work one afternoon to see his sister possessed by a group of demons.

***

2 days ago

"Ash, I'm home," Liam called, shutting the door behind him with his foot as he put the groceries on the table.

The first sign that something was wrong was her non-reply. At first, Liam dismissed it as nothing. She was probably just busy.

He spent the next half an hour preparing the night's dinner – spaghetti and meatballs. When it was finally ready, he called up to her, realizing it was strange that he'd heard nothing from her all day. "Ash, dinner's ready."

Nothing.

"Ash?"

Still nothing.

"You there, sis?" And still, no reply. Now Liam was beginning to worry. That was the second sign.

He walked tentatively up the stairs. Was his sister all right? Was she hurt? Had she been kidnapped? His mind raced.

Liam reached the top of the stairs, turned the corner and stopped at the closed door to his sister's room. He was about to open it when he heard a faint growling sound from within. That was the third sign.

What was that? That wasn't Ashley, was it? There was definitely someone or something in there, though. Liam was sure of it.

"Ash?" He asked nervously and opened the door just a crack. "You in there?"

Silence.

Liam paused for a moment and hearing nothing, was about to step through when a hideous gurgling sound filled the room and something lunged at the door like a crazed animal. But this was no animal, Liam realized. This was his sister.

"Ash, what happened?" Liam asked in fear. Instinctually, he walked toward her – arms outstretched – but stepped back as soon as she lashed out at him for a second time. Liam stared in horror. She seemed rabid – vicious and foaming at the mouth. She circled the room on her hands and knees, glaring at Liam, like a leopard guarding its territory. But she was still clutching her favorite teddy bear like always. Liam never understood why it was so dear to her, but it was and he didn't dare question her about it.

"Y-you, okay, Ash?" Liam whispered, shivering. She bared her fangs in response and hissed at him. Ashley didn't even seem to realize that he was her brother. Liam backed away carefully and hurried down the stairs to the phone. It was not until he had halfway dialed 9-1-1 that he realized his younger sister was being possessed by demons.

***

Present

    Liam's initial reaction was one of shock. At first, he wasn't sure if his crazed, suddenly vicious sister had become rabid or diseased in some way, but it didn't take long for him to realize that it was demon possession. It had been going on a lot, recently, in New York City so he recognized the symptoms after only some consideration.

    His next reaction was one of fury. How dare those demons break into his home, despite the poor security, and possess his little sister? How dare they make her become so deranged? How dare they and their sick, nonexistent minds do this to him and his sister at a time like this?

    As Liam learned from the news, possession of humans was simply the demon's mind taking over Ashley's, making it in control of Ashley's body. Because it was not his sister controlling her actions, those vile demons forced Liam to chain her to the wall of her bedroom. Just the prospect of chaining his own sister to a wall elicited great fury from within Liam but with the mind of a demon dominating her, she was too violent to handle. How dare they do this to Ashley?

    In short, Liam contacted the local exorcist he had heard about on the news to rid the demon's soul from Ashley's body. The exorcist drew the strange circle Liam had seen in movies. He called it a containment circle. Liam didn't see the logic of the containment circle, but he didn't dare question it, since the subject of demons was not his specialty, nor did he fully believe in the existence of demons. That is, until now.

    Once his sister was free from the demon – miraculously, she survived, though the exorcist said that she barely did since the spirit was so strong that it took an alarming amount of energy out of her – by the exorcist's advice, the two fled their home and hit the streets of New York. And things weren't pretty from there.

Liam caught wind of their first demon tail about a day into the journey. The second and third ones appeared a day later. Then the fourth appeared and so did the fifth, sixth and seventh. And they were all after his sister. He had no idea why and didn't really want to, either, but he knew that he needed to protect her. He loved and cared for her too much to let her go. But then the demons started attacking. They might have been easy to fend off for someone with powers of their own, but since Liam was a simple human, he was pretty much useless against them, putting his sister right in harm's way.

***

"Run!" Liam screamed to Ashley, his ten-year-old sister, as the first of the demons attacked. The demon was only slightly smaller than Liam but was still ten times more vicious. It pounced on Liam's back, digging its razor-like claws into his flesh. Liam yelped in pain and threw the demon off of his back in a spasm that was more accidental than it was deliberate. Liam felt a sudden sense of triumph as it skidded across the pavement, thinking that he had won. But the exultation was short-lived. The creature got slowly up to its feet and to Liam's terror, its lips curled into a blood-curdling smile. It seemed almost... amused...

Liam looked to where Ashley was. She was some distance away, but was hesitating to go further. Her cheeks were streaked with tears, her eyes full of fear for her brother. "Go!" Liam shouted just as the demon lunged for him again, knocking him off balance. "Run!"

The hit from the demon was surprisingly powerful, sending Liam skidding across the ground. He groaned in pain.

The creature walked over to Liam, towering over him. It surveyed its prey with a sadistic fascination, poised to strike at any moment. Liam desperately groped for something to defend himself with as the creature drew closer and closer to his face. "Well, well, well," it breathed. "Look who we have here." Liam inched away as the creature approached. He continued to search for a weapon, not taking his eyes off the demon. "Don't worry," it hissed, "I'm not here for you. I'm here for your sister. So your death will be quick and painless." There was a pause. "How about we start... now?"

Liam's hand grabbed hold of a knife just as the demon attacked. He swung it hopelessly at the creature just as its mouth opened around his face. Blood spattered across the wall. But it was not his blood. It was the demon's. Liam watched it slowly crumple to the ground, where it fell – lifeless.

He breathed in and out slowly, trying to restore sense to his brain and relieve himself of his anxiety. But he couldn't. He had been so close to death, there; he nearly died.

And then Liam noticed his terrified sister watching him, her body shaking vigorously. Liam limped over to her. "It's okay, Ash. I'm alright."

She shook her head, clutching her teddy bear against her chest.

"No, don't worry, Ash. I'm fine…" Liam took a step closer to her.

Ashley shook her head again and pointed to his lower stomach. Liam glanced at it quickly to see what the cause of his sister's anxiety was and to his horror, blood was trickling out of a claw-wound. He was hurt.

Liam felt dizzy. He had been attacked and successfully injured by a creature he never believed existed. He was bleeding badly from a gash in his stomach. He could die. Liam's mind raced. Could he die? Did demons have poisonous claws? Was he losing enough blood to die there?

And that's when he noticed them – more demons, but this time coming up from behind his sister.

"Ashley, behind you!" Liam screamed but it was too late. They were already upon her, grabbing her.

"Ashley!" He started to run toward her but only made it a few feet before he was attacked from behind. Liam hit the sidewalk with a sickening crunch and was immediately pinned down by two much larger and much stronger demons.

"Move and we'll bash your head in," one of them hissed. Liam whimpered an "okay" but not without confusion. Why were they keeping him alive? Why did he matter to them? They said themselves that he didn't matter to them and that it was Ashley that they were after. Ashley. They were after Ashley. Why her? What of her did they need? Would they keep her alive? Liam's brain would not settle down.

He turned back to his sister, only to see the larger of the two demons holding Ashley rip the teddy bear from her quivering hands and throw it across the street. Rage coursed through him. That was her favorite teddy bear.

Liam tried to stand up but was held fast by the demons pinning him down. "Uh-uh-uh," one of them hissed. "Remember our deal? Do you want your blood all over the sidewalk?"

Liam whimpered helplessly, knowing he didn't have a choice. He would just have to hope that it would all turn out well, but he knew in his heart that it wouldn't. Not this time.

The demons that were holding Ashley began circling her, chanting. Liam had no idea what was going on. They wrapped her in a tight circle, still chanting. They seemed determined, fierce. They had a goal in mind. The chanting grew louder. Liam could not tell what they were saying but he knew it wasn't good. His sister was in danger.

The demons circled her faster, chanted louder and louder, until... their noises ceased. They stopped. Liam shut his eyes. He couldn't bear to see what was going to happen next.

He gave it a few moments before he opened them again, expecting to see his sister's dead body lying on the ground. But it wasn't there. In fact, his sister was nowhere in sight. And to his surprise, the two demons that were holding him were gone. Liam looked fearfully to where his sister was before. She still wasn't there but in her place was all of the demons, huddled together. They seemed to be bowing to something, or someone. Probably their master, Liam realized with horror. They were probably telling their master that they had successfully killed his sister.

Liam crawled closer, wincing at the pain from the wound in his chest.

"Master, master," he heard them chanting softly. "Rise, my master, rise!"

And the master rose. But it wasn't the master Liam was expecting. Ashley's face shimmered as she rose above the chanting demons. She was beautiful there, pristine, perfect.

Liam gasped and stared, wide-eyed with horror. He opened his mouth to say something but shut it before he could, knowing it was a very bad idea. The ritual went on for a few moments more. Ashley rose, her body shimmering from her powerful aura. And she seemed almost happy to be there.

It took her a moment to notice Liam. "Liam," she whispered. "Now you see, now you see the real me. I am the cause for the demons in New York. I'm what they were looking for."

"Don't say that, Ash," Liam whispered, tears glistening in his eyes.

"I've always been one of them, Liam. Mom was, too. That teddy bear was the only thing that could hide my powers."

Liam gasped. "No, Ash. No, no, no. You're making a mistake here."

Ashley raised her voice. "They have found me, Liam, and this is what I need to do. I was made for this, and you need to let me go."

"Ash..." Liam sobbed.

"I control the demons, Liam. I am their master."

Dark Light

The Flaming Vengeance
by
Linna Drehmel

Tanya shook with fear as she and her younger sister hid under the floor of their bedroom. She could hear her older brother scream in pain and then the sickening crunch of bones as his now lifeless body fell to the floor just above them.

She kept her hand over Gretah's mouth, trying to keep the small weeping girl from crying out and giving away their hiding place.

After the heavy sound of the wraith's footsteps left the room she put her lips up to Gretah's ear and whispered ever so softly. "We will be alright, King Austin will find us."

Chapter 1

It had only been a few months since her family had been slaughtered by the grey skinned wraith. Tanya tried very hard to shut out the memories of all she had seen and heard during the attack that took all but one of her family from her.

She could not get the look of the hideous beasts out of her mind, their long arms and clawed hands, large bat like wings and big heavy feet.

Tanya knew why they had been attacked. It was a stupid promise made to the people by the fire Gods. "Two centuries hence, line of blood next to the king with eyes of green, will protect the planet of the ring." She mumbled bitterly to herself as she finished up her duties in the kitchen.

She hated that promise. It was the reason the wraith killed her family. Her father's line was the only one on the planet with green eyes anymore, but Tanya had the dark brown eyes of her mother's line. Her little sister Gretah had the same green eyes as their father. *"They will not touch you Gretah."* She vowed silently.

Almost as if in response to Tanya's thoughts, her precious little sister hurried into the kitchen where she had just finished with her chores.

"Tanya, are we still going to watch the rings?" Gretah's sweet little voice piped.

"Yes, Gretah. I am done here." She said as she handed her sister a small sack of food that they would share as they do every evening. Then sit side by side on the hill behind the royal household and watch the rings that circle their planet glitter in the light of the twin moons.

Tanya put her arm around her sisters thin shoulders and tried unsuccessfully sneak quietly past the dining room where the royal family sat being served dinner.

"Tanya, Gretah. Please come here." King Austin said in a firm but kind voice.

The two girls walked slowly with heads bowed into the formal dining room and stopped next to the chair of their father's closest friend.

"Every night I ask the two of you to join us and every night you two sneak away." He said looking at only surviving members of his best friend's family. "Why do you leave? I have adopted the two of you into my family. You don't need to act as servants."

With head still bowed Tanya cleared her throat nervously, "You Highness, we…"

"Tanya, look at me." Austin interrupted her. "There was a time when you called me Uncle. Why now that you are a part of my family do you call me Highness?"

Tanya raised her eyes and looked into his kindly face. She remembered the relief she felt when he ripped the floorboards away with his own hands, freeing them after two long days of hiding.

"I can't. I…" Tanya stumbled over her words with tears in her eyes.

Gretah ducked under Tanya's arm and took a bold step forward, "Please Uncle may we go watch the rings? They are so pretty at night."

"Of course child." He said as he reached out and stroked her glossy black hair. "Tanya, be careful. I have heard reports of wraith in the area."

"They would not dare come to your home." Tanya said with fire in her brown eyes.

"All the same Tanya I am going to have my guard watch over you."

Tanya opened her mouth to argue but closed it again when she saw the look burning in his hazel eyes as he gestured the guard standing in the open doorway. "Watch over my nieces, but give them privacy."

"Yes, your Highness." He said with a bow to the king, and then turned to the girls. "Duchess'." He addressed them and gestured to the door way that the came in.

Chapter 2

The sisters lie on their favorite hill after they had finished their dinner, with the Kings own guard keeping a sharp eye on them at a respectful distance.

"Tanya," Gretah asked. "Do you think the souls of our family are on the rings or in the volcano with the fire Gods?"

"Only the souls of the wraith burn for eternity in the fires of the volcano as punishment for their evil. The fire Gods lift up the souls of the good people on our plant to rest forever amongst the beauty of the particle rings." She said reciting what every child learns of the fire Gods that protect their planet. "Our family was good people so they are on the rings."

"But isn't a member of our family supposed to be the protector that rises up out of the volcano? If we are good people then why would our souls be in the volcano?" Gretah asked worry showing in her innocent green eyes.

"Gretah," Tanya said as she turned on her side to look at her sister's innocent face. "The person who is to be the protector must be a good person of our line. That is what the promise says but, they must go into the volcano while they are still alive." She said trying not to let the doubt show in her voice. Tanya just didn't know what she believed in anymore.

Dark Light

"Well that would hurt!" Gretah said her green eyes big with wonder. "What is the protector anyway?"

"I don't know the last protector was about two hundred years ago, all the priests know is that it is some kind of fire beast." Tanya answered her sister and then lay back on the grass hoping that her sister had run out of questions.

"But Tanya…" Gretah started to ask but stopped and the two of them simultaneously turned to the sound of a struggle.

"Wraith," Tanya said with fear in her eyes. "Run back to the house and tell Uncle!"

"But what about you?" Gretah said with tears of dread filling her eyes.

"I have to help him." she said desperately. Not really knowing what she could do but feeling that she couldn't leave this man to be killed by the wraith. "Come on."

Tanya jumped up grabbing her sister's hand and ran to the site of the struggle. Not sure what to do she let go of her sisters hand, gave her a shove toward the house and yelled "Run get Uncle"

Tanya jumped on the beast and wrapped her arms around it pinning its wings to its back and screamed, "Gretah run!"

The wraith was only momentarily surprised by Tanya jumping on its back, but recovered quickly as it cast the broken body of the guard aside. The creature then heaved and pushed its bat like wings out shoving Tanya off causing her to fall back wards hitting a tree.

"What have we here?" The wraiths voice grumbled low in its large chest as it turned to look at Gretah who stood still paralyzed with fear. "Green eyes, I thought my mistress got rid of your family already."

"No, leave her alone." Tanya said weakly as she tried to hang on to conscious thought. "FireLords!" She cried out to the Gods as she lost her fight to stay conscious, but instead of darkness taking her thoughts she saw brilliant green and yellow flames behind her eyes.

"Touch the flames child." Was the command of a multitude of high and low voices. "You called to us and we have answered."

"Help me save her," Tanya begged. "Gretah is the last of the green eyes."

"Have faith child, take the flaming vengeance."

Tanya hesitated only for a moment then reached out to the flames desperate for anything that might help save her sister.

The searing pain of the fire licked her fingers as the heat absorbed into her hands then spread to her whole being. The burning pain jarred her back into consciousness.

Tanya lay on her stomach next to the tree with her arms reaching out in front of her but was startled at the sight of yellow and green flames emanating from her hands. Without any further thought she got quickly to her feet and jumped once again on the beast that was now attacking her little sister. "Get your hands off my sister." Tanya commanded as she wrapped her arms around the wraith and planted her flaming hands on its large chest.

Tanya quickly let go as she felt the wraith fall to its knees squealing in pain. The yellow-green fire consumed the wraith, then it quickly collapsed into ashes as the flames finished its judgment on the evil creature.

"Gretah!" Tanya cried once the wraith was out of the way.

Tanya scrambled to her sisters side and reached out for her sisters still form but quickly with-drew her hands seeing that they still had flames skimming around her fingers. "Stop it." She cried and oddly the fire obeyed her and retreaded to her hands then deeper into her body.

She carefully reached down and gathered her small sister's broken body into her arms. "Hang on baby girl. I will take you to Uncle, hang on."

Gretah began to heave, coughing blood onto her lips. "Your eyes." She gasped as the light that was in her own eyes went out.

Chapter 3

Tanya came home carrying her sister's body. The entire royal household exploded in upheaval with the death of the duchess as well as the death of the loyal guard. No one noticed the change in Tanya's eyes, nor the fact that she quietly slipped away and locked herself in her room for the full night and all the next day.

The young duchess sat huddled in a corner of her room crying. "I should have died, I am not the one. I have brown eyes." She wept.

Standing on shaky legs Tanya went to the mirror afraid to see the truth the image would show her and yet she was compelled to look anyway. She gazed into the lovely dark wood framed mirror that hung on the wall above the matching dresser. She saw her heart shaped face, the same long dark hair but her eyes, they were not her eyes. Instead of the dark brown like her mother had she saw eyes that were a flaming green.

Tanya looked down at her gloved hands, scared of the flames that she knew would flicker on her fingertips. Even though she knew what was under the gloves she stripped them off anyway dropping them on the dresser. She held her hands that were flickering softly green and yellow up by her face further illuminating her now green eyes.

Hot tears began to fall from her eyes again. When she saw the image in the mirror, all she could think of was how much she looked like her younger sister.

"I am not the one, it should have been her." She yelled at her reflection. "I should have been the one to die!" She screamed to her image.

The green flames in her hand began to grow in reaction to the pain in her heart. "No more." She cried and curled up her fire-shrouded fist and smashed it into the mirror, but instead of the mirror shattering, the glass warped and melted from the heat in her fist.

Tanya pulled her hands toward her body in shock at how powerful the flaming vengeance was. "Please stop." She begged the flames but this time the large flames did not respond. Still looking down at her hands that were flickering green she saw her long glossy hair that hung down over her shoulder and could not help but think about how much it looked like Gretah's and her mother's hair.

She could no longer stand the sight of it. Her flaming green hands shook and she reached up and grabbed the dark locks instantly setting her hair on fire. Tanya closed her eyes as her hot tears evaporated on her face while the green and yellow flames quickly burned off her hair.

Tanya knew what she needed to do, even though she didn't understand why the Gods gave her the flaming vengeance. She had to kill the creatures that took her family and took the chances that this planet had for the protector.

Without looking up at the warped mirror she took her gloves from the dresser top and put them back on commanding the flames to stay safely hidden under the layer of dark leather. She reached up with her gloved hand and started to pull off the silver and gold weaved necklace that marked her as a member of the royal family but stopped, instead she brushed the ashes of her once lovely hair from her now balled head. She pulled a hooded cloak on then packed a small knapsack with the essential things she would need on her quest.

Tanya looked to the shuttered window as she thought about how she was going to leave her uncle's house unseen, but a sharp knock at her door shook her out of her thoughts.

"Tanya," call Queen Drea from the other side of the door. "Please open the door my dear. It is almost time for your sister's pyre service."

Tanya could not bear the thought of going to the traditional pyre service. To see her sisters body burned so her soul could be lifted up to the particle rings with the smoke, made her feel sick.

Without a word Tanya pulled the hood of the cloak low down over her face not just hiding her lack of hair but the green fire that burned in her eyes. She quickly unlocked the door and yanked it open keeping her head low. "I am not going to the service Aunt Drea." She declared as she tried to push past her adoptive aunt.

"What are you doing?" The queen asked blocking her way. "Why are you dressed in travel clothing and not mourning clothes?"

"Because I'm not going to Gretah's service" She said with a determined sound in her voice. "I am leaving."

"Leaving? Leaving where?" Drea said with panic in her voice. "You can't go. The wraith is out there and they still want to kill you."

"That is why I am leaving Aunt Drea." Tanya said looking up into her aunt's lovely face. She always thought that the queen and her mother could have been sisters. She had the same big dark eyes and the sweet freckles that were sprinkled across her nose like nutmeg.

"Tanya your eyes!" Drea gasped.

"I have to go." Tanya said as she hurriedly looked down and forcefully pushed passed her adoptive aunt.

"Tanya wait, your eyes are green. Does this mean that the fire gods chose you to be the protector?" The queen pursued her down the hallway as she headed to the busy main staircase.

"No it doesn't" Tanya said as she quickly descended the stairs. "The one who should have been the protector is dead."

"Tanya wait you can't leave." Her aunt gasped as she hurried down the stairs toward the front door. "Austin, come here quick Tanya is leaving." The queen called when she spotted her husband by the door.

"You are not leaving young lady. You are a duchess in my household. It is your duty to be at your sister's pyre service." The king firmly told her trying to block her path.

Tanya lifted her now glowing green eyes to his and could see shock when he saw the new color that blazed powerfully in her eyes. "Uncle I don't know why the gods have given me the flaming vengeance. In spite of the way my eyes look now I am not the protector, but I will do whatever it take to be sure that you and your family are safe. Even if that means I have to leave you." She said as she reached past the stunned king and opened the door. She quickly left the people who had become her family.

After closing the door firmly behind her she quickly removed the glove from her right hand and placed her palm on the wooden door. She surrendered to the flames in her body but at the same time controlled the flow of it to her hand and released it gently on the door. "No wraith will ever enter here." She said as the green flames quickly spread over the large home like a protective green shield.

Tanya took her hand off the door, turned and walked way without looking back. Leaving a measure of protection on the home as well as a swirling green mark on the door where her hand had been.

Chapter 4

Tanya stalked another wraith. This time it was an ugly and fierce female. She knew that she was close. She could smell the wraiths repulsive odor above the usual smells of the city that she now lived in. *"If you could call it living."* She thought.

She still had plenty of money left that she had brought with her from the kings home, but she could never stay in one place for too long if she hoped to kill the wraith without getting killed herself. Tanya lifted her sleeve and saw many the scars on her arm. She wasn't angry that the wraith had given her those scars. In fact she smiled when she saw them on her arms, because she knew that the many wraiths that gave those healed wounds were now dead. She knew that she probably would get another one today but she didn't care, she knew that she was going to kill another wraith female tonight. The males were good to kill but it was the females that could produce thousands of eggs that would turn into a killing horde in a short period of time. So taking one of them out made her smile.

Tanya listened closely to the quiet city street with ears that had been sharpened by the power of the flaming vengeance. At first she didn't hear much of anything, just water dripping and the soft scampering sound of rodents. She strained harder and then she heard it, the deep huffing sound of a wraith looking around for the next human to make as its meal.

"Oh, no you don't." She silently thought as she moved quickly through the streets toward the sound, but another startling sound hit her.

"Looking for a fight, stinking she wraith?" Yelled a strong male voice.

"No I am looking for a tasty human snack, but you will do." The wraith growled at him.

"Well come get me if you can." He taunted the beast just as Tanya rounded the corner of a building and entered the ally that the sound of the confrontation was coming from.

Tanya saw two very different creatures preparing for a vicious fight. The one that she expected to see was the ugly grey skinned female wraith. The other was a beautiful dark haired, dark eyed, young human man.

She saw the female wraith pounce at the young man and felt her heart leap in fear, sure that she would see him killed, but he dodged with cat like reflexes while taking a precision slash with an odd dark bladed dagger at the wraiths midsection drawing a line of sick black blood.

The wraith crouched low pressing a hand over its bleeding belly and growled in anger, "You will pay for that human."

"Sure I will." He said his voice dripping with sarcasm, and also crouched low trying to anticipate the wraiths next attack.

But the wraith did something that he did not anticipate. She deftly picked up a stone and quickly threw it at him hitting him in the center of his chest, knocking him back against the wall behind him. She quickly took advantage of this and leapt the distance between them but fell short of her mark, as he the young man skillfully threw one of his daggers in an attempt to keep her from falling on top of him. The deadly black blade sunk deep into her shoulder and she roared with rage and jumped once again at him taking a wild swing with her uninjured arm hitting him across the face knocking him off his feet. The wraith then descended upon him with a deadly glint in its ugly yellow eyes.

Tanya had never seen anyone else hold off a wraith like that before and was mesmerized by the fight, but she shook herself when she saw the wraith take a vicious swing at him. She quickly stripped off her gloves, and with precise control called the yellow-green flames to flare up powerfully. She quietly ran the distance to the fighting pair.

Using the element of surprise she barreled into the wraith knocking it off the dark haired man. The wraith was unprepared for Tanya's attack landed on its back with Tanya on top of her.

"You will not take another human soul!" Tanya declared as she placed her burning hands on the wraith face. The wraith screamed in pain and slashed wildly at her arms trying to remove the burning hands from her face.

Tanya did not notice the gashes the wraith left on her arms but jumped off the beast once she saw the judgmental flames take hold of the beast. She stood back and watched the flames consumed yet another wraith, and then the screams of the beast stopped as the silent form collapsed into a pile of ash.

"What…who are you?" the young man asked as he got to his feet.

"I could ask you the same question." Tanya responded quickly. "Calm." She whispered to the flames and they obeyed her soft command retreating deep into her body. She bent down and picked up her gloves and put them back on then pulled the hood of her cloak over hear head that had just began to grow some hair.

"What is your name?" She asked him once she finished with her gloves and cloak.

"My name is SeanMarkus. I know who you are in spite of you missing hair." He answered facing her. "You are King Austin's missing niece."

"How would you know?" Tanya asked him with irritation in her voice.

"You are still wearing the royal necklace your Grace." He said reaching forward running his finger along the glinting chain that peaked above the neckline of her cloak.

"Don't call me that." She said slapping his hand away, "and don't touch me."

"Well if I can't call you by your title then what shall I call you?" He asked with a hint of sassiness in his voice and a twinkle in his dark eyes.

"You may call me TanyaLynn." She responded tartly.

"Lynn? Where do you get that name from?" He asked "I thought the royal family didn't take a surname."

"Not that it is any of your business SeanMarkus, but I took the name Lynn back when I left the kings house to hunt wraith." She said with her gloved hands on her hips and a sour look on her face. "Besides I would like to know where you learned to fight like that. I have not seen anyone fight a wraith like that and live."

He ignored her question and asked one of his own, "How did you get the flaming vengeance?"

She ignored his question as well, bent down and picked up the black bladed dagger from the pile of ash that was once a wraith female.

"I will tell you my family secret if you tell me yours." She answered him extending the blade to him handle first.

He was quiet for a moment as he looked into her unnaturally green eyes, then took the dagger and flipped it expertly in his right hand and put the blade in a holster at his left hip.

"I am from a long line of wraith hunters." He admitted to her. "We train secretly from the time we are very young so the wraith don't find out and try to kill us when we are still in training."

"Where did you get those daggers? I have never seen anything like them before." She asked him intrigued by his story.

"They were given to my earliest forefather. The blades themselves were blessed by the Gods."

"They look like volcanic glass." She said gesturing to the second blade in his left hand.

"They are." He said simply as he flipped the blade in the air and quickly sheathed it in the holster on his right hip. "So, your Grace what it your secret."

"I told you not to call me that." Tanya retorted angrily.

"Sorry," He said with a touch of laughter in his voice. "TanyaLynn."

"As you know SeanMarkus, I am the adopted niece of the King. My father was his best friend and adviser." She started to tell him as she led the way out of the alley. "As I am sure you know my father's line passes along the green eyes. My brother and my sister had the green eyes as well but I didn't. I had the brown eyes of my mother's line."

"But your eyes are green." He interrupted her.

"The fire gods changed them when they gave me the flaming vengeance."

"Then does it mean that you are the…"

"No," She said cutting him off. "I am not the protector, I just told you I was born with brown eyes. The one that should have been the protector was killed. I don't know why they gave me the flaming vengeance. I guess I was the only choice they had left."

"Well if you are not the protector then what are they Gods going to do about a protector to rid our planet of the wraith?"

"I don't know SeanMarkus, maybe there is another green eyes somewhere on the planet, but until the FireLords find one I am going to take out as many wraith as I can."

"Well then maybe you and I should work together." He suggested.

"No," she said decisively. "You could get hurt and I don't want to be responsible for that."

SeanMarkus stopped walking and began to laugh, TanyaLynn turned to him with an angry look on her face. "What are you laughing at?"

"You! Your Grace!" He said still laughing.

"I told you not to call me that!" She said getting really angry. "What is so funny?"

"I have trained all my life to fight the wraith." He told her suddenly serious. "I know everything about them, where they live, when they breed, how they eat. Everything, and you a little duchess girl thinks she needs to protect me." Even though his voice was serious his dark eyes still danced with mirth.

"Look here, these creatures are after me just as much as I am after them for killing my family, and I just can't have you getting in the way. You will just get hurt."

"Hang on TanyaLynn," He said putting a firm hand on her shoulder and turning her toward him again. "I can help you, like I said I have been training all my life to take out the wraith."

"I said don't touch me." She warned him shaking his hand off her shoulder.

"Answer me this how were you planning on taking then out? Did you have any kind of plan?" He asked looking intently in her eyes for a moment until she shifted her eyes away.

"I didn't think so." He said. "I have an idea, a way that we can take out a whole clan."

"If you have this great plan for killing the wraith clan in our area, then why haven't you done it already?" She asked him a little snidely.

"Well Duchess I need someone with a little…umm…fire power." He said gesturing to her hands.

"All right SeanMarkus," She said through clinched teeth at the sound of her official title. "Tell me your plan."

Chapter 5

After months of SeanMarkus and TanyaLynn working together and planning their attack on the local wraith clan home, the day had finally come. It was a hot day without a cloud in the sky to interrupt the flow of the large yellow suns waves of high temperature. The heat baked the ground, made every human on the planet beg the Fire Gods for mercy.

The heat was more of a blessing than the people knew. The heat protected them from wraith attacks. The wraith cannot stand the heat. It saps them of their strength, making them sluggish as well as the light of the sun its self, easily burns their grey skin. This is why their clan homes are always deep underground caves that are cold and dark. The two of them worked together pursuing the wraith to find out where the cave was for sure and only killing a wraith when another person's life was at stake. Then they spent time and money tracking down the local alchemist. A woman named SandraKay. She was a tall woman from the north who had bright yellow hair and a friendly smile, but knew her business when it came to the elements that they needed to bring about their plan. Although SandraKay wanted the wraith in their area gone as much as they did her price was still steep for her alchemy services.

TanyaLynn crouched in the pathetic shade of a boulder near the entrance to the wraiths clan home. She pushed her growing dark hair out of her eyes and wished she was down there with SeanMarkus in the nice cool cave. But instead she stayed out keeping watch waiting until the sun just touched the western horizon.

"Come on SeanMarkus." She whispered with more irritation in her voice than she felt. She closed her eyes remembering his beautiful face as he told her to ignite the trail of God-powder the alchemist had given them as soon as the sun sunk beneath the horizon, whether or not he was out.

TanyaLynn opened her eyes and looked up again. The sun was half way down, and she knew he has only moments to get out. "Fire and ashes!" She swore as she pushed herself away from the rock and ran toward the cave entrance. She stripped off her gloves, called the fire to her left hand and crouched down to light the black trail of God-powder.

She closed her eyes and lowered her hand but all she could see in her mind was his beautiful eyes that were the same color as the chocolates the King had always given her. "Fiery ashes SeanMarkus!" She swore again, standing up and hurried into the dark mouth of the wraiths cave. Careful to keep her green and yellow flaming hand away from the black powdered trail she followed it closely knowing that it would lead her to her friend. TanyaLynn held her hand up high now that she saw the direction that the trail leads.

The floor of the cave was a dark smooth rock that was dry and slanting gently downward. The narrow walls of the cave were also smooth dark rock but widened steadily as the channel descended deeper into the ground. Although the air grew steadily cooler, TanyaLynn was surprised that the air and the cave was still dry.

The channel took a steep dip downward as the walls seem to fall away into a large chamber with stalactites hanging from the ceiling and stalagmites pointing sharply upwards. A wonderful sight that no humans have ever lived to tell about, she was mesmerized as she walked through the cave until she heard a deep huffing sound that caused her to freeze in fear.

She looked down to see dozens of sleeping wraith lying curled up all over the cave floor, and she was standing in the middle of this sleeping hoard. Not sure what to do she looked up and saw at the back of the chamber standing next to the sleeping queen wraith was SeanMarkus looking as though he was straining to either hold something up or put it down.

TanyaLynn carefully made her way to where he was and could see right away what the problem was and why he was delayed in leaving the cave.

He was just about to set the last sack of explosive God-powder next to the queen wraith. While trying to avoid stepping on the sleeping male wraith next to her SeanMarkus bumped into a fragile stalagmite, but managed to catch it just before it fell to the rock floor waking an angry throng that would rip him to pieces.

"What are you doing in here Duchess? Why didn't you light the powder?" He said in an angry whisper, even though she saw relief in his eyes when he spotted her.

"Did you really think that I was going to blow this cave with you still in it?" She retorted as she helped him to lower the heavy chunk of rock to the cave floor. "Hurry up chocolate eyes let's get out of here before they wake up."

"Hold up a moment Duchess I have to set the last bag."

"Don't call me duchess." She snapped.

"Well then don't call me chocolate eyes." He retorted pulling the sack of powder from his pocket. He turned to face the large, angry and very much awake queen's wraith.

"Hello tasty snacks." She growled making a swipe for SeanMarkus as he dodged and she only managed to tear open the sack of black powder.

"Run TanyaLynn!" He yelled as he snagged her right hand dragging her stumbling along with him.

She looked over her shoulder as saw the queen wraith extend her wings and lift into the air and begin to fly after them at an alarming rate.

"We aren't going to make it out before she catches us." TanyaLynn puffed as she dodged mounds of waking wraith.

"Just keep running."

"I have an idea SeanMarkus, drop to the floor when I tell you."

"What?"

"Trust me." She begged him as they neared the narrow channel that lead to the surface.

She knew the queen was right behind them when she felt the wind that was stirred up by the strong beat of her wings.

"Now!" TanyaLynn yelled just before they entered the channel and they both dropped to the floor of the cave, causing the queen wraith to shoot past them up the channel and into the night as TanyaLynn's flaming left hand fell into the trail of black powder igniting it in an array of yellow sparks.

"Run!" He yelled desperately as they both got to their feet and dashed through the channel. They fled out of the mouth of the cave just as the first of several explosions rocked the ground under their feet, killing everything that was left down in the cave.

Chapter 6

SeanMarkus stood with his arms protectively around TanyaLynn as the dust and rubble began to settle after the last explosion.

"Duchess? Are you alright?" He said with a scared look in his eyes.

"Yes" she coughed and lifted her head off his shoulder. "But she got away."

"I know what are we going to do?" He asked sounding panicked. "She will be back for us."

"No" she told him vaguely as she looked over her shoulder at the volcano.

"What do you mean no?" He asked her confused.

"I mean that she is not going to come back for us, it's me." She told him taking a step back. "I will give her what she wants."

"Are you saying that you are going to sacrifice yourself?" He asked her with a panicked look on his face. "I will not let you do that."

"No I am not going to sacrifice myself I am just going to draw her off lead her to the volcano then push her in. Then I will come back here for you."

"No TanyaLynn, if we do this we do it together. I will not just sit here wondering if you lived or died." He told her with a firm note in his voice but fear in his eyes. "You have to know I am not just being the wraith hunter here, I love you."

Tanya closed her eyes for a moment when she heard this. She had tried from the time she first saw him not to love him. She had lost so many people that she loved that she could not stand to love and lose anyone else, so she tried so hard not to love him. But she did love him.

"I love you too SeanMarkus." She said when she opened her eyes again. "We will do it together then."

"If we do this together then we truly do it together." He said looking deeply in her eyes and took her right hand in his. "Duchess TanyaLynn before the witness of the mountain of the FireLords I ask you to be my wife."

"Yes!" she said her voice filled with emotion as she let go of his and reached up taking off her necklace and putting it on him. "Let this gift seal our marriage as I am no longer known as Lynn."

Tanya let her hands linger on the back of his neck after placing her royal necklace on him. He took a step forward placing his hands on her hips and drew her close, winding his arms around her small frame. He ever so gently covered her lips with his in a long sweet caress.

Tanya had not felt loved like this before. She felt like she would melt into him. She kissed him back enthusiastically not wanting it to end, but she knew it had to. Gently she pulled back breathing hard, "We have to get moving, the wraith queen will be heading back anytime now."

"I know," He said regrettably but didn't let go of her. "What is the plan?"

"I will need you to cut me, we leave a trail of my blood for her to follow to the mouth of the volcano. You will have to find a place to hide within a few paces…"

"No." He said quickly interrupting her as he let go and turned around for a moment, then turned back. "I will not wound my new wife. Besides the wraith are not blood drinkers."

"Please listen to me Sean." She said desperately. "The wraith may not be blood drinkers but they are after me, they are drawn to my bloodline so the scent of it in the air will draw the queen to where ever I am."

"I don't like this Tanya." He told her with dread in his voice.

"I know but it will work. As soon she shows up I will fight her. Once her attention is fully on me you get her with your blades and then I will push her in the volcano." He looked intently in her face but remained silent not liking the feeling he had in his gut, "Please Sean, it will work." She begged and held up her right hand.

Without taking his eyes from her face he deftly reached down and drew his dagger from his right hip with his left hand and quickly slashed her right palm, cutting her deeply.

She drew as sharp breath in at the feel of the blade cutting her but held his loving gaze, and then curled her bleeding hand into a fist squeezing more blood from the cut. "I love you Sean." She said and leaned forward and kissed him softly on the lips.

As she kissed the man she loved she call only the power of the flames but not the flame its self to her bleeding hand that she had curled into a fist.

Tanya pulled back and smiled at him and without any further warning she smashed her flame powered fist on the side of his head knocking Sean off his feet as well as knocking him unconscious.

She burst into tears at the sight of her beautiful new husband lying on the ground. "I am so sorry Sean." She said as she knelt on the ground next to him. "I love you so much, that I would die if anything happened to you, I have to protect you."

She leaned down and kissed him on the forehead and her tears fell on a bruise that had already began to stain his skin. She sat up straight and grabbed the front of his shirt with her uninjured left hand and ripped it open. She then placed her left palm on his chest and once again called to the power of the flames with in her and controlled the flow from her hand allowing a soft green flame to encircle him like a green shield. "No wraith will ever touch you." She pronounced and lifted her hand from him leaving the same swirling green mark on his chest.

Tanya got quickly to her feet and without looking back she ran as fast as she could toward the volcano. She opened her fist letting the blood fall freely from the wound. She began to ascend the low side of the volcano when she heard the beat of wings. She pushed her tired legs faster, she needed to be at the opening before the wraith queen over took her.

The glowing mouth of the volcano was in sight when she felt the air begin to be stirred up by the powerful beat of the queen's wings and she dove for the ground but just a split second too late as she felt the claws of the wraith slice through her shirt and rake the skin on her back. Tanya landed hard on her stomach and tried not to cry out in pain from the deep gashes in her back. She looked up and saw the queen standing eagerly by the mouth of the volcano, "Come little green eyes, let's end this." The queen wraith growled.

Tanya fully surrendered to the flames in her soul and pushed ever bit of the power to her hands and jumped to her feet and walked calmly to where the wraith stood. "Yes let's be done with this!"

The wraith growled and swung a powerfully clawed fist at Tanya but she ducked quickly and lunged forward and placed her burning hands on the wraith's belly. Squealing in pain the queen wraith shoved Tanya hard causing her to stumble backward. Not deterred from her goal, Tanya lunged forward again but this time the queen wraith was able to land a solid hit on the side of her head causing her to stumble dazed closer to the edge of the volcano.

The wraith seized the opportunity and jumped on the Tanya sinking her needle like teeth into the young woman's neck relishing the taste of her flesh and blood. Tanya knew she hand just mere seconds to do something before the wraith killed her, pushing past the pain in her neck she wrapped her arms around the queen wraith in a tight embrace and whispered, "I'm sorry Sean." As she took a large step back pulling the queen wraith with her into the powerful heat of the volcano.

Even though she was in excruciating pain from where the wraith had bit her she held on tightly being sure to keep the queen wraiths powerful wings pinned so she could not fly out. The beast screamed and writhed as its skin began to burn, but Tanya held on until the wraiths screams stopped and its body turned to ash.

"Let go child."

"Let go of what?" She asked the voices of the FireLords. "How come I don't feel the heat, Why am I not dead? I was not the one."

"Let go of your fear, you are worthy. That is why we chose you."

"But I was not a green eyes until you changed them. It should have been Gretah."

"Gretah rests as she should among the rings, you are our chosen one. Let go of Gretah and let go of your fears and fly child. You are the protector."

Tanya saw amongst the flames the image of her sister's soul happily dancing along the particle rings, then she was finally able to release her fears and let go.

She looked at her arms and saw flames emerge from the scars on her arms, and the flames turned into beautiful yellow and red feathers as her arms became wings. She completely surrendered her being to the flames and her body transformed and became powerful.

"Fly child," The FireLords told her. "You can fly!"

Tanya pushed her new and powerful wings against the hot air and quickly rose bursting free of the mouth of the volcano. She finally knew who she was. She was the promised protector of the world of the ring. She was the Phoenix.

Epilogue

Sean groaned as he began to regain his senses. "Why did you hit me?" He put his hand to where she hit him expecting to feel a painful bruise and swelling but there was nothing, no pain. He opened his eyes and jumped up looking toward the volcano just in time to see the Phoenix rise powerfully.

He saw the Phoenix toss back her head and raise her voice in a song that meant death to all wraiths on their planet, but Sean knew that it was the beautiful voice of his beloved wife.

Dark Light

The Miller's Daughter
by
Stefan Ellery

Tam was not one to indulge in any self-pity. He did not care what others said about him. He just ignored them, what he did instead was put that pity in a form of expression, he was an artist, better than any in his school. Of course, others may think differently of his art, while canvas and paper were the chosen medium for many in the town he lived in. His was brick, stone, wood and pavement. He did not use a brush, and his paint never came out of a tube. He used spray cans to create his art. He could do wonderful things with a can of spray paint. He could create details that were difficult for the average person, when he wanted more complexity, he would use the straight edge of a piece of Bristol board or the curve of an ice cream lid. Everything to him was a tool for his art.

Using the surface of a building was not something most people cared for. Even at fifteen he had run-ins with the law. At worst they would give him a tour of the jail cells in the police station and at best he would just receive a stern lecture. It was very rare that his mother would tell him off. She was a single parent trying to hold down three jobs, just so she could pay the bills and put food on the table.

His mother left before he went to school and returned a couple of hours after he went to bed. Frozen dinners and wearing a key to the house around his neck was normal for him. No one had a leash on him, and he was free to do what he wanted. He was smart enough not to get into drugs and alcohol as others he knew had done.

He just finished creating a silhouette of a group of homeless people sitting on a busy sidewalk. A tin cup was placed in front of them. In color, he painted pedestrians who hurried by them. Not wanting to concern themselves with anyone in need of help. This was painted on the side of a law firm. The kind that did not help people, when this firm won a case, it would often mean people would lose their homes and be sent out on the street. Tam may ignore the rules and authority. However, he still had a rule of ethics he followed.

Tam walked along the river's edge, looking at all the textures on the ground and the buildings he passed. So many surfaces he could work on, his canvas was as big as the world. He halted when he saw the old mill sitting above the water's edge, he looked through the empty doorway and could see the river running underneath it. Stone and timber kept it from washing into the fast-moving water. He touched the stone work and felt the roughness of its surface underneath the palm of his hand. His eye was attracted to the sandy colored stone. There was a tree that rose through the middle of the building, and its green leaves stuck through the glassless windows. A face popped into the window and then disappeared as fast as the breeze that caressed the leaves. Tam shook his head. The foliage of the tree must have been playing tricks on him. Still, he did not feel like confirming if it were an illusion or not, and he hurried home.

Dark Light

His mind fresh with a dream of a haunting girls face made him eager to brush away the image from his head and the best way he could do that was to paint on the old mill's walls. He walked into the local hardware store and grabbed some spray cans. His other source was the recycling bin behind the store. There he found some large plastic lids, a trellis and cardboard. He was quick to leave. He didn't want to be caught raiding the bin by one of the store's employees.

Tam waited for the darkness to envelope the town before he made his way to the mill and waited even longer for the crowd of fishermen that was determined to catch a walleye in the coolness of the dark to. It was past one am by the time the last angler had to retreat from the dampness of the night. Tam never complained about the weather. He was versatile and could paint during a blizzard if he were inclined to. Observing the building from the distance, he turned it over and over in his mind until he managed to fit a picture onto the surface of the mill's walls.

Knapsack in hand he dumped all his tools onto the ground in front of the mill. When he finished shaking a can of purple, he sprayed half of the wall with its amethyst hue. The other half he flattened with the darkness of black. He sat down on the grass waiting for the paint to dry so he could continue with more of the abstract features he intended. Looking up he could see the light of the stars piercing the night. A scream made him push himself up from the ground. He heard it again and again. A streak of reddish fur ran out of a nearby bush and headed for the safety of the shadows. He should have known better. It was a fox that had startled him. The hair on his on arms

397

stood up. He could not shake the eerie feeling the sound of the fox gave him.

Tam started on the next process of his painting, hoping work would keep him occupied and rid himself of any troublesome thoughts. Tam laid down domes and created an array of pyramids with the help of the trellis, in the dark sky, he painted moons tinged with the colors of reds and blues. He finished off the painting by creating stars and adding shadows and highlights to his creations until they could pop off the walls. Satisfied he stood back and admired his work. The act of painting made the bad things go away for him, made his life feel better, even if it were for only the two or three hours he spent working on his art. The end result was less satisfying because it meant an end of his escape, and reality would set back in. Tam jumped back. The girl's face popped into the window. Dull grey eyes stared at him. He thought someone was playing a prank on him, so he moved out of her eyesight and moved to the opposite side of the building. He looked through the window and found he could see the girl through it. He looked at the girl's feet. They did not touch any surface. The girl was floating. She turned her whole body around as if she were standing on a music box. Her feet did not move. She stared at him with the eyes of death.

Tam's heart skipped a beat, and panic rose in his stomach. He ran home as fast as he could. He was afraid of what he saw and afraid of being trapped by the impossible. When he got home, he hid under the covers, like he had done when he was nine. Then, it was nightmares that plagued him, what was happening to him now had nothing to do with sleep. It was all too real. He then realized he left all his paints and the backpack with all his tools behind. He would suffer the loss. He had no intention of ever going back to the mill.

Somehow, he managed to get a good sleep despite what had occurred, the memory was beginning to fade away. He wondered if it was just a dream that he experienced, maybe he did not go out and paint the mill's wall. He wanted to believe that. It was a new day, and he had school to get to. He launched himself out of his bed, but in the process, his foot hit a spray can, and he tumbled onto his back. His head was turned to the side, and he could see spray cans all over the floor. His backpack and tools were also there. He remembered that he had left his pack and paints at the mill. He was happy to see them here. It confirmed that he did have a dream. He breathed a sigh of relief and looked up. His eyes bulged out of his head. He felt nauseous from what he saw. What he found to his horror was a picture of the mill painted on the ceiling of his room. He ran out of the house for the safety of his school.

Tam busied himself with an attempt to go through all his homework he was given earlier in the day. He was not one to do work during his spare, nor did he ever go into the school's library, unless he was told to do so. However, if he didn't do anything, his mind would start dwelling on the painting in his room. Tam pulled out a Math book from his backpack. Before he could crack the text open a delicate hand covered the spine. He looked up and saw Lisa, a girl from his homeroom. He pulled his math book away from her. "What do you want?"

Lisa brushed back her brown hair and set a determined expression "It was you wasn't it?"

Tam looked away from Lisa, she always had a penetrating stare, and he hated how her hazel eyes seemed to see through a person. Himself included. "What was me?"

She sat next to him on the bench and swiveled her body towards him. "The painting on the old mill."

Of course Lisa would know it was him, she took photos of his work. He'd seen them, but he always feigned ignorance. And today would be no different. "Why does that have to be me?"

Lisa let out a short laugh. "Oh come on, when a painting shows up on a building, a fence, anything with a large surface. It's always you. There is no one else in Lindsay that will even attempt what you do. Besides you never sign your work."

Tam shifted on his perch, Lisa was making him uncomfortable. "So what if it was, you going to report me?"

"No, but what you did it was kind of ballsy, you paint on a heritage building and one that is haunted."

Tam stood up, surprise etched on his face. "Haunted? What do you mean haunted?"

Lisa smiled at Tam's reaction. "Haven't you heard of the miller's daughter?"

He clenched his fists, he wanted to run away from anything to do with the mill. "No."

"Wow, you've lived here all your life and you don't even know about that." Lisa was always the one in class to know everything about the towns past and present. She kept tabs on people that she found interesting. Tam was not happy that he was on her list of interesting people.

"I had other things on my mind other than the

400

town's history. So tell me what about the millers daughter."

She looked at him eagerly and he knew she wanted something. "I'll tell you but, I need a favor from you."

Tam never liked doing favors for anyone or owing anybody anything. That's why he kept mostly to himself. "What kind of favor."

Lisa stood up and grabbed his hand, and held on to him. Tam got the impression she was afraid he would run away. "I need you to help raise funds for impoverished kids."

He was right, this charity work was not part of his makeup. He had no interest in bugging people for money. "Forget it, I'm not going to knock on doors for money and I have no desire to talk to people."

Lisa shook her head. "Oh no nothing like that, I just need to make use of your talents."

He gave up, if it was something to do with painting then it couldn't be so bad. At least he wouldn't be going door to door. "Fine, now tell me about the miller's daughter."

"There really is not much to tell. There was a fire that had took the mill, unfortunately a girl was in the mill at the time it burnt down. No one knows who the girl was, but she was given the nickname The Miller's Daughter. They say she haunts the place and once in a while you can catch her face in one of the windows."

Tam had a lump in his throat, the story was becoming all too real for him. He wanted to pass it off as a figment of his imagination or a prank someone had played on him. "I'm out of here, thanks for the story." Tam slipped his hand out of Lisa's grasp and turned his back on her and walked away. He found a secluded spot between the bleachers in the gym, he wanted to be left alone. Arriving home in the afternoon Tam was surprised to see his mother's car parked in the drive. Inside, she was sitting at the kitchen table having some coffee. She looked up when he entered the kitchen and patted the empty seat next to her. Tam sat down. "You're home early."

His mother sipped from her mug. "It's only for a moment, I'll be heading back out, now tell me why have you painted the ceiling of your room."

Tam wasn't going to tell his mom that a ghost did it, she wouldn't believe him and sometimes it's just easier to let people think what they want about you. "I don't know, I was in a mood."

"Well your moods should not include our house. At least it's not unpleasant to look at. Nice touch adding a girls face in the window."

"I didn't paint a face in the window."

"Could have fooled me."

Tam felt chills go through his body, he knew there was no face in the window, at least when he last looked. He ran into his room and the window was empty. His mother came up behind him.

"See I told you so."

He wondered if his mother was losing it. "Ma, there is no face in the window."

His mom looked up at the ceiling in his room. "Are you sure? Cause that window has something in it that looks like a face."

Tam turned around and looked at the ceiling. His mother was right, there was a girls face looking out of one of the windows. Tam chewed on the inside of the cheek. Things were getting crazy, and he didn't know what do to do. That night instead of sleeping in his room, he slept on the pull out couch in the living room. He had no interest in seeing that girls face while he tried to sleep. Even in the living room it became a difficult task. All he could think of was how to stop the insanity. If this kept up, he would go crazy.

His eyelids became heavy, and he managed to get some sleep. Until he felt the duvet tighten around him. He thought his mother sat on the edge of the bed pulling the sheets taught with her pressure. He turned his head to the side, and he saw instead the Millers daughter lying next to him. He tried to scream, but nothing came out. He tried getting out of the bed, but he found his body would not move. He couldn't even move his head away from the view of the girl. It took all his effort and the scream he wanted to release came out as a gasp.

The girl covered her lips with a slender finger motioning at him to be quiet. He did not know how long he laid in bed staring at the girl next to him. He wanted to close his eyes, but it was like they had tape attached keeping them open. The girl stared back at him, her cold grey eyes piercing his soul. He needed to rid himself of this girl. He could not live like this. He could run away but he knew that where he went, she would make an appearance. When the light came through the bay window and landed on the bed the girl disappeared. Tam needed to get rid of the girl's presence and he could only think of one thing that would do it.

At 3:00 am he stood in front of the old mill with a can of graffiti remover and bucket of soapy water in his hands. He looked at his work; it drew him into another world. A world that he must erase and forget. If he was going to have any peace he would have to restore the wall he painted back to its old worn self. He looked at the window and did not see the girls face staring at him. She probably made her home in his bedroom. He wanted his space back. He didn't want to wake up to the cold stare of a dead girl. He sprayed the wall with the cleaner and watched his creation melt from the solvent. The colors dripped down the surface of the wall. He had many of his works painted over or erased by others, but doing it himself was not a pleasant experience. When he was done spraying he took a sponge and cleaned the dripping paint off with the soapy water. In a matter of hours, the old mill was back to its former look. He went home and into his room. The girl stood inside. A smile was pasted on her lips. She faded away leaving only the painting on the ceiling as a reminder of her.

He never erased the painting.

The Transformation
by
Ruth Barrett

Gasping aloud, Paula jerked awake.

"Oh God... not again," she groaned. Another nightmare about her ex-lover Michael had left her bathed in a cold sweat.

With blood pounding in her aching temples, Paula squinted at her bedside clock radio. It was only 6:30 a.m. *Damn it*. Just to really add to her pain, it was Saturday-- but she knew that getting back to sleep would be out of the question. Kicking off the covers, she dragged herself downstairs to the kitchen. Paula banged the kettle onto the stove and slammed open cupboard doors in search of tea bags and a clean mug. No need for her to be quiet, despite the early hour. Her flat-mate Jacquie was away in Bath for a romantic weekend with Marcus, her latest boyfriend, leaving all the more room for Paula to brood in peace. Not that she begrudged Jacquie her bliss, but it was nauseating to witness someone else happily swept up in the throes of a new love affair while she was still mourning the death her own last relationship.

Paula slumped into a chair, staring blankly into space, and waited for the water to boil. A familiar ennui settled over her like a shroud. Outside the window, a foggy drizzle obscured the hilltop view from the deserted North London Street. When the weather was clear, she could spot the dome of St. Paul's cathedral from the back of their rented house in Muswell Hill. No chance of that today. Paula felt like it had been raining ever since Michael had dumped her six weeks ago.

The details of her nightmare were already faded. It hardly mattered. Michael had been just another in a long string of personal disappointments. Nothing good or exciting ever seemed to happen to Paula. Her clerical job at the hospital was dull, she was getting too long in the tooth to go out clubbing, and her social circle was steadily dwindling down to nothing. Most of her friends had married and drifted away to lead idyllic lives in the countryside, or else moved to the continent in pursuit of sexy careers and even sexier European men. No doubt Jacquie would be the next to go, and then she'd be left all alone with the cat. Paula doubted that her life would ever change course: hers was a predictably colorless destiny.

There was a sudden rustle and snap at the front door. The Saturday morning post was early. Paula shuffled out to the front hall in her sock feet, hoping for something other than another letter from her mother imploring her to visit. She didn't need a guilt-trip to add to her overall misery. Her heart sank another notch as she rounded the corner-- it looked to be nothing more than a heap of fliers and junk mail. She stooped to gather it up, fancying that there might at least be a halfway interesting mail-order catalogue to browse over with her cup of tea.

Underneath the pile was an embossed linen envelope. Another love-note for Jacquie from Marcus, she figured... but Paula's grey eyes widened at the unexpected sight of her own name inscribed in an unusual spidery calligraphy. She tossed the fliers unheeded into the recycling bin and hurried to the sitting room.

Eagerly examining the unsolicited mystery, she could find nothing to determine its origin. No postmark. No stamp. No return address. She flipped it over and found it sealed with crimson wax with an indecipherable scroll-mark imprinted in the centre. Someone must have hand-delivered this piece of old-world elegance before the postman's arrival.

Paula's breath quickened at the adventure promised in the offering. Carefully lifting away the seal with a letter opener, she pulled out an embossed invitation card with a message written in the same spidery hand:

My dearest Paula,
Your delightful company is requested on Saturday, 10th
June at 9:00 p.m.
Location: to be revealed.
Dress: to be arranged in the afternoon.
The Occasion: your Transformation.
A car will collect you promptly at 8:40 p.m.

It bore no signature; merely a series of looping calligraphic flourishes underscoring the brief communication. Paula read and re-read the card, utterly mystified as to who could have sent it. Today was the 10th. And whatever could they mean by *'transformation'*?

Glancing up, she met her own eye in the mirror over the desk and smiled.

"Yes," she said to her reflection. "Why not?"

The insistent shriek of the kettle brought her back down to earth. Still clutching the precious invitation to her heart, she padded back to the kitchen. As she waited for the tea to brew, she let Horton the cat in from the back garden. He coiled his lithe ginger body against her bare legs and mewled for breakfast.

" My *'Transformation',* " mused Paula out loud. She rather liked the sound of that. Giving a delighted laugh, she whirled about dancing on the tiles, causing Horton-- a skittish feline-- to dart upstairs and hide under Jacquie's bed.

***

Paula did nothing all day. She simply waited to see what would unfold next. By lunchtime, nothing more was forthcoming and her spirits faltered. It must have been some sort of sick joke of Michael's to get her hopes up. She stomped upstairs to lay on her bed with a novel, inwardly admonishing herself for believing that anything special could ever happen. At 2 p.m., the front buzzer made Paula jump up and rush downstairs. By the time she flung the door open there was no one there, but a huge bouquet of flowers wrapped in paper and tied with a wide red ribbon lay on the front stoop. A small embossed envelope held a note penned in the same script as the early morning missive:

So glad that you'll be able to join me this evening.

It really was happening… whatever 'it' was. It was as though her thoughts were being read; her willingness to go along being taken as granted. Paula arranged the oversized bouquet of roses in Jacquie's best vase and set it on the sitting room coffee table. The blooms were of an unusual depth of red and had an intoxicating scent. The whole of the two-level maisonette was soon filled with their perfume.

At 4 p.m., the front bell rang. Paula opened the door to an older well-dressed woman holding a garment bag. The woman's smile radiated with charm.

"Is now a good time for your fitting, lovey?" she asked in a smooth, warm voice.   Her manner and tone inspired instant trust, and soon they were upstairs in Paula's bedroom, bustling her into a lovely frock. It was perfectly tailored to fit her body, and showed off her curves to advantage without being vulgar by exposing too much skin.

"I do hope that black is all right with you," said the kind woman. "I find it best suits these occasions to go with an elegant simplicity."

Paula nodded knowingly, not wishing to reveal her ignorance regarding the exact nature of the 'occasion'. The woman chatted amiably as she smoothed and fussed over the dress.

"This will be such a lovely treat for you. I know you don't get much of a chance to dress up in your line of work. Hospitals are such dreary places."

"No… how do- "

"You must miss those days when you were dating that nice cellist-- Ron, wasn't it? At least *he* used to get you out and show you off. Such a pity things didn't work between you two, but surely you must realize that it wasn't your fault if the lad ultimately preferred the attractions of his own sex."

"Excuse me, but how did you know about-"

"And you were wasted on that last scoundrel, Michael. How shabby of him to run off with that horrid blonde tart! His loss, my dear. Some men have no idea what's good for them. I dare say you'll not be treated like that ever again-- not if I know my employer."

"Who exactly is- "

"Here, my dear. Slip these shoes on and see if the hemline hangs properly in high heels."

The shoes, like the frock, were somehow perfect. The gentlewoman smiled with pride and stroked Paula's cheek with her cold fingertips.

"Best take off the dress and hang it up. You don't want to end up wearing wrinkles-- tonight of all nights."

Paula obeyed and handed the dress to the woman. As she laid it out gently on the bed and smoothed the silky material out flat, Paula turned away to dig through her wardrobe.

"I'm sure I must have a padded hanger in here somewhere... that will help hold the shoulders' shape, don't you think?"

There was no reply. She peered around the wardrobe door to find the woman had gone.

Paula heard a motor start and a car pulling away. She ran to the window, but couldn't see anything. By the time she'd thrown on a robe and hurried down to the front door, the street was empty. She'd been unable to follow quickly enough to see either the car or the direction it had taken. The stranger had taken her exit while Paula was in a state of semi-undress, ensuring a clean escape.

Heading back upstairs, Paula carefully picked up her dress from the bed, revealing a black satin bag on the bed. Inside was a bar of soap wrapped and sealed in paper, a glass bottle of bath oil and a tiny vial of coordinating perfume. All bore the label *Transformation*. Paula shivered.

***

Paula was too excited to eat supper and opted instead for a long soak in a hot, fragrant bath. As she ran the water, Horton perched on the counter indifferently grooming until the heady scent of the exotic perfume filled the small bathroom. Hopping to the floor, he stood yowling at Paula to be let out, his tail madly twitching.
"All right, get out. I don't want you in here if you're going to cause such a fuss."
Dropping her robe, Paula sank into the silky embrace of the bath. She inhaled the rich notes of the perfumed water. Her senses were deeply stirred, but she could not pinpoint any of the elements that made up the delicious whole of the scent. As Paula soaped each limb, her body grew more languid and her skin tingled with an erotic anticipation. She leaned back and closed her eyes with a sigh. *Please God-- let tonight be wonderful.*

A cynical voice nagged at the back of her skull: *Surely this has got to be some elaborate joke. Do you really think that your life is going to 'transform'? Pathetic fool...* Paula twisted in her bath trying to block out her inner pessimism. She ached with a need to believe. Breathing in the intoxicating perfume of *Transformation*, her mind calmed and her body yearned to be touched. She sensuously trailed the bath sponge over her thighs, enflaming her nameless ardor and stifling her doubts.

***

At precisely 8:40 p.m., a black sedan with tinted windows drew up and its smartly uniformed driver called at the door. He made a small bow to Paula and handed her formally down the walk into the back seat. On the rich leather seat was a corsage of the same lush red roses that made up her bouquet. Beside the flowers sat a black velvet jewelry case. Eagerly, she picked up the box.

"Forgive me, miss," said the chauffeur. "But I think he'd prefer if you'd wait to open it in his presence."

"Of course. I forgot myself." Battling her curiosity, Paula slipped the case unopened into her evening bag as the driver shut her door.

Flushed and nervous, she peered out to see if any of the neighbors were watching as their dear, mousy Paula was being chauffeured away in an expensive European car. The windows were also tinted from within.

***

At 9:00 p.m., Paula was too disoriented by the silent blind journey to know what part of London she was in when she arrived at the shining platinum double-doors of what seemed to be an exclusive nightclub. The place exuded an air of wealth and prestige that she found both intimidating and exciting in equal measures. A tuxedoed host escorted her into a cavernous dining room, and seated her at a round table covered with fine white linen. The room was very dimly lit-- almost black-- and Paula could just make out shadowy figures moving between the tables. There was a continual flow of human traffic: waiters and busboys with trays, and patrons being shown to and from their seats. Each table was cleverly and discreetly spot lit from an unseen source, and glowed like full moons in the darkness.

Paula felt self-conscious. Her central table was large-- too large to be properly intimate-- and she'd noticed that all of the other tables had gatherings of four or more. She was the only solitary figure in the room. Her tightly clasped hands felt damp against the tablecloth.

A handsome young man with slicked-back hair wearing a long apron whisked up to her table and poured her a glass of golden wine. Scooping up her invitation-- she had thought it wise to bring it along-- he gave it a quick glance and broke into a wide grin. He leaned in toward Paula.

"I'll bet you can't wait to finally see him," he enthused. "May I say you look wonderful? Absolutely stunning. He'll be ever so pleased."

Paula mutely gazed up at him, a mix of blurred emotions tugging at the corners of her carefully painted mouth. The waiter's brow furrowed with concern at her apparent discomfort. His voice dropped down a level in volume and became more soothing.

"Don't fret, love. I know it must seem a bit on the odd side, but it's just his way. He'll be along any moment to explain. Relax. Enjoy your wine."

He moved off, gently giving her bare shoulder a reassuring touch as he vanished between the circles of light.

His fingers were cold. Shivering, Paula felt a renewed surge of panic at being stranded alone in such a place. Maybe it was some weird hoax after all. It would be foolish to stay, but she couldn't find the backbone to rise and walk out. To bolster her courage, she took a sip of wine. It was beautiful stuff-- heady and flowery with a glowing aftertaste. Paula had never before tasted anything so perfect, and was a little surprised to find that she'd somehow drained the glass.

"Paula."

A man's voice-- mahogany rich, with a cultured and slightly clipped edge-- spoke her name from the darkness to her left. *It must be him.* She quivered at the sound. He stepped into her pool of light and sat at her table, pulling his chair in close beside her own.

"May I?" he asked, as he lifted her hand to his lips and kissed it. Paula's entire body flooded with heat. She gazed at him, instantly captivated. He was older by a good ten years, but still youthful with a smooth, finely formed face and thick dark hair. His moustache was trim and neat and he wore a goatee, slightly elongated along the strong lines of his jaw, framing his lovely full mouth. His eyes were dark and deep, set off to perfection by long lashes that gave an almost feminine beauty to his face.

The young sommelier reappeared to fill their crystal glasses with more of the miraculous wine. As he grinned approvingly at the couple, her suitor smiled back.

"I'll wager the poor girl thought I was never coming. But I always keep my promises, don't I Thomas?"

"Oh yes, sir. If you say you'll be someplace, then your word is as good as gold."

Thomas winked at Paula as the two men chuckled together like old friends. She felt compelled to laugh along with them-- though haltingly.

"A toast," offered her admirer, as Thomas discreetly withdrew. "To you, my dear one-- for your terribly kind patience."

Paula felt a sensation of confused relief wash through her like a drug. He seemed sincere in his attentions to her-- and she was electrified by her instant attraction to him-- but she was still as much in the dark as she had been that morning.

"I see you are unsure, my pet. How to reassure you? I know... "
Lifting her chin with his cool forefinger, he leaned over and kissed her full on the lips. Paula inwardly reeled with intense desire. Confusion be damned! Nothing else in the world mattered as much as her passion for this man.

"Forgive me," he said, drawing back. "That was too forward."

"No!" she blurted, lunging after him to catch his arm. After a moment of stunned silence, she smothered a giggle with her hand, amused by her own audacity. His dark eyes twinkled as he laughed gently with her. Paula pulled him back to taste his mouth again.

Thomas returned, smiling apologetically for his untimely intrusion. He spoke in a low voice to her mysterious new admirer who heaved a sigh and nodded in reply, waving the sommelier away. He turned back to Paula and caressed her cheek with his gentle, cold fingertips.

"I'm sorry to have to leave you before I've explained myself, but I've been called to another table.

Tonight is a special night for them, and I've been asked to say a few words. I'll be back in no time." He brushed a feathery kiss on her neck, deeply inhaling her perfume as he stood. "You smell wonderful," he breathed into her ear. "I could eat you. Perhaps I shall before the evening is out..."

He receded into the black. Her mind and body buzzing with wine and enflamed lust, Paula strained to watch him emerge from the darkness at a nearby table. Thomas was there, along with several tall waiters clustered about in a semi-circle-- all almost identical with their lean young bodies and long white aprons. They obscured her view of the people who were seated. She could make out muted laughter, a short speech given in *his* melodious baritone voice, a toast proposed. All individual words were swallowed up by the constant background hum of chatter and soft jazz music.

Suddenly, her lover's deep voice was raised in a question. There was an immediate lull in the music and a profound silence as all those present waited for an answer. After a moment's pause, a small murmur came in reply. As if by a signal, the waiters quickly and neatly dispersed back into the inky dusk of the room. A harsh, sulfurous scent of freshly snuffed candles hung in the air.

All else in the room seemed just as it had before: the unseen jazz band resumed their song in mid-verse and the background murmur of dining conversation continued where it had left off. Paula felt a chill like fingers of ice race down the back of her neck. The other table and its occupants had vanished, leaving a gaping black hole like a missing tooth where the table had been just a moment before. She was struck by a sudden instinct to flee. Furtively casting her eyes around in search of a way out, she met the gaze of her lover.

He stood motionless at the edge of a pool of light, his face lit from beneath with sinister shadows playing across his angular face. The expression he wore seemed brutal and cold, silently warning her to stay put... or else.

As she blinked at the apparition, he stepped fully into the light at her table. All traces of the fleeting malevolence were gone. He once again looked irresistibly charming, and in one fluidly elegant move he seated himself and pressed up against her. At the touch of his body to hers, her mind gave over to his overpowering influence. Paula was drunk with need. She wanted only to fuse herself with him and leave all her former dull loneliness behind forever.

"Forgive me," he purred, trailing kisses down her face. He took her hands in his own. "Now: I'm sure you know there's the small matter of a jewelry case in your evening bag. I think it's time you opened it up-- don't you agree?"

Paula nodded, eyes nearly closed, breathing in the absolute beauty of him through her narrowed field of vision, surrendering to this half-formed dream that she so desperately wanted to believe in. She slid her hand into her bag and grasped the nearly forgotten velvet box. He tightened his fingers over hers.

"But first, my Lady, I must ask one question... "

As before, the music and conversation around them ceased. The icy sensation of his hand on hers spread and froze Paula in her chair. She was only dimly aware of the cluster of waiters closing in around their table.

***

On Monday morning, Horton heard the sound of footsteps approaching up the walk and stalked on stiff legs to the front entrance hall. The cat had been driven past all patience by his owners' negligence. Though by nature a solitary beast, he derived much secret comfort from the presence of Paula and Jacquie. He'd been stuck inside the flat alone for two days without fresh food, haplessly watching birds in the back garden through the window. This was a double indignity he did not intend to endure without vigorous complaint. He sat in a rigid pose of contempt and fixed an expectant, stony gaze on the doorway.

The footsteps ascended the front stoop at the door. Horton uttered a loud and peevish meow. His petulant greeting was answered by a fistful of junk mail and bills shoved through the mail slot that showered over his head. Humiliated and shaken, Horton bolted into the sitting room and leapt onto the coffee table with his tail twitching in anger. He'd have to make his point to his owners in a more obvious and destructive way. The cat brushed hard against the vase of roses and deliberately toppled it over, dumping the contents across the oak surface. He shrieked as his paw dipped into the spilled water-- reeling back at the powerful scent of scorched wood and singed fur as his tender footpads were burned to the quick.

Open Your Eyes and See
by
Naomi Bonthrone

Open your eyes and see.

A desert forms about you as you struggle to your feet, a path stretching out from where you now stand. Beside you a shape is erected, the wooden sign pointing down the path as it vanishes over the horizon. Letters are carved into the timber, forming a single allusion to where the path may end; *truth*. Now as you examine the barren landscape, you find your mind falling blank. All memories beyond this very moment are lost within the depths of your psyche. Without any explanation for your presence here, questions swarm through your mind and ravage your thoughts in search of answers. Where are you? How did you get here? Why are you here?

With these questions and many more in mind, you turn, resolving to return from whence you came. But instead you stumble out of your sharp spin, jolting back from the chasm torn through the ground you now face. The edge crumbles under your weight, crashing down into the abyss once you leap back onto solid ground. The rocks tumble further and further into the endless gorge, the crash of their collision with the end never echoing back to you.

You look across at the fog rolling over the chasm, the other side undistinguishable amongst the earth-bound cloud.

You face a choice. There is no way across the bottomless pit; you can either stay where you are or follow the path from the edge. Perhaps against better judgment, you choose to let the path guide you into the unknown. The further you walk, the barer the world around you becomes as the even earth itself, once covered in sand, is now cracked and decrepit.

But you keep walking until you have continued down the perpetual path for what feels like hours. Now your vision slurs, becoming a haze of dull colors as exhaustion sets in. Your legs are weak, fumbling over one another. You collapse, crashing to the ground. Your limbs ache, littered in scrapes as you drag yourself up.

A figure manifests, stepping through the distorted collage of smudges you see. Another assembles and then another, all growing closer to you until each comes into focus. You now see your loved ones standing before you, your mother and your father at your sides. Each challenges you to continue your journey and when you accept, they escort you along the path. As you move with your entourage, a performance plays out along the rim of the road.

With mirrors of your loved ones scattered about the scenes, you begin to recognize them as your forgotten memories. You watch the segments from your past years, your whole life building up before you. Yet there is an oddity about the timeline. It becomes disjointed, your transitional memories absent from the performance.

Before you can question this, the visions draw together alongside the path, merging into a gargantuan board propped up on a wooden platform. Crimson stains are smeared across the blank canvas, curling together to create a warning to passing travelers: "*Welcome to Mermeros.*" A metal fence runs behind the decaying welcome board, a town imprisoned within its bounds. The figures escorting you now move away, evaporating into the fence until it breaks down into an opening.

You follow, trusting your guides as you slip through the rift they forged. The tear slams shut behind you, trapping you in the graveyard of abandoned paraphernalia and deteriorating buildings fusing to form the city, Mermeros. A shiver trickles down your spine as you glance over the town otherwise devoid of all life. To you, it appears locked in a time capsule, the discarded scraps of past civilizations discrepant with your present.

Despite the creeping sensation rushing over you and sending your heart into a frantic rhythm, you find your body maneuvering through the ghost town. It moves out of instinct without your consent, a faint sense of familiarity clinging to the winding alleyways you weave through. You are brought to a sturdy dwelling, the last sliver of vigor left in the desolate city. Now, as you stare down the house, you recognize it as your own, a family home where all the memories you saw occurred.

You enter, breaking through the façade of the pristine exterior. The disease of decay has infected the interior with the furnishings torn open, the walls stripped. You creep over the shrapnel splattered through each room, impulse guiding you through your now deserted home. You slip into a room your parents once inhabited, tiptoeing cautiously as if you may be caught in the intruding act.

Suddenly you tumble to the ground, collapsing over an obstacle strewn across the floor. A shriek breaks through your lips as you face the obstacle. Beaten, battered and bruised, your father lies sprawled out before you, his breathing labored, his features disfigured. You scramble to his side as he clings to life, choking on his last words.

"She did this," he coughs out his claim, his once booming voice now wheezing out weakly. "She did this to me."

"Who?" You stammer over your sobs.

His head lulls to the side, oblivious to your presence as he stares down the threshold. A figure stands there, their identity shrouded by a mask of shadows. A container lies at their feet, a pool of liquid branching out from it to engulf the room. The intruder cradles a lighter in their hand, a flame bursting out of it, lapping up at the air around them. Then in one swift movement, the flame falls free of their grasp. Your heart slams into your chest as the lighter crashes into the fluid river, engorging the room in flames, swallowing you into the inferno.

You wake, your body heaving. You frantically gasp for breath as you grope at your limbs. You gawk, confused as every splinter of your body is intact, not a single blemish in sight. Glancing about, you see an alleyway surrounds your crouching figure. You pull yourself upright, clinging to the wall as you struggle to make sense of the chaos racing through your mind.

Questions bound through your psyche once again. You wonder where you are now, how did you get here and more importantly, who was the hidden figure at your home. The only thing you know, without a doubt, is your father is dead, murdered. A need burns deep inside you, a need to find the truth, to know what happened to your father. But before you can act on this desire, voices flood over you, the speakers huddled several paces away from you.

"Someone now knows what happened," a voice cries, a voice you recognize. "Someone knows what I've done."

You slither closer, confirming your suspicions as the speaker comes into focus, taking the form of your mother. With an anxious look, she stands alongside a towering male, speaking in hushed tones.

"Then there is no reason to stay," the man challenges.

"You want me to run? You want me to leave my home?"

"We can't hide this so why stay? We can leave and make a new life away from everything here."

You sink back as the two continue their muffled exchange. The puzzle of their words floats through your mind, piecing together until suddenly everything snaps into place. *She did this to me. Someone knows what I've done. We can leave and make a new life.* It all makes sense. Your mother is the reason behind your father's death. You were there when he died, the only witness to what she had done and now she needs to run. She knows you know.

But you wonder how. How could your mother bring herself to do this? How could the woman who raised and nurtured you become a cold-hearted killer? Is the man she is whispering away to involved in what happened? Is he involved with her in other ways as well? It all makes sense yet nothing has ever confused you more.

"Okay," the sound of your mother surrendering to the man's suggestion breaks you from your thoughts. "I just need to get a few things. I'll meet you after."

With that, your mother vanishes into the darkness. The man grunts, turning the opposite direction and striding passed where you are hidden. A force of instinct consumes you once again, tugging your body after the man. You follow him as he approaches the outskirts of town, reaching the meeting point agreed upon with your mother. An undetectable witness amongst the looming shadows, you wait as he does. Soon enough someone approaches. The man straightens himself, a smile spreading across his lips.

"I was starting to worry," he says, his voice carrying along the breeze. "Have you got everything you need?"

The figure pauses, their features obscured by a cover of darkness, matching the intruder from your home. You lean forward with interest, nearly slipping out of your hiding as you watch your father's murderer stare down the man, further cementing your mother's guilt. The man speaks up again, his voice now drenched in anxiety.

"What's wrong?"

Before he can question any further, the intruder thrusts a knife towards him, silencing his words. In another swift move, the murderer finishes the attack. The man collapses to the ground, dead, the knife glinting in his back. You stumble, shock racing through your body at the second murder you have witnessed.

Suddenly the figure's head whips upright, staring straight into the shadows where you cower. You feel paralyzed under the stare, breath caught in your throat as you have been discovered. You will join the two fallen men. You squeeze your eyes shut, begging for mercy until you hear the scrambling of feet.

Back turned to you, the figure now runs, fleeing the area. Your body lunges forward out of your control, chasing after the coward at top speed. Adrenaline pulses through you, fuelling your sprint as you charge through the winding maze of discarded buildings. Your mind screeches for you to stop, for your instincts to instead order you to safety, for your life to be secure. But your impulses continue pumping through you as faster and faster you run after the murderer.

It is only when you arrive at a familiar building that you stop, catching your breath as you gaze up at your desecrated family home. The fire is extinguished, but the charred corpse of the room remains, rotting the once unspoiled exterior. This is the final shred of proof; you now know your mother is the murderer. She murdered your father as only she knew you were a witness, she murdered that man as only she knew of their meeting, and now she has fled home one last time.

You swallow your nerves. It is time to face her on equal ground. You crawl inside, moving through each room carefully should she attack. You reach the final room, the only place she can be hidden. It is now or never, it is time to bring your mother to justice. You kick the door open, leaping onto the figure within immediately.

You pin your mother to the ground without resistance, but before you can revel in your victory, crimson stains begin crawling up you. More and more form until you climb to your feet, backing away from your mother. You now see her lifeless body lies limp on the floor. Blood seeps from her many wounds, she must have known you were coming. Maybe she could not face you. Maybe she could not face herself.

You now release your suppressed sobs as you slump over the sink, washing her blood from your hands. Yet no matter how hard you scrub, the scarlet smudges will not fade. Needing something stronger, you glance up at the mirror, a cabinet of cleaning supplies tucked behind it. You press your hands to the reflective surface to peel it open, your horrified face staring back at you.

"Her blood is on your hands." A teasing voice echoes through your mind, cackling at you.

Suddenly, your reflection twists as the manic laughter grows, its lips distorting into a wicked grin. Its features knit together into a demonic mask as its hands lunge forward, breaking free of the mirror. A scream rips out of your throat as it grabs hold of you, dragging you into its domain. You crash through the mirror, plummeting to the ground as the cackling subsides. Chasm walls stand around you, stretching towards the sky, only a sliver of light reaching the pit's end. Your double circles you as a shark trapping you in, eager to tear its prey to shreds.

"Who are you?" You wail through your frenzied breathing as you struggle to your feet.

No response comes, but the demon's appearance
begins to shift into one you all too easily recognize. Its face
becomes a mesh of shadows, matching the mask of
darkness worn by the murderer whose dark deeds you
witnessed. It cackles once more, the cruel sound piercing
through the depths of the gorge.

"You know me all too well,"

It circles closer and closer to you with every passing
second. You whip around after the creature, never turning
your back to it. You cannot let it attack you. You must stop
it before it can murder you as it did the others.

"No I don't!" You protest.

It jolts towards you, its hand curling around your
throat. It holds you prisoner. It draws its face to yours, your
features almost touching as it speaks once again.

"Oh, you do know me. I am the one you have been
searching for, the one who murdered your father, your
mother and her lover. But do you really want to know who
I am?" As you nod, its face morphs one final time,
mirroring your appearance exactly. "I am *you*."

It releases your neck as you scramble back, staring
at your twin. Your heart pound against your chest and your
pulse beats against your eardrums as the words echo
through you.

"Do not doubt my words, you came to this place for
the truth and here I am. This world is you; it is a wasteland
of your banished memories. I simply bring you the truth of
your deeds."

You pray for doubts, for denial, but you know these
words are true. You remember now. You remember
everything. You remember such envy as your mother

bathed in the attention of great men. You remember discovering her affair. You remember such fury. You remember revenge as you chose your weapon. You remember returning to the house, sneaking to the bedroom to defend your father's honor. You remember confusion as you stopped your beating, discovering that your mother and her lover have fled. You remember weeping as you returned to your father's beaten body with fire. You remember burning it all, all the evidence of your misplaced murder.

You remember finding your mother and her consort in the darkness. You remember hearing how she planned to leave you and your father with his replacement. You remember following him to the meeting point. You remember swiftly ending his life without a single sound. You remember fleeing to your house, the one place you felt safe. You remember your mother discovering the murder. You remember pouncing on her in the bathroom. You remember slashing and slashing until all the noise finally stopped. You remember the silence as the men took you away. You remember the doctors and the white walls. You remember the locked doors and the pricks of needles. You remember the pain.

"It is time to return home,"

Your double offers its hand to you as it speaks. You hesitate. You want to forget. You want to stay here. You want to stay the savior. You want freedom. You want forgiveness. But, knowing you can never return to ignorance, you pinch your eyes shut and grasp its hand.

Now open your eyes and truly see.

Alba
by
K.R. Jordan

Darkness surrounds Alba Diaz as she dreams. The light dims more as she traverses a maze of spires that reach to the sky, blocking out the moon. She exhales in a puff of white smoke, her breath freezing from the frigid temperatures. The silence is absolute and she feels as if the shrubs are closing in on her. Suddenly, a beautiful but haunting song fills her ears. She hurries toward it, stumbling through the maze. The clearing she comes to is a field of trees symmetrically spaced and their thin branches are barren. Drifts of knee-deep snow litter the ground causing her to stumble several times. All the while, the lone viola croons out Beethoven's Moonlight Sonata, luring her. She staggers forward under the silvery glow of Queen Luna. There beneath the branches, Queen Luna reveals a lone figure. The shadows of bare branches crisscross the man's countenance. Her body sways with the song that is swelling within her and she walks up to him, standing with her body less than an inch from his, she looks up to see his face but it is obscured by shadows. The moonlight shows his full and flowing dark hair and she reaches up with her hand, caressing down his face. Pleasure pulses through Alba's body as the unknown man bends down to press his lips against hers. Sliding one hand through his hair, she breathes him into her body, their souls dancing together, ululating to the rhythm of the lone viola. Then his hand is in her hair, wrapping it around his fist. He pulls with a firm but gentle tug and then feasts upon her neck, running his hungry tongue down to the pulse point. His other hand holds her tightly to his body and she feels his desire merge with her own.

***

Right after graduation from high school, Alba moved to Randallstown, Maryland to live with her grandmother and attend college. She'd started classes in August and it was not October. The leaves were in their autumnal glory.

Her first day of classes was long and hard, but the one great thing is she met Phoebe. Phoebe Stockton was now her closest friend and would often spend Saturdays with her and her grandmother. The long wooded path to town at first seemed long and lonely but now that she was making friends, it was source of peace to her. Last week they went to a party at the Sigma Delta Psi fraternity and met up with Phoebe's boyfriend Todd and his best friend Sean. Phoebe tried in vain to play matchmaker between Alba and Sean, but neither was interested. Instead they agreed to all be friends and had gone to several parties together since then. Most of the time Alba's friends left her alone while they danced the night away; she wasn't lonely because most of her classmates stopped to say hello and ask her to dance. Unfortunately for them, she was not interested in any of them as a potential boyfriend.

But that night she was restless and stepped outside onto the patio, hoping that a breath of fresh air would make her feel better. It was dark and cold but she could see several couples, some talking softly to each other in corners, others necking like crazy. She turned away from the lovers and made her way to the area beyond the patio.

The freezing grass crackled under her boots as she made her way toward the fence line where the trees met in a natural archway. Raising her face to the moon, she stood beneath the natural archway enjoying the peaceful night.

"Aren't you afraid your posse will miss you?"

The rumbling voice came out of nowhere. Startled, she let out a very embarrassing squeak and spun around.

"Who are you?" she asked breathlessly, frowning furiously at this man whom she'd never before seen. He towered above her tiny five-foot frame with dark hair and eyes, and she noticed a lean muscular build.

"Does it matter?" he asked tersely. "I'm not fawning over you so you can go back inside to your shallow friends." At that, he turned and sauntered away.

How rude, she thought.

Frowning at his back, she was unable to come up with a proper comeback to his rudeness. At that moment her breath hitched in her throat as he jumped the six-foot fence, not even skimming the top of it. Turning her head back toward the patio, she looked to see if anyone else had seen. No one had.

That night she dreamed of him jumping fences and running through the forest that surrounded Gram's home.

After several days she had all but forgotten he even existed. That was when she saw him out on the University lawn. A group of football players were playing touch football on the University lawn. She noticed him right away and stopped by the fountain to watch them.

She was surprised when he turned to her and called out, "Venturing out without your admirers again, are you?" His deep voice rumbled through her and she felt her temper rise at his boorish tone.

"Why do you even care, moron?" she called out bravely. The football players froze in their tracks to look at her, their bodies stiff in a combative stance. Their eyes looked down at her coldly and suddenly she was afraid.

"Guys, go ahead and play without me," he commanded. There was no other way to describe his tone. The football players broke out of their frozen stare, and without giving her another glance they got back into the game play.

He started walking toward her, but she quickly turned away and quickened her pace back to the Science Building, not wanting him to corner her. She shut the door behind her and looked out to see if he would try to follow her in. When she didn't see him at all, she released a nervous breath.

Gathering her backpack tighter to her side she turned to head to Mr. Collier's class, but halfway down the hall, she heard the entry doors open and close behind her.

Goosebumps rose on her arms when she heard his deep voice say, "Why'd you run away, little rabbit?"

Now she was mad, *why was he following her and speaking to her so rudely all the time?*

"Don't call me that," she fumed as she turned toward him, her hand naturally going to her hip. The spark of bravado ended quickly, however, when she realized he was right behind her.

"Little rabbit?" he asked.

"Yes. Who are you? A stalker?" she squeaked, again frowning to give weight to her words.

"Ha! You wish. But if you want to know, my name is Paul."

"Whatever," she said, the single word dripping with sarcasm. "You asked," he said lightly.

"Okay, just stop following me, leave me alone." Turning, she walked to Mr. Collier's door.

"What's your name?" he asked again.

"Why? Why do you want to know my name?" She looked back at him, straight into his beautiful brown eyes.

"Well...you know mine now. I'd like to know yours."

Sighing, she opened Mr. Collier's door and closed it gently behind her, completely ignoring his request.

***

The trees seemed to hang lower that evening as she walked home from classes at the University, as if giant bony hands reached down to run their fingers through her hair. She was not afraid, really. Yet she could not shake the feeling that something was wrong, her skin crawling with goose bumps at the thought that someone may be watching her.

Hurrying along, she wrapped her arms around herself, her backpack strapped tightly to her back. Once she was in sight of the well-lit front doorway of her grandmother's home, she breathed a sigh of relief. Her relief was short-lived however as a huge dog came out from behind the ancient Oak to her right. Stopping in her tracks, she realized it was a wolf as she stood transfixed by its stare.

The wolf's eyes burned with intensity as its brown, gray and black brindled fur stood up in silent rage.

When she saw its lips rise to reveal huge fanged teeth, she extended her hand to hold him off.   It extended one paw to step toward her and she felt the world go dark as she fainted. Upon waking, she felt the intense cold, a cold that seeped into her clothes and drained the warmth from her bones. Opening her eyes she saw that the night was completely dark as the clouds had set in, the nearly full moon and stars no longer visible to light her way down the path. She sat up quickly, a scream escaping her lips. Clamping her mouth shut with her hands, she looked around and saw that she was definitely on the path to Grams, her backpack serving as a pillow while a huge jacket covered her legs. Jumping up hastily, she grabbed her backpack and the jacket in one swift motion and ran home, continually turning to look behind her, fearful of the wolf.

***

Once inside, she looked cautiously through the window. Her heart hammered away against her breastbone, making her chest vibrate. She peered outside. Nothing was there. She let a wisp of breath through her lips as she rested her forehead against the glass. Climbing the stairs to her room she firmly but quietly closed her bedroom door behind her. The last thing she wanted was to wake her Gram and to have to listen to a lecture on the meaning of the wolf.

Alba removed her damp clothing and put her pink robe on, grabbing a book to read while she bathed. The bathroom was next to her room but did not have a connecting door. Running the hot water almost exclusively, the steam began to rise as she sprinkled in some eucalyptus mint bath beads, immediately feeling the change in her stress level. She breathed deeply of the heavenly scent, feeling the intense and healing nature of the eucalyptus and mint oils.

Draping her robe on the towel rack, she entered the steamy bath now filled with frothy white bubbles. Laying back she closes her eyes, the hot steam soothing her nerves. Seeing the image of the strange brindled wolf in her mind, she immediately opens her eyes once more, catching her breath in fear. Fearing to close her eyes again, she finished washing, her book long forgotten.

Rushing through her nightly routine, she skipped sliding the lotion on her legs. Wrapping herself back into her pink bathrobe, she made her way to her room, her body loose and relaxed from the intensely hot bath. Slipping under the warm comforter, she immediately fell into the dream she had been having since the day she turned eighteen.

***

For three days after that, Alba kept her eyes peeled for the wolf, but didn't see it at all. However, she did see Paul around campus, with his group of friends, playing football or running on the track. She didn't stop to watch him anymore after that last incident. After biology, on that third day, she walked out into the bright sunshine and bitingly cold wind. Hearing yelling and arguing she turned and saw a group of three boys kicking another boy that was curled

up in the fetal position on the ground. "Stop that!" she
yelled out. Rushing back into the building, she called out,
"Someone, please help! A boy is being beaten up!"

One of the doors opened down the hall and Mr. Collier
said sternly, "Alba, what is going on?"

"Three football players are beating up another kid!
Send help!" she called out and hurried back out the door.
Before the door even shut, a blur flew out behind her.
Belatedly she realized it was Paul. She had never seen
anyone move that fast! One minute he was at the doorway
and the next he was roughly pushing the bullies away from
the fallen kid.

"Wow," she breathed. Her eyes beamed with
admiration as Paul rescued the poor kid. One of the bullies,
the blond one who she'd seen doing most of the kicking,
decided he wanted his punching bag back. He swung his
arm out as if to punch Paul, but missed by at least a foot
when Paul calmly stepped away from him. At that
moment, the other two football players had somewhat
recovered from their jolt and flanked their "leader."

"This is none of your damn business, Paul," he said.

"It doesn't have to be my business, dirt for brains, now
back off before you get expelled from school." The blonde
leader stepped toward Paul as if to challenge him but he
stopped quickly when he saw Paul crouching, ready to take
him on.

At that moment, Mr. Collier walked out of the hall,
calling out, "Break it up, boys! What is going on here?"

Paul kept his eyes steadily on the blonde leader
sending a silent warning. The blonde boy finally got smart
and pushed the two flanking him back. "Nothing is

happening, Mr. Collier. Edwin must have fallen down." I expected Paul to say something to correct his story, but he kept his mouth shut and his hooded eyes on the three boys.

"Is this true, Paul?"

"Sir, I don't know exactly what happened, but when I came out here, Edwin was on the ground. I was just about to help him up." He glanced quickly at me and continued, "He might have hurt himself. I'm going to get him to the nurse's office." He looked at me imploring me to go along with the story.

"I'll help, Paul," I heard myself saying. Taking a few steps toward Edwin, I kneeled and brushed his coppery brown hair out of his eyes. The most amazingly green eyes stared back and me and I caught my breath and smiled. For some reason, my heart warmed to him and I gathered him in my arms. Well, tried to, but his broad shoulders prevented a complete encircling of him. When he smiled back at me, his tanned face lit up like a light.

"Come on Edwin, we're going to help you to the nurse's office." Paul said sternly. I looked at him curious as to his tone, but he revealed nothing from those hooded eyes.

The nurse proclaimed Edwin healthy as a horse and we all walked out into the hall together. Edwin smiled at me again, with that hundred-watt smile. "Hi, I'm Edwin," he said softly.

"I'm Alba." I smiled. Looking up slightly since he was maybe only five inches taller than me, which would put him at about five foot seven.

"It's very nice to meet you."

"Okay, enough of this. Edwin, what were you

thinking?" Paul said sternly. "You could've really gotten hurt. I've told you a hundred times to stay out of their path!"

"Well," Edwin said calmly, "I have been staying out of their way. But today, they were laying in wait for me. I was outnumbered and out maneuvered."

"Alba, I'm going to take Edwin back to the dorms. We'll see you around, and thanks for, you know, going along with it all." His face flushed a little as he looked down at me from his six-foot frame.

"That's okay," I said quietly and smiled up at him. A smile slowly crossed his face until it seemed as if the sun itself had dimmed in comparison.

"No more *little rabbit*, I see." I grin and make my way down the hall.

Paul ran up behind me, and touched my elbow to get my attention. "Alba, would you want to go out some time, I mean, with me?"

He seemed unsure of himself, not knowing what I would say. "Hmmm, maybe." I said innocently.

"Maybe we could go to the game tomorrow night? I'll call you."

I walked away with a smile on my face.

***

Later that day, as I was leaving campus, Phoebe ran up to me. "Hey, Alba, why don't you stay with me on campus this weekend, we can cram for tests. I need to make an A in all of my subjects; it would be great if you could help. "

"Sure, I just have to clear it with Gram."

Walking home through the woods, the wolf never

crossed my mind: instead, Paul's face and bright smile replaced it. My face flushed of its own accord when I thought of his arm touching mine as we walked Edwin to the nurse's office, his fingertips touching my hair.

That night I asked Gram and she said that it would be okay. "But you know it's the full moon, starting tonight. I know you don't believe, but I would keep clear of any of those boys from the football team, they can't be trusted."

Gram settled comfortably in her seat ready to lecture me, clearing her voice for the story she was about to tell. *Many years ago, before I was born, seven families emigrated here from Italy. They each plotted out a section of land and worked it according to their family's specialty. Some grew crops, some raised animals, things like that. Well, their community grew over the years but for some reason new families never moved to the area. Occasionally, a stranger would come and stay, but it was rare. My great-grandfather was one of the few that came and stuck around, marrying into the Esposito family, and made his place here, flourishing in the process. Over the years our family name, Walker, grew and became respected. Many of great grandfather's children, of which there were twelve sons, became political figures and lawmen. Even so, a lot of the older families were resentful of their success and sought to topple them from their respectable positions. Of the twelve brothers, five were killed mysteriously, their killers never found. The mayor, Peter Walker, was assassinated. The Sheriff, Lucas Walker, was shot in a gunfight in the middle of the town square. Only five brothers survived, preferring to disappear into the background of town society.*

One of those was my grandfather, Cyrus Walker. Cyrus was touched by the spirit, I inherited that from him. He wrote journals from the day he could write, anything and everything that moved his spirit. There were some interesting things in those books. Around the time of all the killings, there were strange stories going around of curses that were put on several of those first families. In return for their commitment they would forever serve their moon goddess, Queen Luna, and she would protect them from harm.

During the time that the Queen would rule the night, the male teenaged children of those families would run amok, carousing in the streets and causing madness and mayhem. People would lock their doors and turn out their lanterns, hoping to avoid a deadly encounter. Mostly people stayed safe but before the Queen's time was over, there would be at least one fatality, and many, many missing people.

"I tell you this for you to stay safe, my love. They have always been a threat to our family. Your mother and father took you from this area at my insistence, to keep you safe, yet truly, only you can keep yourself safe. That is why your brothers fought with you all the time, to prepare you."

"Gram, they tortured me! Mom and Dad let me come and stay with you to get away from them. I begged them for two years to let me come!"

"Say what you want, but you did learn to protect yourself... right?"

"Three years of Karate did not help at all, they still ganged up on me, and I always ended up with bruises. It's

impossible to win with them because they fight dirty.
Really Gram, I don't know how we could all grow up in the
same household and be so different."

"Just promise me you will be alert this weekend, and if
something happens, remember your brothers. Otherwise I
will make you stay home."

"All right Gram," I sighed dejectedly.

Studying that night for three hours straight, Phoebe and
I decided to take a break and go to the basketball game.
As soon as we arrived however, I knew she'd been up to
some matchmaking as Paul and Todd immediately came
walking over to us as we entered the door.

Phoebe smiled over at me apologetically as I shook my
head laughing.

"Phoebe!"

"He really likes you, Alba," she whispered.

Paul smiled down at me when he got close, and I
blushed. Reaching his hand out, I took it while goose
bumps spread across my arm, making me giggle. I cut the
giggle short though when I saw Phoebe and Todd looking
over at me knowingly.

"Hey Paul," I said, trying to take my hand back as he
held onto it firmly.

"Hi Alba, wanna go watch the game?"

"Kay," was all that would come out of my tongue-tied
mouth. He held my hand as we took a seat on the
bleachers. My heart raced and I could feel a blush
spreading across my cheeks.

The game went on, but I couldn't focus on it as feelings
coursed through my body. Paul snuggled in closer and I
looked over at him, my eyes focusing on his lips. I leaned

toward him, the whole while thinking that I should not be trying to kiss him in public, but I couldn't help myself. He leaned down and touched his lips to mine, feeling sparks running across them.

Laughing, I pulled away and touched my fingers to my lips, embarrassed and excited at the same time. I looked up at him and my breath caught in my throat as his hungry look consumed me. Hungry?...yes, there was just no other way to describe it.

His brown eyes almost glowed, showing themselves bright with light. His perfect lips parted slightly so that I could just see the tip of his tongue, my mouth watering at the sight.

"Alba!" Phoebe said with agitation.

Coming back to reality, I remembered that I was sitting in the bleachers and not alone with Paul.

"Wha..what?" I said, clearing my throat and looking at her beside me, my eyes straining to focus on her.

"You're moaning!' she whispered in my ear, "Reel it back to G girl, everyone is watching you!" I looked around and saw that it was true, the guys around me with a glint in their eye, the girls a look that said, *"What a ho"*.

I look back at Paul and we both begin to laugh. "I'm sorry." he mouthed and grinned mischievously.

"Umm, sorry Phoebe," I said as I swatted Paul's hand off my shoulder, determined not to repeat the whole "lost in each other" scene.

For the rest of the game Paul and I just held hands, but my mind kept wandering back to that kiss... and his enticing lips.

I was so lost in my thoughts, I hadn't realized that the

game was over and we had won! People were screaming
and cheering all around us, but Paul and I had eyes only for
each other, his glowing warmth and tenderness, my face
flush with excitement.

"Alba, Todd and I are going to the party, are you
coming?" She looked over at me, pointedly shifting her
eyes meaningfully toward Paul. She was really asking if I
was sure I wanted to go off with him alone.

"Okay Phoebe, have fun! I have the key to your dorm
right here in my pocket." I hugged her and she whispered,
"Are you sure? I feel like you're moving pretty fast." I
squeezed her to say, yes.

"Okay, we'll see you later." I said aloud. Paul grabs
my hand and I take it, not looking back at Phoebe.

As we made our way into the parking lot, mostly
empty now, he wrapped his arm around my waist pulling
me tightly to him. He stopped at a white truck and leaned
against the tailgate. We are inseparable as he leaned down
to kiss me.

I melted into his embrace, my arms around his neck,
pulling so that I am mostly on the tips of my toes. The kiss
becomes oh so much more and we fall apart laughing and
out of breath.

"What do you want to do?" he asks, his voice husky
from our passionate kissing. I know I should say
something else, but I can't help myself.

"This!"

I kissed him again, this time letting my body lay fully
against his. The contact driving me to near madness, and I
don't disagree as he says, "Let's get out of here, go
somewhere we can be alone?"

"Yes, please." I say breathlessly.

We ended up at the parking lot in front of the house he rents a room in. "I want to *keep* you." he says unhappily between kisses and then pulls me onto his lap, his hands caressing my arms. My body quivers with anticipation at the thought of those hands on my naked skin. For a moment the passion recedes and I wonder at my responses to him, feeling the strangeness of it. But then the moment is gone as he kissed me again.

"Should we go inside?"

He pauses, one hand reaching up to my chin to tilt my face up to him, looking me squarely in the eyes. No glowing fever, just honest eyes that were willing to stop if I wanted.

"Yes, Paul, I want you." I whisper.

"Are you sure? I wouldn't be angry if you wanted to stop. I need you to know what you're asking of me."

"Yes, Paul, I understand. I want this," I whisper, kissing the tip of his nose with my quivering lips.

He still looked wary, so I squeezed his hand, "I truly want this, Paul. Yes, I'm excited, but I can think clearly." I laugh, "You're not *all that* with your bristly stubble and messy hair style!"

He laughs as he opens the door to the truck, pulling me out by my waist. Wrapping his arms around me, he kisses me on the nose. "You know I want you, too."

I wrap my arms around his neck, my feet dangling at least a foot above the ground. "Yes, Paul. I definitely want this." I kiss him deeply, letting my tongue dance with his.

He releases me and we laugh as I almost stumble. He pulls me along anxiously through his front door, but I stop cold when I realize we are not alone.

I recognized them as the guys he was playing football with in the University yard. It feels as if cold water is being poured down my back. I look over to Paul, but he is avoiding my gaze. He is looking toward a redheaded guy I recognize from campus.

He doesn't say a word, but redhead says, "Yes, sir," and hurries out of the room. I notice Edwin there, too, also avoiding my eyes.

"Paul?" I say nervously. "What's going on?"

"Ahhh, Alba, it's okay. It's meant to be this way." He reaches out to me. I try to pull away, but he is looking at me with those eyes that I now realize I should've been avoiding. "You made the decision." He takes me in his arms, my mind screaming but my mouth quiet, tears streaming down my face.

Don't ask why I thought of my brothers at that moment: remembering them fighting with me, baiting me, making me lash out and fight them even though they were bigger than me, stronger.

Paul leans his head down and licks the tears streaming down my face, then he kisses me and I think to bite him, but blackness smokes into my vision and I know that I am fainting.

***

I come to consciousness slowly, my body knowing it is morning. I'm cold, in extreme pain, and nude except for my panties. I can only make out the shadowy glow of night with one eye, the other swollen shut and throbbing in pain. They have taken turns beating me like a punching bag, hung by a chain by my arms, wrists bound together. The screaming pain in my shoulders told me that I was still strung up. After each of them took a turn beating me, Paul told them to back off. I guess he wanted all the fun for himself, because he'd spent the rest of the night periodically terrorizing and torturing me.

I heard the chains rattle as Paul lowered me himself, everyone else was gone. Even the trembling Edwin, who had looked on sadly throughout the torture, never lifted a finger to help.

My groans filled the room as he let me fall five feet to the ground, my face smacking the concrete hard. A saltiness I knew was blood washed through my mouth and I hoped I hadn't lost a tooth. I wanted to laugh at the absurdity of that thought but my split lips prevented it.

"It is time to fulfill your destiny, Alba."

My blood boiled at his smugness as I tried to lift myself up or kick at him, but my body wouldn't respond and just lay there helplessly betraying me.

"Fmmff you!" I screamed through my gag.

He laughed.

"I wouldn't soil my body with a half breed mongrel like you!" he hissed, his voice grating in my ears.

I waited for his evil laugh...but it never came. Seeing only his boots from where I lay, I looked on as his body suddenly hit the ground, his head bouncing on the concrete floor with a sickening thud. His head lay mere inches from my face, his eyes closed... mouth slack. I wondered if he was finally dead, but his sour breath reassured me that he still lived.

"I thought he'd never conk out!"

Dark Light

Gram?

I thought I was dreaming at first when I heard her say those words. I tried to turn my head to look in her direction, but it hurt too much.

"That was my strongest spell, it took me fifteen years to master it and it still barely worked on Mister Next in Line for Pack Leader here. Did you know he was a wolf shifter my darling Alba? No, you probably didn't. All you could feel was his compulsion causing you to want him. I know it was strong because he comes from a long line of Pack Leaders.

He was trying to take your spirit for himself, if he did that, he would have no competition for Pack Leader. I counted on his lust for power, knowing that he'd come and incapacitate you.

I couldn't do it, you know. You're too strong, being full-blooded owl shifter, *Lechusa*, although right now you don't think so. But you'll notice that my spell did nothing to you, nothing at all.

Ahhh, there's another revelation for our darling Alba. I know you must be wondering, so I'll explain while I prepare to do away with Paul here.

Lechusa are a breed of angel designed to protect the world from evil, evil like myself. In the beginning, there were masses of *Lechusa*, but now, I only know of you. I killed your real parents, you know. Then, I compelled my daughter who had four sons to adopt you, raising you right even though her sons hated you the moment you were carried into the room as a baby.

Why did I compel her to adopt you? Because you are the most powerful being that I know of. I knew your power

would multiply dramatically as you matured, which is why
I waited until now.

I counted on Paul disarming and weakening you, and
then I put the spell on their compound. It's your power my
dear, the power I worked so hard for all of these years."
Gram finished with a smirk.

I didn't think I could feel any worse, but this woman I
had always known as *Gram* had just pushed me over the
edge, my hope flying away with her words.

I honestly just wanted to close my eyes and die. Not
even the thought of ever seeing my "adopted" family again
could pull me out of it.

Just as she was explaining how she would suck my
power down, Paul opens his eyes. He gazes at me and his
eyes begin to shine with that unearthly glow that I now
knew was his magic. It urges me toward him. I stretch out
to brush my cheek against him, closing my eyes in sick
pleasure. As my skin touched his, Gram's spell was
broken. He smiled mischievously at me and as Gram
swung the ax down to sever his head, he kissed me and in
the next moment he has Gram pinned to the wall, the ax
clanging uselessly to the concrete floor. Letting out a howl
he breaks the spell on his pack as they all coming running
in. He orders the red-headed guy, his second in command,
to grab the ax and walks away to finish what he started, not
even sparing a glance to see that his orders are followed.

I look on in shock, tears running down my face at
Gram's betrayal. Anger bubbles within me, I want to cry
but can't. Paul walks to me, lifting me into his arms in a
hug. He squeezes tightly until I feel my arms begin to
make their way out of their sockets. Leaning down, he

kisses me hard, trying to force my mouth open. Failing, he bites down on my lips, drawing blood.

I flinch inwardly as he whispers, "Thanks babe, for helping me kill your Gram. Now it's your turn." He releases me and I fall on my bound arms, promising myself through the pain that I'll kill him before the hour was up. I close my eyes and play possum, as my brothers had taught me. Slightly opening one eye to look at him, I see him smiling, so full of himself. His eyes glow warm brown and I feel the urge to reach out my hand to caress him.

His magic turns inward, and I know he is about to change to his wolf form. I finally manage to free my bound wrists and know that if I have any chance at all, it would be now. As the magical mist envelops him, and his form changes to that of the brindled wolf I encountered in the woods, my rage becomes intense. He turns and realizes his mistake too late. I pounce on him, straddling his back and effectively pin his paws as they lay on each side of his body.

Closing one hand around his snout and the other behind his head, I pull up and twist with a piercing scream...and he is dead. I feel my strength instantly return, along with my anger and disgust.

Looking around me angrily, I see the pack members staring at me, Edwin smiling knowingly. They don't even touch me; instead, they fall to one knee with a closed fist against their chest in a silent but effective pledge of loyalty...to their new *Lechusa* Pack Leader.

Dark Light

Honest Nightmare
by
Alicia Cannon

The sound of a pen scratching against paper was the only thing that broke the silence that enraptured the pale room. I ran my hands over my arms creating friction in hopes of ridding the feeling of being exposed. I looked through my dark bangs at the woman sitting across from me. She was writing something; I was curious, but too shy to ask, afraid of what it might say. She finally stopped scribbling and looked up. Her eyes were prying; they were searching me for something; two big green orbs attempting to see into my soul. I glanced away; I didn't want her to find anything.

"Lexie, do you have something you want to tell me? This office is a cone of silence and privacy, remember that."

Being a teenager, I wanted to enter the stereotypical mold. I wanted to curse her out and tell her to mind her own fucking business. I wanted to call her a liar and show her that there wasn't anything even remotely private about the office. I wanted to tell her that the walls she called so strong and trusting were paper-thin and anyone sitting in the waiting room could hear what she said. But, I didn't.

"Not really."

Her eyes seemed to smile knowingly. They read my movements as I squirmed uncomfortably in the solid black leather chair. The skin of my legs stuck to the leather and made a rather audible Velcro like sound as I crossed one leg over the other in a poor attempt to seem more calm and together. I didn't want her to think I had something to hide.

"Is everything going well at school?" she inquired, her voice rising to catch my attention, not that she didn't already have it. "How about at home?"

I bit back a scoff and reminded myself not to give anything away—absolutely nothing. I gave her what I thought to be an indifferent shrug of my shoulders. Another silence enveloped the room; she watched me closely, and I did my best to look at everything but her.

I focused on the office. A desk, mostly made of mahogany or oak, and a matching bookshelf filled with books on psychology—big shocker there. A wilted plant in the corner obviously needed some sunlight that it would never get in this windowless room. White walls, excuse me, off white; God forbid something just be white or any other simple color; now instead of purple, its mauve.

Dr. Swindle cleared her throat, interrupting my rather interesting inner rant over the non-existent colors of the rainbow. She reached across to me and invaded my personal space. Her hand gently gripped my chin and she moved my face into what I could only guess was better light.

"Those are rather dark circles, are you not sleeping well?"

I wretched my face from her hand and glared at her bitterly. To say something so rude! For all this bitch knew,

Dark Light

I had naturally dark circles under red, puffy eyes! But, even worse, to hear her say it so blatantly when I had said nothing about sleeping made me angry and scared. I hated that she was able to read what I was thinking. My blood boiled when I saw her beginning to scratch something down in my file even though I hadn't given her a response, like she already knew what kept me awake at night.

When she was done, she looked at me again; her dark hair that sat neatly around her shoulders shone in the dim light as she leaned forward.

"What do you have to tell me Lexie?"

I bit my lip; I wouldn't give her the satisfaction of cracking me, of making me spill my guts. These were my thoughts, dammit! I could feel her eyes on me, waiting for something, anything. I grit my teeth and felt my stomach churn with something unfamiliar.

"Lexie?"

"I've been having nightmares. That's all."

The second the words left my mouth, I wanted to take them back. I hadn't meant to say it out loud, just think it. She scratched something else in her little folder and leaned back, her eyes curious. Maybe my answer had surprised her. Who knows, she was the master of body language, not me.

"Nightmares? What kind of nightmares?"

'The bad kind,' almost said it, but I held it in. I shot a glance around the room. How could I get out of this; where was my escape? I didn't want to talk about my nightmare. It was my weakness, the one thing I was truly afraid of. The churning returned. I placed my hand over my belly; why was it acting so strange?

"Is it about someone in school? A friend? How about one of your classes, maybe someone dies?"

Her constant guessing triggered the memory. I closed my eyes tight trying to block out the images that seemed so real.

"Is that it, Lexie? Someone dies? Who?"

"Please stop guessing," I didn't even recognize my own voice. Even to me, it sounded broken and distant.

"Sweetie, this dream is really hurting you, you got to tell me. I can help you face it."

I shook my head and glared at her, "Why should I tell you? How will remembering make it any better?"

"Lexie if you don't face this, then it will only get worse. Dreams manifest in your mind creating fear. To face a fear, is to defeat it."

"But if I face this fear... then he dies," Face my fear... I can't force him to pass. I won't! I'm just like him; it would be like a part of me would die with him.

"Who dies?"

"Daddy," it escaped without as much as a warning. I felt like a little girl saying it that way, but that's who he was. He was my daddy, my hero. I looked at the woman again; she was staring at me with something new; another thing I couldn't read. She made me feel so illiterate.

"Tell me the dream."

It didn't seem so much of a question as it was a demand. I felt another churn and knew I would tell her the dream. My body was going against me, too much stress? Over eating? I uncrossed my legs and leaned forward putting my elbows on my knees and my face in my hands. I couldn't look at her when I said this—only the floor.

Dark Light

"It starts off in a hospital room. The walls are a blinding white and mirror-like tiles line the floor and ceiling. I'm in the only bed in the room and in a deep coma. The sheets are tucked under my chin and are uncomfortable, like straw. A television is directly across from me playing Looney Tunes, one of the Road Runner episodes. By the window are two dark red chairs with light coming into the room. I can never recognize the first person sitting in one of the chairs. His hair is always somewhat long, falling a little into really blue eyes. He is dressed in all black and something just doesn't feel right about him."

I looked through a little peephole in my hands to make sure she was still paying attention. She was. Her eyes were on me and filled with wonder. I closed my eyes tight and started again,

"The second person I can recognize. It's my Dad. He's standing by the window and dressed in all white, but it's so weird because, my dad never wears white. He is staring out the window into the light, waiting for me to wake up…"

"So you see all of this happening from a different body? Like you're floating above it?" Dr. Swindle asked.

I thought for a moment then shook my head, "I am for the beginning but then I wake up from the coma and then I am apart of everything, not just watching."

She nodded and tilted her head at me, "So what happens when you wake up from the coma?"

"I am sitting in the bed, the blankets around my waist. My dad tells me that he was so scared; he thought I was going to die. He gives me a really big hug and I look over his shoulder at the television just as the coyote falls

455

off the cliff. I smile a little because it's my dad's favorite cartoon; he does the Road Runners 'meep-meep' sound all the time. So, when he pulled away and went back to the window I felt odd. He wasn't laughing or watching with me. The window seemed to be his only interest. I look at the floor and see his reflection as he begins to say he has something important to tell me. It's his time to go. It's," I paused and gripped the chair tightly, digging my nails into the material, "It's his time to pass on and leave! I try to argue with him and tell him no! But he is still standing at the window and I can't get up or stop crying. It's like I'm chained to the bed! And all he can say is it's his time to fucking go!"

My voice broke into sobs as I tried to tell the rest of the story. I clenched my eyes and balled my hands into fists. I felt the tears trail my cheeks and the pain wrap around my heart. I wanted to curl up and die. I shook my head viciously as the memory peaked in my mind,

"He can't die! He swore he would live forever!"

It was stupid, no one could live forever, but I was just like him. I couldn't live without the person who could understand me so easily, someone who showed me everything I knew! He was my daddy, and I was no doubt, a daddy's little girl. A hand rested on my shoulder and Dr. Swindle leaned in close to hug me. Even her embrace felt cold to me; I didn't want it.

"Don't worry sweetie, your Daddy is still here. He is still alive."

I felt my body begin to shake and I pulled back to look her in the eye. A bitter laugh escaped me as the tears kept falling.

"Do you know what the worst part is?"

She tilted her head in question, her precious green eyes soft and sympathetic.

"My dreams always come true."

Dark Light

The Last Picture
by
S.J. Davis

"What do you do at work, Daddy?" Cora asks with the squeaky voice of a young girl, her head peaks around the magazine he is reading. Her kindergarten teacher calls her effervescent. "Do you color?"

"I take pictures," he sighs. His glasses slide down his nose reddened by the sun, alcohol, and allergies. "Photographs." The last word hung in the air. He looked at the ceiling fan as it whirled around their heads, humming in dizzying crescendo.

"Take a picture of me, Daddy!" She twirls around. Her skirt flies up to her hips as she gracefully spins around the living room floor.

"No. Not of you." He stands quickly and rushes from the room.

"Why Daddy? Why?" She runs down the hallway as her mother stops her.

"Let him go, Cora," she instructs. "He is tired. Taking pictures makes him…tired."

Eventually, as the years pass, he takes family pictures again, almost compulsively as if to negate his work for the newspapers.

20 Years Later

Cora is called home to identify her father. As she enters her home she finds a picture taken two years ago. It is the last picture taken of his eldest daughter, strangely labeled 'Picture One'. It is crumpled and smeared with tears as it lies next to her father's dead hand. Beside the camera aimed at her father's dead body rests another manila folder of pictures. 'Picture Two' through 'Picture Six'. She instinctively grabs his camera, the strap is frayed and smells of her father. She scrolls to the last picture. Her father is falling to the floor, halfway to a fall like a dropped marionette. His eyes are open and his temple is bleeding. This is his parting shot.

Picture One

Cora knew what her father expected. Her sister stood under the boy's arm in front of the van, smiling on command. The dusty bumper was warm behind her sister's knees and the remnants of the plumber's name and phone number framed her in the photograph. The lighting and composition could certainly be better. But this is the picture her father deserved, ambushing these two unwilling subjects as they rushed from their house.

Her sister was small and dark haired like her mother. But she had her grandmother's large eyes and quick smile. She wore shorts, flips flops, and a faded gray hoodie. Her smile was perfect - slightly annoyed but still fetching. The boy, he didn't matter. A friend, a lover perhaps, but the relationship was of little consequence – on and off, irrelevant.

None of them will see her again. Her face will be frozen in time, framed by years of smiles, birthdays, and milestones that have been stored neatly on the family computer, classified by year and by event. Thumbnail pictures of a once living girl. In two nights, she will disappear, a few hairs left behind inside that van, and this is the final photograph that her father will take of her.

Picture Two

The house stands behind a rusted For Sale sign. The yard is dusty, the front storm door hangs from its hinges, and cardboard covers the living room window. Three children and their mother stand outside. Their house is in the shadows of a West Virginia mountain. Three-year-old boys smile at the world, their identical faces look like sunshine painted with happy eyes. The mother is gaunt. She is as skinny as the day she will die. While she isn't as happy as her sons, she does seem relieved to be standing outside again. The thirteen-year-old daughter is the most alarming subject. Looking over her shoulder, the girl glances nervously at the house nobody wants to buy. Most of the bad things in the family happened to her. At her feet is a framed picture of a smiling man who resembles the twins but not her. This man was trapped and found dead in the coalmines three days ago. Three days ago, she came back to life. With her right foot, the girl stomps on the picture, leaving her stepfather's face cracked through a tangle of bright lines. The camera clicks as she lifts her foot again.

Picture Three

The eye can't count faces and feel certain about the number. Perhaps fifty Iraqis stand together, no room to spare. They were almost dead for eight months, burned in a club fire set by a man who was angry with his girlfriend. By chance, the girl survived. Alone, she sits on the floor of the hospital lobby before the others, the flesh on her face incinerated by the heat.

She wonders, why should you be able to keep your fingernails and your teeth but not your hair? None of them grow hair anymore. But she is beautiful, and her lovely body wears a fine dress that is a counterpoint to her stretched and pulled skin.

Picture Four

Her face hides in the shadows, make her body more real as a consequence. Sunset flows across a long lovely woman. She sits on cushions and wears nothing. Her breasts and belly seem too large for such a thin frame. They look swollen and dark. Her left hand rests on her swollen stomach, waiting. The baby has been dead for two weeks inside of her yet she still hopes for the next hard kick. The picture jars Cora with the forceful negligence of medical care in parts of Africa. Mothers of malnourished children carry the corpses of their dead babies inside their wombs. Waiting for release, waiting to labor for a child that will never draw breath.

Picture Five
The camera is too distant to show faces or the details of any single body. What impresses is the wash of bare flesh, pale and lovely. Hundreds of bodies stand where they died, closer as lovers.
Aid workers stand on the margins of the clearing in Bogotá, shouting instructions and encouragement in the sea of death and lifelessness.
There is no noise in the photograph, no motion. The quantity of flesh seems infinite.

Picture Six
Cora is surprised to find her own face. A picture from her birth. She is nothing but a round face inside a hospital blanket. The flash from the camera annihilates shadows while her oily green eyes gaze up at a round piece metal that means nothing to her. Torn from the warmth and gentle waves of her mother, she will cry and cry and cry. Five minutes old and she is miserable. This is how her entire life will be.

She drops the pictures, each one heavy with in its story. Each photograph is a moment captured. Each one represents only a mere fraction of the painful images from her father's career. Yet these were the ones he chose to die with.

She looks at the nightstand. The camera had been pre-positioned, connected to banks of strobe lights that throw their glare at the piece of floor where her father crumpled after his self-inflicted gun wound. A note taped to the mirror read, "All my life I took pictures. Pictures of pain, war, poverty, and death. This is the last one."

The Last Picture

Cora scrolls through her father's camera again. Pictures of the sky, of broken glass on the road, and the minutiae of life fill her eyes. The policemen drape the body and the voices of the emergency technicians scramble her thoughts. The oak floor is cleared, but the image of her father remains as the last photo . A picture he took of death. Of his death.

She sees her father's face, unblemished with a closed mouth and open green eyes. His face is blurred yet the body has clear delineation. It seems only halfway real as she holds his camera. Flames lick the still burning fireplace as she pauses. She sets the camera on the logs. Burning plastic and noxious chemicals burn her nostrils as she leaves the camera to die also.

Dark Light

Made in the USA
Charleston, SC
08 March 2012